E S T A T E   P U B L I C

GRAVESEND - D

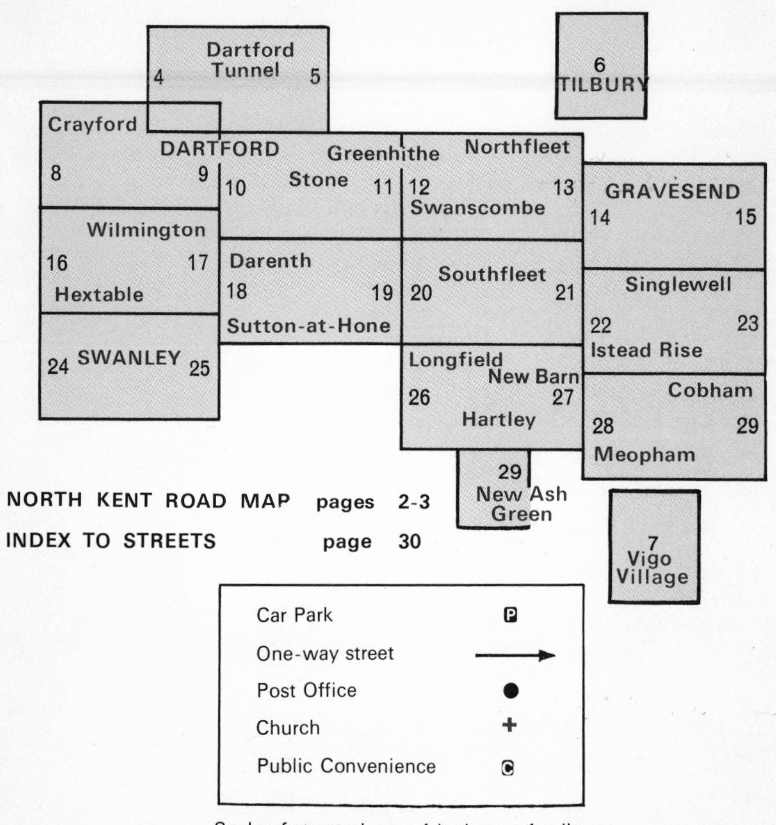

Scale of street plans = 4 inches to 1 mile

Sreet plans prepared and published by ESTATE PUBLICATIONS, Bridewell House, Tenterden, Kent and based upon the ORDNANCE SURVEY maps with the sanction of the controller of H.M. Stationery Office.

The publishers acknowledge the co-operation of Dartford and Gravesham District Councils in the preparation of these maps.

Every effort has been made to ensure the greatest possible accuracy of these maps and the publishers welcome any information that will improve their usefulness.

0 86084 300 9

034 G

ROAD MAP

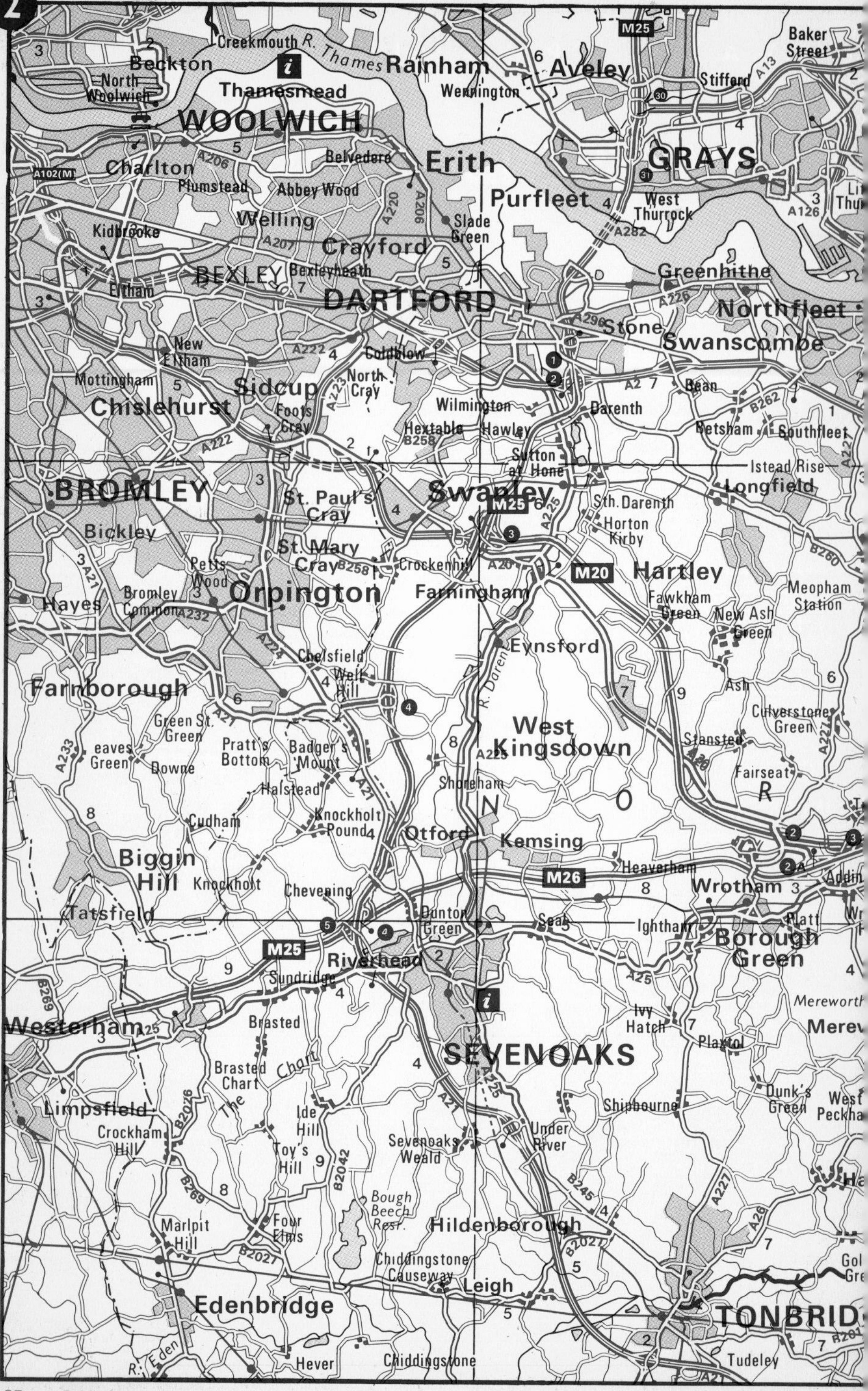

Creekmouth
R. Thames
Beckton
North Woolwich
Thamesmead
WOOLWICH
Rainham
Wennington
Aveley
Baker Street
Stifford
GRAYS
Charlton
Plumstead
Belvedere
Abbey Wood
Erith
Purfleet
West Thurrock
Welling
Kidbrooke
Slade Green
Crayford
BEXLEY
Bexleyheath
Eltham
DARTFORD
Greenhithe
Northfleet
Stone
Swanscombe
New Eltham
Coldblow
Mottingham
Sidcup
North Cray
Bean
Chislehurst
Foots Cray
Wilmington
Darenth
Hextable
Hawley
Betsham
Southfleet
Sutton at Hone
Istead Rise
BROMLEY
St. Paul's Cray
Swanley
Sth. Darenth
Longfield
Bickley
Horton Kirby
St. Mary Cray
Crockenhill
Hartley
Petts Wood
Farningham
Meopham Station
Hayes
Bromley Common
Orpington
Fawkham Green
New Ash Green
Chelsfield
Eynsford
Well Hill
Ash
Farnborough
R. Darent
West Kingsdown
Culverstone Green
Green St. Green
Pratt's Bottom
Badger's Mount
Stansted
eaves Green
Downe
Fairseat
Shoreham
Halstead
Cudham
Knockholt Pound
Otford
Kemsing
Biggin Hill
Knockholt
Heaverham
Chevening
Wrotham
Tatsfield
Dunton Green
Seal
Ightham
Platt
Borough Green
Riverhead
Sundridge
Westerham
Brasted
Ivy Hatch
Mereworth
Plaxtol
SEVENOAKS
Brasted Chart
The Chart
Limpsfield
Ide Hill
Shipbourne
Dunk's Green
West Peckham
Crockham Hill
Sevenoaks Weald
Under River
Toy's Hill
Bough Beech Resr.
Four Elms
Marlpit Hill
Hildenborough
Chiddingstone Causeway
Leigh
Edenbridge
TONBRIDGE
R. Eden
Hever
Chiddingstone
Tudeley

3

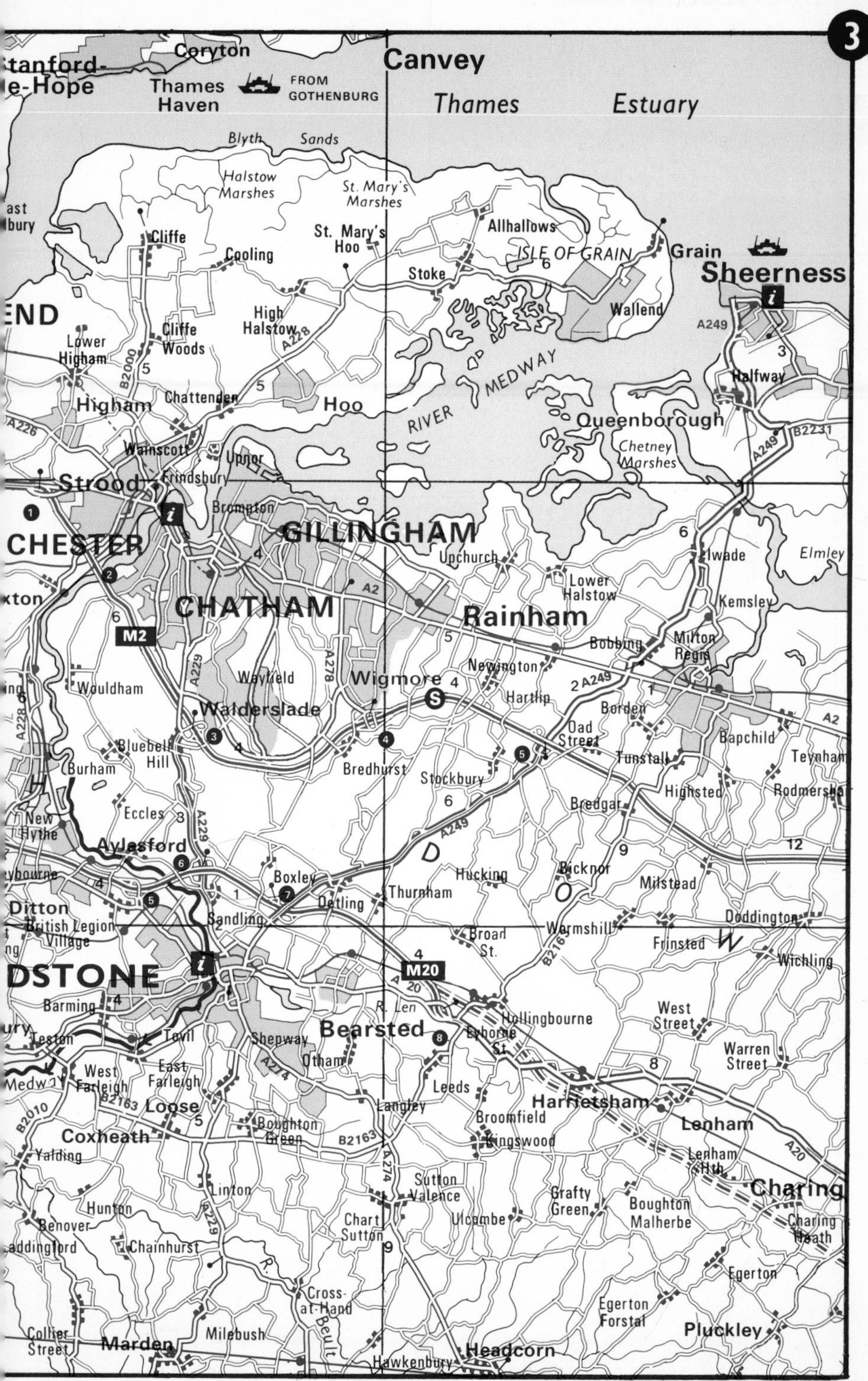

Coryton
Canvey
Thames Haven
FROM GOTHENBURG
Thames Estuary
Blyth Sands
Halstow Marshes
St. Mary's Marshes
Allhallows
Cliffe
Cooling
St. Mary's Hoo
Stoke
ISLE OF GRAIN
Grain
Sheerness
Wallend
High Halstow
Cliffe Woods
Lower Higham
Higham
Chattenden
Hoo
RIVER MEDWAY
Queenborough
Halfway
Chetney Marshes
Wainscott
Upnor
Strood
Frindsbury
Brompton
GILLINGHAM
Upchurch
Iwade
Elmley
Lower Halstow
Kemsley
CHATHAM
Rainham
Bobbing
Milton Regis
Newington
Hartlip
Wayfield
Wigmore
Wouldham
Walderslade
Borden
Oad Street
Bapchild
Teynham
Tunstall
Bluebell Hill
Burham
Bredhurst
Stockbury
Highsted
Rodmersham
Bredgar
Eccles
New Hythe
Aylesford
Boxley
Hucking
Bicknor
Milstead
Ditton
Detling
Thurnham
British Legion Village
Sandling
Wormshill
Doddington
Broad St.
Frinsted
Wichling
DSTONE
Barming
R. Len
Hollingbourne
Teston
Tovil
Shepway
Bearsted
Eyhorne St.
West Street
Warren Street
West Farleigh
East Farleigh
Otham
Leeds
Harrietsham
Loose
Langley
Broomfield
Lenham
Coxheath
Boughton Green
Kingswood
Yalding
Lenham Hth.
Charing
Linton
Sutton Valence
Grafty Green
Boughton Malherbe
Hunton
Chart Sutton
Ulcombe
Charing Heath
Benover
Chainhurst
Egerton
Cross-at-Hand
Egerton Forstal
Collier Street
Marden
Milebush
Pluckley
Headcorn
Hawkenbury
M2
M20
A2
A20
A226
A228
A229
A249
A274
A278
B2000
B2010
B2163
B2231

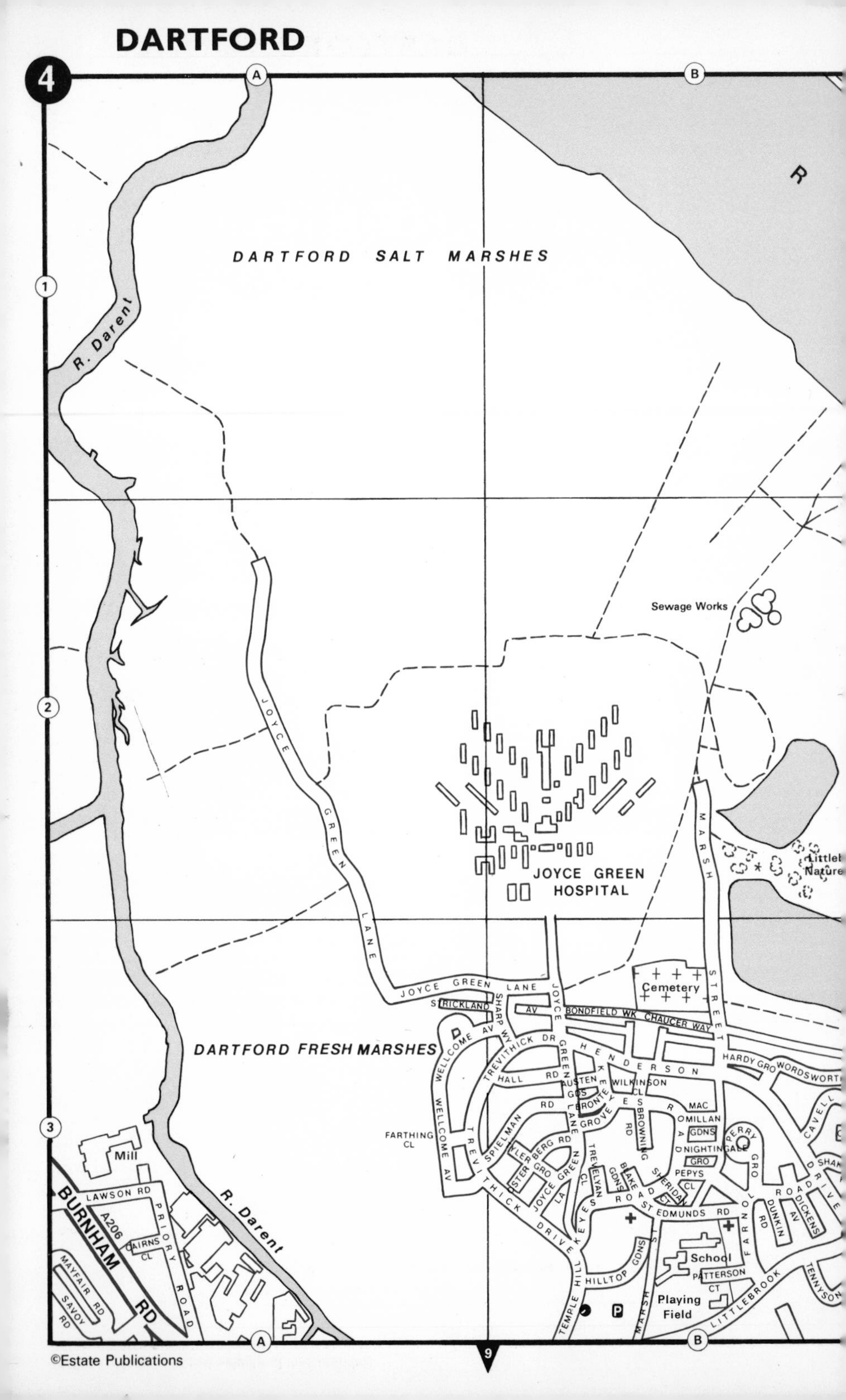
4
DARTFORD SALT MARSHES
R. Darent
Sewage Works
JOYCE GREEN LANE
JOYCE GREEN HOSPITAL
MARSH STREET
Cemetery
DARTFORD FRESH MARSHES
STRICKLAND AV
SHARP WY
BONDFIELD WK
CHAUCER WAY
WELLCOME AV
TREVITHICK DR
HENDERSON
HARDY GRO
HALL RD
AUSTEN GDS
WILKINSON CL
BRONTE
KEYES ROAD
MAC MILLAN GDNS
BROWNING
NIGHTINGALE GRO
PERRY GRO
FARTHING CL
SPIELMAN RD
TREVITHICK DRIVE
TREVELYAN CL
BLAKE GDNS
SHERIDAN CT
PEPYS CL
ST EDMUNDS RD
FARNOL ROAD
DUNKIN RD
DICKENS AV
CAVELL
TENNYSON
School
PATTERSON CT
Playing Field
LITTLEBROOK
HILLTOP GDNS
TEMPLE HILL
Mill
LAWSON RD
BURNHAM RD
A206
PRIORY ROAD
DAIRNS CL
MAYFAIR RD
SAVOY RD
A
B
1
2
3

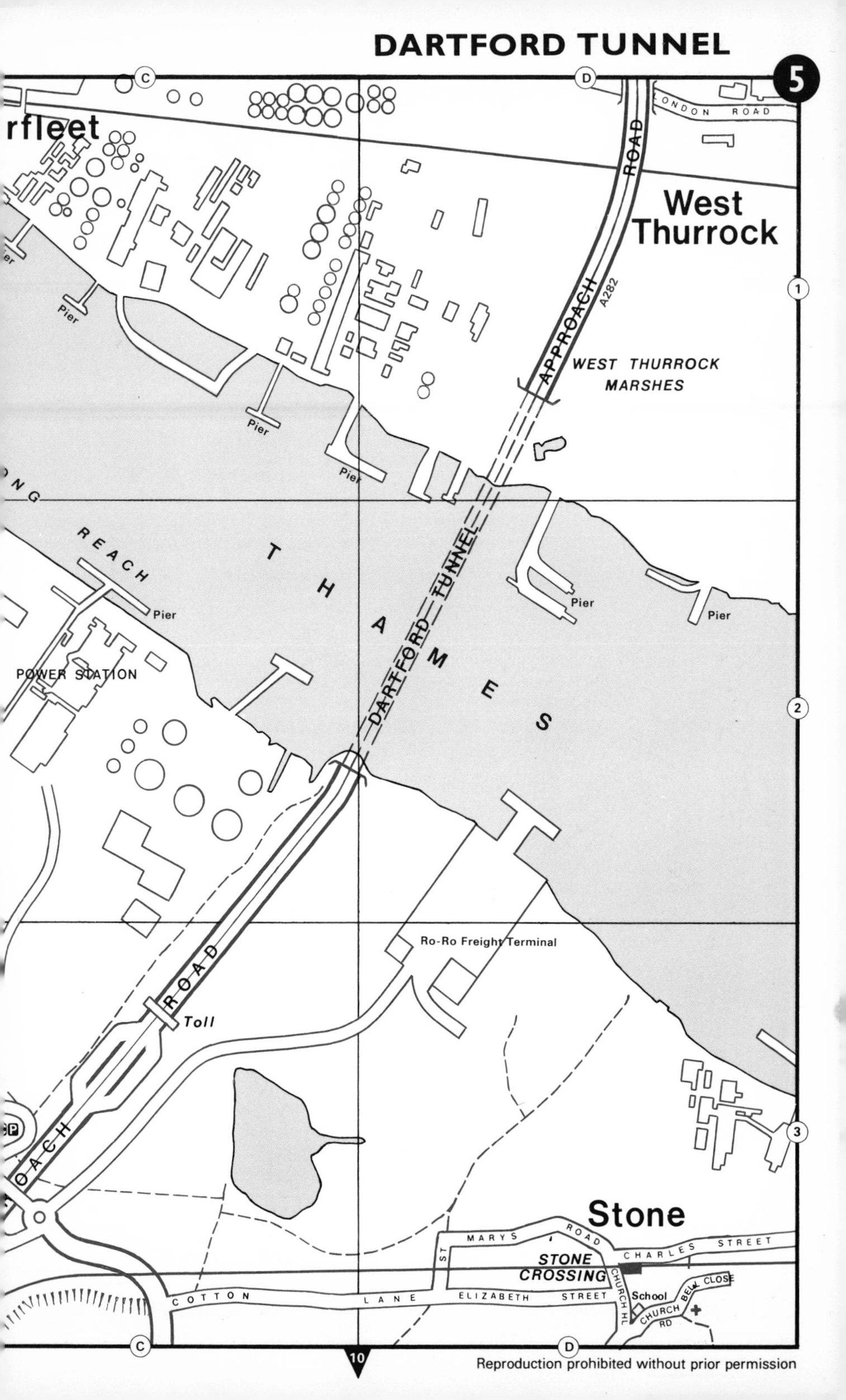
C
D
LONDON ROAD
rfleet
APPROACH ROAD
A282
West Thurrock
WEST THURROCK MARSHES
Pier
Pier
Pier
Pier
Pier
Pier
NG
REACH
THAMES
DARTFORD TUNNEL
POWER STATION
Ro-Ro Freight Terminal
ROAD
Toll
OACH
Stone
ST MARYS ROAD
CHARLES STREET
STONE CROSSING
CHURCH HL
School
BELL CLOSE
CHURCH RD
COTTON LANE
ELIZABETH STREET
1
2
3

TILBURY

DOCK APPROACH ROAD
A1089
MARSHFOOT RD
BIGGIN LANE
BIGGIN LA
SANDY LANE
ST. CHADS ROAD
A128
LAWRENCE GDNS
MILLAIS PL
HANDEL CRES
FEENAN
WREN WK
LEIGHTON GDNS
MELBA GDNS
Tilbury F.C.
CHADFIELDS
SPINDLES
Rec Grnd.
St. Chads School
RAPHAEL AVENUE
SULLIVAN RD
ELGAR GDNS
POYNDER RD
School
DICKENS AV
THACKERAY AV
KIPLING CRES
SHAW
TILLET PLA
FIELDING
GAINSBOROUGH AV
HIGHWAY
King George Playing Field
BURNS PL
Karting Stadium
Prim School
BRISBANE HO
TASMANIA HO
FREEMANTLE HO
LANSBURY GDNS
CENTRAL AV
NTH VIEW AV
STH VIEW AV
THE CIRCLE
ST ANDREWS RD
DOCK
A126
GAYLOR RD
LEICESTER ROAD
SEXTON RD
DARWIN RD
HOBART RD
MELBOURNE RD
RUSSELL ROAD
DUNLOP
FAIRFAX RD
ADELAIDE RD
ADELAIDE ROAD
BEACONSFIELD RD
Athlone House Mission to Seamen
CHURCH ROAD
SEYMOUR
ELLERMAN RD
BROADWAY
SELWYN
ALEXANDRA RD
ROAD
A1089
ST ANDREWS ROAD
TOWN
STEPHENSON AV
COWPER AVENUE
CHRISTCHURCH RD
WALK
MILTON GDNS
SWIN BURNE GDNS
SHAKESPEARE RD
SOUTHEY WK
WORDSWTH CL
SPENCER
ARKWRIGHT RD
MANOR RD
TORONTO RD
OTTOWA RD
QUEBEC RD
ST.
Sch
LANSDOWNE RD
MKT PL
CALCUTTA ROAD
Liby & Mus
CIVIC SQUARE
Anchor PH
Fire Sta
BRENNAN
FEENAN HIGHWAY
PARK SIDE AV
TENNYSON
MOORE AV
LONDON AV
KEATS GDNS
ELIZABETH ROAD
MALTA
BERMUDA RD
CANBERRA
SYDNEY
DOCK RD
Community Centre
Police Station
MONTREAL RD
AUKLAND CL
WELLINGTON RD
NEWTON RD
CROWN CT
KELVIN RD
MONARCH CL
THE BEECHES
HUME
BRUNEL CL
BROWN CL
EDINBURGH MEWS
LISTER RD
FERRY RD
ROAD
Docks
Warehouses
ORIENT RD
FERRY
TILBURY
TILBURY DOCKS
ROAD
FORT
FORT RD
Worlds End PH
QUEEN ELIZABETH PL
QN ELIZ PL
STA APP RD
RIVERSIDE
TILBURY GDNS
Jetty
Cruise Ship Terminal
Sealink Passenger Ferry to Gravesend
A
B
1
2
3

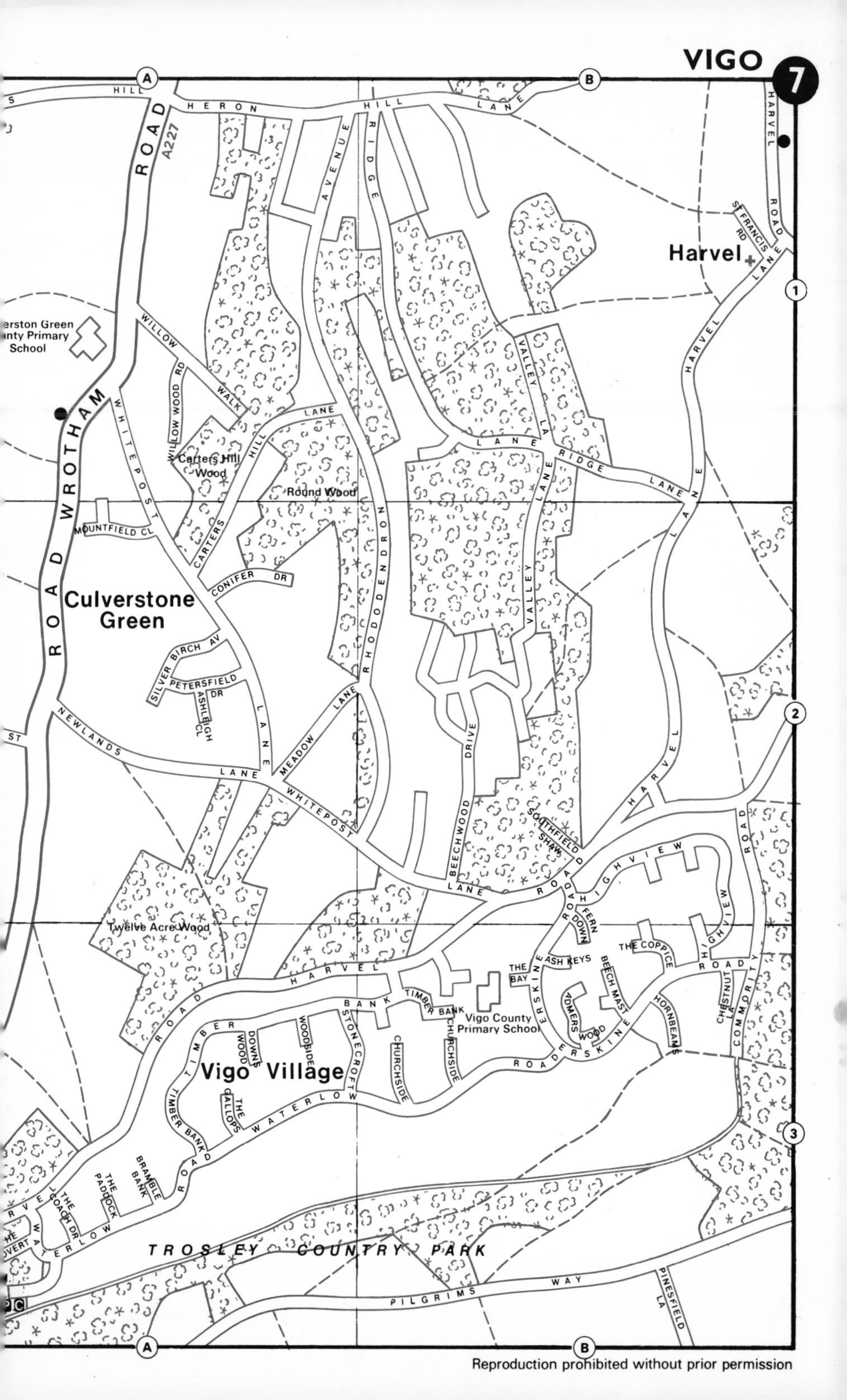

HERON HILL LANE
WROTHAM ROAD
A227
AVENUE
RIDGE
Harvel
HARVEL ROAD
ST FRANCIS RD
HARVEL LANE
WILLOW WALK
WILLOW WOOD RD
Carters Hill Wood
CARTERS HILL LANE
Round Wood
WHITEPOST LANE
MOUNTFIELD CL
CONIFER DR
RHODODENDRON AVENUE
VALLEY LA
VALLEY LANE
RIDGE LANE
Culverstone Green
SILVER BIRCH AV
PETERSFIELD DR
ASHLEIGH CL
NEWLANDS LANE
MEADOW LANE
BEECHWOOD DRIVE
SOUTHFIELD SHAW
HIGHVIEW
FERN DOWN
ROAD
Twelve Acre Wood
HARVEL ROAD
THE BAY
ASH KEYS
BEECH MAST
THE COPPICE
CHESTNUT LA
COMMORITY ROAD
TIMBER BANK
Vigo County Primary School
CHURCHSIDE
STONECROFT
WOODSIDE
DOWNS WOOD
ERSKINE ROAD
HORNBEAMS
Vigo Village
THE GALLOPS
WATERLOW ROAD
BRAMBLE BANK
THE PADDOCK
THE COACH DR
TROSLEY COUNTRY PARK
PILGRIMS WAY
PINESFIELD LA
A
B
1
2
3

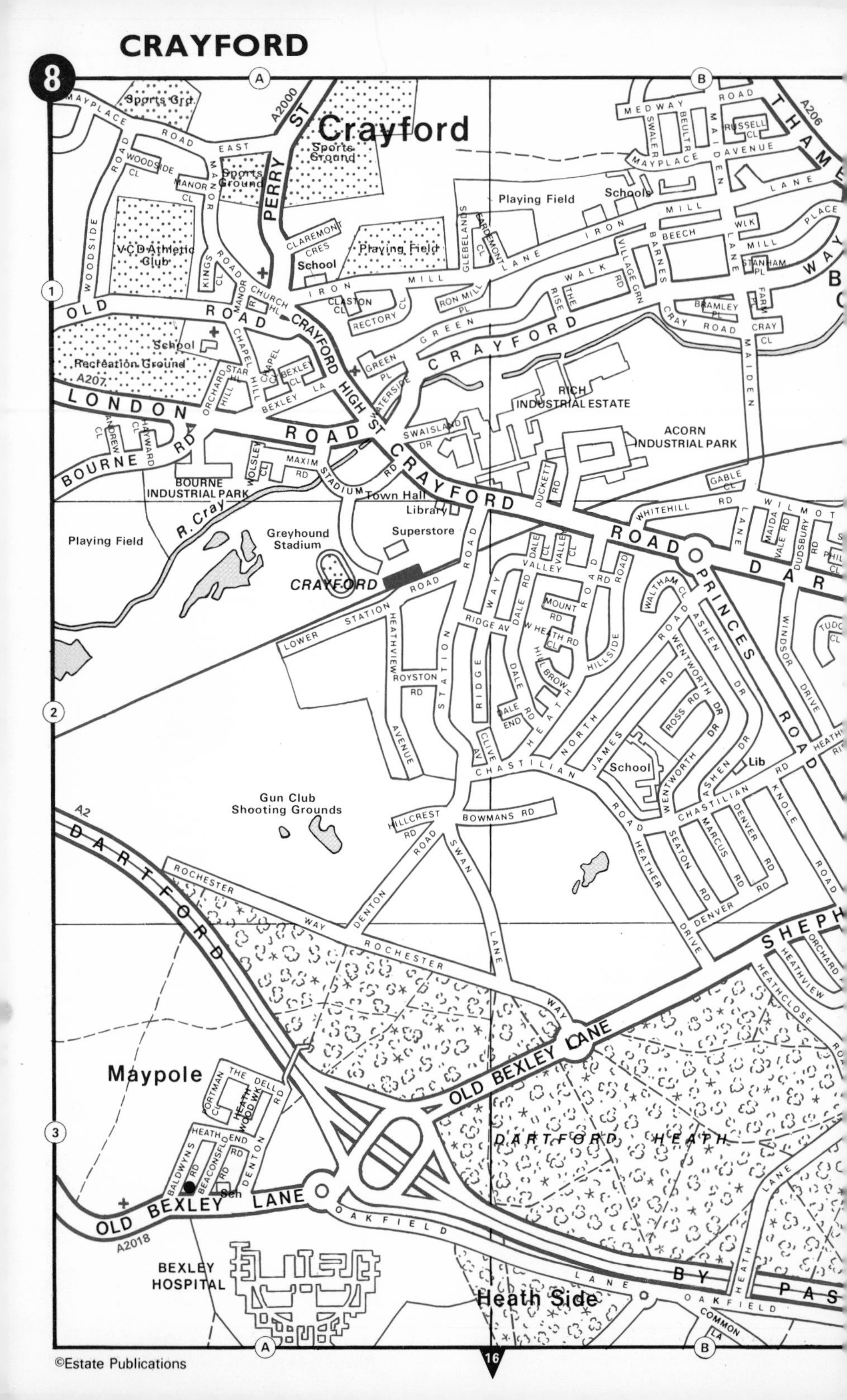

Crayford
Sports Grd.
Sports Ground
VCD Athletic Club
Recreation Ground
Playing Field
Schools
School
RICH INDUSTRIAL ESTATE
ACORN INDUSTRIAL PARK
BOURNE INDUSTRIAL PARK
Town Hall
Library
Superstore
Greyhound Stadium
CRAYFORD
Gun Club Shooting Grounds
Lib
Maypole
DARTFORD HEATH
BEXLEY HOSPITAL
Heath Side
OLD BEXLEY LANE
LONDON ROAD
CRAYFORD ROAD
DARTFORD
ROCHESTER WAY
PRINCES ROAD
CRAYFORD HIGH ST
PERRY ST
MAYPLACE ROAD EAST
OLD ROAD
IRON MILL LANE
MAIDEN LANE
BOURNE RD
STATION ROAD
LOWER STATION ROAD
SWAN LANE
DENTON ROAD
HEATHER DRIVE
A2
A207
A2000
A206
A2018

16

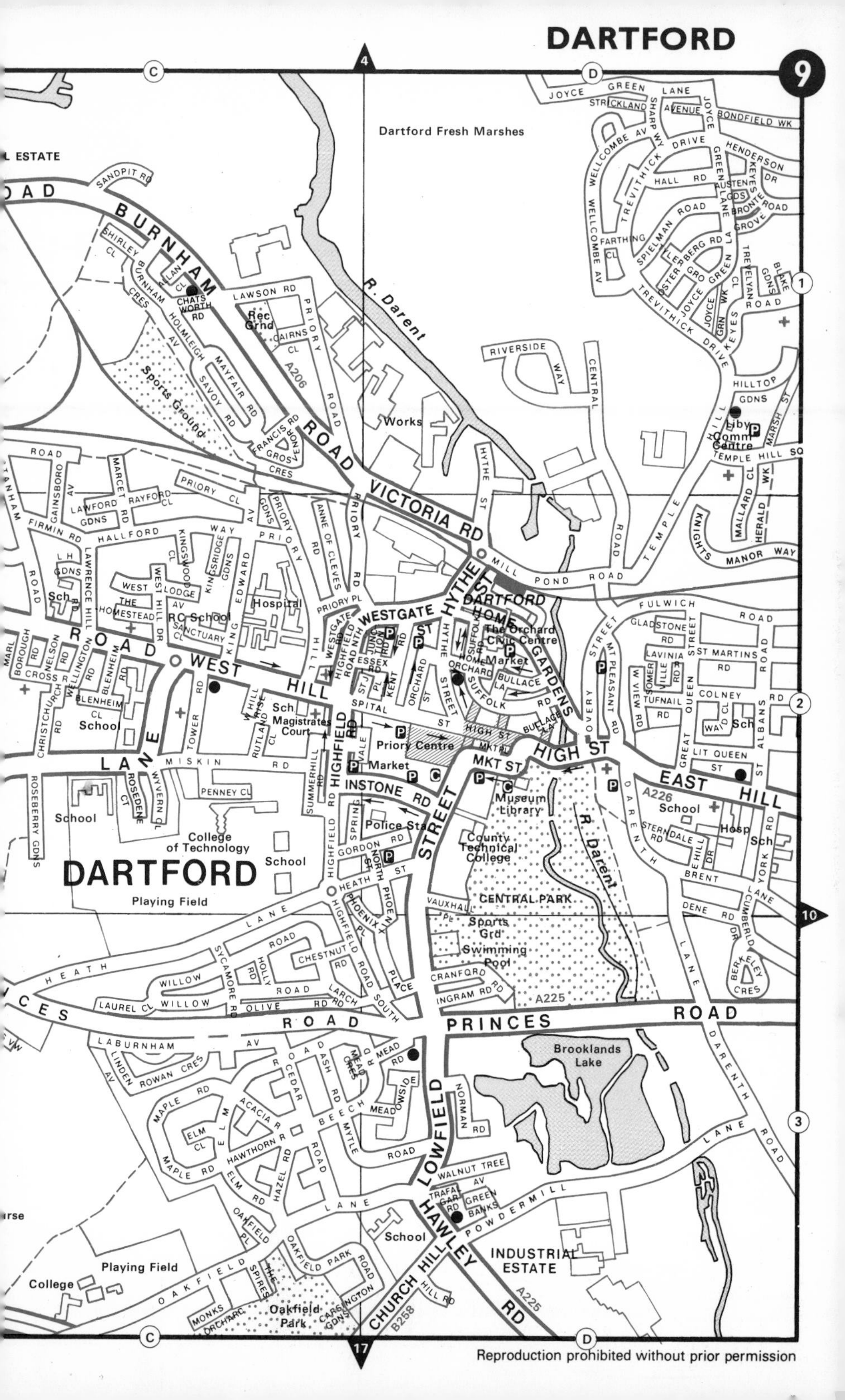
Dartford Fresh Marshes
R. Darent
BURNHAM ROAD
VICTORIA RD
WEST HILL
WEST HILL
HIGH ST
EAST HILL
HYTHE ST
WESTGATE
HOME GARDENS
MKT ST
HIGHFIELD RD
INSTONE RD
LOWFIELD ST
PRINCES ROAD
HEATH LANE
HAWLEY RD
CHURCH HILL
POWDERMILL LANE
DARENTH ROAD
DARENTH LANE
MILL POND ROAD
TEMPLE HILL
CENTRAL ROAD
FULWICH ROAD
MANOR WAY
JOYCE GREEN LANE
TREVITHICK DRIVE
Sports Ground
Hospital
RC School
Priory Centre
Market
Museum
Library
County Technical College
CENTRAL PARK
Sports Grd
Swimming Pool
College of Technology
DARTFORD
Playing Field
Brooklands Lake
INDUSTRIAL ESTATE
Oakfield Park
Playing Field
College
Works
The Orchard
Civic Centre
Magistrates Court
Police Sta
Liby
Comm Centre
A206
A226
A225
B258

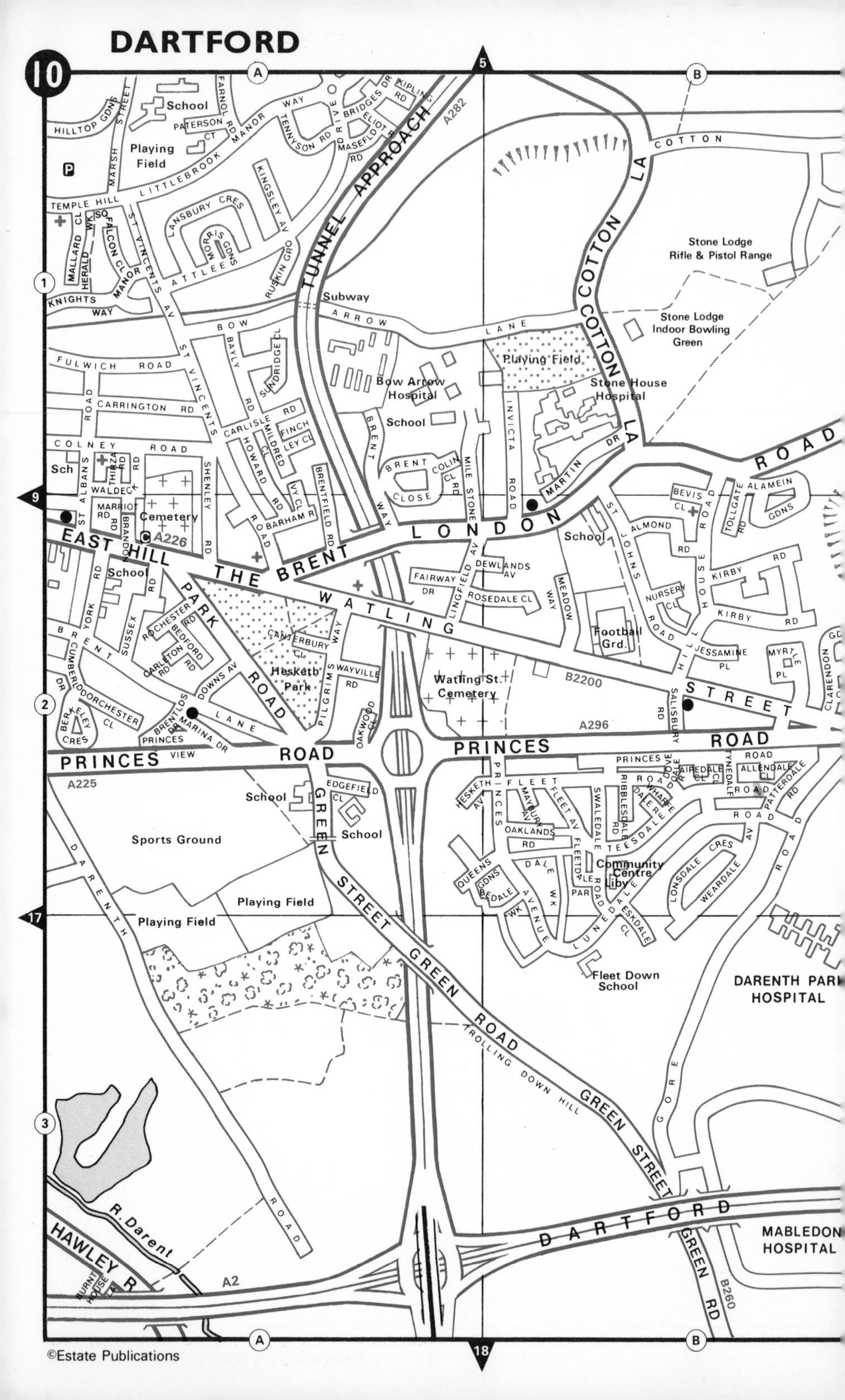
School
Playing Field
Bow Arrow Hospital
Stone House Hospital
Stone Lodge Rifle & Pistol Range
Stone Lodge Indoor Bowling Green
Playing Field
Cemetery
Hesketh Park
Watling St. Cemetery
Football Grd.
Sports Ground
Playing Field
Community Centre Liby
Fleet Down School
DARENTH PARK HOSPITAL
MABLEDON HOSPITAL
TUNNEL APPROACH
COTTON LA
LONDON ROAD
THE BRENT
WATLING STREET
EAST HILL
PRINCES ROAD
PARK ROAD
GREEN STREET GREEN ROAD
TROLLING DOWN HILL
DARENTH ROAD
DARTFORD
R. Darent
HAWLEY R
A282
A226
A225
A296
B2200
B260
A2

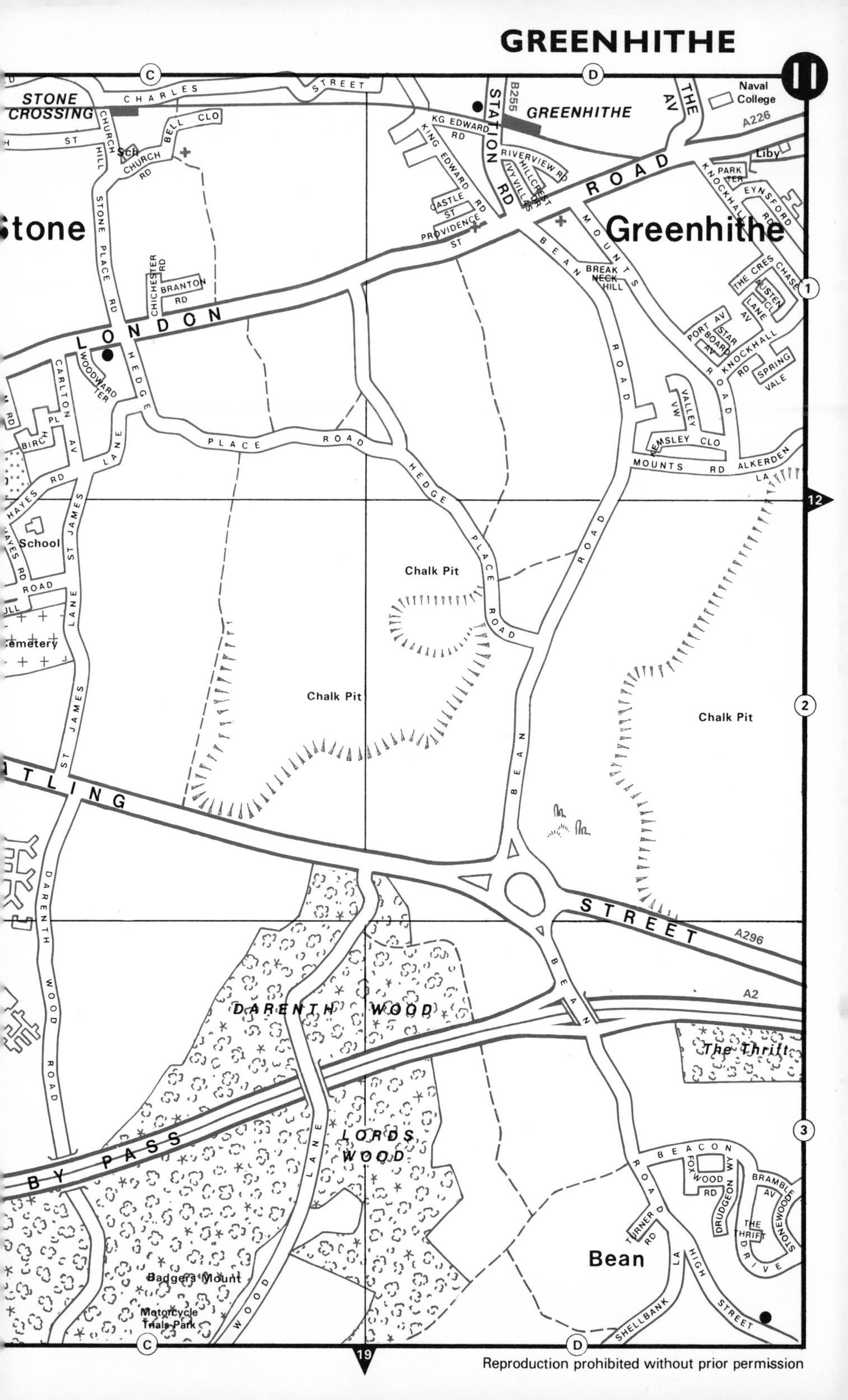
STONE CROSSING
Stone
Greenhithe
GREENHITHE
CHARLES STREET
CHURCH HILL
BELL CLO
CHURCH RD
Sch
STONE PLACE RD
CHICHESTER RD
BRANTON RD
LONDON ROAD
HEDGE PLACE ROAD
KG EDWARD RD
KING EDWARD RD
CASTLE ST
PROVIDENCE ST
STATION RD
B255
RIVERVIEW RD
HILLCREST RD
IVY VILLAS
THE AV
Naval College
A226
Liby
PARK TER
EYNSFORD RD
KNOCKHALL RD
KNOCKHALL CHASE
THE CRES
AUSTEN CL
LANE AV
PORT AV
STAR BOARD AV
KNOCKHALL RD
SPRING VALE
MOUNTS ROAD
BEAN ROAD
BREAK NECK HILL
VALLEY VW
HEMSLEY CLO
MOUNTS RD
ALKERDEN LA
WOODWARD TER
CARLTON AV
BIRCH PL
LANE
HAYES RD
School
ST JAMES LANE
ROAD
Cemetery
Chalk Pit
Chalk Pit
Chalk Pit
WATLING STREET
A296
A2
DARENTH WOOD ROAD
DARENTH WOOD
LORDS WOOD
WOOD LANE
BY PASS
The Thrift
Badgers Mount
Motorcycle Trials Park
BEACON DR
FOXWOOD RD
DRUDGEON WY
BRAMBLE AV
STONEWOOD
THE THRIFT
DRIVE
TURNER RD
Bean
LA
HIGH STREET
SHELLBANK
C
D
1
2
3
12
19

SWANSCOMBE

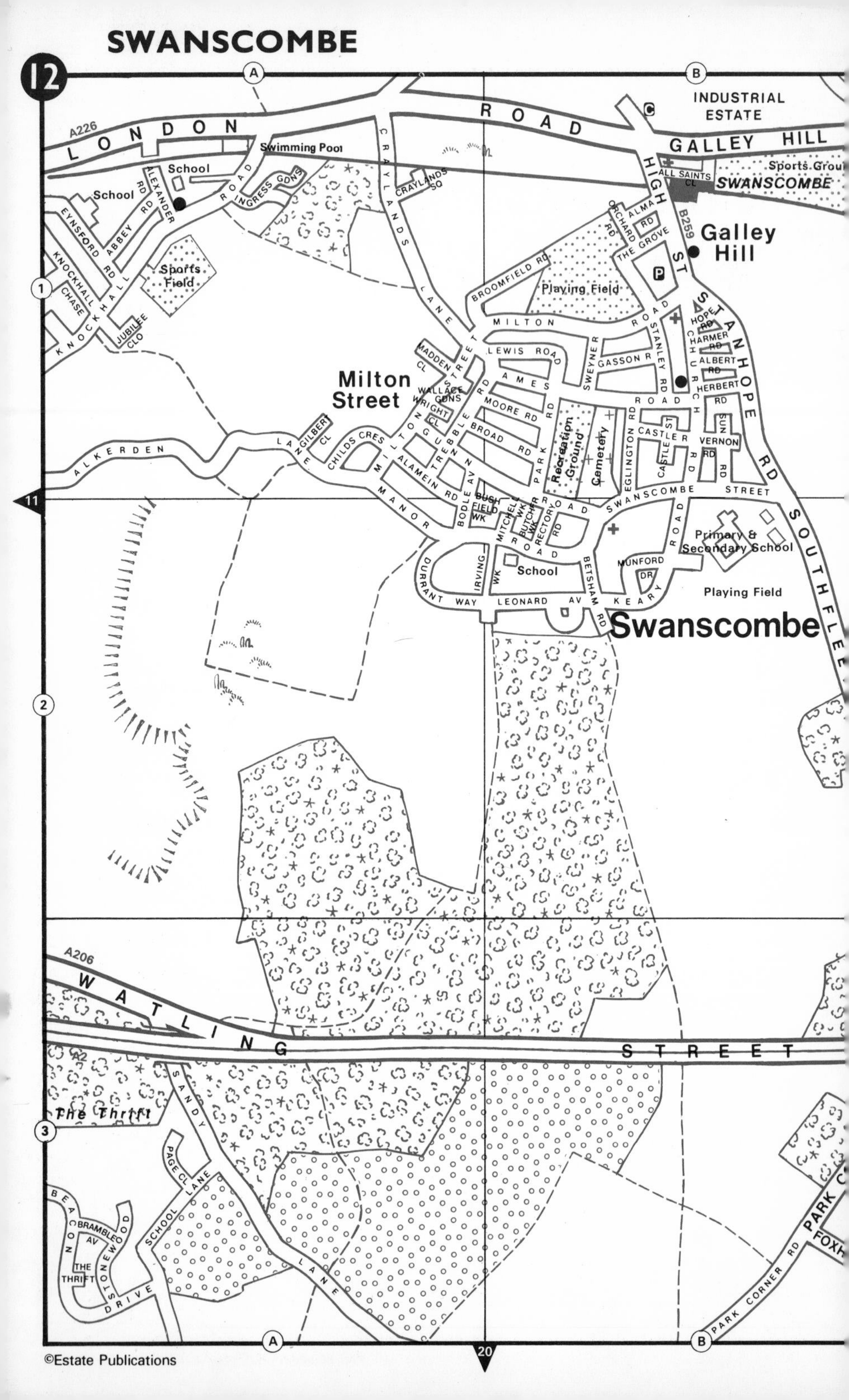
12
A
B
A226
LONDON ROAD
INDUSTRIAL ESTATE
GALLEY HILL
Swimming Pool
School
School
ALEXANDER RD
INGRESS GDNS
CRAYLANDS LANE
CRAYLANDS SQ
ALL SAINTS CL
Sports Grou
SWANSCOMBE
HIGH ST
B259
Galley Hill
ALMA RD
ORCHARD RD
THE GROVE
EYNSFORD RD
ABBEY RD
KNOCKHALL CHASE
KNOCKHALL ROAD
Sports Field
JUBILEE CLO
BROOMFIELD RD
Playing Field
MILTON ROAD
LEWIS ROAD
AMES RD
SWEYNE RD
GASSON RD
STANLEY RD
CHURCH RD
STANHOPE RD
HOPE RD
HARMER RD
ALBERT RD
HERBERT RD
MADDEN CL
Milton Street
WALLACE GDNS
WRIGHT CL
MILTON STREET
MOORE RD
BROAD RD
PARK RD
Recreation Ground
Cemetery
EGLINGTON RD
CASTLE RD
CASTLE ST
SUN RD
VERNON RD
GILBERT CL
ALKERDEN LANE
CHILDS CRES
MILTON RD
GUNN RD
TREBBLE RD
ALAMEIN RD
MANOR RD
BODLE AV
BUSHFIELD WK
MITCHELL WK
BUTCHER WK
RECTORY RD
SWANSCOMBE STREET
SOUTHFLEET RD
Primary & Secondary School
MUNFORD DR
Playing Field
DURRANT WAY
IRVING WK
School
LEONARD AV
BETSHAM RD
KEARY RD
Swanscombe
11
1
2
3
A206
WATLING STREET
A2
The Thrift
SANDY LANE
PAGE CL
SCHOOL LANE
BEACON DRIVE
BRAMBLEWOOD AV
STONEWOOD
THE THRIFT
PARK CORNER RD
PARK C
FOXH
20

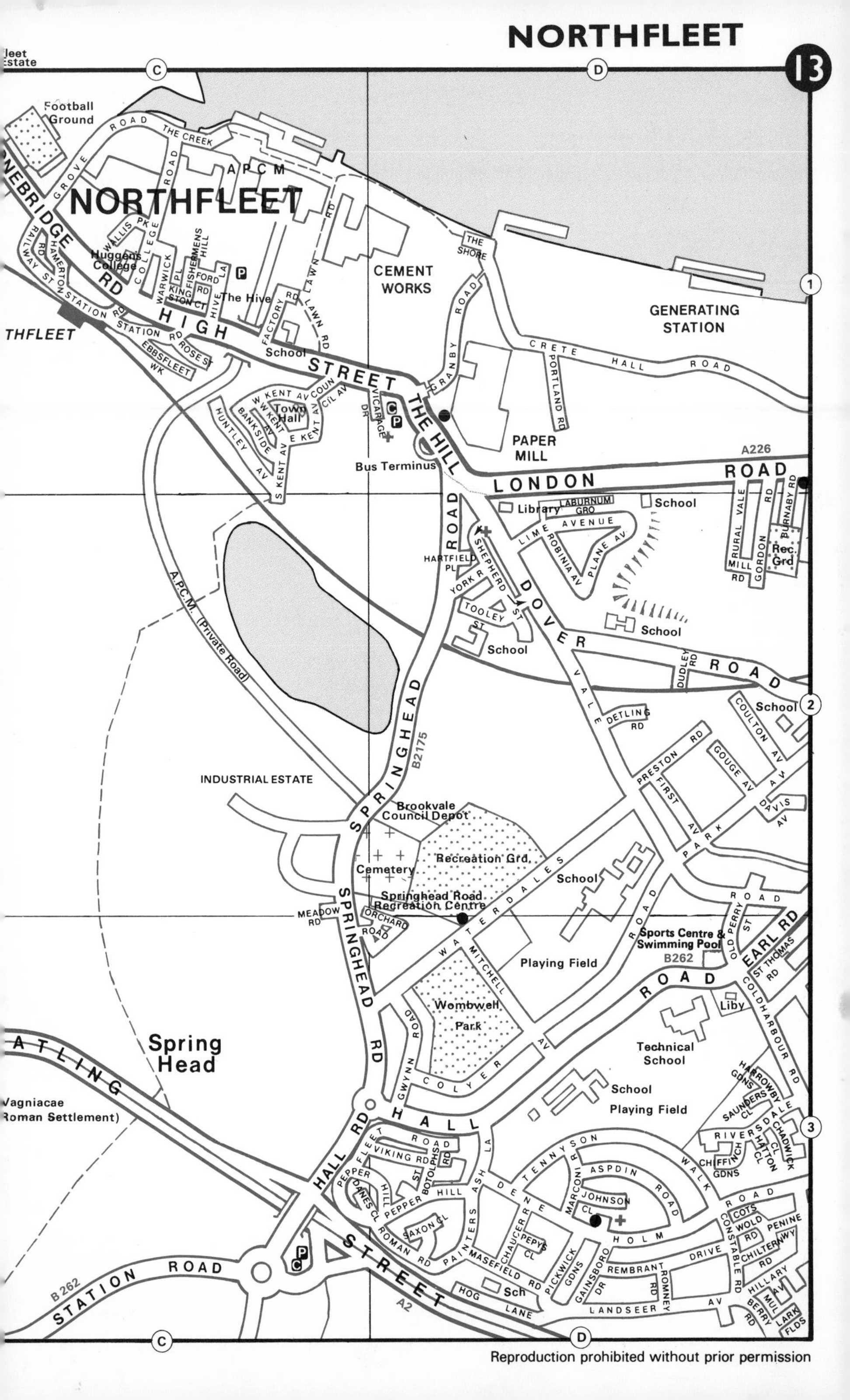
NORTHFLEET
Football Ground
THE CREEK
A P C M
CEMENT WORKS
GENERATING STATION
CRETE HALL ROAD
PORTLAND RD
THE SHORE
GRANBY ROAD
Huggens College
The Hive
HIGH STREET
STATION RD
ROSE ST
EBBSFLEET WK
Town Hall
Bus Terminus
THE HILL
PAPER MILL
A226
LONDON ROAD
Library
LABURNUM GRO
School
LIME AVENUE
ROBINIA AV
PLANE AV
RURAL VALE
MILL RD
GORDON RD
BURNABY RD
Rec. Grd
HARTFIELD PL
SHEPHERD ST
YORK R
TOOLEY ST
School
DOVER ROAD
DUDLEY RD
School
A.P.C.M. (Private Road)
VALE
DETLING RD
COULTON AV
GOUGE AV
PRESTON RD
FIRST AV
PARK AV
DAVIS AV
SPRINGHEAD
B2175
INDUSTRIAL ESTATE
Brookvale Council Depot
Recreation Grd.
Cemetery
Springhead Road Recreation Centre
WATERDALES
School
MEADOW RD
ORCHARD ROAD
SPRINGHEAD RD
MITCHELL
Playing Field
Sports Centre & Swimming Pool
B262
ROAD
OLD PERRY ST
EARL RD
ST THOMAS RD
Wombwell Park
Liby
Technical School
COLDHARBOUR RD
Spring Head
WATLING
Vagniacae Roman Settlement)
GWYNN ROAD
COLYER AV
HALL RD
School Playing Field
HARROWBY GDNS
SAUNDERS CL
RIVERSDALE
CHADWICK
HATTON CL
FINCH
CHIFFINCH GDNS
NORTHFLEET
VIKING RD
BOTOLPHS RD
ST
PEPPER HILL
DANES CL
SAXON CL
ROMAN RD
ASH LA
PAINTERS
DENE
TENNYSON WALK
MARCONI R
ASPDIN ROAD
JOHNSON CL
HOLM
CHAUCER R
PEPYS CL
MASEFIELD RD
PICKWICK GDNS
GAINSBORO DR
REMBRANT RD
ROMNEY
DRIVE
CONSTABLE RD
COTS WOLD RD
PENINE WY
CHILTERN
HILLARY AV
BERRY RD
MUL
LARK FLDS
LANDSEER AV
HOG LANE
Sch
STREET
A2
STATION ROAD
B 262
C
D
1
2
3

GRAVESEND

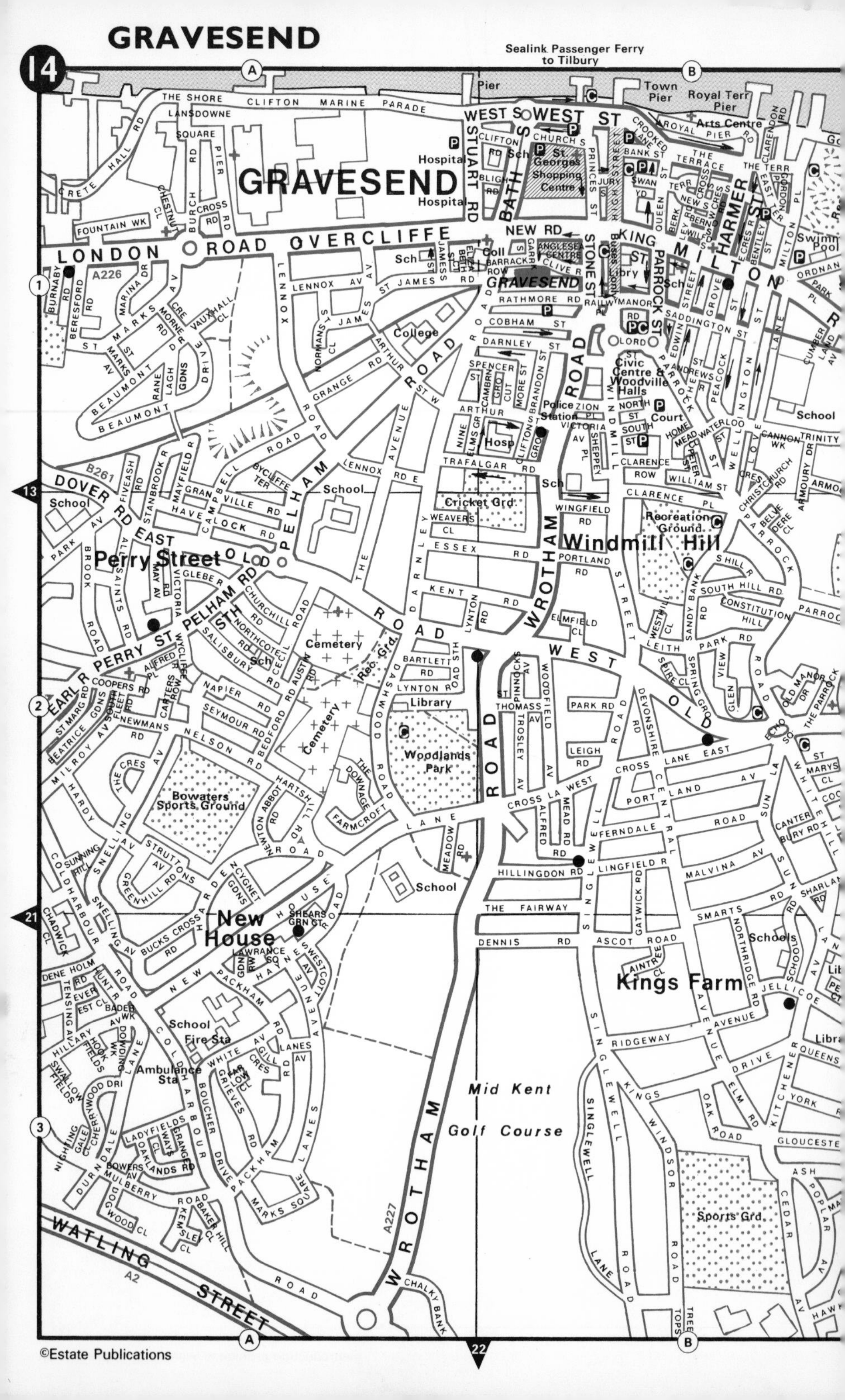
Sealink Passenger Ferry to Tilbury
GRAVESEND
Town Pier
Royal Terr Pier
Arts Centre
St. Georges Shopping Centre
Hospital
LONDON ROAD OVERCLIFFE
College
Civic Centre & Woodville Halls
Police Station
Cricket Grd.
Recreation Ground
Windmill Hill
Perry Street
Cemetery
Woodlands Park
Library
Bowaters Sports Ground
New House
Kings Farm
Mid Kent Golf Course
Sports Grd.
WROTHAM ROAD
WATLING STREET
A2
A226
A227
B261

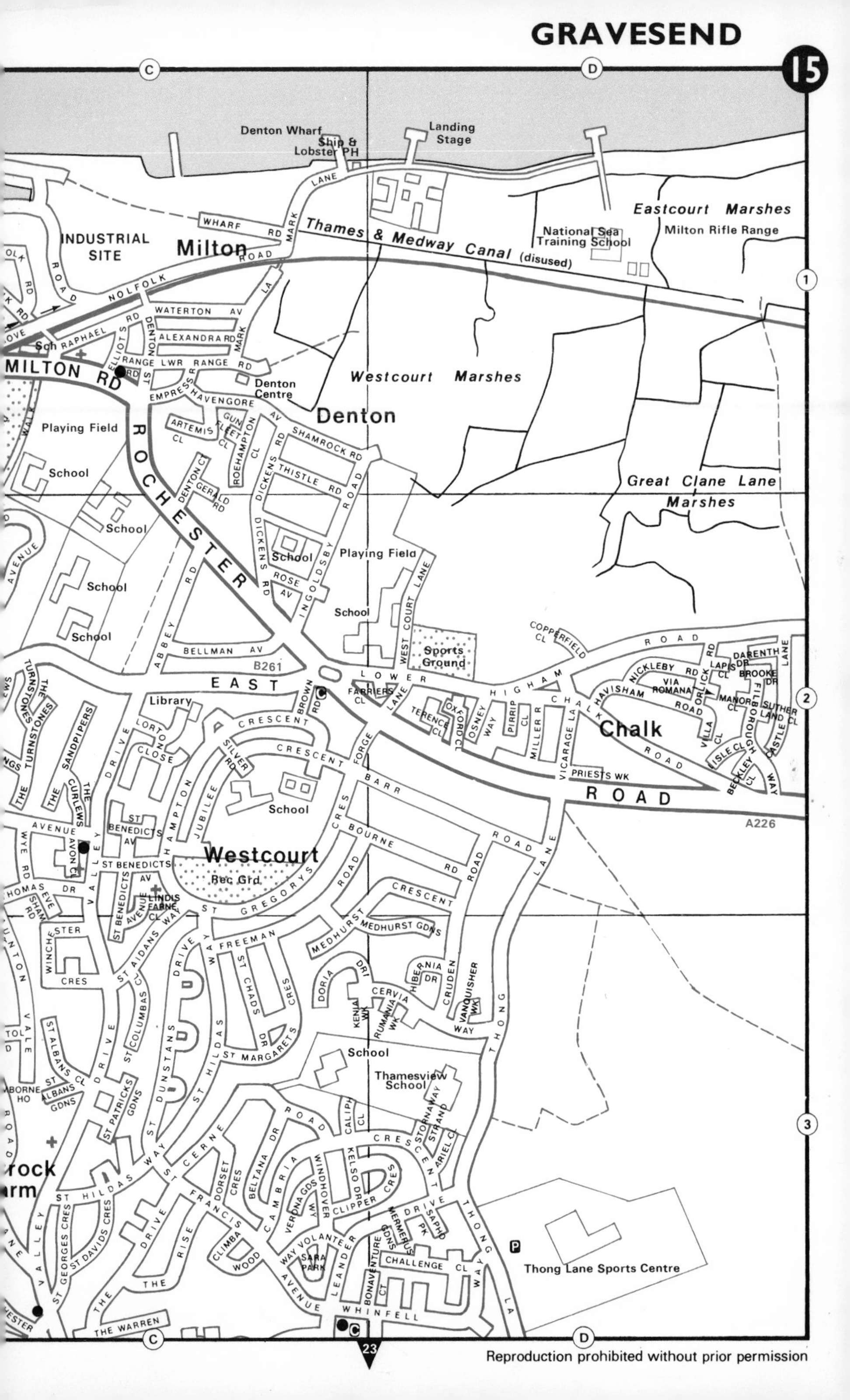
C
D
Denton Wharf
Ship & Lobster PH
Landing Stage
INDUSTRIAL SITE
Milton
WHARF RD
MARK LANE
Thames & Medway Canal (disused)
National Sea Training School
Eastcourt Marshes
Milton Rifle Range
NOLFOLK ROAD
WATERTON AV
ALEXANDRA RD
RAPHAEL RD
ELLIOTS
DENTON ST
MARK LA
RANGE RD
LWR RANGE RD
MILTON RD
Sch
Denton Centre
Westcourt Marshes
Denton
EMPRESS RD
HAVENGORE AV
ARTEMIS CL
GUN FLEET CL
ROEHAMPTON CL
SHAMROCK RD
DICKENS RD
THISTLE RD
Playing Field
School
ROCHESTER ROAD
DENTON CT
GERALD RD
Great Clane Lane Marshes
INGOLDSBY ROAD
ROSE AV
ABBEY RD
WEST COURT LANE
Sports Ground
BELLMAN AV
B261
EAST
LOWER HIGHAM ROAD
COPPERFIELD CL
NICKLEBY RD
VIA ROMANA
HAVISHAM ROAD
ORLICK RD
LAPIS DR
DARENTH
BROOKE DR
MANOR CL
SUTHERLAND CL
FILBOROUGH WAY
CASTLE LANE
Chalk
Library
FARRIERS CL
LANE
TERENCE CL
OXFORD CL
OSNEY WAY
PIRRIP CL
MILLER R
VICARAGE LA
CHALK ROAD
LISLE CL
VILLA CL
BEECKLEY CL
PRIESTS WK
BARR ROAD
A226
BROWN RD
CRESCENT
LORTON CLOSE
SILVER RD
FORGE
THE TURNSTONES
THE SANDPIPERS
THE CURLEWS
JUBILEE
HAMPTON
School
DRIVE
VALLEY
AVENUE
ST BENEDICTS AV
BOURNE RD
ROAD
Westcourt
Rec Grd
AVON CL
ST BENEDICTS AVENUE
LINDISFARNE CL
ST GREGORYS
CRESCENT
MEDHURST GDNS
MEDHURST
WYE RD
DR
ST AIDANS WAY
FREEMAN WAY
ST CHADS DR
DORIA DRI
HIBERNIA DR
CRUDEN
VANQUISHER WK
CERVIA WAY
KENIA WK
RUMANIA WK
THONG LANE
ST COLUMBAS CL
ST DUNSTANS DRIVE
ST HILDAS
ST MARGARETS CRES
School
Thamesview School
ST ALBANS CL
ST ALBANS GDNS
ST PATRICKS GDNS
CALIPH CL
STORNAWAY STRAND
ARIEL CL
CRESCENT
ST CERNE
DORSET CRES
BELTANA DR
CAMBRIA
WINDHOVER WAY
KELSO DR
VERONA GDS
CLIPPER CRES
MERMERUS GDNS
SAPHO PK
DRIVE
FRANCIS
CLIMBA
WOOD
ST HILDAS WAY
ST GEORGES CRES
ST DAVIDS CRES
THE RISE
THE DRIVE
VOLANTE WAY
SARA PARK
LEANDER
BONAVENTURE CT
CHALLENGE CL
AVENUE
WHINFELL
THE WARREN
Thong Lane Sports Centre
23

HEXTABLE
16
Bexley Hospital
Heath Side
Cemy
Playing Field
Dartford Technical College for Girls
Social Club
Secondary School
Joydens Wood Estate
Infants School
Primary Sch
Rowhill Wood
The Ship (P.H.)
School
Playing Field
Furness School
Hextable
Horticultural College
Comp School
Oakfield
Common
Clayton Croft Rd
Wilmington Ct Rd
Tredegar Road
Wallis Clo
Manor Road
Leyton Cross Road
Hook Green Road
Rowhill Road
Tile Kiln Lane
Baldwins Park
Wickstead Cl
Staple Cl
Dykewood Cl
Hanbury Walk
Cameron Cl
Stedman Cl
Maryfield Cl
Faesten Way
Park Way
Wood Road
Red Lodge Road
Red Lodge Cres
Summerhouse Drive
Briar Road
Woodberry Gro
Ferndall Av
Eden Cl
Eden Road
Joyden Wood
Vanessa Way
Hillbrow Cl
Stevens Cl
Green Wood Rd
Woodlands Pk
Avenue
Bankside Cl
Brackendene
Birchwood Drive
Dene Cl
Rosewood
The Chenies
Woodside Dr
Birch Wood Dr
Silver Birch Cl
Chalet Cl
Spurrell
Squires Way
Chestnut Grove
Norfield Rd
Summerhouse
Fernheath Way
Grnfld Rd
Drive
Alfan Lane
Road
Birchwood Road
Puddledock Lane
Top Dartford Rd
Lower Road
Maud Rd
Nuffield Rd
Fens
Durant Rd
Laura Dr
Bower Road
Plantation
Princes Rd
Home Hill
Rowhill Road
St Davids Road
Rowzill Rd
Mansfield Rd
Herongate Rd
Claremont Rd
Claremont Road
Malyons Rd
Rollo Road
Main Road
Panters
New Rd
Egerton Avenue
Casstine Cl
Spring Vale Cl
Nutley Cl
Stuart Cv
Victoria Hill Rd
Millbro
College Road
B258
Hook Green
A
B
8
24
1
2
3
©Estate Publications

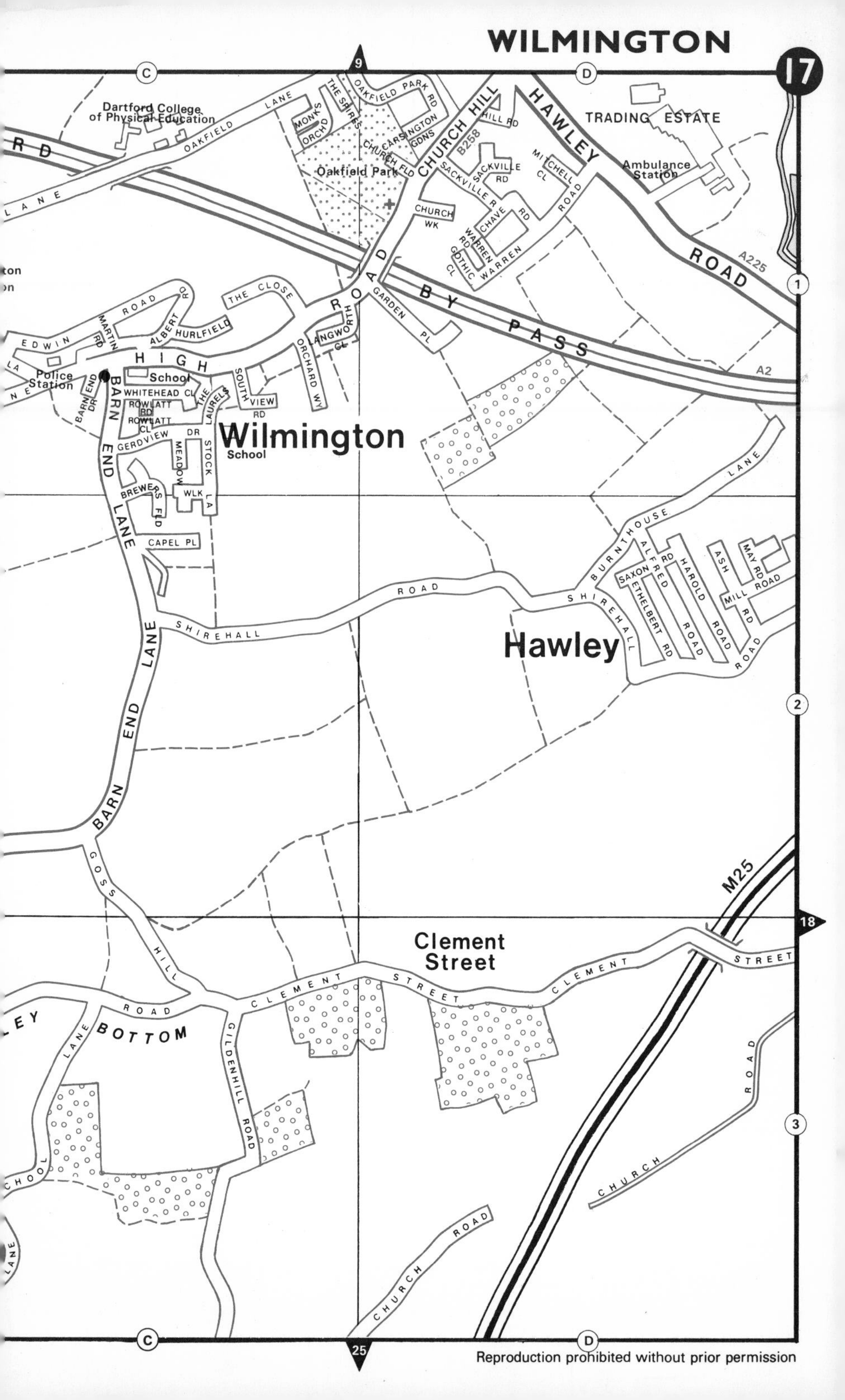
Dartford College of Physical Education
OAKFIELD LANE
MONKS ORCHD
THE SHIRES
OAKFIELD PARK RD
CARSINGTON GDNS
CHURCH FLD
Oakfield Park
CHURCH HILL
HILL RD
B258
HAWLEY ROAD
TRADING ESTATE
Ambulance Station
A225
SACKVILLE RD
MITCHELL CL
SACKVILLE R
CHAVE RD
CHURCH WK
WARREN RD
GOTHIC CL
WARREN
MITCHELL ROAD
BY PASS
A2
GARDEN PL
THE CLOSE
ROAD
LANGWORTH CL
ORCHARD WY
EDWIN ROAD
MARTIN RD
ALBERT RD
HURLFIELD
HIGH
Police Station
School
BARN END DR
WHITEHEAD CL
ROWLATT RD
ROWLATT CL
THE LAURELS
SOUTH VIEW RD
Wilmington
School
GERDVIEW DR
MEADOW
STOCK LA
BREWERS FLD
WLK
BARN END LANE
CAPEL PL
SHIREHALL ROAD
BURNTHOUSE LANE
ALFRED RD
SAXON RD
ETHELBERT RD
HAROLD ROAD
ASH ROAD
MAY RD
MILL RD
MILL ROAD
SHIREHALL
Hawley
M25
GOSS HILL
Clement Street
CLEMENT STREET
BOTTOM ROAD
GILDENHILL ROAD
SCHOOL LANE
CHURCH ROAD
C
D
9
25
18
1
2
3

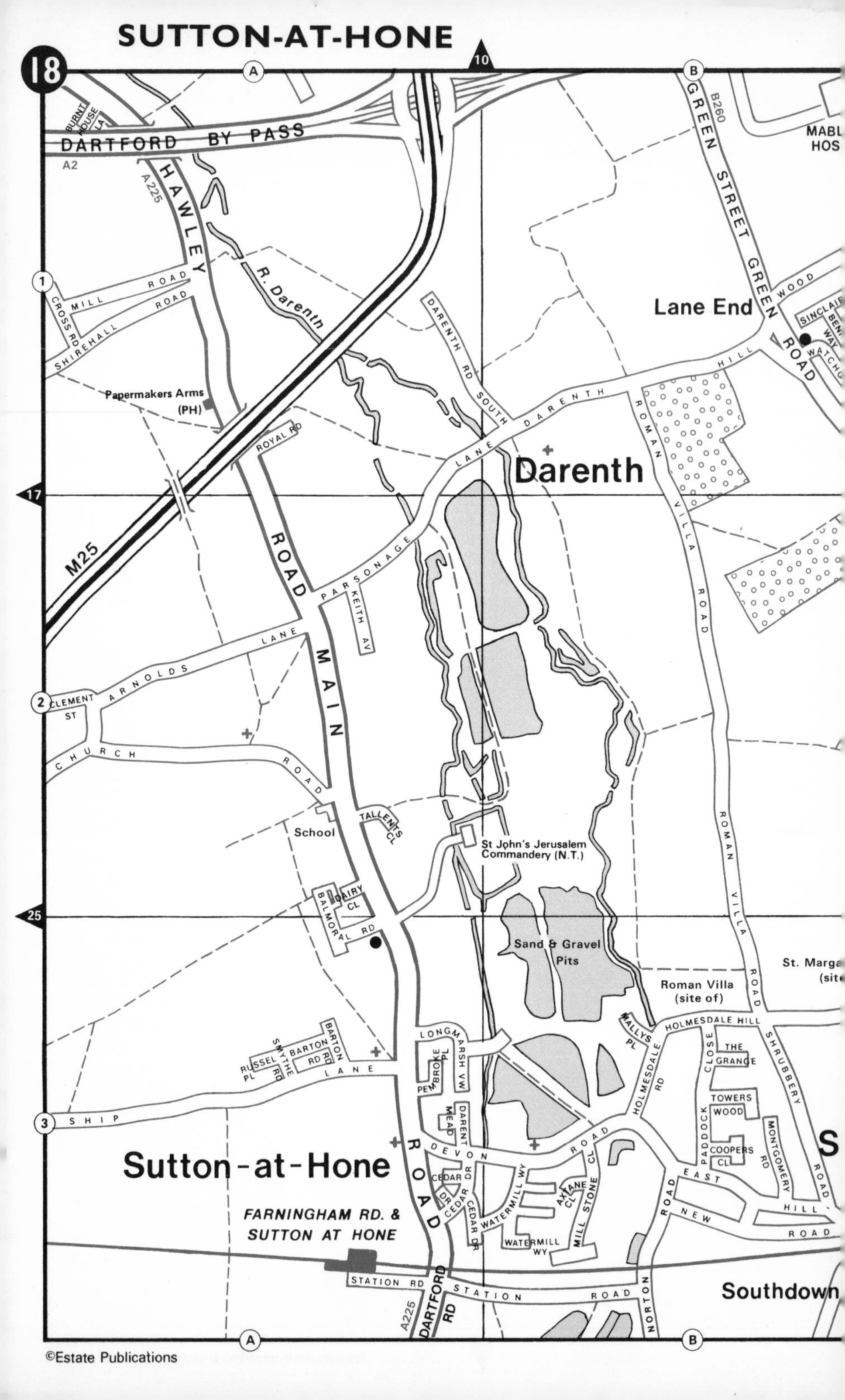
DARTFORD BY PASS
A2
BURNT HOUSE LA
HAWLEY
A225
GREEN STREET GREEN ROAD
B260
MABL HOS
MILL ROAD
SHIREHALL ROAD
CROSS RD
R. Darenth
DARENTH RD SOUTH
Lane End
WOOD
SINCLAIR
BENN WAY
WATCH
DARENTH HILL
Papermakers Arms (PH)
ROYAL RD
LANE
Darenth
ROMAN VILLA ROAD
M25
ROAD
PARSONAGE
KEITH AV
MAIN
ARNOLDS LANE
CLEMENT ST
CHURCH ROAD
TALLENTS CL
School
St John's Jerusalem Commandery (N.T.)
DAIRY CL
BALMORAL RD
Sand & Gravel Pits
Roman Villa (site of)
St. Marga (site
MALLYS PL
HOLMESDALE HILL
HOLMESDALE RD
CLOSE
THE GRANGE
SHRUBBERY ROAD
BARTON RD
BARTON
SMYTHE RD
RUSSEL PL
LANE
LONGMARSH VW
PEMBROKE PL
TOWERS WOOD
PADDOCK
COOPERS CL
MONTGOMERY RD
SHIP
MEAD
DARENT
DEVON ROAD
Sutton-at-Hone
CEDAR DR
WATERMILL WY
AXTANE CL
MILL STONE CL
EAST HILL
NEW ROAD
FARNINGHAM RD. & SUTTON AT HONE
STATION RD
STATION ROAD
DARTFORD RD
NORTON
Southdown
A
B
1
2
3
10
17
25

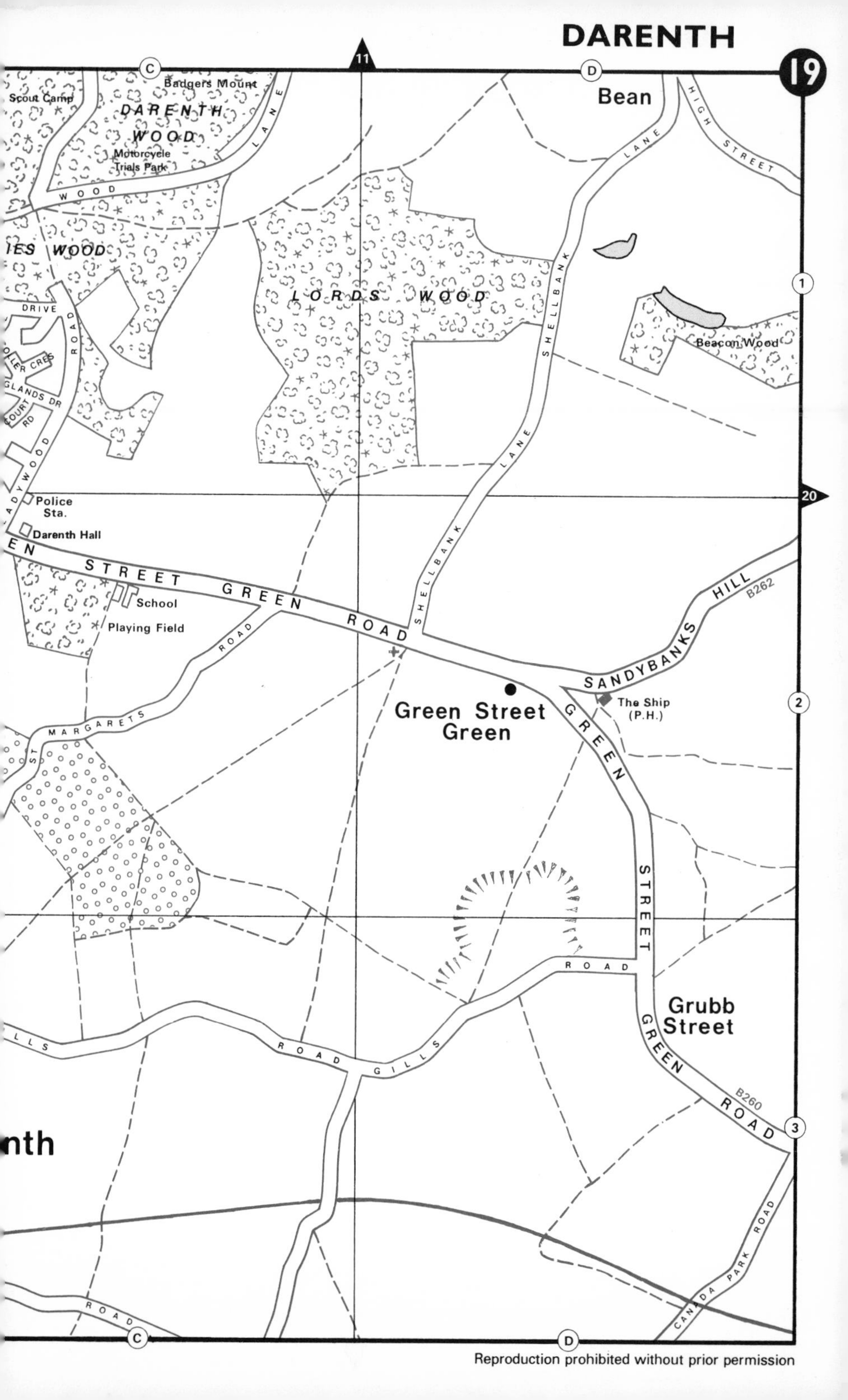
Scout Camp
Badgers Mount
DARENTH WOOD
Motorcycle Trials Park
WOOD
LANE
IES WOOD
LORDS WOOD
Bean
HIGH STREET
LANE
SHELLBANK
Beacon Wood
DRIVE
ROAD
OLLER CRES
GLANDS DR
COURT RD
ADYWOOD
Police Sta.
Darenth Hall
EN STREET GREEN ROAD
School
Playing Field
SHELLBANK LANE
ROAD
HILL
B262
SANDYBANKS
The Ship (P.H.)
Green Street Green
ST MARGARETS
GREEN STREET
ROAD
Grubb Street
GREEN ROAD
B260
LLS
ROAD GILLS
nth
ROAD
CANADA PARK ROAD
C
D
11
20
1
2
3

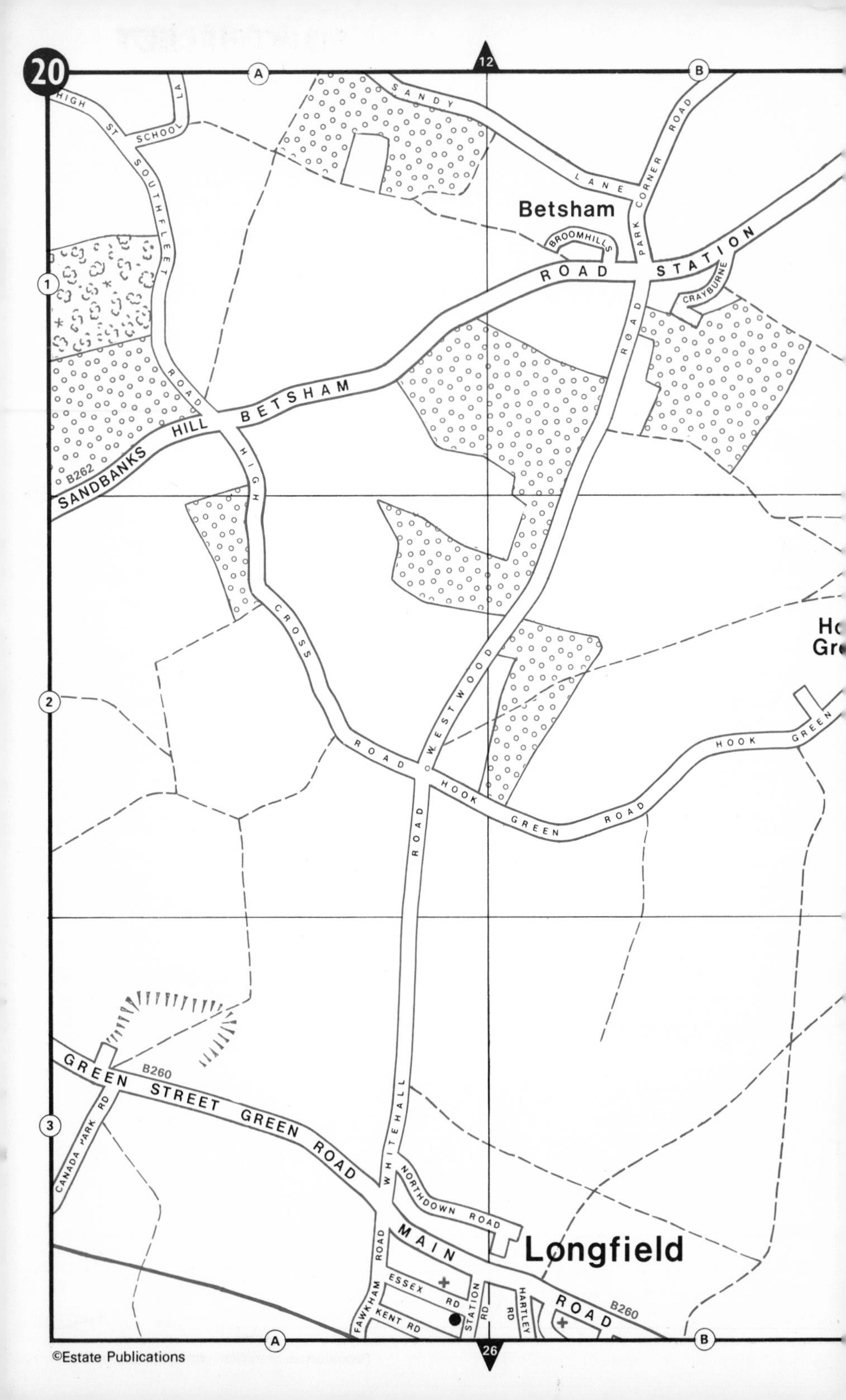
A
12
B
HIGH ST
SCHOOL LA
SANDY LANE
PARK CORNER ROAD
Betsham
BROOMHILLS
SOUTHFLEET ROAD
STATION ROAD
CRAYBURNE
BETSHAM ROAD
SANDBANKS HILL
B262
HIGH CROSS ROAD
WESTWOOD ROAD
HOOK GREEN ROAD
HOOK GREEN
1
2
3
GREEN STREET GREEN ROAD
B260
CANADA PARK RD
WHITEHALL ROAD
NORTHDOWN ROAD
MAIN ROAD
Longfield
ESSEX RD
KENT RD
FAWKHAM ROAD
STATION RD
HARTLEY RD
B260
A
26
B

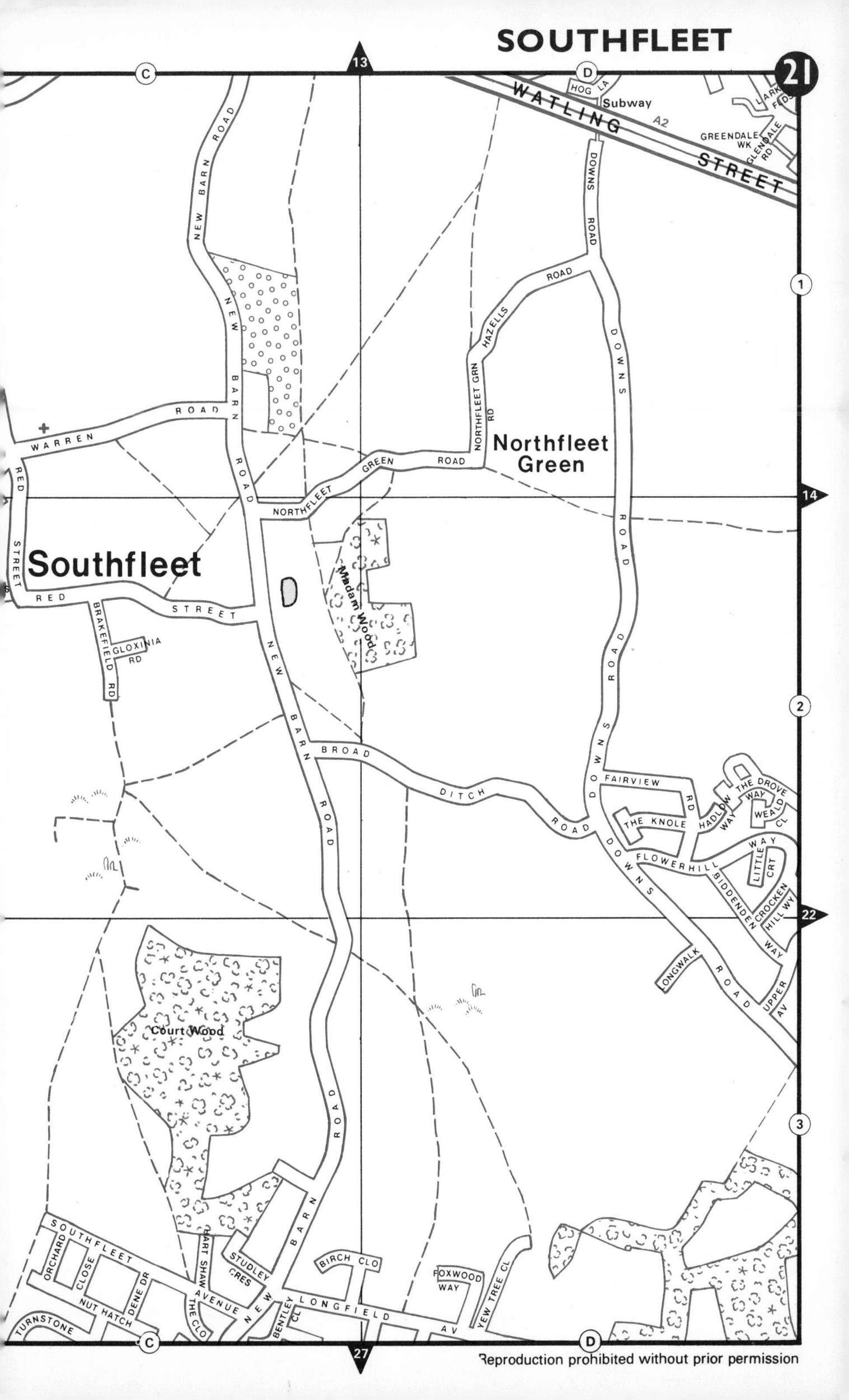
Southfleet
Northfleet Green
WATLING STREET
A2
Subway
HOG LA
LARK FLDS
GREENDALE WK
GLENDALE RD
DOWNS ROAD
ROAD
HAZELLS
NORTHFLEET GRN RD
NEW BARN ROAD
WARREN ROAD
RED STREET
NORTHFLEET GREEN ROAD
Madam Wood
BRAKEFIELD RD
GLOXINIA RD
BROAD DITCH ROAD
FAIRVIEW RD
THE KNOLE
HADLOW WAY
THE DROVE WAY
WEALD CL
FLOWERHILL WAY
LITTLE CRT
BIDDENDEN WAY
CROCKEN HILL WY
LONGWALK
UPPER AV
Court Wood
SOUTHFLEET AVENUE
ORCHARD CLOSE
DENE DR
NUT HATCH
TURNSTONE
HART SHAW
THE CLO
STUDLEY CRES
BENTLEY CL
BIRCH CLO
LONGFIELD AV
FOXWOOD WAY
YEW TREE CL
13
14
22
27
C
D
1
2
3

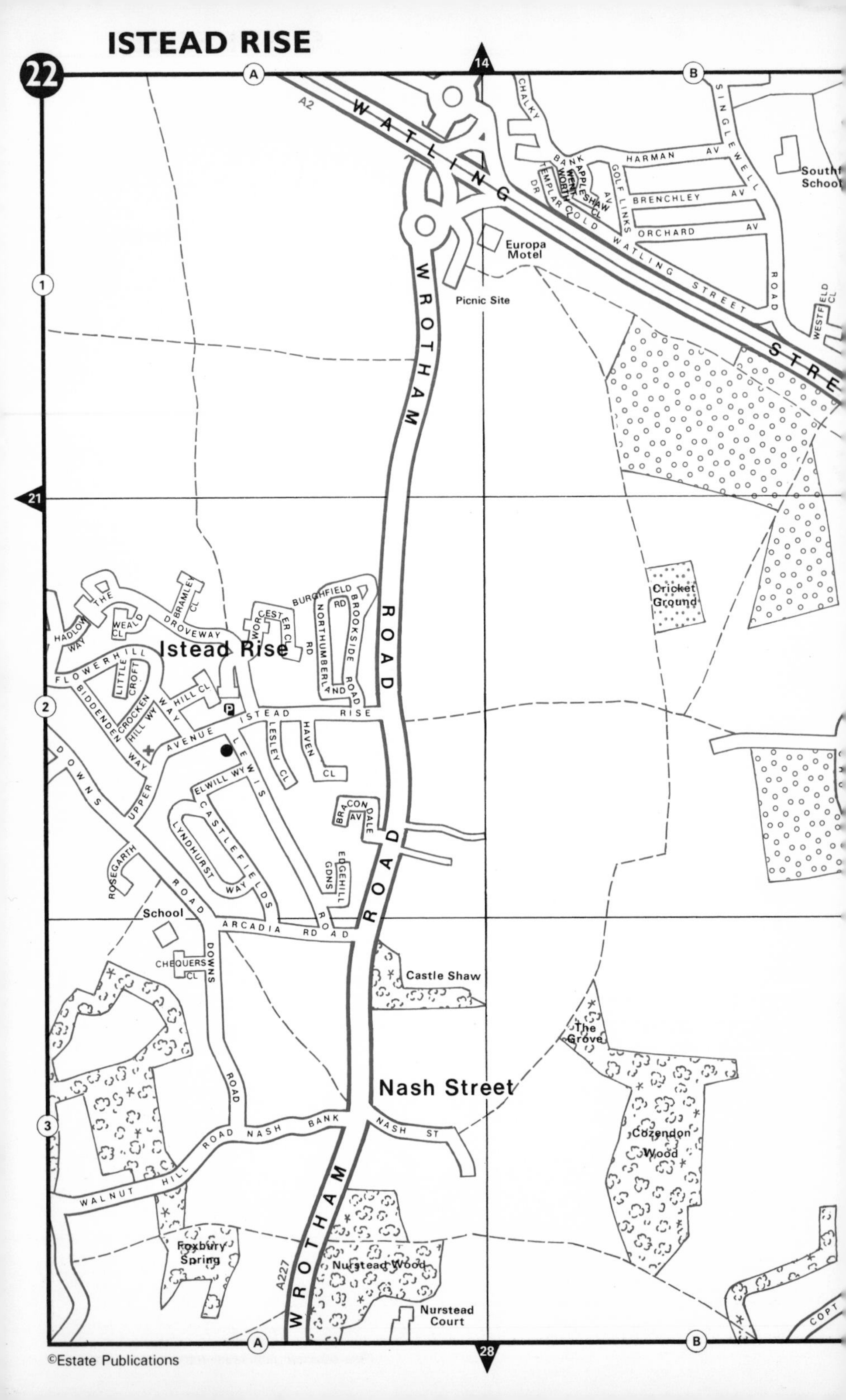
Istead Rise
Nash Street
WATLING STREET
WROTHAM ROAD
A2
A227
Europa Motel
Picnic Site
Cricket Ground
School
Castle Shaw
The Grove
Cozendon Wood
Foxbury Spring
Nurstead Wood
Nurstead Court
Southfleet School
HARMAN AV
BRENCHLEY AV
ORCHARD AV
SINGLEWELL ROAD
GOLF LINKS AV
CHALKY BANK
APPLESHAW CL
WENTWORTH DR
TEMPLAR DR
COLD WATLING STREET
WESTFIELD CL
BURGHFIELD RD
BROOKSIDE ROAD
NORTHUMBERLAND ROAD
WORCESTER CL
ISTEAD RISE
LESLEY CL
HAVEN CL
BRACONDALE AV
EDGEHILL GDNS
ARCADIA ROAD
LEWIS ROAD
CASTLEFIELDS
LYNDHURST WAY
ELWILL WY
UPPER AVENUE
DOWNS ROAD
ROSEGARTH
CHEQUERS CL
HILL CL
CROCKEN HILL WY
BIDDENDEN WAY
LITTLE CROFT
FLOWERHILL WAY
HADLOW WAY
THE WEALD
WEALD CL
THE DROVEWAY
BRAMLEY CL
NASH BANK ROAD
NASH ST
WALNUT HILL ROAD
COPT
A
B
1
2
3
14
21
28

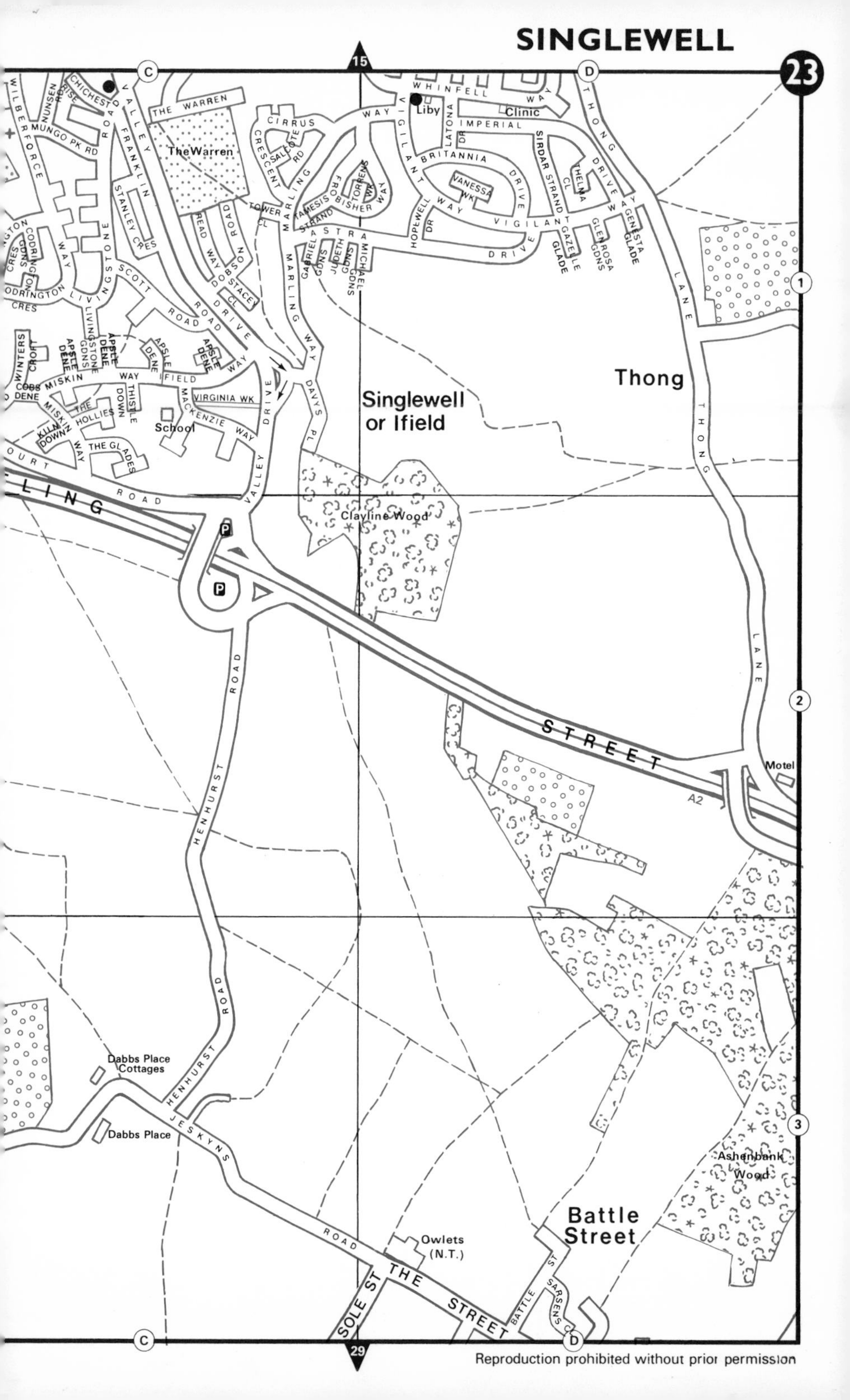
Singlewell or Ifield
Thong
Battle Street
The Warren
Clayline Wood
Ashenbank Wood
Dabbs Place Cottages
Dabbs Place
Owlets (N.T.)
School
Liby
Clinic
Motel
STREET
A2
HENHURST ROAD
JESKYNS ROAD
THE STREET
SOLE ST
BATTLE ST
SARSENS CL
THONG LANE
THONG DRIVE
VALLEY DRIVE
MARLING WAY
VIGILANT WAY
VIGILANT DRIVE
BRITANNIA DRIVE
IMPERIAL
WHINFELL WAY
CIRRUS CRESCENT
SALCOTE RD
FROBISHER WAY
TORRENS WK
TAMESIS STRAND
ASTRA DRIVE
GABRIEL GDNS
JUDETH GDNS
MICHAEL GDNS
HOPEWELL DR
LATONA DR
VANESSA WK
SIRDAR STRAND
THELMA CL
GAZELLE GLADE
GLENROSA GDNS
GENESTA GLADE
TOWER CL
DAVYS PL
THE WARREN
READ WAY
DOBSON ROAD
STACEY CL
FRANKLIN
STANLEY CRES
VALLEY
SCOTT ROAD
LIVINGSTONE
LIVINGSTONE GDNS
APSLE DENE
IFIELD WAY
MISKIN WAY
THISTLE DOWN
MACKENZIE WAY
VIRGINIA WK
THE HOLLIES
THE GLADES
KILN DOWN
COBS DENE
WINTERS CROFT
CODRINGTON CRES
CODRINGTON GDNS
WILBERFORCE
NUNSEN RISE
MUNGO PK RD
CHICHESTER ROAD
COURT ROAD
LING
C
D
15
29
1
2
3

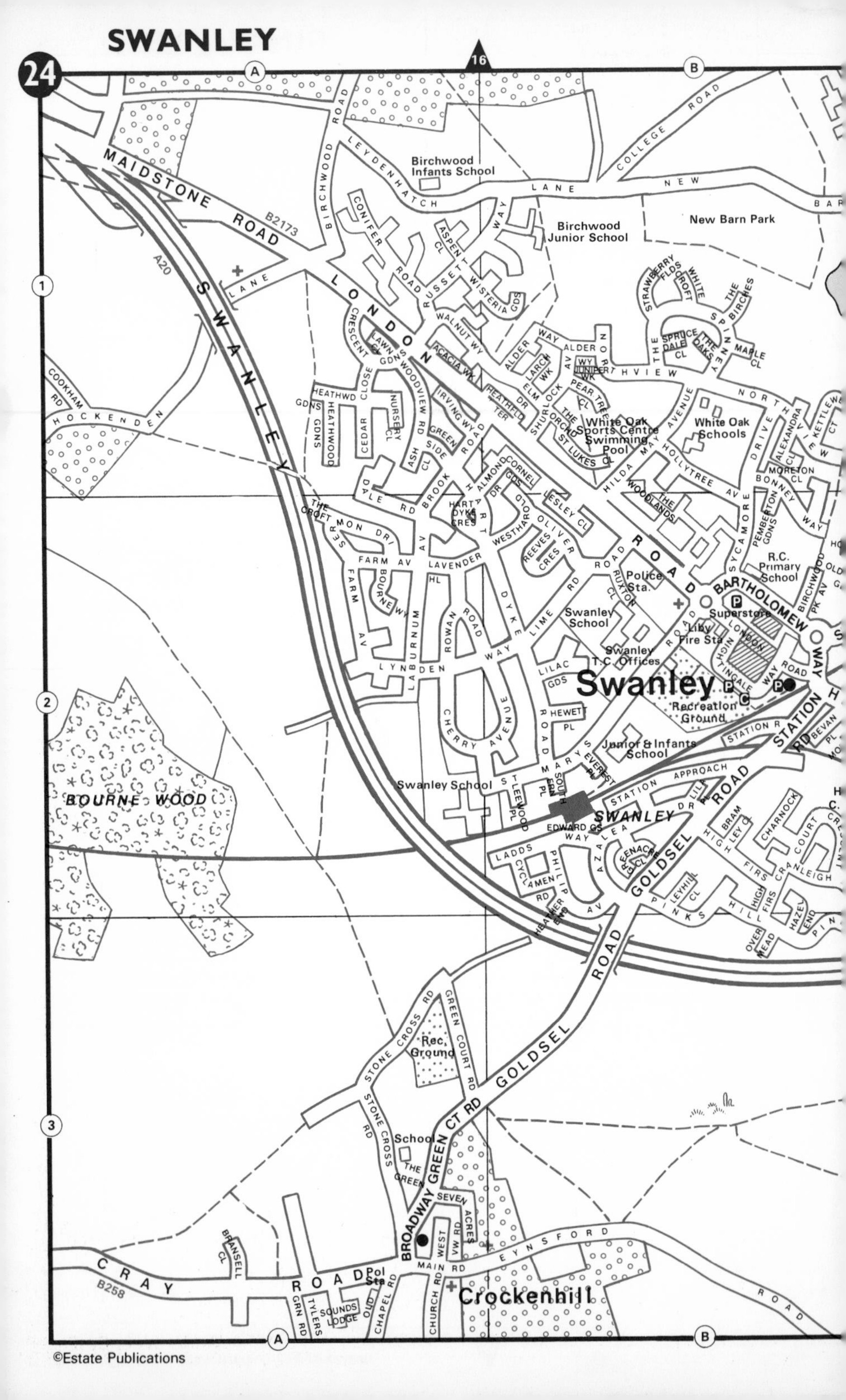
MAIDSTONE ROAD
B2173
A20
SWANLEY
LONDON ROAD
BIRCHWOOD ROAD
LEYDENHATCH LANE
Birchwood Infants School
Birchwood Junior School
NEW BARN
New Barn Park
COLLEGE ROAD
HOCKENDEN
COOKHAM RD
CONIFER
RUSSETT WAY
ASPEN CL
WISTERIA GDS
WALNUT WY
ACACIA WK
ALDER WAY
LARCH WK
ELM
SHURLOCK AV
JUNIPER WK
NORTHVIEW
STRAWBERRY FLDS
WHITE CROFT
THE SPINNEY
THE BIRCHES
THE SPRUCE DALE CL
THE OAKS
MAPLE CL
HEATHFIELD TER
PEAR TREE CL
THE ORCHARD
White Oak Sports Centre Swimming Pool
ST LUKES CL
HILDA MAY AVENUE
White Oak Schools
HOLLYTREE AV
THE WOODLANDS
SYCAMORE DRIVE
ALEXANDRA
MORETON CL
BONNEY WAY
PEMBERTON GDNS
R.C. Primary School
BIRCHWOOD PK AV
KETTLEWELL CT
LAWN CL
CRESCENT GDNS
WOODVIEW RD
HEATHWD GDNS
HEATHWOOD GDNS
CEDAR CLOSE
NURSERY CL
IRVING WY
GREEN SIDE
ASH CL
ALMOND DR
CORNEL GDS
HART DYKE CRES
HART DYKE ROAD
DALE RD
BROOK AV
THE CROFT
SERMON DRI
FARM AV
LAVENDER HL
BOURNE WY
WESTHAROLD
REEVES CRES
OLIVER CRES
LESLEY CL
ROAD
RUXTON CL
Police Sta.
BARTHOLOMEW WAY
Superstore
Liby
Fire Sta
NIGHTINGALE WAY
LAURNUM
ROWAN ROAD
LYNDEN WAY
LIME RD
Swanley School
Swanley T.C. Offices
LILAC GDS
Swanley
Recreation Ground
HEWETT PL
CHERRY AVENUE
ST MARYS ROAD
EVEREST PL
Junior & Infants School
STATION R
STATION RD
BEVAN PL
Swanley School
ST LEWOOD PL
SOUTH FRM PL
STATION APPROACH
SWANLEY
EDWARD GS
WAY
AZALEA DR
LILAC
GOLDSEL ROAD
GREENACRE CL
BRAMLEY CL
CHARNOCK
COURT CRESCENT
CRANLEIGH
HIGH FIRS
LADDS
CYCLAMEN RD
PHILIP AV
HEATHER END
LEYHILL CL
PINKS HILL
OVER MEAD
HAZEL END
BOURNE WOOD
STONE CROSS RD
GREEN COURT RD
Rec. Ground
GOLDSEL RD
GREEN CT RD
School
THE GREEN
SEVEN ACRES
BROADWAY
WEST VW RD
BRANSELL CL
CRAY ROAD
B258
Pol Sta
MAIN RD
EYNSFORD ROAD
GRN RD
TYLERS
SOUNDS LODGE
OLD CHAPEL RD
CHURCH RD
Crockenhill
A
B
16
1
2
3

17
C
D
Swanley Village
St. Pauls C of E School
SCHOOL LANE
ANTHONY LA
HIGHLANDS HILL
SWANLEY VILLAGE ROAD
WOOD ST
PARK LA
BUTTON
M25
BEECHENLEA LANE
FIVE WENTS
B258
ROAD
LANE
AV
School
Olympic Leisure Centre
Downsview Junior & Infants School
WEST VIEW RD
MOULTAIN HILL
ABBOTTS CL
MANSE WAY
Bus Station
BREMNER CL
ROGERS CT
Broom Hill
FARNINGHAM WOOD
STREET
BEECHENLEA
ROAD
SALISBURY AV
MAYES CL
WANSBURY WAY
MEAD CL
MARK WAY
PEDHAM PLACE INDUSTRIAL ESTATE
WESTED LANE
LONDON ROAD
BUTTON
FARNINGHAM HILL ROAD
M20
A20
M25
1
2
3
C
D

LONGFIELD

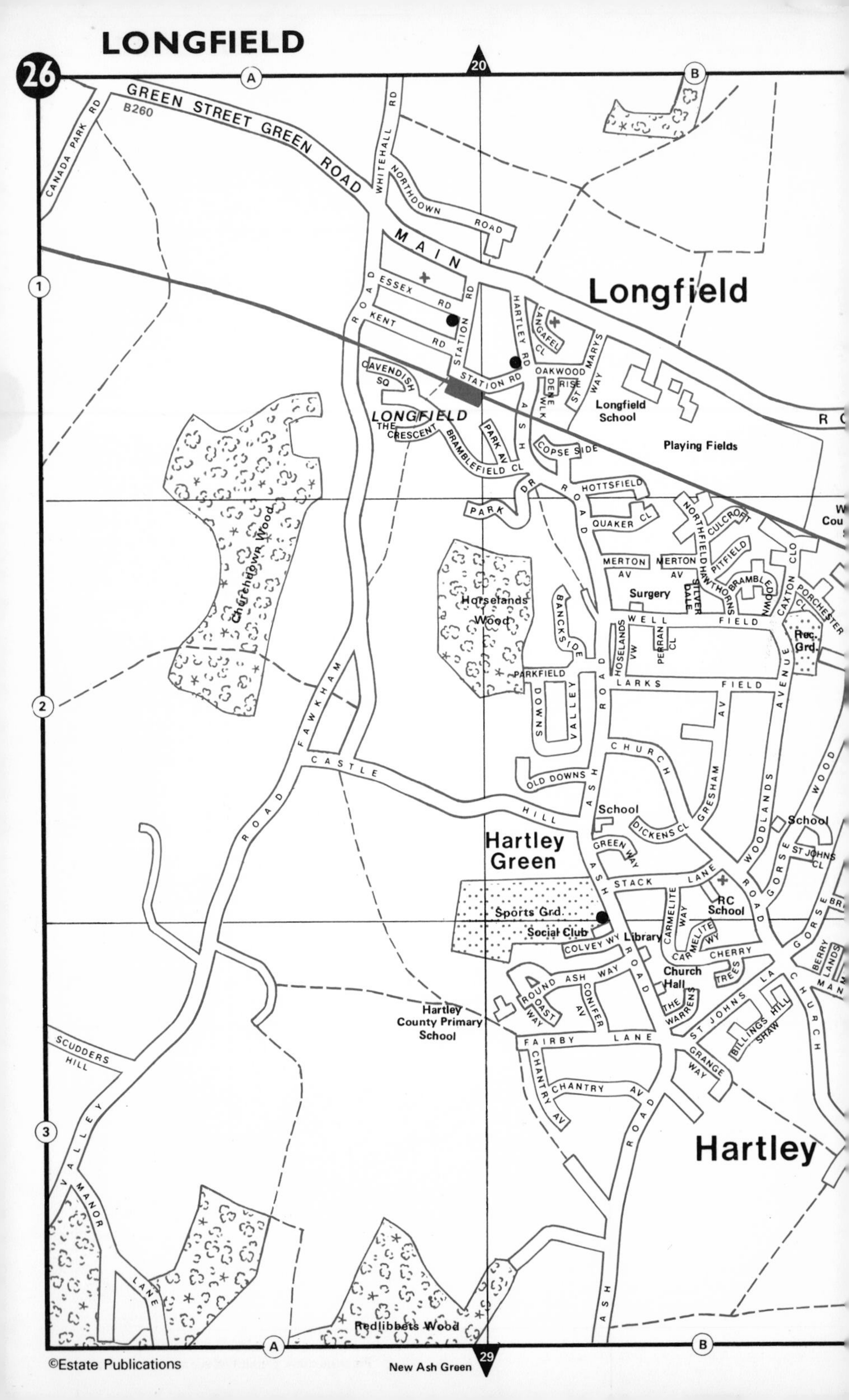
26
Longfield
Hartley Green
Hartley
GREEN STREET GREEN ROAD
B260
CANADA PARK RD
WHITEHALL RD
NORTHDOWN ROAD
MAIN
ESSEX RD
KENT RD
STATION RD
HARTLEY RD
LANGAFEL CL
OAKWOOD RISE
DENE WLK
ST MARYS WAY
CAVENDISH SQ
LONGFIELD
THE CRESCENT
BRAMBLEFIELD CL
PARK AV
COPSE SIDE
PARK DR
ASH ROAD
HOTTSFIELD
QUAKER CL
MERTON AV
NORTHFIELD
CULCROFT
PITFIELD
HAWTHORNS
BRAMBLEDOWN
SILVER DALE
CAXTON CLO
PORCHESTER CL
Longfield School
Playing Fields
Surgery
Rec. Grd.
Horselands Wood
Churchdown Wood
BANCKSIDE
WELL FIELD
HOSELANDS VW
PERRAN CL
PARKFIELD
LARKS FIELD
DOWNS VALLEY
AVENUE
FAWKHAM ROAD
CASTLE HILL
CHURCH
GRESHAM AV
OLD DOWNS
WOODLANDS
WOOD
School
DICKENS CL
GREEN WAY
GORSE
ST JOHNS CL
STACK LANE
CARMELITE WAY
RC School
Sports Grd.
Social Club
Library
COLVEY WY
CHERRY TREES
BERRY LANDS
Church Hall
ROUND ASH WAY
CONIFER AV
OAST WAY
THE WARRENS
ST JOHNS LA
BILLINGS HILL SHAW
Hartley County Primary School
FAIRBY LANE
GRANGE WAY
CHANTRY AV
SCUDDERS HILL
VALLEY
MANOR LANE
Redlibbets Wood
20
29
A
B
1
2
3
New Ash Green

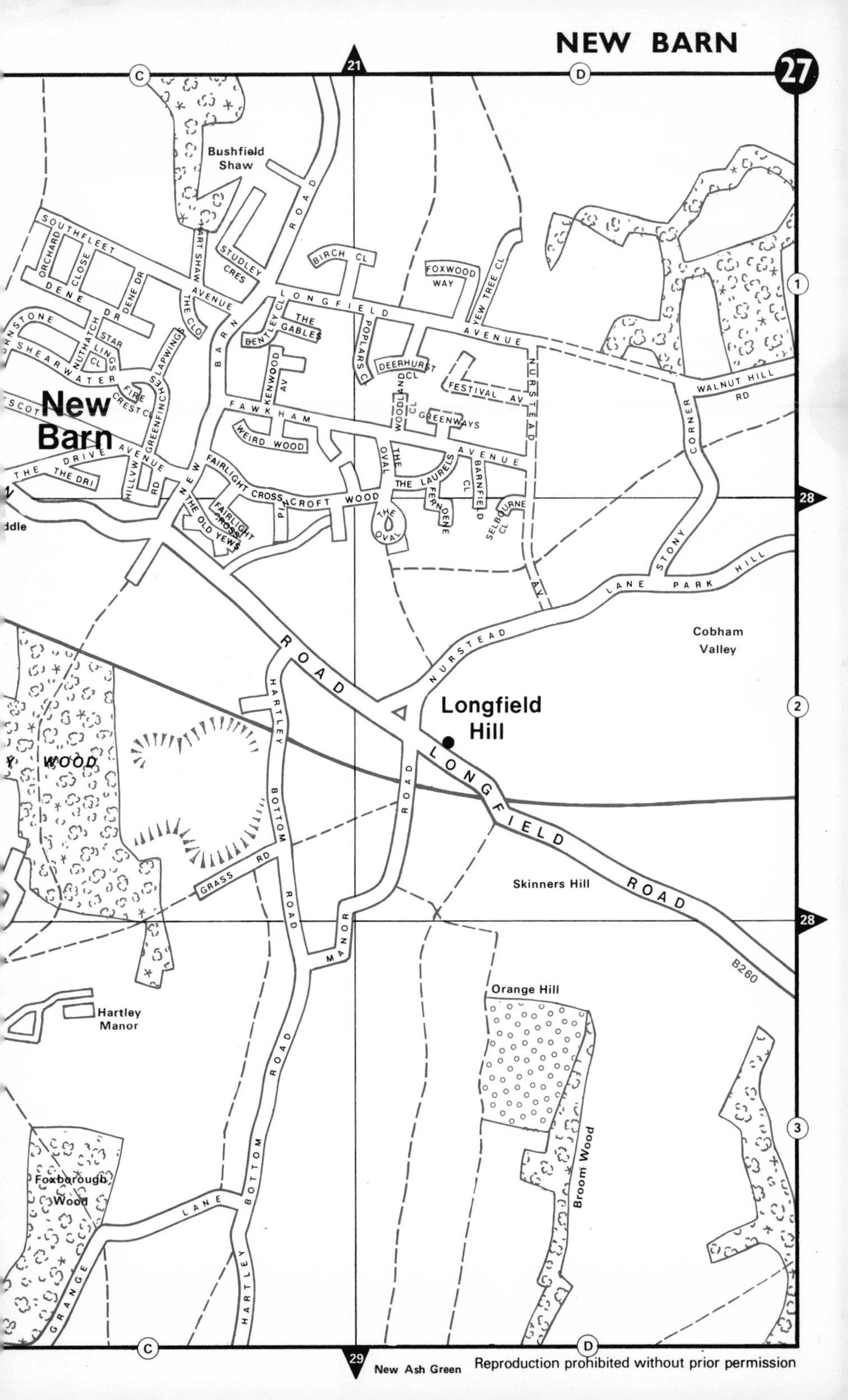
Bushfield Shaw
New Barn
Longfield Hill
Cobham Valley
Skinners Hill
Orange Hill
Broom Wood
Hartley Manor
Foxborough Wood
WOOD
SOUTHFLEET AVENUE
ORCHARD CLOSE
DENE DR
DENE
NUTHATCH DR
STAR LINGS CL
SHEARWATER
FIRE CREST CL
LAPWINGS
GREENFINCHES
HART SHAW
THE CLO
STUDLEY CRES
BARN ROAD
BIRCH CL
LONGFIELD AVENUE
BENTLEY CL
THE GABLES
KENWOOD AV
POPLARS CL
DEERHURST CL
FOXWOOD WAY
YEW TREE CL
FESTIVAL AV
WOODLAND CL
GREENWAYS
NURSTEAD AV
FAWKHAM AVENUE
WEIRD WOOD
THE OVAL
THE LAURELS
BARNFIELD CL
FERNDENE
SELBOURNE CL
THE DRIVE
THE DRI
HILLVIEW RD
NEW FAIRLIGHT CROSS
FAIRLIGHT CROSS
THE OLD YEWS
PINCROFT WOOD
WALNUT HILL RD
CORNER
STONY
LANE PARK HILL
NURSTEAD
ROAD
LONGFIELD ROAD
HARTLEY BOTTOM ROAD
GRASS RD
MANOR ROAD
B260
LANE
GRANGE
HARTLEY BOTTOM
C
D
21
29
28
1
2
3
New Ash Green

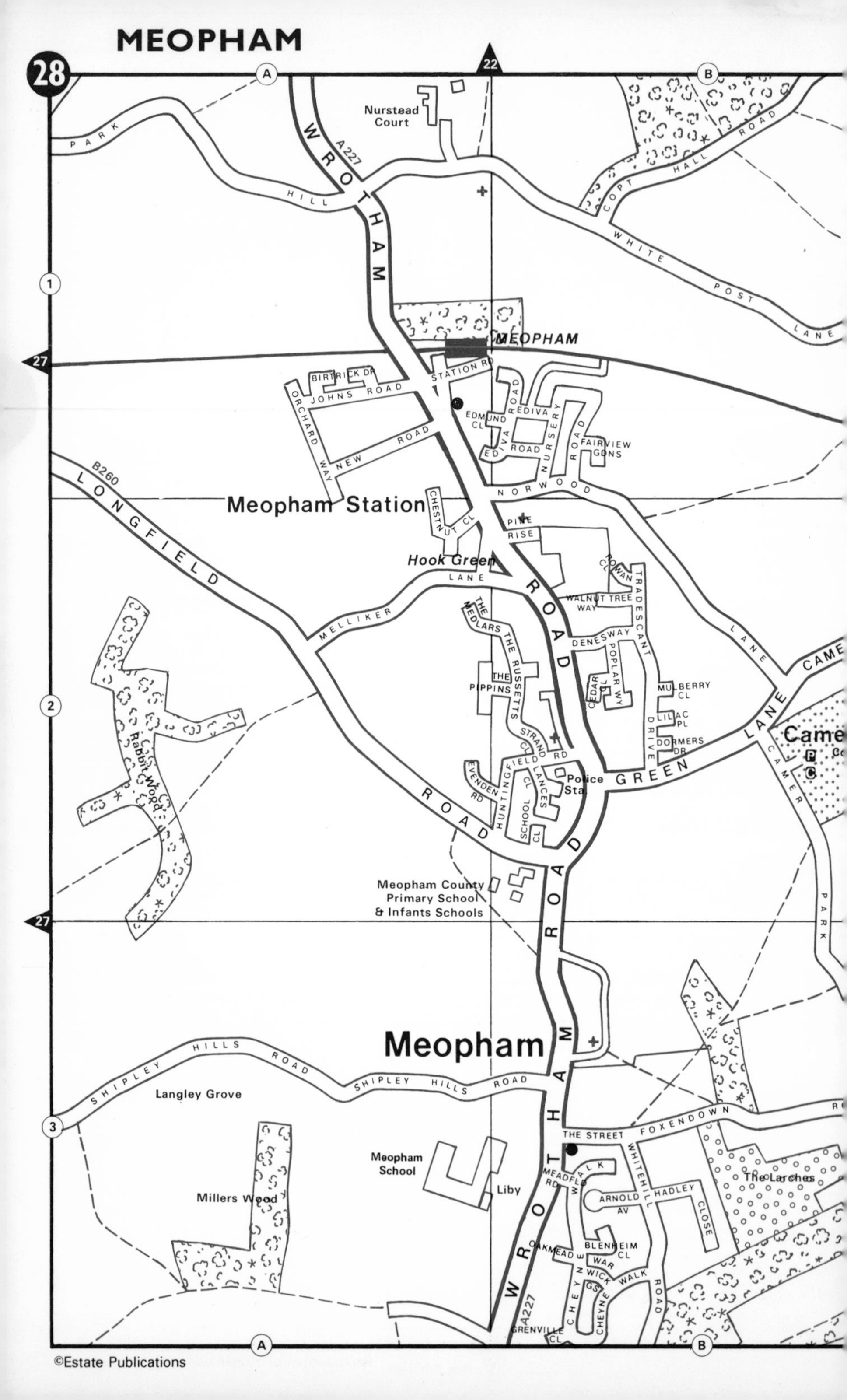

MEOPHAM
28
A
22
B
Nurstead Court
PARK HILL
WROTHAM
A227
COPT HALL ROAD
WHITE POST LANE
1
MEOPHAM
27
BIRTRICK DR
STATION RD
JOHNS ROAD
ORCHARD WAY
NEW ROAD
EDMUND CL
EDIVA ROAD
EDIVA ROAD
NURSERY ROAD
FAIRVIEW GDNS
NORWOOD
B260
LONGFIELD
Meopham Station
CHESTNUT CL
PINE RISE
Hook Green
LANE
ROAD
ROWAN CL
TRADESCANT
WALNUT TREE WAY
MELLIKER
THE MEDLARS
THE RUSSETTS
THE PIPPINS
DENESWAY
CEDAR CL
POPLAR WY
MULBERRY CL
LILAC PL
DRIVE
DORMERS DR
LANE
CAME
Came
2
Rabbit Wood
STRAND RD
CL
EVENDEN RD
HUNTINGFIELD
CL
LANCES CL
SCHOOL CL
Police Sta
GREEN
LANE
CAMER PARK
ROAD
ROAD
Meopham County Primary School & Infants Schools
27
Meopham
HILLS ROAD
SHIPLEY HILLS ROAD
SHIPLEY
Langley Grove
3
THE STREET
FOXENDOWN
Meopham School
Liby
MEADFLD RD
WALK
WHITEHILL ROAD
ARNOLD AV
HADLEY CLOSE
The Larches
Millers Wood
OAKMEAD
BLENHEIM CL
WARWICK WALK
CHEYNE
GS
CHEYNE
A227
GRENVILLE CL
WROTHAM
A
B
©Estate Publications

COBHAM

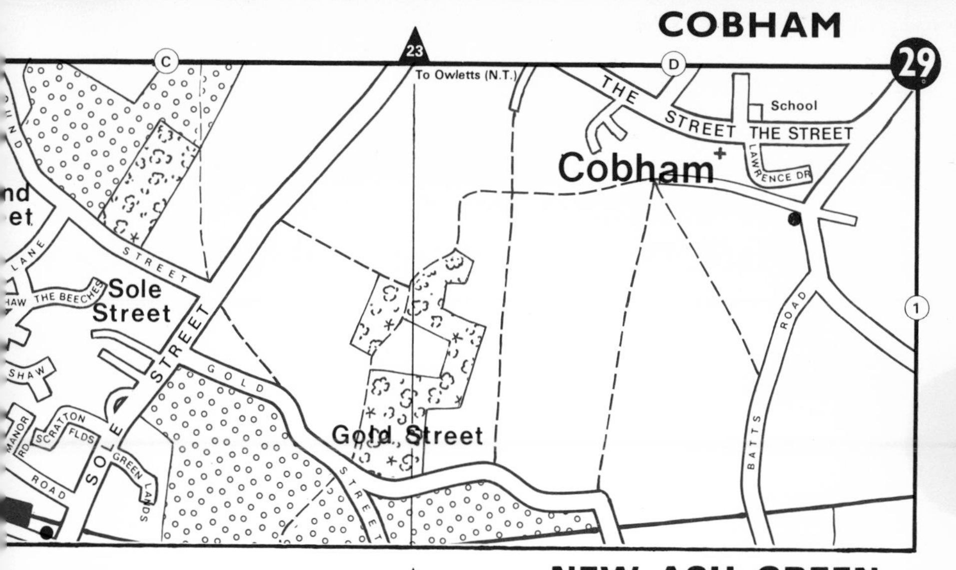

NEW ASH GREEN

INDEX TO STREETS

TH
SAXON KNIVES

The Song of Ash
Book Two

JAMES CALBRAITH

FLYING
SQUID

Published January 2020 by Flying Squid

Visit James Calbraith's official website at
jamescalbraith.wordpress.com
for the latest news, book details, and other information

Cover photo: Oleksandr Zamuruiev, Peter Lorrimer via Shutterstock

BRITANNIA SUPERIOR, c. 450 AD

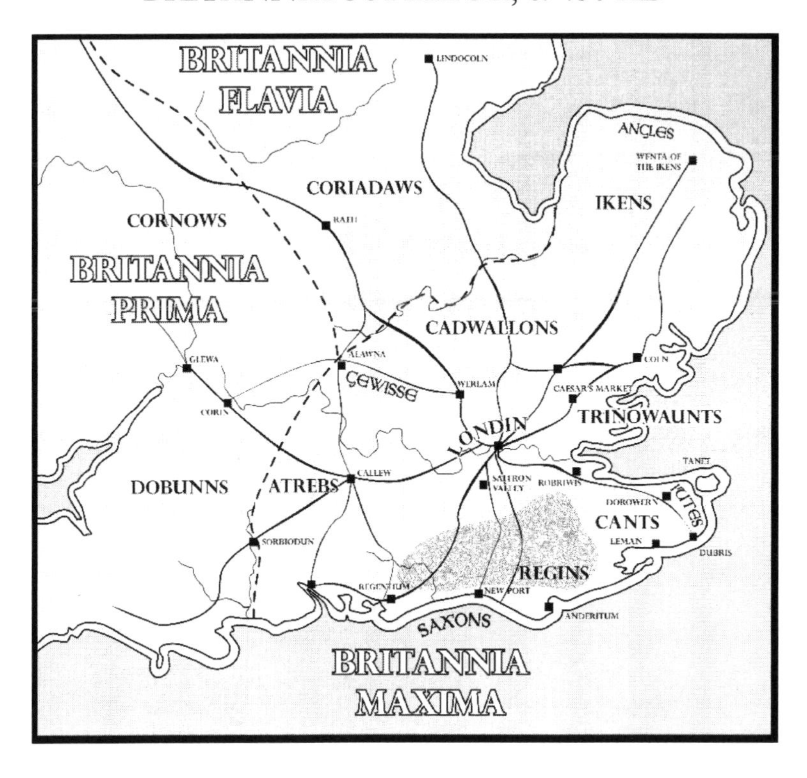

BRITANNIA MAXIMA, c. 430 AD

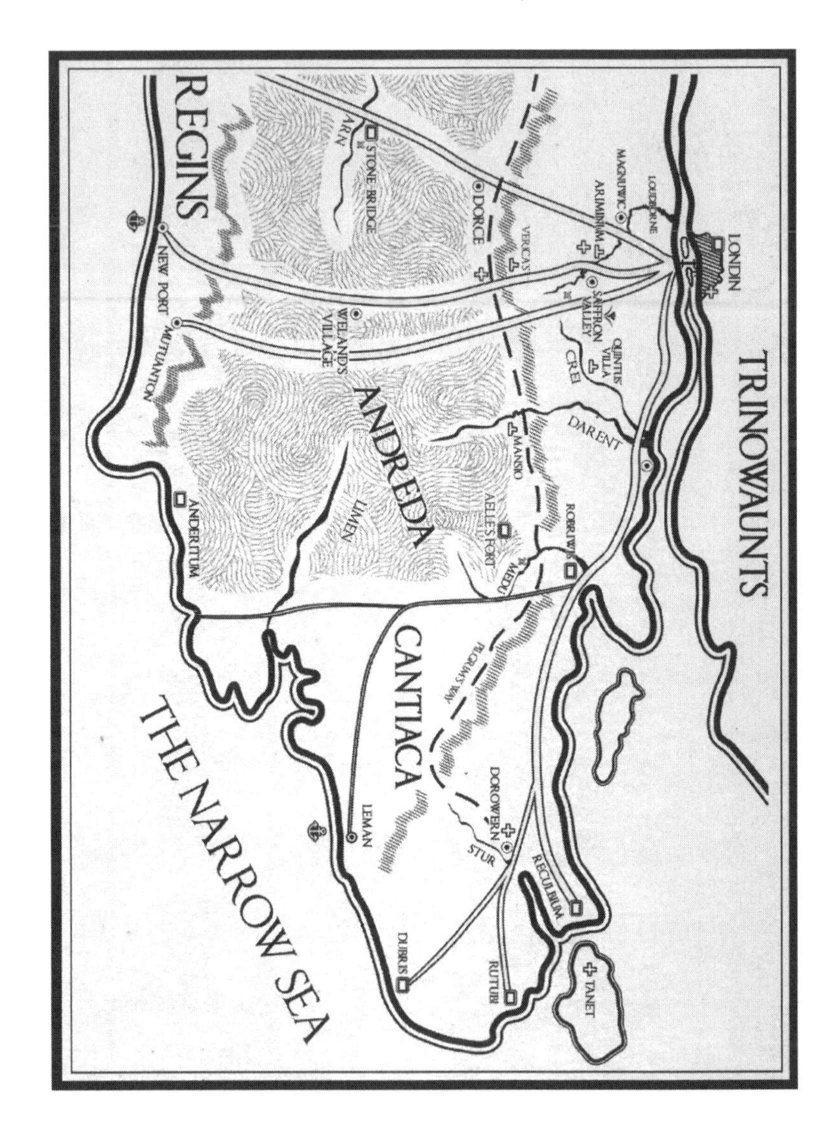

CAST OF CHARACTERS

Londin

Brutus: Centurion of Londin *praetorium* guards
Deneus: Oyster merchant
Fastidius: Vicar General of Londin, Ash's Brother
Fatalis: Bishop of Londin
Postumus: Senior Councillor
Wortigern: *Dux* of Britannia Maxima
Wortimer: Younger son of Wortigern

Ikens, Angles, Picts

Angenwit: *Drihten* of the Angles
Cunedag: a Pict prisoner
Drust: King of the Picts
Una: *Comes* of the Ikens

Britannia Maxima

Elasio: *Comes* of the Cadwallons
Catuar: *Comes* of the Regins
Masuna: *Comes* of the Atrebs
Odo: *Decurion* of the Gaulish cavalry in Cantiaca
Peredur: *Comes* of Trinowaunts
Worangon: *Comes* of Cantiaca

Britannia Prima and Rome

Ambrosius: *Dux* of Britannia Prima
Donatus: Bishop of Ebrauc
Germanus: Bishop of Autissiodorum
Riotham: *Praetor* of Ambrosius
Severus: Bishop of Treverorum

Iutes

Three brothers:

Eobba: lost at sea
Hengist: chief of the Iutes of Tanet
Horsa: chief of the Iutes of Londin

Beadda: commander of Hengist's household guard
Beormund: commander of a coast defence warband
Haesta: Hengist's cousin
Rhedwyn: daughter of Eobba

Saxons

Pefen: chief of the Saxons, unifier of tribes
Aelle: chief of the Saxon warbands in Andreda
Weorth: chief of a Saxon tribe
Bucge: chief of a Saxon tribe

GLOSSARY

Aesc: Saxon spear
Ceol: Narrow, ocean-going Saxon ship
Centuria: Troop of (about) hundred infantry
Centurion: Officer in Roman infantry
Comes, pl. Comites: Administrator of a *pagus,* subordinate to the *Dux*
Decurion: Officer in Roman cavalry
Domus: The main structure of a *villa*
Drihten: War chief of a Saxon tribe
Dux: Overall commander in war times, in peace time — administrator of a province
Fulcum: Roman shield wall formation
Hiréd: Band of elite warriors of *Drihten's* household
Gesith: Companion of the *Drihten*, chief of the *Hiréd*
Mansio: Staging post
Pagus: Administrative unit, smaller than a province
Praetor: high administrative or military official
Pugio: small Roman dagger
Seax: Saxon short sword
Spatha: Roman long sword
Villa: Roman agricultural property
Wealh, pl. *wealas*: "the others", Britons in Saxon tongue

PLACE NAMES

Andreda: Weald Forest
Anderitum: Pevensey, East Sussex
Ariminum: Wallington, Surrey
Callew: Silchester, Hampshire
Cantiaca: Kent
Caesar's Market: Caesaromagus, Chelmsford, Essex
Coln: Colchester, Essex
Corin: Corinium, Cirencester
Dorowern: Dorovernum, Canterbury, Kent
Beaddingatun: Beddington, Surrey
Britannia Maxima: a province of Britannia, capital in Londin
Britannia Prima: a province of Britannia, capital in Corin
Ebrauc: York
Eobbasfleot: Ebbsfleet, Kent
Lindocoln: Lincoln
Londin: Londinium, London
Medu: River Medway
New Port: Novus Portus, Portslade, Sussex
Regentium: Chichester, Sussex
Robriwis: Dorobrivis, Rochester, Kent
Rutubi: Rutupiae, Richborough, Kent
Saffron Valley: Croydon, London
Sorbiodun: Salisbury, Wiltshire
Tamesa: River Thames
Tanet: Isle of Thanet, Kent
Wenta of the Ikens: Caistor St Edmunds
Werlam: St Albans, Hertfordshire

PART 1: 445 AD

CHAPTER I
THE LAY OF RIOTHAM

Two pairs of bare feet stomp on the beach. The one at the back is heavier, burdened with the weight of a sack full of plunder. The one in front is fleeter, but limping, every step leaving a bloody spurt on the sand.

The two men are desperate to reach the boat, bobbing in the rising tide. I give them no chance. My boat pony fares well in the wet sand, and soon I reach the blood-splattered trail and overtake my prey.

I draw the *seax* and point it at the runaways. They pause. Their eyes dart around, seeking another escape route, but all they see are more riders — two ponies approaching to their left, and a black horse to their right, its rider brandishing an *angon*, a Frankish javelin.

The two men split: while the younger one tries to pass me to my rear, the stockier, older warrior drops his haul, draws a short, curved knife from a sheath at his thigh and lunges at me. I leap down to face him; I fight better on foot. The old man is swift for his size, and no doubt has seen his share of fighting, but I have the range over him. I parry and twist, and the knife flies from his hand. He clutches a bleeding wrist.

I turn to face the younger raider. He limps away towards the boat, but he's too slow. The boat's lone helmsman decides not to wait any longer. He heaves away, pushing out with a long pole. The horseman throws a well-aimed javelin straight into his chest. Before long, the empty boat drifts off in a tide of purple froth, towards a small ship which stands watchful on the horizon, beyond the range of our missiles.

The older raider grunts a command at his younger comrade. They both kneel in the sand, their heads low, ready for an executioner's sword. At last, I can now take a closer look at the captives.

The Romans called them Picts — the Painted People; but I can't see any more or less body paint and scars on them than on any battle-seasoned Saxon warrior. They're both short and stout, and both are wearing drab tunics and brightly coloured plaid capes, torn in the fight. Other than that, I doubt I'd be able to pick them out from a crowd on a Londin street. Their speech is a coarse-sounding, rural form of the standard Briton tongue.

The other horsemen trot up to us and dismount. Two of them are Iutes from Tanet, *Drihten* Hengist's men. The third rider, who threw the deadly missile, approaches from the south, his long black hair flowing in salt-dried clumps over his shoulders: Odo, the Gaul cavalry *decurion*. He takes one last scowling glance at the ship on the horizon.

"This must be the last of the raiding party," he says. We encountered three other boats on the nearby beaches — all of them managed to get away before we reached them, though we've recovered most of the plunder.

He steps forward, drawing the long *spatha* sword. The younger of the Picts — he looks a few years older than myself — flinches inadvertently, but the older one grunts at him to act like a man.

"How many of you are still out there?" he asks. The older Pict stares up at him, defiant. Odo's mail-clad fist meets his face. The Gaul picks up the bloodied captive. The Pict spits red sand.

"He'll talk," Odo says, after studying the old man for a while. "But I need to take him with me back to Dorowern. You can do what you want with the other one."

The two Iutes look to me for decision — not as their leader, but as a guest on this raid. The Iutes are not taking prisoners if they can help it — but I don't feel too keen about slaying the young man in cold blood. The Pict raiders this season have been more interested in plunder and pillage than killing, and I can see in the youth's eyes that he has never bloodied his blade before.

"Get up," I say, kicking the younger Pict's backside. "You're coming with us."

By nightfall we reach the Iute war camp. Nine tents cluster atop a low, grassy cliff overlooking the Tamesa Estuary to the north, not far from where the old Reculbium road turns a sharp corner. There were eleven tents here at the start of the summer, but two warriors have since perished fighting the raiders.

The losses did little to endear the Iutes to our young captive. Knocked about and spat at, the hapless youth slumps from my pony and plops down, staring dejectedly into the sea. I stand between him and the curious Iute warriors, to shield him from further abuse.

"What do you need him for?" asks Beormund, the chief of this small warband. "He's not going to tell you anything. He doesn't look like he even knows why he's here."

"I'm taking him to Londin," I reply. "To take him before the Council."

"You're going home?" asks Beormund. "How fortunate you are. We're supposed to stay in this dump until the full moon."

He barks at his men to stand down and sits beside me and the Pict thrall. "When you arrived at *Eobbasfleot* with Worangon's men, back in the spring…" he starts, "I thought you only came to mock us."

It has been a difficult summer in Cantiaca. The Picts have been coming in great numbers — greater than anyone alive remembered; after the war with Aelle last year, the treasury and the manpower of the small *pagus* were all but depleted. Odo's Gaulish cavalry could not be everywhere at once, swift though they were, and the *Dux*'s Council in Londin stubbornly refused to acknowledge the seriousness of the raids — not that they would have much to send in the way of reinforcements, even had they wanted to.

Even a *Comes* as loath to ask pagans for help as Worangon was eventually forced to confront the reality of his situation. There was only one place left he could reach out for help, one that was right at his doorstep: the Iute warriors on Tanet, bored, impoverished and seeking the kind of glory that their more fortunate brethren found the year before in Andreda.

As the Council's representative to the Iutes, I took part in Worangon's hastily assembled emergency mission to Hengist's mead hall at *Eobbasfleot.* But the proposed deal was not what the Iutish chief had hoped for. The Cants would still not let the warriors settle in their land — only to set up a war camp for the duration of the summer campaign, for a dozen men, paid for their effort in a share of the spoils, and a handful of unclipped bronze coins each, to spend however they wished in Dorowern's shops and taverns once the fighting was over.

"Did you know the *Drihten's* cousin, Haesta, almost rebelled against Hengist?" says Beormund.

"I did not know that," I reply. "What did he plan to do?"

"Cross the Stur channel and invade Cantiaca — or die trying. He wanted me as part of his conspiracy, but too many remained loyal to Hengist." He sighs.

"It was the most we could convince Worangon to grant you," I say. "You have no idea how difficult — "

"It doesn't matter. I see now that Hengist was right. If anything, we've been here too long."

"Is it that much worse than Tanet?" I ask with a wry smile, remembering the filthy, crowded squalor of the island.

"At least there are women on Tanet," replies Beormund with a bawdy laugh. "The only ones here are Helge and Inge — and they're only interested in each other!" He laughs again, but more bitterly this time.

"It is hard to live in a place where you're not wanted," he says. "We've all heard how happily Beadda's men have settled among the *wealas* — but it's different here. I may not understand what the Cants say, but I can hear the repulsion in their voices, I can see the loathing in their eyes, even as they smile."

I nod. I know all too well what he means — I have seen it, not only here in Cantiaca, but in Londin, too, some of it aimed at myself.

"You should… join us…" croaks the prisoner. This surprises me even more than Beormund's revelation of the rebellion threatening Hengist's rule. Beormund is equally shocked.

"*Join* you?" he asks. "You're just another *wealh*."

"*Riu*… Drust… respects all warriors…" says the Pict, struggling for Saxon words through swollen lips. "We have some… Anglians — a handful, by Ebrauc. All… united — under the Boar's Banner…"

Beormund and I look at each other, then the Iute smacks the Pict in the face to shut him up.

"What do you need this boy for, anyway?" he asks me.

"To show what we're dealing with here, and how you Iutes are helping. The Councillors fail to appreciate the threat these raiders pose to our shores, and refuse to send help. Some of them have never even seen a Pict in the flesh before."

Beormund scratches his chin and nods. "It may seem a long way from here to Londin for someone used to travelling around on a litter — but it's only a day's sail for a Pict ship."

"Precisely," I say, content that I don't need to belabour my point any further.

In truth, there is another reason for me wanting to bring a captive to Londin. I need to show *something* for all my efforts. I am neither part of the Iute party, nor one of Odo's cavalrymen, and so I have been allocated neither a share of the plunder, nor a salary. I have been sent here to observe and report, not to fight — that I found myself unable to stand idly by as the Iutes fought back the raiders was nobody's problem but mine…

I have spent the better part of the year on these observation missions — first in Beadda's village, throughout the winter, then the spring in the two newer settlements south of Londin, and now here, in Cantiaca, in the summer. As the Council's representative to the Iutes, it has been my duty to see how our new allies have been faring — but I knew the real reason for my continuous absence from *Dux* Wortigern's court had nothing to do with tribal diplomacy.

All through the winter I have watched, helpless, how Wortimer, the *Dux*'s only surviving son, through intricate political manoeuvring, throwing a praise here, a threat there, or a promise of wealth and power where neither sufficed, gained a sufficient majority in the Council to push through any decision he wanted, as long as it wasn't directly opposed by his father. And whatever other plans he may have had for himself and for Londin under his quasi-dominion, one thing, I knew, was always on his mind: to get *me* out of the city for as long as possible.

He could never outright banish me — I was far too cautious for that, and I had the backing of too-powerful figures at the court, my foster brother Fastidius among them. But he could send me on distant missions I could not refuse, one after the other, and so he did; all so that he could be alone at the *Praetorium*, the Roman Governor's Palace, now turned into Wortigern's court house — alone with Rhedwyn…

The thought of him lurking about her, leering at her pure bright face, slobbering at her slender frame makes me shudder with nausea — as, I know, it must her. We barely had time to talk after her arrival from Tanet, but I soon gathered she was as repulsed by Wortimer as I was; not by his visage, which, as I understood, was a fairly handsome one for a Briton, but by what he stood for — and by the hypocrisy with which he pursued her, while striving to make the lives of her fellow Iutes in his father's land as miserable as he could.

"I have been away for too long," I say, more to myself than to Beormund. "It's time to return home."

I didn't exactly expect a triumphal parade into the city, bringing with me nothing but the single bound prisoner and a pack of letters to the Council from *Comes* Worangon and Hengist — but I am still annoyed and surprised by how little attention I'm granted upon my return.

There is so much commotion at the *Praetorium*, so much noise, so many people pacing to and fro down the half-ruined corridors arguing with each other about some ceremonial minutiae, that my entrance is barely noticed. At first I worry that the news of some new attack has reached the city in my absence — but I detect no fear in the voices of the courtiers, more agitation and irritation. Something other than war has stirred this nest of hornets, and they do not like it.

I stand at the door of the audience hall for a good minute, my Pict unceremoniously squatting on the mosaic floor behind me, before the *Dux* wearily summons us in.

"You have dealt with the raiders in Cantiaca, Councillor Fraxinus?" he asks, referring to me with my baptismal name and, before I can answer, swats me away with impatience. "Good, good."

"My Lord, I bring with me — "

"I will read your report in due time, Councillor."

"But the situation in Cantiaca — "

"I'm sure you believe it's all very serious, but it will have to wait."

"Why? What's going on here?"

He looks up. "Oh. You haven't heard. Why don't you go to your brother — he's as busy as everyone else, but I'm sure he'll find the time to explain everything for you."

He glances at the Pict. The young warrior straightens his back and defiantly returns his stare. The *Dux* smiles lightly. I grasp the meaning of that smile in an instant. I've been at the court long enough to know not to miss a chance to ingratiate myself before the master of the city and everything around it.

I bow, and say: "My Lord, at least let me present you with this gift. A young Pictish captive, from the dark North."

His smile grows. He nods, appreciatively. "I will put him to good use, Fraxinus. Now, go to your brother. We'll need you both here soon."

I find Fastidius leaning on the table, his head in his hands. Ink and wine stains splatter the pile of parchments scattered before him, next to a half-empty goblet.

"What's wrong with everyone?" I ask, after we exchange greetings. "They're all running about as if our Lord himself announced His return."

He rolls his eyes. "It would be easier if He had," he replies, then makes a quick sign of the cross. "No, it's just Riotham. And the Bishop has tasked *me* to prepare a welcome for his arrival."

"Riotham?" I've heard the name mentioned at the court before — but never thought it was anyone I should be aware of.

"He's Ambrosius's *Praetor*," he explains. "His right-hand man and second in command."

"Why is he coming here? Why now?"

In the few years I've been at the court, we've never had an official visit from any representative of the court of Ambrosius, Wortigern's counterpart in the western part of Britannia.

"It's the thirtieth anniversary of the Treaty of Sorbiodun. He's coming to celebrate and to renew the accords."

"What's the problem, then?" I ask.

"The problem is, it will have to be a ceremony the likes of which Londin has not seen in a decade. The problem is, we have no money or men to spare. Our borders are unguarded, our roads and bridges untended, our stores are empty. The Picts you fought have all but halted our trade with Gaul and Frankia. I'm trying my best, but it will take a miracle to make this work."

"Then you're the right choice," I say, rubbing his shoulder. "You're the only miracle-maker I know."

"That's blasphemy," he replies with a smile.

"Can't you ask Beadda for help? I'm sure he'd be more than happy to do something to further improve the reputation of his Iutes."

He gives me a weary, impatient look, and I feel like the younger kid again, not grasping some basic tactics during one of our mock battles.

"Even among Ambrosius's men, Riotham is known for a particular… distrust of pagans. He fought against the Scots on Ambrosius's northern border for years. If he found out we had to ask them for assistance, we'd be a laughing stock. Besides…" He reaches for the pile of parchments and blows the dust from the top. "I hear there's rumours of Aelle's bandits returning to Andreda."

"I haven't heard anything of the sort," I say, surprised. "And I was at the border just a few weeks ago."

There has been no news, good or bad, from the southern border of Wortigern's realm since our hard-won victory at Saffron Valley. As agreed, Aelle and his Saxons have been keeping mostly to themselves, licking wounds, gathering allies and waiting. I knew he was watching with great intent the development of relations between the Britons and the Iutes, but I also knew he and his father, the Saxon *Drihten* Pefen, were too shrewd to risk a new conflict so soon after the last one. If there was news about the bandits in the Andreda Forest, it was either falsehood spread by Wortimer, or… some new force had entered the vacuum left by Aelle.

"As I said, it's just a rumour," says Fastidius. "Meanwhile, I have all these documents to go through, and I fear I'm running out of time."

"I understand." I stand up. "I'll be in my quarters. Let me know if there's anything I can help with."

Fifty slaves precede and another fifty follow the column of mounted soldiers and officials, and carriages plated — thinly, I notice — with silver and gold decorations. At its end, eight mighty *lictors*, all Scots captives from distant Hibernia, their hair and moustaches daubed white with lime, carry the *lectica*, an oak box lined with bronze, marked with the Imperial Eagles, laurel wreaths and other symbols of old Rome.

A gawking throng lines both sides of the Callew Highway, the main road west out of the city. Even the noble landlords from the *villas* along the route — those who were not invited to the *cena* at the palace, at least — come up to the borders of their properties and lean nonchalantly against the hedges and fences as the carriages and the litter move past. They might be curious of the procession, but it does not sit well with them. Most still remember how Ambrosius's father, Aurelius, and his court departed the city — in infamy, fleeing, taking all their treasure with them, to the west, to their new capital at Corin. The return of the *Praetor* is almost triumphant, as if he was back to survey the city for his master's conquest, rather than graciously allowed a one-time anniversary visit.

All along the road, young slaves, dressed in theatrical costumes, present fancy tableaus, living sculptures, illustrating the events leading to the Treaty of Sorbiodun, the reason for Riotham's visit. It all happened long before my birth, before even the serfs' rebellion and Wortigern's arrival in Britannia. I learned some of this story from Paulinus, back at Ariminum, and the rest of it during my time at the court, but to many in the crowd, those from Wortigern's and Pascent's generation, these are all still vivid memories.

The first tableau, set up at the city gate, shows the Roman Legions leaving Britannia: soldiers in gleaming mock armour, with brightly painted wooden spears, led by Imperator Constantine onto boards of their striped-sailed ships, never to return. This is followed closely by images of a weeping populace, abandoned to barbarian raids and other calamities.

At the next crossroads stands a reconstruction of the last united Council of all Britannia: the two conflicted factions, one led by the last Governor, Aurelius, the other by rebellious nobles, demanding a Britannia free of Roman rule and taxes; the crucial final vote, and the expulsion of the loyalist Magistrates from the city.

The tableau that follows is not flattering to Aurelius and the other members of the losing faction: their ignominious escape to the West. Though the slaves in the living image do not represent any particular individuals, I imagine Riotham must see himself somewhere among the refugees. The fleeing loyalists established themselves first just off the western border of Britannia Maxima, and from there launched attacks on the new regime, hoping to sustain the campaign only for as long as was necessary for Rome to come to their help.

But Rome never came back. Several amphorae of red paint and pigs' blood has been used to prepare the largest of the tableaus, along the final stretch of the road leading towards the *Praetorium*: the five-year-long civil war, bloody, cruel and ultimately inconclusive, culminating in the Battle of Guolopp, where the flowers of both armies fell. By this time, the exhausted serfs in the eastern part of the island rebelled, and the economy of the west, cut off from its usual markets, was in tatters. Any further conflict risked plunging both sides into an irrecoverable disaster.

On a hill of Sorbiodun, shown at the entrance to Wortigern's palace as a tall heap of dirt with a clay model of a fortress on top, Aurelius's court and their Londin counterparts signed a ceasefire, which was supposed to be only a temporary respite, until the two enemies were ready to resume the fighting and settle the matter, once and for all.

The ceasefire has now lasted thirty years.

The procession reaches the entrance to Wortigern's palace. Bare-chested female slaves scatter rose petals before the litter, as Riotham climbs out of the vehicle. The crowds gasp; it seems, like me, everyone was expecting to see some fat old dignitary. Instead, Riotham is a handsome, athletic man in his early forties, with a chiselled jaw, sharp aquiline nose and well-trimmed salt-and-pepper hair. A slave boy carries the hem of his cape of bleached wool, lined with a stripe of purple, to keep it from the filth of the street. Under the cloak glistens the bronze of a sculpted breastplate. A *spatha*, its hilt studded with jewels, hangs at his belt. It's as if one of the old statues of Roman heroes has come to life and descended upon Londin.

With his hands behind his back, he treads, alone, the path of cracked paving stones which runs through the middle of what was once the palace courtyard. He stops halfway and takes in his surroundings with a scowl. Nothing is left of the arcades which once encompassed the main square, the rubble of the foundations grown over by hedgerow and thorn. Beyond the path, the yard is dirt and mud; the worst filth has been washed and dusted away for the visit, but very little here tells the story of the old Roman grandeur. A small group of town folk waits in line before the *quaestor's* stand to pay their annual tax in kind, too tired and confused to pay heed to the commotion around them; they hold on to their lambs and goats as if they were made of gold.

The *Praetorium* looks even more squalid and dilapidated than when I first saw it — or maybe I've just grown so used to it over the years that I can see better past the remnants of the ancient splendour. A timber construction now rises in the place of the western wing, a roof on oak pillars, a poor imitation of the old arcaded market. A few merchants have set up their stalls between the oak pillars, counting on Riotham's visit to bring in some badly needed trade. Ducks and goats bleat and quack and shit all over the place, only adding to the filth. Everything around us is crumbling, falling apart in the wind.

"It's worse than I remember," Riotham says to himself. His voice is clear, ringing, stentorian; he speaks in a lofty-sounding mix of Vulgar and Imperial tongues. "Does nobody care to repair these old walls?"

He shakes his head and moves on. Wortigern steps forward to greet him at the threshold of his palace. The two men eye each other warily. Riotham takes a long glance at Wortigern's jewel-studded diadem.

"On this auspicious day, I bring greetings from my lord Ambrosius, son of Aurelius," declares Riotham with a slight nod. "Governor of Britannia Prima, *Dux* of the Britons in the West, *Comes* of Dobunnia, Cornovia and Durnwara — to Wortigern, Governor of Britannia Maxima, *Dux* of the Britons in the East, *Comes…*"

"Welcome back, Riotham," interrupts Wortigern, his manner far less formal than Riotham's. "I hope your journey was swift and pleasant. You must be wanting a bath."

"Have you travelled all the way in the *lectica*?" asks one of the younger courtiers.

Riotham chuckles and wipes the wine from his lips — not the sour local drink, but one poured from Wortigern's own cellar, from the ancient amphorae he'd brought with his army from Armorica.

"I doubt my rear would have survived it," he says, and we all laugh, as we do on his every joke. Charm and confidence are oozing from his every pore. I glance to my left, where Rhedwyn is sitting, resplendent in her finest linen gown and a sheer veil; the only female at the table, as a sign of respect to her uncle. Even she appears impressed by Riotham's demeanour, even though she can't possibly understand much of his antiquated speech.

"I dismounted at the ford at the old tidal mill," he adds, then leans towards Wortigern. "Wasn't there a bridge there once?"

The *Dux* shrugs and twirls the point of his grey beard. "The road is not as frequented as it used to be."

"I've noticed." Riotham nods. "It's a pity — we should work on increasing the trade between our provinces. We have many goods to offer, as you can see."

He points to his plate. Like all the crockery on the table, it's a piece of coarse black pottery, glistening with mica and decorated with scenes of deer hunting rendered in white enamel. It's part of a set Riotham brought with him as a gift to Wortigern. It's not as delicate and precious as the old Roman ware, but it's well made — and, what's more important, it's a brand-new pattern, something not seen in Londin for years.

"As long as your master insists on only taking coin in exchange, we have nothing to pay you with for these goods," the *Dux* replies.

"Then it's true — your treasury is empty." Riotham looks to the damp, cold, bare walls of the hall. "I should've guessed."

"We have enough for our needs." The *Dux's* voice grows snappy. "But not enough to spare for buying pots that are a slightly different colour to ours."

"And what about *your* treasury?" asks Wortimer. "Where does Ambrosius get the coin? He can't be minting it all himself — that old mine at Iscalis must be all but depleted by now."

"Unlike in some places, our people have not forgotten their duties and continue paying tax the usual way." Riotham reaches to his purse and throws a handful of coins on the table. There are two gold pieces among the silver, and none are clipped. "You won't find bleating goats before Ambrosius's palace in Corin."

The Councillors eye the money with greed, but Wortigern makes a secret gesture round his ear: *he's bluffing.*

"Our people have always prized their freedom over gold," replies old Postumus. "As well you remember."

"Yes, I remember." Riotham's face twists in an unpleasant grimace, the first time this evening. "Though I was just twelve when the townsfolk came before the Council, demanding *freedom* from Rome and her taxmen, even as the rebels ravaged the countryside."

"We all voted," Postumus reminds. "Your master lost his case fairly."

"*Fairly*? You were too scared of the mob outside to think of the future!" Red-faced, he raises his hand towards the door. "The mob you yourselves whipped into a Rome-hating frenzy! You squandered your wealth and the safety of your children, for what? Damp, crumbling walls and wind howling in the streets! This crown should, by right, be on Ambrosius's head!" he shouts, pointing at Wortigern's jewel-studded diadem.

He catches Wortigern's warning eye and calms down. "I'm sorry. What's done is done — there's no point bringing it up all over again. You know better than I do what really happened — after all, most of you were here when the vote passed."

The *Dux* sits quietly throughout this exchange, not showing any emotion. These are old animosities, in which he took no part — he was still fighting the Bacauds in Armorica when Londin voted to break its ties with Rome. To him, Ambrosius is just a ruler of a neighbouring country, not the *traitor* and *coward* some of the courtiers call him.

Riotham looks around until he spots me and Rhedwyn. "Though our Saxon friends might want some of these matters explained."

He speaks that last sentence in pure Imperial, in a deliberately lofty manner. Rhedwyn stirs, noticing she's being talked about, and irritated that she can't understand his words.

"Thank you, *Praetor*, but I'm well aware of what you're talking about," I reply, in similar style, coldly. In an instant, he's lost all my sympathy. I can see Fastidius was right — he's no different to Wortimer, or rather, he's what Wortimer *wishes* he could be. "Also, we're Iutes, not Saxons." My pronunciation is coarse through lack of practice, but still, I can see I've made a desired impact, not only on him, but on all the courtiers. I glance at Rhedwyn; she, too, seems suitably impressed.

Wortigern smiles lightly.

"You haven't met Fraxinus yet, have you?" the *Dux* says. "He's a ward of one of my best officers. And this is Rhedwyn, the niece of the chieftain of our Iute *foederati*. A guest, like yourself."

Riotham flinches. Being compared to a barbarian does not sit well with him.

"*Iutes*," he repeats. "Forgive me, I'm not familiar with the divisions among your pagans."

"Of course." Wortigern nods. "You must have your own share of problems with the barbarians. Scots, I hear? And Picts?"

"Yes, though unlike you, we fight them, not *dine* with them. The Picts have not bothered our borders for years."

Riotham picks up a grape and pops it in his mouth, looking straight at me. I glance at the *Dux* and our eyes meet. Is this why the Picts have come to our shores, instead — looking for an easier quarry?

"You have an army?" Wortimer asks. His eyes gleam. "A proper army — not just mercenaries?"

"A mere two Legions," Riotham replies. "Led by my master's two sons. Utir, the younger, took my old command in the west, while Aurelius holds our northern border against the Brigants and the Picts. Why do you ask? How many Legions does *Dux* Wortigern command?"

There is silence around the table. This is an outright challenge — Riotham must know Wortigern has no army beyond his own household guards and the unreliable militia. The tribal *pagi* under his ostensible rule must look to themselves for defence.

"Enough for our needs," replies Wortigern.

"I'm sure, I'm sure." Riotham swallows another grape and gulps some more wine. "Oh, I'm sorry, I all but forgot — my master sends condolences for the loss of your son. We always respected young Catigern in Corin."

Wortigern's face reddens. The cheese knife in his hand clanks on the black plate.

"You have my thanks," he says through teeth.

Riotham's confident smile vanishes as he senses he's overstepped his mark. He hides his face in the wine goblet and for a while, he's saying nothing, letting the courtiers and Councillors pick up the discussion of taxes and standing armies. I've heard this debate several times already in my time at the palace and the consensus is always the same — soldiers need a salary, and there is none to give. The nobles of the *villas* and landlords of the palaces of Londin, even those who sit at the Council, are unwilling to part with what silver and gold they still might have in their chests. The only levy they agree to pay is the Wall upkeep fee. Ever since Aelle's attack on their countryside *villas*, they have been steadily moving their businesses behind the safety of the mighty Roman defences and war machines, leaving their serfs and slaves to tend to their property beyond this secure perimeter. The only offensive unit at Wortigern's disposal — other than the veterans of the war with the rebels, who have by now all grown too old to be of everyday use — is Wortimer's cohort, a mere *centuria* of bored noble-borns, who provide their own weapons and armour. After the victory over Aelle's Saxons, for which they took full credit, their ranks have swollen — but there are only so many young nobles in the city willing to waste their time on training to fight a phantom enemy. Those on the Council who did not fall for Wortimer's charm know full well his soldiers would not stand a chance against a real threat.

I catch Rhedwyn stifling a yawn, and smile at her; she smiles back, and it's as if every lamp in the hall turned into a sun. I don't notice that the table has fallen quiet, and everyone is staring at me expectantly.

"I'm sorry?"

"Our guest was asking about the Iutish villages," says Postumus. "You've visited them recently, have you not?"

The suns turn dark. My heart sinks. I reach for the wine cup, as my mind races. How much do they know, and how much do they want me to say in Riotham's presence?

"I have indeed," I reply.

"Twenty families, is it?" asks Riotham. "And they are all warriors?"

"In Beaddingatun, yes. Half that number in Orpedda's village, and in Waerlahame…"

I glance at Wortigern. Is this information we want to give out freely? He notices my concerned look.

"I have an idea," he says. "Why not have young Fraxinus prepare a written report, not just about the village but about the Iutes in general? I'm sure that'll be of interest to you and Ambrosius — and it will help Fraxinus make a name for himself in the West."

Riotham agrees, though with a hint of reluctance — he's lost a chance to catch me unprepared. It's clear that the report will be censored by Wortigern's scribes according to what they will deem proper to divulge. After all, there is only a ceasefire between us and Ambrosius — not peace.

"Now," the *Dux* continues, "I notice some of my older comrades grow weary of feasting and merry-making. I propose to end the festivities for today." A murmur of agreement ripples throughout the hall. "I myself might retire to my quarters soon, and I advise you all to do the same. We have a busy schedule tomorrow."

"Sound words," says Riotham, and raises his glass. "I'll drink to that, one last time."

James Calbraith

CHAPTER II
THE LAY OF PEREDUR

A bat zooms across the face of the Moon, swerves to catch a stray moth, and disappears into the shadow of a low-hanging eave. A toad belches a loud croak in response and plunges into a puddle. Somewhere beyond the river wall, the Tamesa laps at its muddy banks, calm and lazy, waiting for the swollen rush of the morning tide.

There are no other sounds. Everyone at the palace is sound asleep, except for the guards; but there are none here. I sit by a small folding table amidst tall, unmowed grass in the middle of the palace gardens. The flame of my lamp flickers. I pour some more oil into the bowl, sculpted in the shape of a scallop's shell. I dip the reed pen in the ink and put it to the birchwood. The copper nib splits, leaving an ugly mark, but I don't care — this one doesn't go into the archives, it can be messy.

The frogs fall silent. They sense someone approaching before I do; the rustle of linen on grass alerts me to a presence a moment later. I look up to see Rhedwyn glide across the meadow. She wears no veil, and her unbound hair cascades like a golden waterfall. In the silvery moonlight she looks like a pale spirit; a goddess.

"I didn't think anybody else was coming here this late at night," she says, quietly.

I lick my suddenly parched lips. Despite living in the same palace, we haven't had many opportunities to be alone. Rhedwyn spends most of her time in her quarters, guarded by a silent, armed Iute; when she's outside, she's always accompanied by a gaggle of female servants.

"I'm having a hard time writing this report for Riotham," I explain. "I needed quiet."

"Riotham," she repeats. "Who is this man? Where did he come from?"

I remember how little she understood of our conversation at the feast. I explain briefly about Ambrosius and how there came to be two countries and two rulers where once was only one Roman Britannia.

Her eyes widen when I speak of the vote. "These people *wanted* to cut themselves from Rome?"

"Why are you so surprised?"

She looks around the garden, and towards the palace. "I don't understand. To all of us — the Saxons, the Iutes, the Angles — Rome was always an unattainable dream. My uncle told me legends of its riches… Its merchants, its warriors… That glass horn of his was a symbol of what we could never have. We envied the Goths and the Franks, for being allowed to live within Rome's borders…"

She shakes her head. "We always assumed the Britons must have committed some inconceivable transgression to be thrown out of the Empire. I never would've guessed they did it of their own volition."

"It was a different time," I try to explain, with little conviction, remembering what I've learned during my time at the palace, from talking to old veterans and reading yellowed parchments in the library. "Rome was in a worse shape than she is now. Barbarians sacked the city, rival Imperators led mercenary armies against each other… Everyone thought the Empire was as good as vanquished. The Legions had left. There didn't seem to be any reason to pay the taxes and abide by the old rules."

"What if the Legions came back?"

I see the dreamy naïveté in her eyes, and recognise it. I used to be like this myself, confronted with the past glories, wishing for them to return, to bring some semblance of order into these confusing times, asking the same questions of Pascent, Paulinus and, later, Wortigern. None would give me a clear answer. I doubt any of them believed it possible, not after all those years. Rome does not forgive, but she easily forgets.

I tell her as much.

"But some still believe," she replies.

I shrug. "They're not of Rome anymore, either. They just want to be, like you and the other Iutes. Rome has abandoned *all* of us here — we are left to fend for ourselves. I suppose even Ambrosius understood it at last. That's why he's sent his man for these peace talks. That's why I'm writing this report."

She leans over to see the tablets. Her hair brushes against my hand. My mouth and throat turn dry. My face burns as if in fever.

"What are you writing about?" she asks.

"It's about your… our people," I say, my lips trembling. "I have to explain where the Iutes came from, who they are, and what the *Dux* hopes for our alliance to achieve."

"You'll write the truth about the Saffron Valley?"

I raise an eyebrow. Of course, she'd know the Iute side of the battle from the songs the *scops* wrote about the victory. No wonder Wortimer's boast failed to impress her…

"I doubt I'll be allowed. This will go through the Council's scribes. But they will have to let me mention the Iutes' valour in combat, both there and against the Picts, otherwise it would seem the *Dux* made the wrong choice."

"I wish I knew how to read and write Roman letters," she sighs. "I would be of much more use to my uncle then."

"I can teach you!" I exclaim, a little too eagerly.

"Could you, really?"

She looks at me intently and her face lights up in a smile that would melt steel. *If only she knew…* But I could never tell her how I felt. I don't understand why myself; any other girl, I'd confessed my love to, and asked her to lay with me, a long time ago. Even if she'd refuse me, so what? I'd just move on to another. But with Rhedwyn … I don't even think of such things. She's like a delicate, warm jewel to me, shining with inner light, innocent and cherished. I'm content with just being in her presence. I feel as if by confessing my feelings, I could ruin something precious, mar what little friendship there is between us.

"Of course." I stare down at the tablet and am reminded of the cold reality. "As soon as I'm finished with this thing. We could start tomorrow."

"I would love that." She smiles again and turns back; her hair spins and swirls, gleams and glints in the flickers of the oil lamp. As she walks away, the long hem of her dress makes it seem as if she's hovering over the dew-damp grass.

I realise I forgot to ask her what *she* was doing in the gardens, this late at night.

Several months passed after I started living at the court before I first dared to see the old amphitheatre up close. It's always seemed to me a foreboding, ghostly place, a dead relic, shrouded in the mists exuding from the moors that surround it and into which it is slowly, inevitably, sinking.

It's not that far from the palace — half a mile to the west, maybe, a man-made hollowed-out hill looming over its part of the city in the same way the ruined *basilica* looms in the east: both buildings of inhuman scale, fit for gods — or demons — rather than mortals. But it's a different world here from that of the *villas* and palaces of the Callew Highway or the densely packed tenements of the Cathedral hill. No roads lead here anymore, other than the old cattle track out to the moor pastures; nobody lives in its shadow other than shepherds, beggars and vagabonds, eking out a measly existence in huts built on the ancient foundations. Further to the west, a straight line of tangled hawthorns masks the remains of a boundary older even than the Wall: the fort of the Legions, abandoned when Constantine took the last Roman soldiers with him to the Continent. Now the only army that dwells there is a horde of feral dogs, engaged in daily battles with the shepherds over their herds.

Between the ruined fort, the desolate moor and the empty amphitheatre, this corner of Londin feels as if it was tacked on to the rest. Its only connection to the otherwise vibrant city is the Wall, bounding it from the north-west, thinner and in worse shape here than anywhere else. No enemy has come this way in centuries. Fastidius once explained to me that even in the Roman days, this area was never as developed as the ancient planners had wished — and fell into ruin as soon as the city's prosperity began to wane. If anything, it was now starting to regenerate slowly after decades, if not centuries, of decline, since Wortimer made it a centre of his *centuria*'s operations.

The amphitheatre did not share the sad fate of its counterpart in Dorowern, quarried for Roman stone into near oblivion; rather, it was allowed to age and die gracefully, its weathered stone walls cracking and falling apart at their own speed. As we approach it, I spot some scaffolding growing over the widest crack in the eastern gate tower; the builders, recruited no doubt from among the local vagabonds, are sealing it with wattle and daub, and plastering it over with lime. Riotham smiles and nods at the sight.

"I see you haven't let *all* of Londin's old glory fall into ruin," he says. His words are scornful, but a genuine, nostalgic admiration lingers in his voice.

"Do you have a theatre like this in Corin?" I ask. It seems Riotham has finally accepted that I'm not just some illiterate pagan, despite the appearances; he's seen me keep up with the discussions in the Council as an equal, he's heard me recite ancient speeches and poetry without so much as a stutter.

Even so, he can't help but patronise me at every opportunity. He's allowing me to march beside him today, not just because he sees me as an exotic curiosity, but also because it gives him an opportunity to gloat about what life is like under Ambrosius's rule. I suspect he'd prefer to do it before Wortimer, ever eager to hear how superior western Britannia is compared to his father's domain — but the *Dux's* son is not with us today.

The *Praetor* laughs. "Not like this. Ours is smaller. There was no greater amphitheatre than Londin anywhere north of the Alps. But ours stands proudly on top of a quarry hill just outside the city, not in the middle of a stinking moor. Its walls gleam white in the sun…" His eyes mist up as he stares into the distance. "Every major feast day, we have games of bear-baiting and slave combat. Thousands come from all over the province. I can't wait to see what kind of entertainment your master prepared for us."

I don't answer, but I predict he's going to be disappointed. In all my time living in Londin, I have never seen a feast at the amphitheatre. I'm not sure myself why we are headed there today, having crossed the entire city straight from the Cathedral hill, where Fastidius conducted the morning Mass. The Cathedral, at least, appeared to have made a suitable impression on our guest — though he did not omit to mention that the construction started long before Wortigern's days, at the behest — and funding — of Imperator Maximus.

"The last of Rome," he tells me after the Mass. "Makes you think, doesn't it, boy? What this city would've looked like if we hadn't abandoned the Empire…"

"It's the Empire that abandoned us," I remind him, but he only shakes his head.

"You wouldn't know what it was like back then, boy."

Neither would you, I think, remembering he was also just a child at the time.

At last, we reach the entrance to the theatre. The timber of the gate is long gone, replaced by a curtain of cloth, painted with the Imperial Eagle and the letter V flanked with two dots. Riotham raises a mocking eyebrow at the sight. He points to the Eagle.

"What is this? Are you staging a re-enactment play of Roman times?"

"It's Wortimer's mark," I explain. "His militia wears it on their armour."

Inside, the amphitheatre looks more worse for wear than it did from the outside. All of the wooden benches have rotted away in the wind and rain of the passing years, except for the single row nearest to the arena, where new seats have been installed for our benefit. All the draining channels are filled with muck, dust and dry leaves; the moor is encroaching on the arena from outside and from below, and as a result, more of its two hundred feet expanse is mud and puddle than sand. The air, enclosed within the round walls, is stale and smelling of farts and cabbage. Riotham covers his nose with a handkerchief.

"Judging by the state of the arena," he says, wiping dust from his bench, "I'm guessing we're going to see a *naumachia*."

"What's that?"

"A staged sea battle. I'm joking, boy. There's never been a *naumachia* in Britannia, as far as I know, not even in the old days." He sits down. "But I'm sure whatever is prepared will be just as exciting."

The boar squeals and grunts one last time as the third javelin penetrates its thick hide. Blood spurts from its nose and between its tusks, already red after an encounter with an enemy's calf.

Following a show of jugglers and dancers, the mock hunt has been, so far, the most interesting part of the spectacle. It is the first time any blood has splattered the arena's mud, and I notice Riotham's nostrils flare as the injured slave is dragged away, screaming, leaving a crimson trail in his wake.

A trumpet blows, announcing the next stage of the show. Sixteen men enter the arena through the rear gate, each wielding a different set of weapons and wearing a different suit of armour, each an imitation of an ancient warrior: a Gaul, heavily armoured, with a short *gladius* sword and a rectangular shield; a Samnite, wearing bronze greaves and a crested helmet; a Thracian, with a round buckler and a curved long knife; a Greek, with a long infantry pike…

Wortimer himself leaps out of his seat and lands heavily on the sand. He bows and introduces the men as the best of his militia, here to fight for our entertainment, but also as a test of their strength. A bizarre sense of having seen all this before washes over me; this is just like the *Hiréd* fighting in

Beadda's village… Would Wortimer have organised all of this just to mock the Iutes? Or could it be just a coincidence?

Riotham, to my surprise, looks disappointed. "Nobles fighting each other for show?" He shakes his head. "This is not proper."

"How do you do it in Corin?" I ask.

"We have slaves fight — to the death," he replies. "It's much more exciting that way. How can you enjoy combat if there's no danger of death?"

Our exchange is overheard by Wortigern, sitting above us on a rug thrown over bare stone. He leans down. "We don't condone gladiatorial bouts here," he says. "It is against the teachings of our Lord. I'm sure Bishop Fatalis will agree."

The Bishop, seated to our right, nods. "'Thou shalt not kill'," he recites.

"They're just slaves," scoffs Riotham. "We would never allow free men to kill each other."

"Slaves or free, all men were born equal," the Bishop replies. "Only God has the right to decide how long their life should be."

Riotham scowls. "I see Germanus did not cleanse *all* roots of the heresy. Perhaps another visit is warranted."

Heresy — whatever can he mean? All the Bishop does is quote the same writings of Pelagius as Paulinus taught me. I look to the *Dux* and the Bishop, bewildered. At the mention of Germanus they both sit back, their faces red with anger, unwilling to pursue the matter further.

Down in the arena, the first of the eight bouts, happening all at once, is over almost as soon as it started; the Gaul towers over the other warrior, who was wielding a fishing spear and a net, in which he is now tangled. Not a drop of blood was spilled in this fight. Riotham boos and raises a hand with his thumb down.

"We don't do that here, either," remarks Wortigern.

Further in the arena, however, the fighting continues, and grows more brutal with each minute, as the warriors grow tired and impatient. There is a marked difference between this fight and the one at the village. The Iutes relished their mock battle; they played at war with pure joy and enthusiasm. For Wortimer's men it appears to be a cruel burden, almost as if they were forced to do it for our entertainment. In this, they are no better than the slaves from Riotham's tale.

Eventually, one by one, eight of them emerge victorious, and immediately start fighting with each other in another round of combat. This time, blood spurts from the cuts and scratches, and Riotham is, at last, immersed in the spectacle, cheering the victors and jeering the fallen.

I glance at the other spectators. Most of the nobles join Riotham in the applause, taken in by the bloodlust. *Dux* Wortigern and those of his court who'd seen real combat in their life, observe the fight with a calm detachment; there isn't much that can impress a veteran of so many wars. Meanwhile, the Bishop's face has turned a sickly shade of green; he's not enjoying himself at all, and when another fighter falls with a deep gash in his thigh, he stands up and excuses himself.

At the far end of the row of seats I spot Rhedwyn. She's thrown back her veil; her face is red with excitement. She's cheering the loudest, hurling Iute insults at those of the fighters who don't perform to her satisfaction. This shocks me at first, until I remember she was raised in a village of warriors, where bouts like this were a common occurrence. Of course, she's become used to the sight of blood and men hacking each other to pieces. Once the initial surprise passes, I'm starting to enjoy watching her act so naturally; it's as if she's taken off some unwieldy disguise. She catches me looking at her and sends me a challenging grin. I grin back.

When the second round of fighting is over, Wortimer announces a change. The remaining four will not fight against each other. Instead, the gate opens again, revealing two giants of men, both fair-haired, sunburnt and dressed only in loincloths, and both with chains at their feet; one is holding a two-handed battle axe, the other — a *seax* and a round shield.

"Who are these men, son?" Wortigern shouts a question.

"Captives from a raid on Andreda," replies Wortimer. "Aelle's men."

It's a lie. Not only am I certain there have been no bandits in the forest for months, I doubt Wortimer's men would be able to capture any of them alive, a feat not even Beadda's *Hiréd* managed back when the attacks were more frequent. These two are Saxon warriors, no doubt, but the only way Wortimer could have got his hands on them was by buying them off a slave market in New Port.

"Is this safe?" Wortigern casts a worried look on the muscles rippling on the two warriors. Even naked and in chains, even swaying from side to side due to some numbing herbs they were no doubt served before the fight, they present themselves much more terrifying than any of Wortimer's four winners.

"Don't worry, my men will make short work of them," replies Wortimer. "But just in case …" He waves his short sword, and six archers step out into the arena, their bows drawn and aimed at the Saxons.

The two are pushed out into the sun. They are still chained together, and so can only move in short, awkward steps. They stand back-to-back to face the incoming enemy. Of the four Britons, two are "Greek" spearmen, the other two wield long *spatha* swords; the spearmen charge at the Saxon with the battle axe. The swordsmen carefully flank his comrade from either side.

A spear thrust digs deep into the Saxon's side, spilling his guts out, but he doesn't flinch. He drops the axe down onto the skull of one of his enemies. The blade is blunted, but the impact itself is enough: the Briton falls in an instant, blood and brain gushing from his ears. The nobles gasp. Even Wortigern frowns and stirs in his seat. Riotham cheers, just as the other of Wortimer's men falls on his back, with his ribs crushed. The power of that blow breaks the shaft of the axe, leaving the Saxon with just a wooden stick to defend himself from the remaining pair of swordsmen. A flash of the blade later, his head rolls on the sand.

His comrade now turns and, with the same indifference as the first Saxon, accepts a sword slash to the leg; a harmless wound, in exchange for which, he manages to get close enough to the third Briton to stab him in the neck. It's a perfect cut, neat and fast, executed with such prowess that even Wortigern claps at the sight, recognising a fellow professional. There is no blood — the *seax* blade was also blunt; but the stab is enough to smash the Briton's windpipe. He doesn't even know what hit him. He staggers a few steps away, holding his neck in surprise and gasping, before loss of air makes him drop to his knees.

There are only two of them left now, the grinning Saxon and the last, cautious Briton, the latter circling the former warily. The archers step forward, but Wortimer orders them to wait. Instead, he picks up a discarded *spatha* and waves it a couple of times, clearly readying himself for a fight with whoever survives the duel.

The Briton leaps into the air, with the setting sun in his back, in an attempt to catch the Saxon by surprise; but he's too slow. The Saxon dodges as far as the chains allow him, his *seax* whistling through the air and hitting the enemy precisely under the chin, cracking the jaw and pushing it into the brain. By the time the Briton reaches the ground, he's dead.

In stunned silence, the Saxon turns to us, his audience, with a mocking bow. Wortimer roars a challenge and charges at him from behind. The Saxon parries the first blow, then the next; but he's already weakened from the injury and the dumbing herbs. Wortimer cuts at his left arm; the Saxon responds with a well-aimed blow to the chest, but his blunted blade only slides off of the metal armour hidden under Wortimer's tunic. The *Dux's* son cuts at the Saxon's other arm and then finishes him off with a slash across the stomach.

The Saxon staggers and drops to his knees. His *seax* plops into the mud. Wortimer grabs him by the flaxen hair and with one sharp slice, cuts his head off.

He raises the head and the sword in his hands, triumphant; the eagle on his chest splattered with the blood of the captive. Riotham is the first to lead the applause, then the others join. I see now that everything happened according to Wortimer's plan. It doesn't matter that the fight cost him four men. He never cared about any of them. He is now a hero, the vanquisher of the unruly Saxons, the strongest man in the arena. He closes his eyes and drinks in the cheers. There may be only twenty of us in the audience today, but by the look of bliss on his face, in his head he hears an ovation of the immeasurable crowds that used to gather in this place, sensing their ghosts still filling the thousands of seats.

"Now that's the sort of man I'd like to see in our Legions!" shouts Riotham.

I'm the only one who doesn't join the applause. Not even Rhedwyn is immune to the fervour, though it's *her* two distant kinsmen, the Saxons, who lie headless in the mud before a victorious *wealh*. My own feelings are a confused mess. If it's true that they were Aelle's men, then they were among those responsible for the deaths of Pascent and Catigern, and countless others. I should be glad of their demise. But I feel a certain kinship to them nonetheless; a remnant of the time when I served in Aelle's army, perhaps. After all, one of the fallen could have been Eirik or Hilla, my one-time comrades in battle. And I find their brave last stand far more inspiring than Wortimer's deliberate butchery.

I can't bear seeing Wortimer gloat over their bodies anymore. Without thinking, I leap into the arena and pick up the blunted *seax*.

"One more duel?" I ask. "If you're not too tired."

He turns to me with a wry smile. "I'm never too tired to fight you, Fraxinus."

I'm not sure why I'm doing this. Part of me feels the unfortunate Saxons deserve more than a drugged, chained death at the hands of a pampered Briton prince, even if they were our enemies. Part of me just wants to teach Wortimer a lesson, avenge the humiliation I suffered from his men on the day of my baptism.

No shields — just the swords: his *spatha*, long, slender, with a mahogany grip stamped with the Imperial Eagle on the pommel; and my old *seax*, short, broad, heavy, the blade not only blunted but chipped now on the bones of the fallen. Wortimer takes an ancient stance, the sword over his head, like a scorpion's sting. It looks imposing, but without the shield in the other hand, it leaves him too open.

I glance at Rhedwyn — she stares at us with bated breath, ruddy-cheeked, clutching her fists at her breast. Wortimer notices my glance and his face, mocking until now, turns deadly serious. I feel the blood rush hot through my veins, as if a floodgate was opened. I strike first, testing his response. His parry is accurate, but slow, and he doesn't manage a follow through before I leap back. It's his try now, and I don't even bother blocking, just let the blade swish past me. I stab at his side, but he dodges. I slash again, and this time our blades clash, grinding against each other until we reach the hilts. I can feel his breath on my face; it smells of meat. I hook my leg behind his, trying to bring him down, but he wiggles out and pushes me away.

I take a step back to gain enough space for a heavy, whirling blow — and my foot gets entangled in a body lying behind me. I don't fall — but I get distracted; I catch the glimpse of Wortimer's *spatha* aiming for my head and parry at the last moment. With a resounding crash, both our blades crack: the flying *spatha* shard digs a groove in my shoulder; a splinter of my *seax* scratches his neck, inches from an artery.

Wortimer's fist lands on my face. I drag him down, and we start to wrestle in the bloody mud; the years of pent-up rivalry exploding in a fury of snarls, blows and scratches.

"Enough!"

Wortigern's yell shatters the air. I look up — he is standing tall, red-faced, his jowls shaking with fury. Wortimer, like me, must think he's angry with us, for we both stop and leap up from the mud, full of remorse, ready to apologise. But our behaviour is not the reason for his wrath — or at least, not the only reason. I spot now a messenger boy at his side, panting; he must have run all the way from the palace with some urgent and dire news.

"The Picts have invaded Cantiaca," the *Dux* announces with grave voice. "They sacked Dorowern. *Comes* Worangon is dead."

The news comes fast from Dorowern throughout this and the next day; at first, they seem exaggerated, fearful rumours, but as more eyewitnesses and refugees reach Londin, the full extent of the disaster soon becomes clear.

The Picts we knew from the years past were no more than pirates, sea raiders, harassing Frankish merchants and fishermen, robbing the small chapels by the coast, frightening villagers, abducting sheep from the tidal pastures. But not these Picts; they came as an invading army, a fleet greater than any seen in a generation, a multitude of swift, sleek boats filled with bloodthirsty warriors. They struck at dawn, swooping with the morning fog, when Dorowern was asleep. They knew when to attack, too — their spies must have told them that Beormund's Iutes would have already returned to Tanet, and most of Odo's Gaulish cavalry would be out of the city pursuing an alleged incursion into southern Cantiaca by forest bandits; another rumour that proved to be unfounded too late.

"It was a military operation," says Wortigern, explaining his finds before the Council. "I wouldn't have planned it better myself." He draws a quick map on the parchment, with the deftness of someone who's been doing this sort of thing all his life. "They arrived in two columns: the first one raided the *villas* outside the city walls and waited for the town guards to march at them in the field. Then the other column struck at the river harbour and entered the city from there."

"What about the church?" asks Postumus.

"Plundered. Acolytes killed. They spared the priest, but took all the silver and gold. The boats heaved with plunder as they sailed off — before any of the town guard even realised what was going on."

Gasps of disbelief erupt around the table.

"Why now?" asks another courtier. "We've been safe from the major raids for so long. I almost hoped the Picts had become civilised. A people we could trade with, not fight."

"Picts will never be civilised," scoffs Riotham. "Filthy, painted barbarians. Rome never saw any use for them. But good fighters, mind you — we've been barely keeping them at bay all these years."

Wortigern gives Riotham a weary look. The *Praetor* should be preparing for the long journey back, his visit cut short by two days, but he insisted on attending the Council this one last time. In the chaos and uproar, the reason for his coming has been all but forgotten. The anniversary accords have been quickly signed off, with a promise of more discussion later, as soon as the situation is more stable. He and his servants have since been wandering forlornly along the palace corridors, moving out of the way of the messengers and couriers.

"They must have decided we would be an easier target than Ambrosius," says Wortimer. "I did warn you, Father…"

"It's their new *Drihten*," the *Dux* interrupts. "Thanks to young Fraxinus, we've been able to get our hands on one of the Pict raiders, from what we now know must have been the vanguard of the attack." He nods at me. If Wortimer's stare could kill… "I've spoken to him — though it wasn't easy, given how these people mangle our tongue — enough to gain some idea of the situation. The Picts have a new leader, called Drust — he's been uniting the Northern tribes for at least the past decade, and now feels strong enough to strike at us." He turns to Riotham. "I'm surprised you haven't heard of him, *Praetor*."

Riotham shrugs. "Who would bother to follow what goes on beyond the Aelian Wall… The barbarian chieftains come and go, while the might of our arms — "

"Yes, yes, we know, you've always fought them back," Wortigern says, impatiently. "It doesn't matter now. We have a war on our hands, noble lords. The Picts will not just go back to their mud huts beyond the Wall, now that they've tasted Southern blood. If left unchecked, they will strike again, before winter comes — and this time, we must be ready."

"A War Council, then?" asks Postumus, raising his wine glass. The others join him, a visible majority of the gathered, to announce their support for whatever decision the *Dux* would make.

"As much as it pains me… yes." Wortigern nods. "Send out the heralds. Prepare the guest rooms at the palace. Call on the War Council!"

CHAPTER III
THE LAY OF ELASIO

"What does it mean, exactly?" I ask Fastidius. "A War Council? I thought we already had a Council."

"This one is different," he explains. "All four *Comites* are called in, as well as all the prominent men of Londin. I suppose you'll be needed, too, to speak for the Iutes. How many *will* come, though…" He pinches his lower lip. "A war means expenses, maybe even new taxes."

"Don't they want to defend themselves?"

"We'll see, but I wouldn't hold my breath. We've been at peace for so long, it will be hard to convince them the threat is real enough."

"Even after what happened at Dorowern?"

"Dorowern is far away — so is Coln, and any other place the Picts are likely to strike at. I hear last time, they all found one excuse or other not to do anything, and the War Council disbanded without making any decisions."

"When was that?"

"Six years ago, when the Armoricans revolted again. Fortunately for us, they were soon suppressed and the rebellion didn't spread to the islands. Otherwise…" He shrugs. "Get dressed and let's grab something to eat on the way. There will be no feasting today."

Fastidius was right. The Council table is half-empty — fewer courtiers are interested in discussing war with the new and terrible enemy than there were at Riotham's welcoming feast. The representatives of the tribes have not yet had a chance to arrive, and it is doubtful if they will; the Cants are still reeling from their defeat, and the others no doubt are making ready to defend their lands on their own.

Only Peredur, the *Comes* of the Trinowaunts, reaches the city before nightfall; he lives the closest, in Coln, on the far end of the Augustan Highway, but it still takes him the better part of the day by fast carriage. Nobody pays him much attention at first, as his tribe and land are far too small and weak to matter in this conflict. The Trinowaunts have always relied on whoever ruled in Londin for protection, not the other way around. Instead of soldiers, Peredur brings news, and it is dire, though not unexpected.

"The enemy ships were sighted at the mouth of the River Coln," he says.

"Already?" exclaim the Councillors.

"It was another fleet — this one came from the North, out of the mist… They joined with those returning from Dorowern just off our coast."

"God spared us," says Bishop Fatalis, raising his eyes to heaven. He sits at Wortigern's left hand — as owner of the greatest treasury in the city, his voice is decisive when it comes to funding the war chest. "At least they passed Londin."

"They know they're no match for our Wall," says Wortigern. "No army has ever breached it. But what about Coln?"

"The forts at the rivermouth are already besieged. They are manned only by small Saxon detachments," the *Comes* warns. "If they get past those forts, there is nothing standing between them and Coln."

"I'm well aware of your strategic situation," replies Wortigern. "What about your tribal militia?"

"They're gathering, but won't stand long against the Picts."

"But they can harass them. A siege takes its toll on the attackers as well as defenders. I know those forts, it will take days to seize them, even with just a skeleton crew." The *Dux* beckons a messenger and scribbles orders on a piece of parchment. "Get these to Coln." He glances at the *Comes*. The man knows better than to argue; nobody in the room knows the art of war better than Wortigern.

"We should pursue them while they're still this close," announces Wortimer, slamming his fist on the table.

"Pursue with what?" asks Councillor Postumus. "It will take us days to organise the tribal militias into a coherent force."

"Elasio's Cadwallons are the nearest," remarks another Councillor. The scars on his face mark him as one of Wortigern's old comrades at arms. "Order them to march out."

"I don't think they'll be eager to attack," replies Postumus. "Elasio believes in the strength of his fortifications more than the arms of his men. If he's heard the news, he's likely making himself ready to defend his borders."

I sneak up to the table to take a look at the map he's pointing to, but I can't make out any clues out of the complex network of roads marked in red and navigable rivers marked in blue. The veteran notices my glance; his finger draws an almost straight line leading from Coln to Werlam, the capital of Cadwallons, bypassing Londin's mighty walls at a safe distance. I nod, acknowledging that I understand the situation.

"Doubtful the sea raiders would go this far inland," murmurs Wortigern, rubbing his chin. "But you're right, Elasio won't be taking any chances."

"Then we are toothless, for now," says Postumus.

"Send me, Father," Wortimer volunteers. "Me and my *centuria* will face the barbarians."

Wortigern hides an eyeroll in a head shake. "No, son. Your men will need to stay to guard the city." I catch a grimace running through Wortimer's face. "This all might be a ruse, like in Dorowern, to draw us out into the open. Who knows how many more such fleets they've hidden from us. Besides, you wouldn't get to Coln in time. I'm sorry, Peredur, I fear your city must fend for itself —we will fight the Picts somewhere else."

"What did you have in mind?" asks Postumus.

"You can't bring so many ships such a long way in one go, and hope to return before winter with all the spoils. They must have a base somewhere near, somewhere they will stay to divide the plunder. We must find out where it is, and intercept them there."

Wortimer slams the table again. "I will not stand for it! I will not let our allies face the barbarians alone!"

A few murmurs rise around the table in agreement, but they are a minority. There is no one here who would dare to accuse Wortigern of cowardice — not even his own son. The *Dux* knows what he's doing.

"How will we know where to find them?" I ask.

"I was hoping you'd help us with that, Fraxinus…"

"You're being fed well, Pict?"

The captive lifts his head wearily. A bowl of half-eaten porridge lies at his feet. He's chained to the floor, but even without the chain, there would not be enough strength in him to strike at me. I see fresh scars on his back. Somebody must have "prepared" him for our conversation.

"I did not ask them to do this," I say, pointing at the scars. "I'm sorry."

"I'm not a Pict."

"What?"

He spits a bloody globule.

"I'm a Wotadin."

"What's that?"

He rolls his eyes. "You Southrons think anyone north of the Aelian Wall is a *Pict*."

"So Wotadin is the name of a tribe you're from?" I crouch beside him. "I'm a Iute, myself. What do they call you, Wotadin?"

"Cunedag."

"What other tribes are there, Cunedag?"

He closes and opens his eyes, slowly. His gaze is drawn to the narrow opening in the vaulted ceiling. The *Praetorium* has no prison — it may have originally been in the ruined wing, if ever — and so the *Dux's* captives are being held in a half-ruined bath house in the eastern part of the city, the bathing and dining chambers divided into small, damp cells with brick walls.

"Wertriu, Kirkins, Kaiths, Aers…" he replies. "Too many to mention — too many to care. We all fought each other for whatever meagre scraps our land provided… Land that even Rome did not want to take."

He spits again and looks at the bowl with disgust. "Porridge. I've had enough of it in the North. Oat is pretty much the only thing that grows there."

"And so you'd ride the South."

"Riding parties, sneaking over what was left of the Aelian Wall, or striking the fishing villages along the coast… We'd steal just enough food and weapons to sustain ourselves in the wars with our neighbours." The boy is filled with self-disgust. I sense his youth must have been a terrible time.

"Until this… *Drust*? United you all under his banner?"

"*King* Drust," he replies, using an old Briton word, *riu*, to denote his leader's position. "Drust of a Hundred Victories. Drust of the Wild Boar." He looks up. "All land north of the Wall is his. Now it's the time of the South."

"Conquer the South?" I scoff. "That's bold."

"My grandfather was a Roman officer on the Wall," he says. "He'd tell us stories of the riches that lay beyond it. But we saw none of it on our journey here. Your cities are wide open, your fields lie fallow, your walls have crumbled. Only the churchmen at Ebrauc and Lindocoln are still growing fat, while everyone else is as poor and starving as we are. If not us, someone else will conquer it all."

I'm intrigued by what he's saying — especially his mention of a Roman officer in his family — but I have no time to discuss it right now, not when there's crucial information to extract from the boy.

"You've seen a lot of the South, then," I say.

He purses his lips, realising he's said too much. It finally dawns on him that I haven't come here for a friendly chat.

"It's like this, Cunedag," I say. "You will tell me where your fleet's base is, and I will let you go free. You can go back home. Or, you stay silent, and somebody else comes here to squeeze the answer out of you — someone with much less patience than me."

"I don't know anything. I'm just a foot soldier — I go where they take me."

"You must have seen *something*. You've come all this way. There had to be stops."

"I don't know anything."

"A warrior's honour," I say, nodding. "I understand. But nobody will know. We can make it seem like you've escaped this prison, if you want."

"*I* will know."

"You're too young for this. Trust me. There will be plenty of chances for you to prove your worth as a warrior. This is not it."

He hangs his head and stays silent for a long time. I'm about to prod him again, when he speaks.

"It was a great marshland…" he says. "A day's sail north from the Tamesa Estuary."

"There are marshes all over the coast. You'll have to be more precise."

"I don't…" He looks up. "There were cliffs. Striped red and white. Red at the bottom, white on top. I've never seen any like it. We passed them the day before the marsh."

"Anything else?"

"A rivermouth with two Roman forts on either side — both long abandoned… We camped in their shadow. We… were told not to stray too far from the beach. The natives were fierce warriors. More dangerous than those further south. That is everything I know."

I nod. "This should be enough," I say. "I might come back with some more questions later. I'll tell the guards to give you something else to eat than porridge."

"Hey — " he cries as I turn to leave. "You were supposed to let me go!"

"And I will. As soon as we've defeated your King Drust."

At dawn the next day, before the Council is gathered, I'm summoned before Wortigern, alone. He tells me more bad news.

"The Regins refuse to send any help. They claim they need their warriors to defend themselves from the bandits at Andreda."

"There are no bandits at Andreda," I reply. "I would know."

"I suspect as much. Catuar is just a coward, hiding behind his Saxons."

Wortigern is one of the few people with whom I shared the truth about where Aelle and his warband came from:

recruited from among those same Saxons who serve as allies and protectors of the southern province of Wortigern's domain, the *pagus* of the Regins.

"But others will believe the rumour," he says, "and think it's a concerted plot, the barbarians threatening Britannia from all sides."

"Why are you telling me this first, lord *Dux*?"

"I need you to ride out to Beaddingatun and see to it that the Iutes answer our summons. If they're here, this will be the proof there is no conspiracy."

"You would send them against the Picts instead of Wortimer's *centuria*?"

The *Dux* scowls. "I don't know how long I can keep them in the city. I can order Wortimer to stay — if he chooses to listen to his father — but his men are not under my command. The young men want their glory."

"If they go against the Picts alone, they'll get slaughtered."

"That's why I need those Iutes here as soon as possible."

He lays a hand on my arm — a fatherly gesture, showing the trust he's putting in me, though I know him well enough to see through such façade.

"Be quick, Ash," he tells me. "Everything hinges on this."

A sudden thought strikes me.

"It would be easier for me to convince the Iutes if I took Hengist's niece with me," I say.

A chuckle. "The girl? Yes, why not." A mischievous glint. "Wortimer is going to hate it."

"You lived in this palace as a child?" Rhedwyn asks, staring wide-eyed at the cracked rubble of Ariminum.

I conceal a chuckle. My heart beats faster than the hooves of the horses we rode here from Londin, just the two of us and the silent Iute guard. The rush of air painted her face a ruddy red, and brought a bright glint to her eyes.

"Me and Fastidius," I say. "And the entire family, and servants and slaves…"

She runs inside and lets out a yell, revelling in it echoing in the *villa's* empty chambers. After a moment, she falls silent, then comes out serious and downcast.

"Ten Iute families could fit in here," she observes.

It's an exaggeration. Ariminum is one of the smaller properties still existing along the old ridge south of Londin. But she's right that we should be doing more to accommodate the Iutes. If only it was up to me… But even as the heirs to the *villa*, neither I nor Fastidius can let any more of them settle on the property's grounds without the Council's permission.

I urge us to move to Beadda's village, across the river. It's getting late — we rode slowly, since Rhedwyn is unused to the tall Briton horses — and I need to talk to the Iute *Gesith* before nightfall.

"You haven't seen it yet, have you?" I ask.

"It will be the first real Iute village I'll have seen in my life," she replies.

"Don't you remember anything from the Old Country?"

She shakes her head. "It's all a blur. I was too little. Born just before the Crossing."

"What about your family?"

"Not much," she replies with a slight, sad shrug. "I was only a baby when my family perished on the whale-road. I didn't even have a name chosen yet — it was Uncle Hengist who called me Rhedwyn, after *Hredmonth*, when I was born. He told me many stories about life in the Old Country, but he spent most of his youth in Frisia, so wasn't there when I was born."

"Your parents must have been important, to lead a ship of their own."

She tilts her head and looks to the ground. "Hengist told me once my mother was the most beautiful and graceful of all the shieldmaidens in the tribe. And that my father was stronger than either he or Horsa. He could snap a ship's oar with one hand. When my uncles went to seek fortune in Frisia and Daneland, he was the one who remained to fight the marauders harassing our villages."

"Was he a *Drihten*, then? Like Horsa and Hengist?"

"We had no need for *Drihtens* in the old land, before the war… The *witan* of elders would choose strong men to command the warriors for each battle, as needed."

I'm embarrassed at not knowing any of this — it is part of my legacy as a Iute, yet I'm learning this from this fledgling, who's barely entered adulthood, as if I was a child and she my tutor.

"You were an only child, then?"

The question, obvious though it might seem, results in a surprising frown and a pause. "I think so," she says at last. "I mean, they would've told me otherwise, wouldn't they? They never mentioned any brothers or sisters I could've lost in the storm."

"But there were other relatives, no doubt."

"A five-score people went down with that boat. Three villages, all clansmen of Eobba."

I nod. "My family among them."

"I'm sorry." She takes my hand. Her skin is soft and warm. "I can't even imagine what it must've been like. I had my uncles, and all the Iutes, around me growing up — you were all alone…"

For a moment, I imagine the life we both could have had if the coming war hadn't pushed the Iutes out into the sea. Would we have known each other? It's likely — those who came on those first three *ceols* all came from neighbouring villages. But we probably would never have been able to meet like this, to talk, alone. Rhedwyn would have been a chieftain's daughter, and I — maybe a warrior in training…? A hunter? A farmer's son? A blacksmith's apprentice? I don't know what else a boy of my age and predisposition could do in a Iute village. There were no scholars of Roman history in the land of Iutes, no Christian priests like Paulinus, no army quartermasters like Pascent…

Once we cross the Loudborne, I slow down and let her mount pass mine. This way I can watch her slender form closely without her knowing, bobbing up and down in the saddle… I feel like I should tell her something, something about what I feel when I look at her, when I hear her speak. Otherwise, what was the point in dragging her all this way? Just to have her near me? What a selfish notion. But then, isn't everything we do for love, selfish…?

I open my mouth. "Rhed — "

"Do these all belong to Beadda?" she exclaims. "I knew he was doing well, but I didn't think…"

I look to where she's pointing and see a dozen horses grazing on the glade between the village and the cemetery. They're all war mounts, tall and muscle-bound, twice as large as the ponies of the Iutes.

"No," I say. "These are not Iutish."

I tense up and scan the village for signs of attack, but nothing seems out of the ordinary. The smoke rises from the chimneys, not from smouldering ruins; the cries are of playing children, not of terror and panic. The livestock moos and bleats just as it did the last time I was here.

I relax a little as we enter the village. Seeing Rhedwyn gawp at the roofs heaving with thick thatch and solid timber walls of the Iute houses makes me chuckle. She seems even more impressed with Beaddingatun, the newly built work of her own kin, than she was with Londin or Ariminum, the magnificent ruins created by the demi-gods of legendary Roman past.

I spot another couple of horses, tied up in front of Beadda's hall. I recognise the larger one, and at last I breathe a sigh of relief. I dismount, tell Rhedwyn and the silent guard to wait, and rush inside.

"Odo!" I cry out. "What are you doing here?"

"We ride from Leman," Odo says. "The entire *ala*, forty men. The others are staying the night at Saffron Valley."

He looks haggard, road-weary. They must have ridden here without stopping. The port of Leman lies on the other side of Cantiaca, at least two days away on fast horse. What made them race here in such a hurry?

"We had to make sure the return of the bandits was just a rumour," he explains. "Nobody's seen or heard from them in months, anywhere along the forest border. I spoke to the Regin merchants at Leman. The Saxon mercenaries are busy fighting each other for who gets to control the *witan*."

"Have you heard of the man called Pefen?"

Odo nods. "He is the strongest of the *Drihten*s — but some of the others united against him, and the Regins are supporting both sides. It's a dangerous game *Comes* Catuar plays," he stops to take a bite out of a piece of dark bread, "but at least it's keeping everyone in the South too busy to bother us."

This must be the real reason why we haven't heard from Aelle all this year — and why the Regins refused to send us any troops, too busy trying to keep the peace in their own land… The Picts have truly chosen the worst possible moment to strike. It's almost as if their knowledge of what goes on in the South is better than that of Wortigern's own Council.

I turn to Beadda. The *Gesith* sits at the top of the table, slowly sipping the mead from a large bronze goblet. It's a vessel I haven't seen before, of foreign shape — must be a gift from a passing merchant.

"You will answer Wortigern's summons, then?" I ask. "Now that you know there is no threat to your village."

I can only see his eyes over the goblet's rim — hesitant, calculating, no longer the hot, eager eyes of a warrior.

"We have sworn to defend Londin from its enemies," he says, his voice echoing inside the goblet. "Are the Picts threatening the city?"

I admit that they do not — they've moved on to Coln and, by now, likely beyond it. I understand his hesitation. It was one thing to fight the Saxons who encroached on his territory and threatened his links to Londin and Tanet; it is another to send warriors on a distant raid to some other province. He may be a *Gesith*, chief of Hengist's household troop, but he's now also a leader of a thriving settlement; he has a responsibility to protect the children born in the village, and their mothers, the prosperity and well-being of all people under his command.

Rhedwyn's voice rings out clear and bright in the silence. "I will gladly relay your dilemma to my uncle, *Gesith* Beadda. I'm sure he will agree to send some other, more eager commander in your place. Orpedda, perhaps?"

The tips of Beadda's cheeks go red. Being called a coward by a woman — not even a shieldmaiden — must leave an indelible stain on his honour. He gulps the last of the mead and slams the goblet on the table.

"Even without the summons, we would march to Londin's aid!" he booms. "Let your *Dux* know we will be ready in three days. By Donar, those *wealas* will learn the true might of a Iutish *Hiréd*!"

I return to Londin in the wake of Odo's *ala*, forty lancers galloping across the Bridge with their white horse cloaks flapping in the twilight breeze like angel wings. The blessed tidings they bring make the Bishop send Fastidius rushing off to the Cathedral to prepare a thanksgiving Mass.

They have still more good news than they shared with us at Beaddingatun, this one meant for the Council's ears only.

"*Comes* Worangon is alive," Odo announces, triumphant. "But he's gravely injured. He'd gathered what remained of his household guards and tried to intercept the Picts further up the river, but his troops were overrun."

"I'm guessing you saved them?" asks Wortigern.

"You're guessing wrong, Lord *Dux*. We were too late to join any battle. No, the *Comes* and his men fled to Tanet, into the protection of Hengist and his Iutes."

"The Iutes?" I hate the incredulous tone I hear in the Councillors' voices. "They stood their ground against the Picts?"

"They beat them back three times," replies Odo. "I have seen the dead myself, scattered on the grounds of the monastery where the Iutes made their stand. The Picts lost three men to each fallen Iute until they figured out there was nothing on the island worth dying for and turned north."

He is itching for a fight; I can see it in his gleaming eyes. The lancers blame themselves for having been fooled into pursuing the non-existent foe in the woods of Andreda and are now yearning for revenge.

"Hengist's men are now protecting Cantiaca's coast — and thanks to them, the *Comes* released us from our obligations. My Gauls will ride against the Picts alongside whatever army you muster, *Dux*."

Odo looks at me across the table and nods, reminding the others they have one of those valiant Iutish warriors in their midst already. I beam; for the first time in a long while I feel proud to have the Iute blood flowing through my veins.

"Should we send for the Iutes, then?" asks the scar-faced veteran. "But it would take a long time for them to get here…"

"You need not wait," I say and, with the *Dux's* silent approval, add: "the warriors of Beaddingatun have heard our plea and are already preparing to march to our aid. Others will join them soon."

In the morning, on the tenth day after the fall of Dorowern, they arrive: the *Hiréd*, led by *Gesith* Beadda, all twenty of them, resplendent in polished mail and steel helmets. As they enter the city through the Bridge Gate, the heads of their spears blaze like flaming torches in the rising sun. They sing as they march, a rousing song that starts with an invocation to Wodan and Donar, but soon turns into a lewd tribute to the beauty and laying prowess of their women. Their compatriots from the Forum trading camp, and Saxon merchants from the harbour, join them in song, if not in the marching; the chanting and stomping and rattling of weapons resounds throughout the entire city.

Wortigern and I meet with Beadda in front of the palace to hear his report and relay it to the War Council. Another, smaller band of Iute warriors, from Orpedda's hamlet, is also heading for the city and is a mere half day away.

"We will assign them to the Wall," announces Wortigern. "And send those of our men they replace after the Picts."

"Have the barbarians man the Wall?" rage the Councillors from Wortimer's faction. "This has never happened! This is tantamount to surrender!"

Wortigern glowers. His son sits silent at his right hand, but his nostrils are flared. He's letting the others' ire blaze for him. I can see in his eyes there's another topic he's more interested in than the Wall arrangement, one that he's saving his rhetoric energy for.

"There will only be a dozen or so of them," replies Wortigern, coolly. "And they will not be on combat duty. Hardly a threat to our great city. Would you rather we'd send your son to the *ballistae*, Eusebius?"

"You know very well my son is of frail health, Wortigern," scoffs the Councillor.

"I'm sure we can manage without the pagans, father," Wortimer interjects. "Or, for that matter, without the Gauls, or your Wall-men. My *centuria* will do quick work of the Picts. We're ready to march as soon as you give orders."

"You will wait until everything is ready."

"The longer we wait, the greater the danger to Coln!"

"Coln's walls are almost as old and mighty as ours. The Picts will raid the countryside and then move further north — where we'll be waiting for them."

"You are a stubborn old fool, Father! I will not share my God-given glory with pagans and barbarians!" Wortimer rails.

"You mean, plunder," I hear a courtier's voice. Wortimer swivels around and searches for the source of the remark and, not finding it, returns to facing his father, now openly seething with ire.

"My lords," Wortigern says, his voice cold like a winter stream. He looks towards the door.

We take the hint and leave the father and son alone in the Council hall. For the next hour all we hear from behind the closed door is Wortimer's shouting. The *Dux* only raises his voice once, to demand obedience from his son; there's a long pause, and then the door slams open as Wortimer walks out, his face contorted in a furious grimace.

Overnight, the militia camp empties. By dawn we learn that Wortimer has taken his hundred men through the Old Gate, leading them towards Coln.

There are seven gates in the Londin Wall, not counting the one that guards the Bridge — not because there are seven directions worth going from the city, but because it was considered a fortunate number by the Romans; indeed, only four of them lead to other cities, rather than fizzling out into the surrounding moorland. Of these, the Callew Highway, which leads west, and the Augustan Highway to the east are the oldest and most important. The third highway links Londin with the ancient burial mounds and, further, the old capital of the Regins in the south-west. Finally, the fourth of the great highways begins at the northern end of the Forum and ventures north, across the hills of the Cadwallons towards the marshes of the Coriadaws, Ikens, and further still, across the mist-covered moors of Lindocoln and Ebrauc, until at last it reaches another mighty barrier built by the Romans: the Aelian Wall, a place known to most only from legend, a single line of stone a hundred miles long and twenty feet tall that once separated Britannia from the windswept wilderness that the Picts call home.

It is this road that our "Legion" takes out of the city. The name is one that we gave ourselves in mockery: in the old military manuals, a legion is a force of thousands; we are little more than a hundred altogether: Odo's Gauls, Beadda's Iutes and the Briton contingent, consisting mostly of the veterans from Wortigern's old army and the Wall guards combined. But then, our enemy is neither Parthian nor Dacian, nor any of the great foes Rome had to scuffle with in the old days; the Pict horde may be a large one compared with what they usually muster, but they are still just a bunch of cowardly barbarians from the frozen Northern wastes, their recent success a matter of fortune and surprise rather than might of arms. Our spirits are high, our pace is good: everyone here knows how to march long distance, and even the veterans, burdened with mail armour, long shields and heavy weapons, have no trouble keeping up to the mounted Gauls up front, though some of them are nearing fifty, and have lived peaceful, boring lives for the best part of the past three decades.

Besides, we're hoping our numbers will grow from local recruits by the time we reach the northern coast. We're not headed for Coln, like Wortimer. Just as the *Dux* intended from the start, we're marching up the Iken Way, along the northern coast, towards the briny marshes of the Iken folk. Their coast, with its red cliffs and its many abandoned Roman forts, is what the scholars at the court have identified as the location best fitting the description given us by the young Wotadin captive.

"You have chosen me to lead you in war," the *Dux* reminded the Council, as he explained his decision. "And until you relieve me of my duty, the army we've raised is under *my* command."

With Wortimer absent, there was no one eager to argue. Like everything in war, it's a gamble: we put all our trust into

Cunedag's word; what might wait for us in the Iken marshes could be a trap — or, worse, nothing at all, the Pictish fleet gathered elsewhere, laughing and counting the spoils.

But first, we have to reach the border of the Iken *pagus*, and that means leaving Wortigern's domain and entering the territory under control of the fierce tribal lords of Middle Britannia.

"They are still Christians there, right?" I ask Fastidius, who, to my delight, has joined our small army to serve as its diplomat and chief scribe. "And Romans?"

"This used to be Rome, yes, and I'd hope they would fight with us against the pagans — but they do not acknowledge Londin's authority, other than in matters of faith."

Most of our journey will be through the *pagus* of Cadwallons, under *Comes* Elasio, one of Wortigern's subordinates. But beyond the next crossroad the old province of Britannia Maxima ends — and so does the *Dux's* jurisdiction.

"There used to be two more provinces between here and the Aelian Wall," Fastidius explains. "Each with its own Governor, though all subject ultimately to the *Praetor* in Londin."

"Who rules them now?"

"Nobody. It all fell apart after the Romans left. Now it's every tribe for themselves. The only authority that remains are the two Bishops, still set in the old provincial capitals of Lindocoln and Ebrauc — but what power they hold over the land, I cannot tell."

There is a glint of excitement in his eyes as he talks of these things. He's yearning to see the distant lands he's only been reading about until now. He was not ordered to join us — indeed, he himself insisted on going on the long journey instead of some other court clerk, and pleaded with Bishop Fatalis to relieve him of his duties for the time being.

"I had to promise I would try to convert the Pict captives," he says with a chuckle, then turns serious. "And of course, I will, for it is my duty to spread the light of God."

"But that's not why you wanted to come," I say.

"I needed to get away from Londin," he replies, rubbing his forehead. "The intrigues, the plotting, the pettiness of it all… Sometimes it feels as if the entire world has been reduced to just the ring of the Wall, as if there was nothing of interest beyond it."

"I know what you mean," I say, recalling my time at the court. For the first few months it was all new and exciting, but soon I noticed that most of the "work" that went on in the palace consisted of pursuing trivial rivalries, inducing minute changes in the hierarchy, and tedious day-to-day administration. There was no greater plan beyond immediate survival, no splendour, no thought for the future. The everyday running of the city, and of the four *pagi* under Wortigern's rule, was left to lowly clerks and educated slaves, as if it was a task beneath the Councillors. No wonder Londin was falling apart at the seams…

"But I thought it was different in the Church. What about Rome — what about the Pope?"

Fastidius sighs. "We haven't heard from the Pope in years. I don't know whether it's become too difficult for the messengers to come through Gaul and Frankia, or we are simply not important enough to warrant a response. To think, my — *our*," he corrects himself quickly, "father fought at Arelates with Constantine, while we two are confined to this tiny island and an occasional trip to Armorica."

I never thought of myself as *confined* to Britannia before. To me it has always been a vast enough country, compared with what I knew at Ariminum — I've never ventured further than Tanet Island or Coln on court business, and I never felt I needed to. But Fastidius's words open my eyes to the truth. I remember the maps Paulinus showed me. The world used to be vast — not just in the days of the ancients, who travelled with ease from one of its corners to another, but even in our fathers' youth, *Dux* Wortigern and Master Pascent saw all of Gaul in their service with Constantine, a country at least twice as broad as Britannia. In those not so long gone days, the pilgrims were still free to reach Rome and back, the merchant ships still plied the great ocean, free from the pirate threat, and the couriers still brought news from places as distant and exotic-sounding as Africa or Thrace.

It wasn't just that between then and now the pagan hordes overran Gaul, cutting us off from the rest of the Empire, or that the pirates took control of all but the least profitable sea routes. All this had happened before, and would happen again, and while it certainly made the travels more difficult, it did not render them impossible. Something else has changed in our generation. It was our minds that shrank, not the world. We are all thinking in terms of here and now; we are more concerned with what goes on in the suburbs of Callew, than in the great cities of Iberia; the rise in price of duck eggs in Rath sends more ripples through the court than the news of a new Imperator in Rome. We've learned to "get by" with what we have, rather than pursue new crafts, new ideas. Our mosaics are all recycled from old ones, our churches are built from stone stolen from ancient temples, rather than quarried anew. Even Riotham's new black pottery failed to rouse anyone's interest once everyone decided it was no better at holding soup than our old pots and bowls — and that only came from a neighbouring province, not from far across the seas.

I'm now annoyed at Fastidius; all these sobering thoughts mar my enjoyment of what should be a fascinating and exciting journey. I've never been this far north, and I've never been outside of Wortigern's province before, and I was looking forward to seeing the marvels of these distant lands, before Fastidius reminded me this kind of journey used to be routine for most people of our status in Britannia, no more than a lifetime ago.

CHAPTER IV
THE LAY OF UNA

We stop overnight in a village that sprawls around a crossroad of Roman tracks, marked with a great cross of red sandstone, raised here by the followers of Martinus in place of a pagan milestone. Fastidius looks up from a thick book he's reading, notices my brooding, and disappears for an hour. He returns with a mug full of steaming brew. I sniff it. The heady herbal scent seems familiar. I blow and take a sip.

"What is it?" I ask.

"Hypericum," he answers. "I picked it in the heath. It does wonders for melancholy."

"Isn't this what Father Paulinus used to drink?"

"He taught me how to make it. Now it's no longer enough for him — so he drowns his sorrow in the Saxon mead… But it should work for you."

"Thanks."

He sits beside me and picks up the book again. I notice the title — *On Military Matters*, the same book on the art of war he used to read when we were kids.

"I'm glad you came with us," he says.

"Me too. Though I didn't have much choice."

It was Wortigern's idea — followed by an order — for me to accompany the "Legion". More than that, he's made me a nominal commander of the unit, though due to my lack of experience or any knowledge of warfare, it is only an honorary position — the real generals are Odo and Beadda. I don't know whether it is the *Dux's* idea of a joke, or a political manoeuvre I don't understand… or is he just playing me against his own son at the Council, now that Catigern is gone? I'm sure he would've preferred Fastidius to lead the army, but the Bishop insisted his role in this expedition must be strictly civilian.

The evening mist rising from the heath makes the crossroad village seem as if it was floating in the air. The night before we left Londin, the fog was even thicker. It crept up from the river, into the palace gardens, obscuring the Moon and dimming the lanterns. It was no night for reading lessons, but Rhedwyn came nonetheless, her slender frame tucked in a woollen cloak.

"I hear you're off to war," she said. "Are you going to fight, or just watch?" She was no longer the timid, quiet creature I'd first fallen in love with — but that did not diminish my feelings for her.

"The Picts might be gone by the time we get there," I replied, hiding the anxious enthusiasm in my voice. "We may not even get the chance to fight."

"But if you do …?"

I pushed my chest forward. "I am a Iute. I'll make my ancestors proud."

To my surprise, her shoulders slumped and her face sagged with sadness. She bit her lower lip and touched my chest with her long fingers. "You — you will take care of yourself out there, won't you, Ash?"

Remembering the way her blue eyes pierced me that night makes my heart race, but it only serves to bring my spirit down further. And we are not the only ones engulfed by melancholy. The Iute camp is shrouded in gloom: there is no more mead, and the men are already missing their wives and children. They would all be here if it was a band on the march in the Old Country, Beadda tells me, the women fighting alongside their husbands, the weaning babies tied to their breasts; but things are different in these new, strange times. The Iutes cannot live off the land during their march — they are mercenaries in the employ of those who own the fields and pastures; and, with the harvest so near, the fields around the village need constant tending. There are other women in the camp now, from the town at the crossroads, used to servicing passing travellers, but they bring only passing joy to the warriors.

Odo's Gauls are the only ones keeping their spirits up; they've seized both of the town's inns for their use, and found a barrel of old Aquitanian wine in one of them and a wheel of some ancient mouldy cheese in the other. This brings them untold amount of joy. Their jubilant songs drown out the lamenting recitations of the Iutes, but instead of lightening my mood all they do is remind me of Fulco, the Frank who taught me how to fight, and I grow even more despondent. He was just as fond of the Aquitanian wine and mouldy cheese as these Gauls.

"Is this the border of Wortigern's domain?" I ask, looking north across the fog-shrouded fields. In the dusk, it's no longer possible to make out any details of the flat landscape, just a sea of desolate, damp grey. Are we even still on God's Earth? It feels more like we're in some realm of the dead, waiting in the directionless space for some final judgment.

"Borders are more ideas than lines on the map here," replies Fastidius. "Three tribes lay claim to this crossroad town — Cadwallons, Coriadaws and Ikens. Elasio, chieftain of Cadwallons, is subordinate to the *Dux*, but the other two are masters in their own right… The locals certainly don't seem to care who their lord is."

A shrill neigh cuts through the fog, followed by cries and a clash of arms. Fastidius and I jump up. I reach for my Anglian spear and run towards the source of the noise — the stables by one of the inns occupied by the Gauls.

As the fog clears, I see the scene of carnage: two men lying in pools of blood, one of them a stable boy, the other a slain warrior with unkempt bushy beard and long black hair, wearing tatters of a padded undercoat and shin guards; his sword — a good, well-kept sword, I notice immediately — lies in the dirt beside him.

Two Gauls are holding on to the slain man's comrade, forcing him to kneel. He's silent, solemn and downcast. An old, dented helmet sits askew on his head, and a chipped hatchet lies at his feet. One of the horses looms over him, with pain in its big, sad eyes; a stray scratch drips red all over its dappled grey flank.

"We caught them trying to steal the horses," says one of the Gauls, though an explanation is hardly necessary. "Pict marauders, I bet!"

"We're not Picts," says the kneeling warrior in a clear voice. "We're Britons. And this is our land."

"What do you mean, this is your land?" asks Fastidius. "This town belongs to Elasio, the *Comes* of the Cadwallons, by grace of *Dux* Wortigern."

"It used to be a village of the Ikens," the prisoner says, defiantly. "And it will soon be ours again."

Fastidius looks around helplessly, but none of us can help him. We are not here to settle border disputes — indeed, we were not aware of there being any this near Londin.

"When you say, *used to be…*" asks one of the veterans. A small group of spectators has gathered around the stables, gawking at the kneeling warrior. "I've been here as a youth, it was a Cadwallon town even then."

The Iken scoffs. "I'm talking about the *old* time. Before the Romans came and set the borders up as they wished."

Gasps of disbelief ripple through the crowd. "But that was four centuries ago!" says Fastidius.

"We remembered," says the Iken. "We waited."

"Remembered? How?"

"Our women told the stories, mother to daughter, for generations. Of Iken armies burning down Roman cities, Iken warriors destroying the Legions. Our land spread from the sea to the Tamesa. And it will again!" His eyes glint.

"He's right," murmurs Fastidius. "The Ikens did do all those things — back in Imperator Nero's times."

I nod, remembering the story from Tacitus — but it's hard to believe anyone today would still consider these old tales, from a time as old as myth, worth not only remembering but used to support some new land grab.

"Shouldn't you worry about the Picts raiding your shores, rather than some ancient feuds?" I ask.

"Picts?" He blinks, as a narrow trickle of blood from under his helmet reaches his eye.

"We've been sent from Londin to fight them," explains Fastidius. "We don't care about your squabbles with the Cadwallons."

"You're not Elasio's army, then?" The Iken warrior stares at us, then he spots Beadda and a couple of his Iutes. "But you have the Saxons among you!"

"They are Iutes," I say, but I see the word makes no impression on him. "Don't you know anything that's been going on outside your borders?"

He shakes his head. I cannot blame him. This Iken didn't even know of the Pictish invasion occurring in his own tribal lands, how can I expect him to know about what goes on in the land of Cants or Regins? The extent of his wildest ambition is for his tribe's lands to one day reach Tamesa — a few days away on horseback. What does he know, or care, of more distant places like Gaul, Rome, or the Saxon lands?

It is just as I feared: the world in people's minds has shrunk, and in the darkness beyond the edges of the bright light shining from Londin, the dim torches of distant towns and villages serve only to illuminate their most immediate surroundings.

Is it the same in Ambrosius's realm in the West, I wonder? Or are they even more cut off from the real world, sucking on the marrow of memories until there's nothing left? Any ruler who would wish to restore Britannia to any semblance of its old glory would need to first tackle this darkness engulfing people's minds — to expand the horizons of their thought, to have them consider the world beyond their tribal borders. I truly doubt whether Wortimer, for all his bluster, could be the man to do it…

We take the Iken from the cold of the stables — more for our convenience than his — and into the inn, where we bind him with rope and investigate him further. We learn that the quiet conflict has been bubbling away along the border between the three nearby tribes ever since the Roman Legions departed for the Continent. That the Germanic mercenaries — the *Gewisse* tribe of Saxons in service of the Cadwallons, and the Angles in service of the Ikens — rather than protecting the outer borders of the province from barbarian raids, are being used to settle the ancient scores, and push the Briton villagers and townsfolk from homes in which they lived for generations. The warrior we captured, and his slain comrade, were survivors of one such raid, and planned to steal our horses to get back to Wenta of the Ikens with the dire news.

"Elasio is the worst culprit," the Iken says. "If it wasn't for his *Gewisse* harassing us and the Coriadaws as far as Rath, we wouldn't need to pay the Angles so much for protection."

"Elasio has no right to do this," says Fastidius. "I will need to report it all to Wortigern."

"Your *Dux* knows about everything," says the Iken. "Our *Comes* sent him messenger after messenger. We were told to look to our own defences."

"So you got the Angles to fight for you," I note. This angers him. He stirs in his binds.

"We got the Angles to fight his Saxons! We would manage the Cadwallons alone, like we always have. The Iken lands were never subdued, not even by the Romans!"

"That is true," says Fastidius with a nod. "You were always the most troublesome of tribes."

The Iken is placated by the faint praise. He seems glad to recognise in Fastidius one as fond of ancient history as he is — even if the only ancient history *he* knows is that of his own tribe, no doubt transformed beyond recognition from the truth by generations of retelling. He asks for something to drink, and Fastidius generously shares with him the last cup of the Gaulish wine.

I pull Fastidius aside. "What are we going to do with him?" I ask in Imperial tongue.

Fastidius rubs his chin. "We need the *Comes* of the Ikens on our side, if we are to defeat the Picts."

"You want to set him free?"

"He didn't know who we were. Attacking your enemy is no crime."

"Do you believe all that about Elasio? How come we've never heard anything at the court?"

He shrugs. "There've always been rumours about all those Saxons settled around Dorcic and in the hills, those … *Gewisse*, as they call themselves. We thought Elasio brought them there to protect his northern borders."

"And do you think Wortigern really knows of it all?"

"Even if he does, there's nothing he can do. Keeping peace within his own domain, balancing power between the Cants, Regins and Cadwallons must be taking his entire energy. The Ikens don't acknowledge him as a ruler, so they can't count on his support."

I glance at the Iken warrior, and he glances back at me — or rather, the spear that's still slung over my back.

"Yes, it's an Anglian design." I anticipate his question. "But I'm not an Angle."

"You look like them, though," he says, and I sense hostility in his voice.

"You don't like the Angles?" I ask. "I thought they were protecting you."

He spits. "And they're bleeding us dry in exchange. *Comes* Una gives them all they ask for."

Fastidius steps between us. "I don't want to hear anything more about it. It's obvious you have your share of problems here in the North, problems that one day will need solving, but *my* only problem right now is how to defeat the Picts quickly and go back home." He cuts the warrior's ropes. "You're free. Tell your *Comes* to await us in two days — if she's at all interested in defending her own people."

The Iken rubs his wrists and gives us a surprised look, then nods awkwardly and runs out of the inn into the night.

Fastidius shakes his head. "What a mess. I don't know about you, but my lust for adventure is all gone. The sooner we're back in Londin, the better."

We are about to leave the red cross town, and embark on the long trek down the Iken Way, when we are once again disturbed by yet another unexpected arrival.

This new visitor rides up in a strange machine: a wobbly, four-wheeled chariot pulled by two weary dray horses. A troop of soldiers follows in its wake, some twenty men altogether, guarding a column of slaves; the soldiers all in red cloaks and brown tunics, the slaves all in chains and loincloths, beaten up and scarred from whips. The slaves are Britons; the soldiers are Saxons.

Odo and Beadda order their men to stand in a crescent across the road and make ready for battle, while I and Fastidius step forward to meet the man on the chariot. He looks as peculiar as his vehicle: thick red hair spills in braids from under a high-peaked bronze helmet, splotched with green patina; a red beard rests on his chest, protected by a rusted mail shirt and a pleated plaid robe. He carries a heavy leaf-bladed spear that appears more a ceremonial device than weapon of war. His arms are bare, covered with blue paint. A thick golden ring clasps around his neck, a relic from some old treasure chest.

He is, in short, a ghost of ancient past, a statue of a Briton warrior, come to life.

"*Comes* Elasio!" Fastidius greets him with a bow. Although I'm supposed to be the commander of the expedition, I stand back and let his natural authority shine.

Elasio eyes us carefully, then disembarks from the chariot, leaving the spear and helmet in the hands of a wretched-looking slave.

"Father Fastidius! We met last year at the Cathedral. And you are?"

"Fraxinus, my brother, and a courtier of *Dux* Wortigern," Fastidius answers before me. He does not give Elasio the chance to wonder why we look so different, if we're siblings. "We did not expect to meet you this far from Werlam, *Comes*."

"I was out on patrol nearby, and heard news of your passing through my land. I thought I'd pay you a visit."

"We appreciate it." Fastidius points to the slaves. "Who are these?"

"Just some Ikens I caught sneaking through my borders."

"I take it you're about to release them back to their land."

Elasio scoffs. "So they can return and harass me again? No, I'm going to sell them to Frisian merchants. I need to recoup my losses somehow. Keeping the Saxons happy isn't cheap."

Fastidius blinks. His face turns stern. He straightens his back. I spot a fire light up in his eyes which I haven't seen in a long time. He comes up to the *Comes* and though Elasio towers over him by half a foot in his tall helmet, he steps back, apprehensive of Fastidius's sudden burning passion.

"No Briton is to sell another Briton into slavery!" my brother declares, in his fiery preacher's voice. "Such is Wortigern's law — and you are still Wortigern's subject!"

"Wortigern!" Elasio scoffs and raises his hands in the air. "What does *he* know of life out here! He's safe behind the walls of Londin — walls he didn't build. We're fighting for our survival every day. The Ikens, the Coriadaws… I'm the one who has to protect Wortigern's borders, and I will do anything that's necessary to keep them safe."

"And what of the Picts?" I interject. "We were hoping for your assistance in defeating them."

"The Picts harass our enemies more than us," he answers with a shrug so mighty it makes his helmet drop to the side. "If they can take a bite out of the Ikens, they're welcome to it. I'll have less of them to worry about."

"I'm not here to discuss the law," says Fastidius. "I command you to release those captives — or we'll fight you for them."

Elasio stares at him, then at the crescent of warriors behind us. These *Gewisse* of his may be fierce fighters, but they look tired and disorderly after the battle. One charge from Odo's lancers would be enough to scatter them into the marshes. Elasio tries to plea and bargain one last time, but Fastidius and I are insistent and, at last, he relents.

The Saxons scowl, annoyed at the order: there goes their salary for the battle. I notice Elasio is sweating under the helmet. The Saxons murmur among each other, and then their leader calls for the *Comes*. From the way Elasio skulks off in a hurry, it's clear who's the master and who's the servant in this relationship.

"These Picts…" he asks when he returns to us, "…will they have much plunder?"

I hear Beadda grunt behind me. The Iutes don't feel like sharing their reward any more than Wortimer's men did.

"They robbed the church at Dorowern," says Fastidius, and Elasio's eyes light up, for the wealth of the Cantish priests is well renowned even this far north. "And the *villas* around Coln. But our men are promised the greatest share of the reward — or what is left of it once we return the sacred vessels, of course."

"Of course." Elasio returns to his warriors, and after a long, swearing-studded exchange, the Saxons finally agree to release the prisoners. The Ikens rush to us with thanks, calling our praise to God — and to the *gods*, I notice, hearing the names of Wodan and Donar among others I don't recognise. Fastidius blesses them with the sign of the cross, choosing to ignore the pagan invocations.

"Have the innkeeper feed them," I order. "And make sure they remember it was Father Fastidius of Saint Paul's who freed them."

"Please, Ash, it's completely unnecessary — " Fastidius opposes, but I stop him.

"You were supposed to spread the light of God, remember?" I say with a smile.

"I can spare a dozen of my best warriors in the fight against the Picts," Elasio interjects. I glance at the Saxons — they have already chosen among themselves who's going to join us, without waiting for the *Comes's* decision; or ours, for that matter. "If you promise the Ikens will not attack us while you're there."

"I'll make sure of that," Fastidius says, though we all know he has no way of keeping the promise. "Are they ready to march? We were just about to leave."

"We are," says the Saxon leader. Disregarding all ceremony, he pushes Elasio out of the way. "We go in front," he adds. His Vulgar Tongue is even rougher than that of Beadda's men. "Is dangerous on Iken Way."

"Dangerous?" I glance at Elasio.

"Bandits and marauders coming from all over the North," the *Comes* explains. "They hide in the wetlands. But I'm sure they'll have more sense than to attack a hundred-strong army of such mighty warriors," he adds with a crooked, sycophantic smile.

Behind me, I hear somebody spit into the mud in disgust.

If meeting the *Comes* of the Cadwallons was an unusual experience, talking to Una, the chieftain of the Ikens, is doubly so. She is dressed in a similar antique fashion to Elasio, but she dons a precious Saxon helmet, inlaid with weaving patterns of silver and gold, and a breastplate of bronze rendered so that it imitates the curves of her mature body. With her wild mane of black hair, deliberately unkempt, and piercing black eyes in a sharply chiselled face, she looks more like a living form of some pagan goddess than a human female.

Her capital, Wenta of the Ikens, is so tiny, it could fit whole in Londin's Forum. Most of the space inside the rectangle of Roman walls is taken by a marketplace, though there are only a few stalls today, and it doesn't seem like there would be many more on a market day. A ruin of a quaint *basilica*, smaller than the *Domus* at Ariminum, serves for Una's headquarters: the stone walls replaced by oak beams, the tiled roof patched with reed thatch. There is no church, only a small roofed altar, no larger than a field chapel, attached to the eastern wall. A couple of the old stone houses still stand; the rest of the town is a jumble of wooden shelters and wattle huts built on top of old foundations, same as I've seen in so many places elsewhere.

It's a different story outside the walls. A vast settlement sprawls all around the Wenta and along the Iken Way; for the best part of the day we've been travelling through smaller villages, some of them grown so large they ended up linked to each other almost seamlessly. The damp, peaty soil of this flat swampland is fertile enough to ensure the prosperity of the farmers; smoke rises thick from the forges and smithies, cows and pigs have grown fat and content, the houses are large, with thick timber walls — but they are not Briton in design. And these are not Briton villages. We've heard little of either the Vulgar or the Briton tongues today, only a strange, guttural dialect similar to Saxon and Iutish. As we pass a herd of woolly sheep on their way to the Wenta market, Beadda remarks how it all reminds him of their homeland across the sea — before the horse archers came.

"We left all that wealth to come to Cantiaca's mud," he says wistfully. "We should've sailed north instead. This is like Frige's garden."

Little wonder, then, that the first question we ask of *Comes* Una, even before we mention the Picts, is about the opulence of her countryside.

"I have nothing to do with that," she replies. "The Angles rule themselves. All I did was give them some empty land, in exchange for defending our borders from the Northern raiders and Elasio's *Gewisse*."

"Who is their *Drihten*?" asks Beadda. He's not even trying to hide his excitement. What we saw in Wenta is the fulfilment of his people's dreams — a fertile piece of soil to call their own, enough to fit the entire tribe.

"Angenwit. You'll have to discuss the military matters with him," she tells us. "Though from what I hear, he's already sent men into the swamps, looking for the pirate ships."

"Aren't there any Britons in your army?" I ask.

"Only my palace guard." It's a lofty name for the handful of spearmen standing watch in front of the timber hall.

"What about the men we released from Elasio's chains?" asks Fastidius.

"They gather in bands of their own volition, and play at war on the western frontier. I forbid this, but I cannot enforce my orders so far from Wenta."

"It seems to me you hold no power over this land at all," I note. "You don't rule over the Angles, you can't control your own people…"

Her nostrils flare, and her lips narrow. In fierceness, her cold beauty shines even brighter. "I'm doing what I can under the circumstances," she says. "I'd like to see you try better, squashed between the sea and the Cadwallons. We Ikens never asked for anyone's help. Not even the Romans."

"You asked the Angles."

"They're mercenaries. We're paying for their assistance, not begging for it."

"Paying with your best land, from what I see," says Fastidius. "How long before they ask for more — before they ask for your palace? Your throne?"

Una stands up and dismisses us with a wave of her hand. "Enough. I will not be questioned in my own home by a priest and a fledgling boy. I believe we've discussed all we had to discuss. Go to Angenwit to talk about the Picts — and leave me be."

She wraps her plaid cloak around her, leaving only her black eyes brooding from under the helmet, and sits back on the creaking throne.

"I had no idea things were so bad in the North."

Fastidius and I are taking a stroll around the desolation of Wenta. The town was larger once: there is another, wider border around the town, marked with an earthen embankment studded with remains of a stone wall jutting out from under the grass like broken teeth. But there are no houses inside this border, and it seems whatever deal Una struck with the Angles forbids them from settling in the empty space. Our "Legion" sets up camp on the southern meadow, as we wait for news from Angenwit's vanguard. The conversation with the Anglian *Drihten* proved easier and more fruitful than with Una. He's got a hundred men already under arms, gathered from all over the *pagus*; some are little more than farmers armed with pitchforks and clubs — but the core of his army are his *Hiréd*, household guards, armed and trained at least as well as Beadda's men.

By evening, when the last carts leave the market, the town falls dark and quiet. The only lights and noises are coming from Una's "palace'. A couple of empty boats bob on the river by the wharf. The inhabitants of the few remaining stone houses shut their doors and shutters at dusk, uninterested in our visit. The people from the huts and lean-tos are more curious, but they, too, are fearful and cautious, and watch our camp from behind the safety of the town wall.

"The Ikens were always a bit of a backwards tribe," Fastidius replies. He skips over a flat boulder — too flat to be a natural outcropping. "Never truly conquered, never fully a part of the Empire. It's not them I'm worried about — but Elasio."

"Did he always dress like that?"

"When he came to Londin last time he looked just like any other nobleman. No idea where he got that ancient costume from. It must be a show for his own people, but — why?" Fastidius shakes his head. "You'll need to bring this up at the Council. It's not our job to worry about these matters."

"I think the Council will be more interested in those *Gewisse* warriors under his supposed command," I say. "They didn't behave like mercenaries at all."

Silently, I wonder if this is what the land of Regins will look like when Aelle's father unites the Saxon tribes under his command. Will *Comes* Catuar become the same meek weakling at the whim of a pagan warlord as Elasio?

"I know." Fastidius stops. "Do you think this is why we two were sent here? To report on the Cadwallons and Ikens? After all, neither of us is exactly about to change the tide of a battle."

"Wouldn't Wortigern have told us that?" I reply; I'm wounded at the suggestion of my uselessness — I fought at Saffron Valley, after all, and survived! — but I can't disagree with Fastidius's logic.

"The Bishop would never have agreed to send me on a spying mission among fellow Christians. As for you — " He scratches his cheek, unshaven since we left Londin. "Maybe you're not as trusted at the court as you think."

"I don't think I'm trusted at all. They all still treat me like a Saxon slaveling."

"Well, then we're both — " He trips over something in the tall grass. I catch him from falling. He kneels down to examine the obstacle. "And what do we have here?"

We uncover a tightly packed cluster of flat stones, half-sunken in the peat, stretching from east to west. They don't look like a foundation of a building, rather …

"It's a military path," I say. "Must be from when the Romans had a fort here."

"Where does it lead to?"

We dig in the peat some more and, since Roman roads are always in a straight line, we soon figure out that its destination must be the thick clump of junipers on the riverbank. Judging by the age of the trees, nobody has bothered to clear it for at least a generation. I push away the branches and venture deeper into the dark, dense grove, until my hand meets a cracked stone surface. We scrub out the lichen and vines, to reveal a sandstone pillar, supporting a rotting frame of an oaken gate of a barn-like building. The timber wall disappears into the undergrowth. The right leaf of the gate, what we can see of it, is carved with the design of a bull, and the letters 'COH I AQV'.

"First Aquitanian Cohort," whispers Fastidius. "I've seen that name on the list of units that went with Constantine."

"A legionary storehouse!"

I begin to clear out the rest of the door from under the vines and bramble; the thorns dig deep into my skin. "It's probably empty," says Fastidius. "It must be." But I can hear the anticipation in his voice. He gets down on his knees and digs out the soil and roots from under the threshold. Soon we clear enough to make an attempt at opening the door. The threshold stone is marked with a scratched cross and an undecipherable name of some long-forgotten soldier. Another inscription, covered with lichen, reads under my fingers: *revertemvr.*

We will return.

I feel a tingling at the back of my neck.

"It must be locked," doubts Fastidius.

"The lock would have rusted away by now, surely."

We both hang on the round brass handle and pull with all our might. It creaks, but doesn't budge. We pull again. A small fissure appears between the leaves: enough to insert a sword blade. I tell Fastidius to hold on to the handle as hard as he can, and then I slide my *seax* into the crack. I whack at the latch and push, then again, until I hear a crash of metal giving way. A plume of red dust puffs from inside. The gate swings open and Fastidius flies away into the junipers.

I help him up and we peek inside; it's pitch-black — the light of the dusk does not penetrate into the grove and the barn. Fastidius reaches for the fire-steel at his belt. I take a sniff and stop his hand.

"It's full of peat dust," I warn him. "No flames."

We have to let our eyes get used to the dim light before we can start exploring the interior. The origin of the peat dust is soon clear: there's a great pile of it taking up most of the barn, rotting on the surface, but warm and dry inside. I cover my nose and dig my hands in up to the elbows.

"Timber," I announce. "Hard, square beam."

Fastidius rolls up his sleeves and throws off heaps of peat from the pile. It's hard work, but soon we are able to make out the shape of the device hidden underneath: the long wooden beam, the iron frame at one end, a winch on the other, and a heavy tripod in the middle. It looks similar to a greatly magnified version of Aelle's black bolt-thrower. Whoever left it here, knew what they were doing. The peat pile preserved the wood and metal in near-perfect condition. There is barely any rust on the iron, barely any rot on the wood.

"A *carrobalista*!" exclaims Fastidius. "I read about it in Vegetius. I never thought I'd see one in real life!"

"Can it be used still?" I ask. I don't need to know the name; I can tell it's a powerful weapon, similar to those standing on the turrets of the Londin Wall. I'm trying to imagine the size of the missiles it hurls — the bolts must be as big as my spear.

"All we need is some rope — and bolts. There must be some under all that peat."

He crouches to dig deeper, but I lay my hand on his shoulder. "It's too dark — we need to go back to the camp."

"We'll have to come back by daylight," he says. "It's a sign, Ash. Not all of Rome's might is yet lost, not all of God's light is extinguished — not even in a place like this."

CHAPTER V
THE LAY OF ANGENWIT

There's a handful of people waiting for us back at the camp; or rather, as it soon turns out, for Fastidius. They are Britons — poor serfs, bent in bows, dressed in simple, patched-up clothes.

"Is it true?" asks one of them with trepidation, clutching a woollen cap.

"Is what true?" I reply. He speaks in the gruff peasant way, like the Old Man and Woman back at the hut of my childhood; I don't think Fastidius can understand his mumbling.

"We heard there was a *Pater* here…"

I start translating, but Fastidius stops me with a raised hand. "I am Father Fastidius of Saint Paul's," he replies. "What do you want with me?"

"We were wondering if, maybe… you could conduct for us a Mass. We haven't had our holy communion for a year…"

Fastidius frowns. "What about that chapel we saw in the town?"

The serfs look at each other. "Our *Pater*, he — he's been dead since winter."

"What? And you haven't had a priest come by since then?"

The peasant shakes his head.

"Why didn't your *Comes* send a message to the Bishop at Lindocoln? This is an outrage!"

"Please," the peasant grasps his cap tighter and casts a worried glance around. "We don't want any trouble."

I nod and invite them all into our tent. I offer them some ale, and the peasant leader downs a mugful. We sit on the floor — the only furniture here are my and Fastidius's beddings and a small folding table.

"Now, tell us what's going on," I ask.

"The *Comes* said we don't need a Roman priest anymore," he replies. "Now that we have the Anglian ones. She said all the Church is good for is stealing money from poor serfs like us."

I notice Fastidius's knuckles go white on the edge of the table. "Anglian ones? You mean pagans?"

"Yes, lord. They've built a shrine over at the old theatre, by the mead hall. That's where most of our folk now go to have their fields and livestock blessed. But not us, no. We're faithful."

"Do you all live in the town?" I ask. They shake their heads vigorously.

"We've come from the hills over yonder." He raises his hand to point, but inside the tent he can't tell where his home is and the pointing finger hangs in the air. "We used to live in the villages along the stone road, before the *Comes* gave them to the Angles."

"Then the land was not empty after all," I note.

"How many of you are there?" asks Fastidius.

The peasants confer and count on their fingers, but soon give up. "Many," their leader replies. "In the swamps upriver, in the woods uphill… We live by the old faith and the old law, but it's difficult without a priest — or a judge."

The mention of "old law" piques my interest. I ask what he means by that.

"The law of the Legions, sir," the peasant mumbles. "From when they used to stay in the shore forts."

"They promised they'd return," murmurs another. "We've waited so long…"

"You mean the Roman Law? But — what other law is there?"

"The Anglian Law," he replies, surprised at my ignorance. "The *Comes* says it only applies to the Angles and their land, but when they own *all* the land, what's the difference?"

"The *wergild* is the worst," adds another serf, a woman, her face and body ravaged and twisted by time and hard work, though she can't be more than thirty years old.

Wergild. I heard that word before — when Horsa saved me from Wortimer's men; and again, after the rescue from Aelle's hillfort. A payment for life — saved or taken.

"A Briton's life is worth only half that of an Angle," the woman explains. "His possessions worth half of theirs. So they treat us like half humans. Like slaves."

"How can the *Comes* tolerate this?" Fastidius asks, though the answer is obvious, considering the number of Anglian warriors settled around Wenta. "I admire your tenacity in coping with these conditions."

"He means you're doing well, all things considered," I translate Fasitidius's lofty phrase, seeing the serfs' bewilderment.

"Not all do," the peasant leader replies. "Many are tempted and fall."

"How so?"

"If you join the Angles, if you become one of them, you are counted as fully human again," says the woman. "You can settle in their villages, and trade in their markets. But you have to worship their gods, and let your daughters marry their men." She spits.

I can see the impact the peasants' tale is making on Fastidius; I've never seen him so perplexed. But I remember how Wortimer's men treated the Iutes in the Londin Forum; how the Saxons had to hide with their faith in ruins and underground shrines; how the only thing that prevented me from being seen as nothing more than another Saxon slaveling was the baptism and Master Pascent's good word.

Here, the situation is reversed; here, the Angles are strong and numerous, and it's the Britons, the Christians, who need to skulk in the woods. But it's their own choice: they could get back their rights and their land, it seems, without too much bother: all they have to do is acknowledge their new masters. Isn't this better than what the Iutes were offered in the South?

"*Once a Saxon, always a Saxon…*"

"What?" asks Fastidius. Everyone is looking at me in confusion, and I realise I spoke out loud.

"It's nothing. So, what are you planning to do about them?"

"I cannot change the laws of this land, but I can still perform my duties." Fastidius turns back to the serfs. "Is two days enough to gather all of you here?"

"It is enough," says the peasant leader with confidence.

"Then I will hold the Mass in two days, in the field between the new and old walls." His lips move silently as he counts something in his head. "I will need bread for the communion, I haven't brought enough with me."

"We will bake it."

The peasant faces are now beaming with joy and relief. I have never experienced what Fastidius calls the "grace of faith"; I'm still not even certain which gods I should be praying to… So I don't understand why the prospect of a Mass brings the peasants so much delight. But I'm happy for

Fastidius — this is his vocation; this is why he came all this way from Londin.

One thing still bothers me. "What if we have to go to battle before the Mass?" I ask when the peasants leave.

"Then you will go to battle," he replies. "And we will pray for your success here. I'm sure God will listen to the pleas of all those lost souls with more attention than just to that of some young priest."

The Anglian patrols return the next day. They're not alone: they bring two captives from the Pictish camp. One of them has an injured leg and has been beaten within the inch of his life; the other, whipped a few times, is more eager to cooperate.

The injured one looks more like I imagined a Pict would look like than the men we caught in Cantiaca. He has an elaborate skin decoration of a spiralling dragon on his right shoulder and chest, and his hair and moustache are daubed white with lime. But when he opens his mouth, he speaks in Briton similar to that spoken in the South.

Comes Una points to the uninjured warrior. "You're not one of them. You're a Brigant, aren't you?"

She arrived at the interrogation in her full regalia, in a hay cart disguised as a battle chariot, with steel plates attached to the front and spikes nailed to the wheels. *Drihten* Angenwit allowed her to sit in the chair of honour, in his place, though it is his house we're all in — his mead hall, raised in the ruins of an amphitheatre, south of the town walls; a building greater than the one where Hengist met us, as the Angles are richer and mightier than the Iutes. The oak beams and pillars are all carved in fanciful shapes. Painted shields and dyed cloth hang on the walls for decoration, and fur and sheepskin lines the long benches. The smell of roast meat drifts through the air, not from any meal, for we didn't have time to eat anything other than some bread and cheese, but from the hecatomb made to the gods of war in the adjacent pagan shrine.

The prisoner shrugs. If he's a Brigant, that means the Picts have already been recruiting warriors from south of the Aelian Wall. Suddenly, Cunedag's boast doesn't seem so far-fetched.

"Is he here?" Una prods. "Is Drust truly leading this fleet?"

Fastidius and I glance at each other. "You've heard of Drust?" I ask Una.

"The glory of his victories has reached even here, I see," the Brigant remarks, boastfully, before the *Comes* can reply.

Angenwit slaps him in the face. "Answer the question, *wealh*."

"Yes, Drust is here. We're *all* here. You'd be wise to let us go our way in peace — your little war band stands no chance against Drust's combined fleet."

"Why are you in his army?" asks Fastidius. "You live in the South. You should be allied to *us*."

The Brigant captive scoffs. "Allies of Londin? Allies of that tyrant, Wortigern? He doesn't care for us, why should we care for him? Drust may be a Pict, but at least he's there for us when we need him. He travels with his court all over the North, visiting his subjects, looking after his land. He's the best ruler we've ever had."

"You know much," says Una. She turns to Angenwit. "He's no ordinary footman. Where did your men find him?"

"In the woods on the southern hills."

Una's eyes narrow. She steps up to the captive. She reaches into his tattered tunic and tears off a cord hanging on his neck, revealing a small crucifix, similar in shape and size to the one I found on the Pict we caught in Cantiaca — except this one is made of bronze and meticulously carved. Fastidius stirs at the sight.

"You're a Christian," she says. "Why are Christians fighting for the King of Picts?"

"Drust is a Christian too," the captive replies. "Baptised by Ninian himself. Which is more than can be said for your army of pagans."

Una looks at Fastidius. He shakes his head. "I've never heard of any Ninian. You'd have to ask the Bishop at Lindocoln."

"You were sent here to plot, weren't you?" Una accuses the Brigant. "Raise my own people against me. I know what's been going on here. I know the fools in the woods hearken to the old days of Rome." Unexpectedly, she turns to Fastidius again. She pokes him in the chest with the crucifix. "I bet that's what they've sent *you* for, too. It's all a conspiracy — you're not here to fight Picts at all!"

"There is no conspiracy," I say firmly. "All we want is to help you defeat the invaders. And we're not all Christians. I worship Wodan and Donar, just like the Angles."

Fastidius looks up at me with a pained, shocked expression.

"Then why send a *priest* with the army?"

"He's not here as a priest," I reply. "He's here as a war commander."

"Him? A commander?" Una stares mockingly at Fastidius's feeble frame. "He couldn't even hold a sword!"

"He doesn't have to. His weapon is his mind." I tap my skull. "He studied all the Roman generals. He's the finest strategist I know."

Angenwit rises heavily from his woollen seat. "The Roman soldiers are no longer here," he says. "What good is studying their ways to anyone?"

"Some principles remain valid always," says Fastidius, composing himself. "Wherever men gather to fight each other."

The Angle grins. "That is true."

"You don't believe them, do you?" asks Una, her eyes flashing in anger. There is a dynamic between them that's quite different from what we saw with Elasio and his *Gewisse.*

Are they lovers, I wonder? Neither the Anglian *Drihten*, nor the *Comes* have other spouses, as far as I can tell…

"The priest, I don't much care for. But I believe the Iute." He nods at me. "They were always honest folk back home. Bad craftsmen," he adds with a smirk, "but good people."

"He's not a Iute — he's Wortigern's spy!"

Angenwit shakes his head. "Maybe so, Una. Maybe so. But we have a battle with Drust of Hundred Victories on our hands, and these boys have brought a hundred good warriors to help us, and that's all I care about for now."

The *Comes* tries to protest, but he stares her down, in exactly the same way Wortigern stares down his Council. "You promised you wouldn't interfere in matters of war — well, *this* is a matter of war. Until we defeat the Picts, I need the Iute here."

"And the priest?"

"Leave him be for now. If he's as good a strategist as the Iute claims, we might find a use for him. If not — " He shrugs. "A single priest can't do us harm."

"I hope you know what you're doing," says Una. She casts us another murderous look and rises from the throne. "This tires me. I'm going home. Let me know what else you find out from these traitors," she adds, nodding at the captives. "Especially the Christian one. I need to know what he's been plotting in those hills — and with whom."

The swamp of the Ikens stretches from horizon to horizon, north to south, growing thick with tall grass, reed, willow and black, twisted marsh trees. An entire legion — an actual legion — could be hiding there in plain sight. Our few hundreds of men don't even make a mark on this gloomy landscape.

First into the marsh go Angenwit's household warriors, the *Hiréd*. They make no effort to conceal their ranks as they march through the tall grass. Sunlight bounces in dancing silver glints off their polished helmets and spear tips, sharpened into needle points.

Unlike the veterans and militiamen of Londin, but much like the Iutes, these warriors had no gear of their own, other than the simple weapons with which they trained. The day before our departure, I witnessed these mighty hulks line up orderly before their *Drihten*, as he opened a great chest and gifted each of his men with a fine mail coat and a good helmet. Those who had no swords, were each given a long *seax*; those whose shields were dented, or spear blades chipped, were presented with new ones. They offered me a spear, too, to replace my old one, but I'd grown too fond of it to part with it. It is the only reminder of Fulco and the days of my youth back at Ariminum… and besides, it can still pierce a man through when thrown right.

I had seen Beadda perform a similar ceremony on the morning before the Battle of Saffron Valley, but I did not think to ask then what it meant. I posed the question during the Anglian proceedings, which he observed with misty eyes.

"This is a memory of how things used to be back in our homeland," he told me. "Only the *Drihten* had the right to give out arms and armour; he controlled the smithies, he owned the iron fields and the charcoal pits. We had no metal of our own. In return, we swore loyalty to him greater than that between blood brothers. This is what it meant to be a part of a *Hiréd*."

The smithies and forges owned by Angenwit must have been working ceaselessly for days to prepare this bounty, and Fastidius and I wondered aloud where all the iron was coming from. The day before battle, Una and Angenwit took us to the coast to the north of Wenta, to show us the cliffs of red and white stone that the young Wotadin captive mentioned in his tale. On the top of the cliffs spread a vast smelting field.

"These forges stood here before the Romans came. We used the ore to make weapons with which we slaughtered Londin," said Una, licking her lips, as if remembering something that happened in her own lifetime, rather than an ancient legend. "Just as we will slaughter all who stand against us." I felt uneasy when she said that, not sure whether she meant us or the Picts — or both.

I observe Angenwit's march from the cracked ramparts of an old Roman shore fort, overlooking a broad rivermouth, which the Angles have made their base of operations. Just like the Wotadin prisoner said, there is another fort just like this one, a mile to the north, on the other side of the estuary, but it's been taken by the Picts; other than a narrow, easily defended causeway, the northern fort is only accessible by sea, and with Drust's entire fleet gathered on the coast, there's no chance of recapturing it, even if we had the manpower.

I have seen some of those Northern boats up close, patrolling the shoreline: broad in the middle, low-decked, with a single sail on a single mast, and thirty oarsmen, who must also double as warriors, for there is no space for anyone else on board; the vessels are poor and primitive compared to the Saxon *ceols*. It's a wonder how they reached this far from the Pictland in one piece. But they are many; our patrols report at least twenty of these boats dragged onto the beach by the enemy's main camp. This matches what we know of the strength of Drust's combined fleet from other reports. They must all be here now — those who raided Cantiaca, those who besieged the forts at Coln, and many others.

Their numbers may be greater than ours, but numbers alone don't win a battle. Each of Odo's lancers must count for five footmen at least, and both Angenwit's and Beadda's *Hiréd* are a terrifying force, especially once they drown themselves in henbane wine. We have local guides on our side, who know secret paths through the moor; we have Wortigern's veterans, who know this might be their final battle and will fight to relive their glory one last time; and we have Fastidius, helping with the battle plans. The thought of defeat not even once crosses my mind.

Drust's forces are no less of a medley of peoples than ours. Apart from the Brigants, drafted into the Pictish army by force or promise of plunder, there's easily a dozen other Northern tribes, each sailing under its own banner and chieftain. Animal figures are painted on the sails of the boats, or carved in wood and set on tall poles to mark the campsites, scattered throughout the moor and beach: deer, bear, eagle, beaver … We know that Drust's own tribe, the Wertriu, carries the badge of the wild boar — just like Beadda's Iutes; but our patrols have as yet failed to locate them. Not that we're lacking for enemy to slaughter, once the killing begins.

We don't have much time. An army this size can't stay in one place for long. We've intercepted a few foraging parties, but the others have evaded us, carrying away sheep from the pastures and wheat from the fields. Now they know we're on the move, they will soon set sail. Their next destination, according to the captives, are the shores near Ebrauc, a mighty Brigant fortress in the far north. There, the Picts will be back among allies; Drust's fleet — and, more importantly, the plunder and the slaves they captured in our lands — will be out of our reach.

Several *ceols* set sail from the beach. The Angles once came here on those ships, but that was a generation ago, and now they are more farmers than sailors; but there's just about enough of them still remembering how to hold an oar and how to shoot a bow from the deck. They will be the first to enter the fray, hoping to draw the Picts out to the beach. We need as many of them on that sand as possible, for Odo's cavalry to then mow them down. Those fine Gaulish horses are no good in the swamp; they will charge down the old Roman causeway and trample any man in their path, but only on solid ground. It is down to the *Hiréd* and the veterans to push the enemy out of the marshes.

The entire plan was devised by Fastidius, who pored over the observation reports, maps hastily sketched on birchwood, and his copy of Vegetius, all through the night. But he's not with us. He remained in Wenta, preparing for the Mass he'd promised the hill folk, even though *Comes* Una still regards him as a spy, plotting with the Christians to overthrow her rule.

I could see my confession in Angenwit's hall bothered him greatly, even as I tried to convince him it was only a ruse designed to gain the Angle's trust.

"I sensed the truth in your words," he told me, almost teary-eyed, "and so did Angenwit. That's why he believed you."

I had no response to that. He must have seen deeper into my soul than I myself have, for I was still of two minds on which god appealed to me the most. I wanted to believe in Christ — for Fastidius, for Master Pascent, even for old grumpy Paulinus. But despite the best efforts of the priests, despite all the incense and mosaics, despite all the ancient glory of Rome tied to the Church, He simply didn't speak to me in the same way as the Grey Wanderer and his *Ensi* kindred. He never appeared to me in a dream; He never spoke to me about my fate, never helped me with my confusion, always a distant, silent figure, no matter how much I prayed for guidance. Above all else, I grew convinced that drinking mead in Wodan's Hall and frolicking with his shieldmaidens was a more fitting way to spend eternity for a young warrior like myself than whatever Christ had prepared for me in Heaven; I could never really get a straight answer on that from Fastidius.

"You've inspired me, brother," he said with a sad smile, as I prolonged my silence. "I know what to talk about in the Mass."

"Are you sure it's wise to say anything except prayers?" I said. "We don't want Una to banish us from her land."

"It won't matter after the battle. Our task here will be over. The least I can do is strengthen the hearts of the faithful."

"You're going to tell them about me? What good will that do?"

"I will tell them not to worry about their temptation — that a fall can happen to even the best of us." He smiled again. "And that we must always hope for their redemption."

"I'm not sure I appreciate being made a bad example for your sermon," I say, only half-joking.

"But I will also tell them that, in the end, it doesn't matter which god you believe, as long as you're a decent man." He laid a hand on my shoulder. "What good is faith, if it's not reinforced by good deeds? And if good deeds are performed in the wrong name, does that invalidate them?"

"Paulinus would have your arse whipped if he heard you say that."

He pulls back. "Paulinus used to believe all this too, when he was younger."

"Pelagius," I say, recalling the teachings instilled in me prior to my baptism.

"The greatest scholar this island has ever produced." Fastidius closes his eyes and recites: "*Omnes voluntate propria regii…*"

I flash back to Ariminum, to the first lessons of the Imperial tongue with Paulinus, to the stylus digging into the wax tablet.

"'Each man is ruled by his own will'," I repeat in Vulgar Tongue. "I know what the words mean, but …"

"It means God has given us hearts and minds so that we can raise ourselves to salvation of our own accord. It means the will to do good is more important than rituals and formulas." He leaned over the birchwood. "Now, I just need to put all of that into words simple enough for these folk to understand…"

I wonder how the final preparations for the Mass are going as I trudge through the swamp behind the Iutes, my boots sinking in the mud. My spear and helmet are wrapped in rags to conceal their glint. I have joined Beadda's *Hiréd* in the attack, rather than the Britons, just like at Saffron Valley — not just due to the tribal affinity I feel with them. Wortigern's veterans fight in the old Roman way, with long *spatha* swords, heavy spears and large oblong shields, and I would only be in their way with my short *seax*, my light throwing spear and a small round buckler.

The Iutes have not fought alongside a Roman-style army before. In battle with Aelle, the two armies were separated by the palisade — and Wortimer's treachery. Here, we will at last join our forces in the field, like the legionnaires and their *socii* allies, side-by-side, as it always was and always should be… if all goes well.

Beadda stops and points north. A plume of thick black smoke rises in the distance. That's our signal: the Angles have reached an enemy forward station and set it on fire. We leap to a run — as much as we can run in the mire. The mud splashes all around me. I struggle to keep up. I trip; one of the Iutes helps me up, but by now I'm already at the rear of the pack.

I hear the sword slashing through flesh; a second later, I pass the Pictish guard, kneeling in the tall grass and gurgling in agony. Our guide did well: he led us straight onto the enemy foraging camp. We emerge from a clump of gnarled willows onto a meadow of tents, circling a campfire. The surprise is ours, but the Picts recover more swiftly than we expected. Three big men run out to meet us at the edge of the camp, each waving a giant iron-studded mace. The Iutes, wary of getting too close to the mace heads, pierce them with javelins; by the time the three men fall and we can get past them, the rest of the camp is ready for us.

Beadda leads the charge, hacking and slashing his way towards the centre, where the tribal pole stands with the figure of a fox on top. The *Hiréd* fight like mad men, frenzied, foaming at the mouth, whirling and kicking, biting and punching. They're showing off, rather than seeking the opponent's death, but the display works. The Picts, though valiant, are soon forced to pull back before this insane onslaught. Some of them notice we're only attacking from one direction, leaving the way out to the beach wide open. Before long, their ranks thin out as the Picts flee for the perceived safety of the shore; one by one at first, then suddenly, the line breaks and they all turn and run, pursued by our javelins and throwing axes.

We halt to rest and laugh at the easy victory. We lost no men, and slew eight — two more are found in the reeds when the Iutes go to pick up their missiles. The *Hiréd* pat each other on the back, proud and amused at their own acting skills. They have not yet drunk the henbane — that is something that can be done only once, before the main battle; but they knew well enough how to act as if they had, and the Picts must have recognised its frenzy-inducing effects to have fled so rapidly.

There is little to plunder in the camp except for what food the raiding party foraged from nearby fields and woods. The most valuable item is the bronze fox on top of the pole, but it's too heavy to carry, so we bury it along with the rest of the spoils in the bonfire ash, wash our throats with Pictish ale and set out again, this time ready for a proper fight.

The beach is wide and long, a perfectly flat ribbon of golden sand as far as the eye can see, bound with the red cliff far to the north, and dissipating into low dunes to the south. Our timing is impeccable: the tide is out, and the ocean is a hundred feet away, stranding most of the Pictish fleet and its crews in the midst of a sea of mud. The core of the enemy army, their animal banners fluttering in the breeze, huddles around the boats, protecting their only means of escape from a fierce attack led by Angenwit and his *Hiréd*. The rest of the Anglian host, the Iken militia, and the small *Gewisse* band, are scattered all over the beach, searching for whoever would emerge from the dunes. Some even rush towards us, waving their clubs and pitchforks, until they realise we are on their side.

To the north of all this chaos, I see a straight, thin line of red stretching across the beach: Wortigern's veterans. They've locked their great shields, stamped their feet in the sand, and stand firm. Holding a gap between two wedges of timber posts used for trapping fish, they bar any Pictish reinforcements from reaching their brethren. It is a marvel to behold, the old Roman *fulcum* formation in its full glory. In complete deployment, there would be a second line of soldiers holding shields over their comrades' heads to guard them from arrows — but the Picts have no bowmen, and there aren't enough of the veterans to complete the tortoise.

It doesn't matter. The enemy crashes against this wall of shields like sea against a cliff, each wave met with the heavy Briton spears thrusting forth in unison, almost mechanical in motion; each wave receding leaving a line of dead bodies in its wake, like flotsam at low tide. As long as that wall of men stands, our northern flank is safe.

Beadda puts on the boar helmet, raises his sword and lets out a battle cry. The Iutes have already drunk from their goatskins, and now their eyes are bloodshot and burn with real, rather than pretend madness. We run down the dunes and sweep away any Picts who stand in their way. Like an armoured fist, we punch through their defences, crumble their ranks and soon, we reach the anchorage. While we push forward, clearing a widening path through the enemy, the Anglian militiamen follow us with axes and hatchets, and proceed to destroy whatever boats they can get at, hacking at their bottoms, hewing down the masts and shattering the oars.

The Picts raise a mournful cry and launch into battle with renewed strength, but their counterattack soon falters. There is no stopping the Saxon warriors once they're in the henbane frenzy. They become monsters in man flesh. They feel no pain, they ignore all wounds; they don't even see their enemies as human anymore, but as twisted, black beasts who need to be vanquished from the Earth. They see gods of war in the sky above them, and goddesses of death on the ground, helping them with the victory.

I'm the only one who didn't drink from the goatskin. I seek in vain for an enemy whose blood my spear could spill: the Pictish army withers like leaves in flame faster than I can keep up. Still they don't flee — they have nowhere *to* flee to, trapped between us and the sea.

"Where are those riders?" I hear a familiar voice. "They won't get their share of glory at this rate!"

I turn to see Angenwit, leaning on his knees, breathless. His mail coat is bent and torn in places, his helmet is dented on the crown, but he seems uninjured. The Angles were fighting long before we got to the beach, and some are now taking a brief respite as the Iutes push forth in their place.

The *Drihten* is right — the battle seems almost over. Odo and his Gauls should be here already. Did they get lost in the marsh? Was the causeway too narrow for them to pass? I feel a sudden shiver. I realise we still haven't seen the wild boar banner of Drust's household guard; something must have gone wrong with Fastidius's plan…

The shiver passes, replaced by reprieve, when I hear — and sense — hoofbeats, thumping on the firm sand. A heartbeat later the riders dash out from between the dunes, their armour glistening, their cloaks flowing in the wind, their red helmet plumes fluttering like fire, their horses like four-legged demons of vengeance, bringing destruction on all who dare stand in their way…

All four of them.

"Woe!" they cry. "Woe!"

I notice with relief that one of the four riders is Odo. He halts before us and tears out an arrow stuck in his shoulder.

"We've been ambushed," he cries.

Angenwit doesn't wait to find out the details. He calls for his *Hiréd* to gather around him. There isn't anyone else who can respond to his summons: the Iutes are too deep into the Pictish host by the ships, and the veterans can't move from their post, still guarding our northern flank. The *Gewisse* hear the order, but ignore it, not yet aware of the danger, busy with robbing armour and weapons from the fallen enemies.

A new Pictish horde, at least eighty-men strong, pours forth from the dunes in grim silence. At its head, astride a sturdy grey pony, rides a warrior wearing a tall helmet of polished iron topped with a golden boar, waving a long, slashing blade: King Drust of the Hundred Victories.

At his order, the horde splits — thirty men rush to strike at the Briton veterans' rear, trapping them in a deadly pincer. But we have no time to worry about them: the remainder of Drust's force runs straight at us, ignoring the scattered militias, ignoring the confused *Gewisse*; Drust knows Angenwit's *Hiréd* are the only remaining force worth fighting on the entire beach.

The Anglian chieftain picks up a large shield from the ground and hands it to me. "Prove your worth, Iute," he commands. The *Hiréd* line up in a wall of shields, similar to the veterans' formation, but more crude. Following their example, I kneel in the damp sand — the tide is back, coming in tiny rivulets of brine between our feet — and raise the spear over my head. Angenwit's heavy hand grips my shoulder. "Stand firm, boy," he says. "Make your fathers proud."

Fathers… For a moment, I wonder how the *Drihten* could know I had two sets of parents, before realising that's not what he meant. Then my mind clears, and all I can see, hear and think of are the enemies, charging at us, still in that unsettling silence. The warriors in front hold strange shields shaped like the Roman letter H, with which to counter our oval ones; the ones in the back only wield small leather-bound bucklers. I spot slingshotters at the back, behind the swordsmen and axemen, and make ready to avoid their stones.

The Angles let their missiles fly, but the throwing axes fail to bounce off the sand, and the javelins get blown off course by the sea breeze. Only then do the Picts raise a war cry: a shrill, disconcerting, haunting howl. It sends a shiver down my spine. Drust leaps off his pony and leads the final charge on foot. The slingshots twang; bullets fall on our heads like spring hail. I raise my shield at the last moment. A man to my right falls, struck on the temple; another takes his place. Then the enemy closes in and I have to pull my shield down to meet a charging Pict. For a moment, I'm stunned by the sheer force of his impact.

I reach over the shield and thrust my spear blindly until I hit flesh. I pull back, and blood spews on my head and shoulders. This baptism feels more real than the one at the Cathedral. I am now a warrior; I am now worthy of Wodan's Hall.

My shield rattles again, and an axe-head wedges itself in the board, an inch from my head. I push back, but whoever is on the other side is stronger than me. I thrust the spear once more and I feel it graze the enemy. The pressure on the shield lessens. I drop it, grab the spear in both hands and shove it with all my strength. The barbed blade goes through limeboard and straight into the stomach of the man behind it. I don't even see his face; I only hear the thud as he falls dead.

Our wall falters at the flanks. Angenwit orders his ranks to tighten up into a crescent. But the Angles are not Romans, and the manoeuvre breaks the line. The Picts break through to my left. I draw the sword and join the fray defending the breach, hacking and slashing with both hands, without looking, until the hilt is slippery with blood, until my arms can no longer rise to a blow.

A stray slingshot stone strikes my head.

CHAPTER VI
THE LAY OF DRUST

Dawn renders the sky over the Governor's Palace a sharp red. A nightingale's trill announces the day's arrival. But the gardens are still shrouded in the thick silver fog of the night, which mutes all sounds and scents until all that's left is an unearthly numbness of the senses.

She is here, as always, gliding over the dew-wet grass, her emerald dress clinging tight to her frame, showing every curve of her slender body. Her face is blurry in the fog, but I see the sadness in her eyes.

We meet by the empty table.

"No lesson today?" she asks quietly.

"There will be no more lessons," I say. She lets out a short, dignified gasp.

"I'm sorry," she says. "I… enjoyed them."

Why am I being so formal? Why can't I just tell her how I feel… Even now, in these final moments, I'm afraid to spoil what's between us.

I never told her this, but I feel there is a bond between me and Rhedwyn, stronger even than the one between lovers; I feel as if I've known her forever. And maybe I have… Hengist never did find my parents among the Iutes on Tanet, which made it more likely that I fell out of Eobba's ship, which had barely any survivors except Rhedwyn herself.

Now I will never find out — unless Wodan keeps records of the fallen in his Hall. I feel my hands and feet grow cold, wet with approaching death. The fog grows thicker; the light of the dawn turns brighter. A raven crows in the distance.

"I have to go," I say, my throat tightened.

"I wish you could stay longer."

"I… I wish so too." The pounding of my heart is deafening in my ears. "Rhedwyn, I… "

She puts her finger to my dry lips, then leans forward and kisses me. She opens up and pulls me in. The inside of her mouth is wet and salty.

"By Donar's hammer, get up, boy!"

Beadda grabs me by the tunic and hauls me up to my feet. I splutter and rub sea water out of my eyes. I have just enough sense to grasp the hilt of the sword before we start to run. I wade and splash through the mud and surf of the rising tide; around me are the Iutes, the Angles and the *Gewisse*, all jumbled together, all fleeing for their lives. The Picts chase after us, howling, waving their weapons, singing in victory. We are defeated, vanquished…

But we live.

I reach to my forehead. The blood is already dried. How long have I been out? What happened in the meantime? The Iutes must have recovered from their frenzy just in time to come to our rescue… But only ours. I glance around, and don't spot any of the veterans' red cloaks, or the drab tunics of the peasant militia.

We reach the dunes and I stumble in the weeds that grow over them. It's a slow, sinking slog up the sand slopes, in our wet boots, blood-soaked clothes and heavy armour… Our only hope is to reach the line of low pines at the crest of the dune ridge; beyond it stretches a dense forest where we might lose our pursuit. But the Picts are lighter and faster; they run up our flanks, to cut off our escape. I hear Beadda groan; he raises his sword to show his men a new direction to strike, but few heed his command. Panic has set into our ranks. It is terrible to behold; I see warriors who, mere minutes ago, slaughtered all in their path, now run blind, straight into the spears of the enemy.

As I face the prospect of certain death, I reach an odd clarity of mind. Everything I see is sharp, slowed down. Every man around me is a separate soul, a candle, burning brightly within the flesh. A sword blow here, a spear thrust there, one by one the candles are extinguished, but still we press on. Honour is only a word. Life is the only thing that matters. Without life, there is nothing. I must survive.

A gap opens in what's left of our line, and three Picts leap through it, armed with clubs and axes. They separate me from Beadda and the others. I swipe my sword before me, to keep them at bay, but we all know this won't last long. I lock my eyes with one of them, letting him know I chose him to go down with me. This makes him lose his step. I leap forward and thrust my sword with both hands into his throat. I strike with so much impact I nearly slice his head off. The blade bends, close to snapping. I turn to face the other two and see a fourth enemy has now joined them.

How many of them are there?

I hear a strange sound, a loud twang followed by the rush of a javelin zooming through the air at great speed; the missile strikes one of my adversaries, goes right through his body and lands in the chest of another. The third is too dumbstruck to react as I cleave his skull with my sword. I then look to the beach in astonishment, to see what giant managed to throw a javelin with such might.

Out on the beach, Una turns her battle cart around. In the middle of the cart, pulled by four black Anglian ponies, stands a heavy tripod, and mounted atop it I recognise the old Roman weapon: the *carroballista.* Three men are busy operating the device: one loads the ash-wood bolts, the other two turn the crank that tightens the sinew springs, and pull on the lever releasing the bowstring. The fourth man stands in front, pointing which way and at which angle to turn the weapon.

That fourth man, distinctive in his priestly robes, is Fastidius.

The *ballista* shoots again. The bolt, four feet long and tipped with bronze, flies straight and true, and takes out another couple of warriors. The Picts now notice the chariot's arrival. Some turn to attack it, but most ignore it even as another missile tears a whole arm off one of their own. The Iutes and Angles climbing the dunes are still the main prize, and I fear even Fastidius's ingenuity and Una's stubborn bravery will not be enough to turn this battle around.

At that moment, the pines on top of the dunes come to life. A hundred or more men pour down from the forest, all dressed in white linen, descending from above like vengeful seraphim or Wodan's shining maidens. They wield the most primitive of weapons: large sticks, kitchen knives, sickles, butcher's cleavers… But they are numerous, unexpected, and full of vigour, while the Picts, like us, are already weary of fighting. A heartbeat ago, they were certain of victory, already celebrating our defeat; now, in a blink of an eye, the tide has turned.

The enemy fall into disarray. Their ranks break. It's not yet a panic that would turn to retreat, only confusion, but Beadda and Angenwit are quick to exploit the sudden change of fate. They rally as many of their exhausted, battered *Hiréd* as they can for one last contest. At the bottom of the dune King Drust does the same; he blows a twisted ox horn, and the Picts gather to him, his boar banner, his polished iron helmet. The two weary, bloodied hosts, two wild boars, face each other as around them the world is engulfed in the chaos of a tired, inglorious battle, peasants against soldiers, clubs and pitchforks against swords and spears; blood and splattered guts turn sand into red, slippery mud. The Pictish king raises his sword. So do Beadda and Angenwit. I stand with them, though my legs feel as if they were on fire, and my arms hang heavy as lead.

Una's battle cart pulls up between us and the Picts. Fastidius leaps off and stands in front of King Drust with his arms spread wide. In his right hand glistens a large silver cross.

"In the name of God Almighty, cease this senseless slaughter!" he booms.

Drust hesitates, then looks at the cart and the *ballista*, its string still drawn, the weapon aimed at his chest. This, more than Fastidius's plea, convinces him to throw his sword in the sand. He takes off his helmet and kneels before the silver cross. The rest of his army does the same, as do the white-clad peasants who came to our reprieve. Fastidius then turns to face us, the Iutes and the Angles. Beadda and Angenwit order the *Hiréd* to drop their weapons and bow.

But their knees don't bend at the sight of the cross; and neither do mine.

"These are harsh terms," says Drust.

He takes a gulp of water, wipes his moustache and wrinkles his nose. A gust of wind blows in a sour smell of smoke from the beach, where the remains of the destroyed boats were made into a pyre for the fallen warriors.

"But fair, and you know it," replies Fastidius. A pile of silver and gold lies between him and the Pict. The surviving Saxons and Angles eye it greedily. Another pile, equal size, is being loaded on Drust's ships in the dancing light of the pyre. Separate from it all is the church silver from Dorowern, laid neatly into a chest padded with white linen. Fastidius keeps his hand on the chest's lid, as if keeping it from being taken by some phantom enemy again.

"We could fight again for these trinkets, and you would lose even more men. Maybe even the whole battle. What would your subjects in the North say then?"

Drust smiles wryly. "Keeping the name of Drust of a Hundred Victories means more in the North than any gold," he says with an unhappy nod. "I have buried enough warriors in this bleak place. You…" He stares into Fastidius's eyes. "You would count this as a loss for your side?"

"You sail away freely, with half of the silver — I wouldn't call this battle a triumph of Briton arms."

"What about your reputation in the South?"

Fastidius laughs. "I am just a humble priest at Saint Paul's. My reputation is counted by the number of the souls I help save, not men I help slay."

Drust rubs his chin. "I have been stalled by a priest and a child," he says, glancing towards me. "And to think I was promised an easy plunder."

"Promised?" I interject. "By whom?"

He gives me a mocking glance. "You'll find out soon enough, boy." He stands up and extends a hand to Fastidius. "I grant you the share of the warriors you slew. They won't need it in Heaven."

Fastidius seals the deal with a handshake. "I bow before your skill in battle, King Drust of a Hundred *and One* Victories."

"I will have my bards tell the story of your valour throughout my kingdom, Fastidius of Saint Paul's. It was a fine *loss*."

They both laugh a forced laugh.

I breathe a deep sigh of relief once the last of the Pictish ships disappears beyond the northern horizon.

As Drust's men boarded their boats, the crowd of serfs gathered in the knee-high surf of the ebbing ocean to jeer and cheer. To them, it was a victory they would tell their grandchildren of; but we, the real warriors, knew what we had avoided. None of these people would've survived our defeat. The Picts will make sure the tale of their wrath spreads far and wide, and the fastest way to spread the news is through slaughter. Fastidius saved all of the villagers' lives, but they will never realise it.

A skein of bewildered seagulls searches for a place to land, but can't find it on a beach filled with plunder, flotsam, burning pyres and men drunken with ale and glory.

"I thought a confession was confidential," I say.

"It is. I never told anyone what I heard," replies Fastidius.

"It won't take Una long to figure out what happened."

"I cannot account for that."

We both know it's obvious how he obtained the knowledge of the Pictish ambush, how he knew he needed to come to our aid. One of his flock must have confessed to helping the enemy, divulging our secret battle plan. Drust waited for Odo's lancers on the narrow causeway with ropes strewn across, and other traps; the riders stood no chance even to fight back, most of them thrown off or crushed under their mounts.

Beadda climbs up to meet us on the dune ridge. He's holding a fistful of silver and gold jewels in his hands.

"You haven't come to get your share," he says, "so I thought I'd bring it to you."

I search through the jewels and pick out an elaborate necklace of woven silver with five golden coin-shaped pendants, something a Cantish noblewoman must have once worn to feasts. I imagine how it will look on Rhedwyn's breast, and my heart starts racing again.

I nearly died in this battle — without telling Rhedwyn how I felt. This cannot happen again. There's no point delaying things that really matter. I have decided to confess my love as soon as we're back in Londin. The necklace, I hope, will go a long way towards ensuring a sympathetic response.

I pick up one more small trinket. "Give the rest to your men," I tell Beadda. "They deserve it more than I do."

"As you wish. What about you, priest?"

"Thank you, *Gesith*," Fastidius replies, raising his hand in blessing, "but please, give my share to the chapel at Wenta. Maybe it will help find a new priest."

Beadda raises an eyebrow. "Your God would accept the blood money? I thought you weren't supposed to kill."

"We are allowed to defend our faith and protect the peace," replies Fastidius, then recites: "'But if thou do that which is evil, be afraid; for He beareth not the sword in vain.'"

"The Picts were Christian, like yourselves," says Beadda, a frown on his face showing he did not understand the citation. "But, I'm sure you know more about your faith than I do. I'll let the *Comes* know of your decision."

"'For he is the servant of God, an avenger who carries out God's wrath on the wrongdoer'," Fastidius adds quietly when Beadda leaves us alone.

"You're not sure we did the right thing, after all," I guess.

"One minute I teach them about peace and turning the other cheek. The next, I lead them into battle, stopping only to pick up the tools of murder."

"You saved us all," I remind him.

"Their holy white robes were splattered by blood," he says. "That's not an easy sight to remember. It's like the blood of our Lord, Christ, on…"

"You saved us all," I say again. "Maybe it was God's plan all along. Think of the victory you've won in His name. Even if we did win without your help, it would have been pagans defeating Christians."

He chuckles. "For a pagan, you make a surprising lot of sense."

I'm stunned by how matter-of-factly he says that; accepting my choice of faith without as much as a blink. Me standing straight before the cross must have finally convinced him of my fall from grace.

"I'm no pagan," I say. "At least, I don't feel like one."

"And yet you're not a Christian."

"No. I guess I'm somewhere… in between?"

"That won't work. Not in these days. Everyone will have to declare themselves on one side or the other."

"I'd rather stay on your side, no matter what, brother."

He smiles and wraps his arm around my shoulder. "Of that, you can be sure."

The Angles and the Iutes may be weary of fighting, but they are never weary of celebrating. They don't care that Fastidius wrote the battle off as a loss; they live, and they have enough of the spoils to make the deaths worthwhile, and that's all that matters. Now it's time for ale and mead — and women.

They come from the neighbouring villages, Anglian and Briton alike, those who did not take part in the battle themselves. They come to bask in the glory of the victory, to join in the feasting, to search for mates. The shieldmaidens observe them with condescending smiles from their seats of honour by the ale barrels. They don't need to search — they can choose; it is a warrior's honour to lie with a woman who fought at his side.

I hide in the shadow of an oak with a mug of mead, away from the bawdiest of the festivities — but one of the Anglian girls spots me. As she approaches, something stirs within me. She wears her golden hair in twin braids, and her body is clad in a similar kind of linen tunic that Rhedwyn sometimes wears, but dyed onion brown. A small, rat-like dog follows her, running between her legs back and forth.

"You're the boy who came from the South?" she asks. Her gentle voice softens the rough way the Angles pronounce words.

I nod. She sits down beside me and leans forward to look me in the eyes. Up close she doesn't look so similar to Rhedwyn anymore — her eyes are wider, her nose bigger, her smile not as bright; a smudge of freckles paints her cheeks, almost up to her ears.

"Tell me about it," she asks. The closeness of her breath on my face makes my blood rush like a mountain stream.

How do I describe Londin to a girl who's never seen anywhere beyond Wenta? I try my best to paint the picture of the broad avenues, the mighty palaces, the Forum as broad as her entire town, the *basilica* taller than any hill she might know in this flat, marshy land; of the Tamesa, roaring brown at high tide, spanned by a bridge fit for the gods; I tell her of the crowds of people in the streets, and the vast amounts of goods traded at the market, but I see she has no grasp of the numbers I'm talking about, having grown up in a village of fewer than a hundred souls. Her eyes glaze over when I go into detail, but still she listens; I'm not sure she believes everything I tell her. To her, all this might as well be a fairy tale, a myth I made up to impress her.

I pause to take a breath and a gulp of mead. The little dog presses itself between our knees. I scratch it behind the ears, and it licks my leg. My fingers meet hers on the dog's neck, and we dance a dance of fingers as I speak; the strokes grow bolder and more sensuous. Our breaths quicken. I suddenly notice the forest around us is heavy with the moans and groans of those who already found themselves in the dark. The dog notices we've lost interest in it and runs off, and there is nothing between us anymore other than sweat of the hot, humid night.

She takes my face in her soft, eager hands and her tongue assaults my mouth with all the passion of youth trapped in a bleak, hopeless life; I know it's not me she yearns for, but for what she sees in me — a promise that somewhere out there, there can be something greater than her own meagre existence.

I let her take me into the woods, and there I mount her in the stuffy darkness, a clumsy and sweaty union of two unhappy people, searching in each other for something the other cannot offer. As we near the climax, the girl repeats in frantic gasps the superlatives with which I described Londin: "the greatest! The tallest! The widest!" Her face blurs in my eyes, and resembles once again that of Rhedwyn. I raise my head and howl my love's name into the forest.

I hear a galloping horse, approaching down the Londin highway. Quietly, I slip out of the Anglian girl's embrace.

She's still asleep, calm and sad even in dreams. I never learned her name, and don't think she's bothered to remember mine. I lay the trinket I took from the Pictish hoard between her breasts, put my clothes on hurriedly and go to see the new arrival.

I find Fastidius already on the road, waiting. He did not partake in the pagan festivities, of course — but he looks just as weary as everyone else. All through the night he's held prayers for all the fallen in the battle at the beach, on both sides. His robe is worn out on the knees.

The horse rounds the last bend. I'm hoping to see another of Odo's men; a few have returned after the battle, miraculous survivors from the ambush, finding their way through the marsh. But the mount is a chestnut mare and the rider is clad in a white cape, lined with red, a combination I have not seen among the Gauls.

"It's a messenger from Londin," says Fastidius, whose eyes are sharper than mine. "Something dire must have happened."

The rider halts before us. He looks at me, then at Fastidius, with a faint glimmer of recognition. I think I've seen him at Wortigern's court before, but I can't be sure.

"You are Fraxinus of Ariminum and Fastidius of Saint Paul's?" he asks, catching his breath.

"That we are," replies Fastidius.

"I bring summons from *Dux* Wortigern. You two must return to Londin at once."

Fastidius grabs the reins of the horse and helps the messenger dismount. "Calm down — have some water — tell us what's happened?"

"*Wortimer*." The name sounds on his lips like the name of some foul demon. Hearing it sobers me up better than a pitcher of cold water poured over my head.

"He and his *centuria* never reached Coln in time," the messenger says when we return to the others at the feast meadow. Odo's remaining men and the old veterans have already heard of the rider's arrival and have gathered to hear the grave news.

"What happened to the Trinowaunts?" asks one of the Britons.

"The walls saved the city, just like the *Dux* predicted — but the Picts ravaged the countryside all around it."

"That explains why there were so many of them left to fight us here in the North," I murmur to Fastidius. He nods in agreement.

"So Wortimer's cowards returned to Londin without any glory," I say out loud. "What of it?"

"They didn't just return to their homes. They marched straight into the heart of the city and laid siege to the *Dux's* palace, demanding Wortigern gives the throne over to his son."

Fastidius waits for the uproar to die down. The Briton veterans gather together and murmur among each other, already hatching a plan to march on the city.

"A *siege*, you say?" Fastidius asks. He's calm on the surface, bringing a semblance of order into the chaos that erupted on the meadow, but I see a bulging vein and a thin trickle of sweat on his forehead. "But the palace has no fortifications, or enough guards to withstand an assault — with so many of the *Dux's* men here…"

"Orpedda's Iutes have joined the defenders," replies the messenger. "But they will not hold out long. I was the last to leave the palace before Wortimer's roughs closed all the roads from the capital."

"How long did you ride?" asks Odo. He glances at the chestnut mare with a worried eye.

"Three days. There are no post stations past Wortigern's border, I had to spare the horse," the rider adds, apologetically.

"Then the palace must already be in Wortimer's hands," says Fastidius.

Along with everything and everyone in it…

"Is Rhedwyn still there?" I ask, my fists clutched. "The Iute girl. Fair hair — "

"I know who you mean. Wortigern sent her back to Tanet as soon as we got word of his son's return."

At least she's safe from Wortimer's grasp. If he'd laid a hand on her, I would tear him limb from limb…

Fastidius touches my shoulder, but says nothing. He asks Odo to come nearer.

"We will need two of your horses," he says.

The Gaul quickly agrees. He has mounts to spare left after the disaster at the causeway.

"I have just the thing."

He takes us to a couple of docile grey mares tied up before Angenwit's hall.

"These are the most gentle of my horses," Odo says. There's a mournful melody to his voice. "Chariulf and Agrippin always complained about them. Not great for fighting — but will be more than enough to take the two of you to Londin." He strokes the nearer mare's mane. A stable boy brings out two saddles; I notice one of them is still rusted with blood.

"It's a long way back," says Odo. "Keep to the beaten track. And stone, once you reach it. The shoes should hold until you reach the city. And don't gallop or canter, no matter how much you might be in a hurry. A decent trot will take you much farther over the day."

When we return to the meadow with the horses, we discover the remaining veterans have already marched off. We bid a hurried farewell to Angenwit, Una, and the villagers, and ask them to take care of our wounded.

"We will send them your way as soon as they can walk," says Angenwit.

"Have them sail to Cantiaca," says Fastidius. "They'll be safer there."

"My *Hiréd* will also march out today," says Beadda. "We should reach the city not long after you. If you decide you need our help in dealing with Wortimer…" He punches his palm with his fist, letting us know without a doubt what he plans to do with Wortigern's son, given a chance.

"Thank you," I reply. "But first, Fastidius and I need to find out what's really happened at the capital in our absence."

"Pray to your gods that there will be no need for any bloodshed," adds Fastidius. "As I will pray to mine."

CHAPTER VII
THE LAY OF DENEUS

"Is that young Fraxinus and Fastidius I see?"

I search for the source of the voice among the crowd thronging the inn in Caesar's Market, a small harbour town just a day's ride from the walls of Londin. The town is filled with travellers and refugees from Londin; we've listened to enough of their excited chatter to get a clear idea of what's been happening in the capital. Just as we suspected, the siege of the *Praetorium* didn't even last a day. In the morning, Wortimer's troops surrounded the city centre, and by evening, Wortigern ordered Orpedda's surviving men to stand down and abdicated in his son's favour. There was barely even any blood spilt — Briton blood, at least, as that's the only thing the locals care about.

The man waving at us from across the inn's main room is Deneus — "Dene to his friends" — the salt and oyster magnate we know from occasional visits to Wortigern's court. He's wearing a brown travelling cloak, stained with fresh dust, and leather riding gloves.

"You shouldn't be here," he tells us in lowered voice, when we sit at his table. "We're too near to Londin. Your names are at the top of the purge list."

"A purge?" asks Fastidius with a deep frown. "How many dead?"

"The brat doesn't feel strong enough for executions," the merchant scoffs. "Wortigern's loyalists have only been banished out of the city. But for you two… I'm sure he'd make an exception."

"What about the people of Londin?" I ask. "Surely they will rebel against the usurper."

The look on his face tells me I said something ridiculous.

"Wortimer is a shrewd man," he says. "He announced a week's holiday on tolls, so the people love him, for now. Nobody cares what happens to one group of nobles or the other — the townsfolk hate all of them equally. Other than that, nothing's changed in the city, except for the guards and barriers on the main approaches."

"Guards?" I ask. "How many?"

"Enough to keep the lot of us out. If you're looking to sneak into the city, forget it. They might let the priest in, if the Bishop vouches for him — before Wortimer finds out." He nods at Fastidius. "But no Iute or Saxon can enter, not even one who once was a member of the Council."

"And the Council — they aren't protesting?" asks Fastidius.

"Most of them couldn't care less. Wortimer was destined to take over after his father, anyway — all he did was just hasten the process."

"You cared," I say.

"I'm an old-fashioned man," Dene shrugs. "If we don't abide by the law, if we don't follow the correct order of things, what difference is there between us and the barbarians? No offence." I nod, though I don't see why *I* should take offence for that. "Besides, I suspect there were other forces here at work. Wortimer wouldn't have come up with such a plan by himself. He had help — and not just from inside the palace."

"What do you mean?"

He smiles mysteriously, takes a glance around and decides he's said enough. "I don't want to have to move out even of Caesar's Market. It's enough of a hole as it is. I'll tell you this, though: consider the timeline of recent events, and you will have all the clues you need."

Despite Dene's warning, we decide to join the long column of commoners trying to pass through the barrier on the ford across the River Lig, on the Trinowaunt border — more to assess the general mood and gain intelligence, than actually try to get into the city. We don't know how thorough the checks are, but if Wortimer knows of the messenger sent out before the siege, he must have ordered the guards to expect our return… And we're not keen to find out what he's told them to do if they spot us.

Not that it's easy to spot anyone in the crowd. The Augustan Highway is busy on most days; the barrier and the border checks have made it tenfold more so. The usual traffic across the ford, the only place for miles to cross the marshes of the River Lig, is made up of merchants from the Northern lands, local peasants carting goods to the Londin market and shepherds moving their flocks from pastures on one side of the river to the other. It is now joined by twin currents of refugees: those heading west, still fleeing the rumours of Pictish invasion, and those going back, having already learned of the enemy's departure. Where the two streams meet, at the river crossing, erupts a chaos such as I've only seen in battle before. A cart lies overturned in the ditch, having failed to bypass the traffic, its load scattered in the mud; a pair of mules bray desperately, whipped senseless by the draymen; the poor city folk, carrying all their belongings on their backs jostle for space with bodyguards of a rich trader, pushing through with clubs and fists; a half-naked urchin darts underneath it all, pinching whatever she can get her hands on — apples and turnips from the sacks, rather than silver from the purses.

"I don't envy those border guards," says Fastidius. "Wortimer must be paying them a fortune to keep them from deserting."

So far, however, we have seen and heard little to indicate that all of this is anything more than a temporary nuisance to the regular townsfolk. To them, it doesn't matter who the ruler is in Londin; many aren't even aware of the change. Most of the travellers we talk to believe the barrier is a necessary precaution against the Picts and other marauders encouraged by the lack of troops at the capital. Some loudmouth even blames Wortigern himself for sending the army off instead of defending the city. "No wonder the young *Dux* had to come back and take over!" he cries. I feel like I know him from Wortimer's band of roughs. "What business did our boys have marching off to the North, when the Picts ravaged the country right *here*?"

"What are we even doing here?" I ask Fastidius after another peasant shrugs off the news of the coup with as much interest as if we told him of a cow giving birth outside calving season.

"*Dux* Wortigern requested our help. We responded to his plea."

"Help with what? The two of us will not overthrow Wortimer. And I'm not even sure we should try. He seems as capable a ruler as any."

"Wortimer? Capable?" Fastidius scoffs. "He couldn't rule his way out of the latrine. That the city hasn't collapsed yet is all down to the Council."

"But he *is* the rightful heir. If Wortigern died today, we would have no reason to oppose him. We haven't heard from the *Dux* since the coup," I add. "Perhaps he doesn't even want our help anymore."

"There's only one way to find out."

It takes us hours to get close enough to the crossing to see the guards and the barrier itself: a fence of brushwood fascine, with a gap in the middle, big enough to let a single cart through at a time. One such cart is now stuck in that gap, with the driver arguing loudly with the guards over what he deems an exorbitant toll for crossing.

"I never had to pay for coming through here before!"

"*Dux* Wortimer's orders," explains the guard, tiredly.

"And who in hell is *Dux* Wortimer? Who are *you*, for that matter? You're not from around here, son!"

The cart driver is a Saxon — not one of the recently arrived mercenaries, but one of those whose ancestors arrived here as Rome's allies generations ago and who is now just a common peasant in one of the Trinowaunt villages. He's more at home here than the guard, whose accent and entire manner are strange; he's a Briton, but not from our part of the island.

"Let's get closer," says Fastidius. We step off the causeway and wade through the marsh until we can see the markings on the guards' cloaks and the cloth thrown over the fascine.

"Imperial Eagle," I say. "Wortimer's mark, as expected."

"No. It's a different design. And Wortimer's is not surrounded by laurels. Where have I seen this before …?"

"Riotham's *lectica*," I remember. I grind my teeth. "They're Ambrosius's men."

"So that's what Dene meant. *Other forces*. Ambrosius wants to return to power in Londin, with Wortimer's help." Fastidius rubs his chin. "But… Not even Wortimer is stupid enough to not see this. What is *he* getting out of the deal?"

The guard and the driver finally come to a grudging agreement. The cart is waved through, and the next one is stopped in the gap. The guard stifles a yawn.

"I'm going to go in there," says Fastidius. "I need to talk to the Bishop."

"I'll go. Your face is too well known in the city," I oppose.

"And you're a Iute."

"I speak like a native. I know how to get around. The blockade isn't as thorough as Wortimer thinks — if they let that Saxon driver through, they'll let me in, too."

"And if they don't?"

"Then I'll talk my way out of trouble, as always," I reply with an uncertain smile. "Go back to Caesar's Market and wait there for Beadda. Looks like we might need their help after all."

Just as I'd predicted, marching through the guard post at the river crossing is the easiest part of the plan. Ambrosius's soldiers, despite having clear orders only to let the natives into the city, are not prepared for a Iute who looks them straight in the eye, speaks perfect Imperial Latin and pays the toll in unclipped bronze. Murmuring confusedly among each other, they let me pass with a wave.

There is another outpost at the gate in the Wall, but this one is more concerned with looking out for an incoming invading force than with individual travellers; the crowd here is too thick and rushing too fast for them to notice a stray fair hair among the blacks and reds. There are fewer soldiers, I note, manning the great *ballistae* than when we left for Wenta. Did the loyalist's purge involve even the Wall Guard?

Once inside the city, I am supposed to seek out the contacts from a list compiled by Fastidius and Dene — but first, I want to find out what the people of Londin really think, and there is no better place for it than at the Forum.

The Iute camp in the north-western corner lies empty, the overthrown stalls and strewn potsherds a testament to the haste with which it was abandoned when the order to expel the newcomers came. I can only hope no one was badly hurt in the process. No Briton traders took over this stretch of the market, as if still fearing the return of the rightful owners.

The unhappy rumours from the North, combined with the uncertainty created by the coup, resulted in a more subdued and doubtful mood in the Forum than that which I saw outside the city. The trade continues, and the goods pour in, but the traders and the customers glance anxiously at the new guards posted in the main alleyways of the market, and hush their voices whenever one of Wortimer's roughs, easily recognisable by their armbands and their haughty, challenging stares, walks past.

"I've heard that everyone we sent to fight the Picts is dead," one of the blade merchants says. "And that Coln itself was burned to the ground."

"That's not true," replies the clam vendor. "I went to Coln two days ago; it was untouched. What *I* heard was that the Picts allied with the Brigants and were gathering in the marshes of Werlam, to strike us from the west."

"It's not the Picts we need to worry about," interjects another voice, "it's those damn Iutes and Saxons. *They* killed all our men on the way to Wenta — slaughtered them in their sleep. And they would do the same to us, if it wasn't for Wortimer!"

There are more rumours and tall tales rushing about the market, each more incredible than the other, but I soon begin noticing the pattern — whenever the crowd grows too thick and agitated with worry, a voice appears that blames all the real and imagined woes on Wortigern and his Iute "friends", and praises Wortimer for the quick and effective way with which he's dealt with the menace. Most of the time, the voice would turn out to belong to someone wearing Wortimer's mark, or Ambrosius's colours on their cape. I cannot tell how many people in the Forum believe them, but it is clear these men did not appear at the market by accident.

Having heard enough, and satisfied that none of the roughs have spotted or recognised me, I sneak out into the outer streets of the eastern *villa* district, where Wortigern's courtiers have their dazzling palaces, to search for the addresses from my list. The first two properties have their gates boarded up, and guards posted at the entrance; the third one is half burnt down and plundered, shattered marble statues strewn across the lawn.

Losing hope, I approach the fourth address. I don't expect anyone to be home — the palace belongs to Postumus, one of Wortigern's oldest and most loyal followers. To my surprise, it is neither boarded up nor robbed, though there is an armed guard by the gate, eyeing suspiciously all who venture too near to its thick hedge wall. But the guard is one of the Westerners, and he doesn't know the backstreets of Londin as well as I do; it doesn't take long for me to find what would seem to most people like a cut-off dead end, from which, climbing over the roof of a nearby tenement, I can leap into the *villa's* back garden unseen.

Postumus is as surprised to see me in Londin as I am to see him safe and sound.

"We were told none of you survived," he tells me.

"And I heard you were all banished," I retort.

He laughs. "Wortimer would never dare touch me. I wedded one of my daughters into Ambrosius's household a long time ago. I haven't lived this long without being prepared for every opportunity."

By a flask of heady Aquitanian wine, we share our stories, and for the first time I hear the full tale of the aftermath of the coup. The fighting was not as bloodless as I had hoped; a dozen at least of Orpedda's Iutes perished in the siege, and in the chaotic fighting at the Forum, before a cohort of Ambrosius's soldiers appeared in the city to bring a semblance of order. Though Wortimer's militia were more numerous, they had no wish to stand openly against the highly trained Westerners. Before long, the soldiers with the Eagle's emblem occupied the main avenues and gates in the city, with Wortimer content to control the *Praetorium* and the trade district.

"It all happened so quickly," Postumus says, "Ambrosius's men must have come with Riotham, and waited just outside the walls for the signal. It's as if everything was prepared long before the Picts attacked — but how did Wortimer know they would? The raids came as a surprise to everyone at the court, myself included…"

"I don't think it was a surprise to Wortimer at all," I say, and repeat the words of King Drust: *this wasn't what I was promised.*

Postumus's face twitches. He leans closer. "I would keep an allegation like this to myself, boy," he says. "Unless you have solid proof. It's one thing for Wortimer to seek help of other Britons to gain power — most on the Council would do the same, given a chance. But to ally yourself with the barbarians is treason of the highest order. This would be an even greater blow to his credibility than the missing crown…"

"The crown?"

"Wortigern's golden diadem — the insignia of the Governor of Britannia. The mark of a rightful ruler — if the succession was orderly, it would pass from Wortigern to his son."

"This is what Riotham was so angry about when he was here."

Postumus nods. "It went mysteriously missing on the day of the coup — and they've been looking for it ever since." His gaze falls on a locked ironbound strongbox in the corner of the room. He turns back to me with a mischievous gleam in his eye.

As we speak, a servant approaches and whispers something in Postumus's ear. The old Councillor stands up and walks to the window.

"Are you sure you haven't been followed?" he asks, with his back to me.

"Pretty sure," I answer, "why?"

"There are four men out on the street I don't recognise. All armed. I think it will be best if you left me alone now."

"Is there another way out?"

"Of course," Postumus scoffs. "I told you I had ways to stay alive longer than most. There's a tunnel to the docks under the kitchen floor. Sextus will show you the way."

Not knowing when or how I would be able to find safety again, I gulp the last of the wine, even as Postumus urges me to leave with increasing anxiety.

"Tell me one last thing," I ask, just before descending into the secret tunnel. "Why does Wortimer obey Ambrosius at all? He didn't need the Westerners' help to capture the *Praetorium* and the Council. I would have thought he would have wanted to rule Londin alone, after all that effort…"

"He was promised an army," replies Postumus. "To bring the fight to the Iutes and Saxons. It's always been his obsession — now he's got the means. *And* a motive."

"A motive?" I ask. "What have the Iutes done to him now? They've been nothing but good neighbours ever since we fought the Saxons off."

"Too good, perhaps. After Hengist defeated the Picts at Tanet, even Worangon saw merit in settling some of them on Cantish land. Wortimer's men claim the Iutes *forced* him to give the land away, and now must be pushed back before they take even more. Now go! I can hear them at the door!"

What I wouldn't give for a mug of the warm, soapy ale from Caesar's Market inn.

I scratch my cheeks and stifle a sneeze. I haven't shaved in four days. I haven't eaten in two. That Aquitanian wine was the last time I had anything to drink that wasn't puddle water gathered in the cracks of my shelter.

Outside, another dawn breaks with the noise and bustle of Londin's harbour; the seagulls shriek at the sailors, the sailors shout at the porters, the porters curse at the amphorae and crates they heave from wharf to deck and back again. Like the night before, I huddle inside a fisherman's storage hut, the wet nets and ropes coiled around me and under me, hoping no one will bother looking in.

When Sextus, Postumus's most trusted slave, left me at the wharf, he promised he would find a way to get me out of the city as soon as possible. But now, two days later, I fear I may never see him nor his master again. I cannot wait any longer.

The threat is real; twice already I have tried to reach the city gates, and twice I was spotted by Wortimer's roughs and had to lose them in the harbour's narrow pathways. They know now I'm here, hiding somewhere. If they could, they'd turn the place inside-out to find me; but they do not dare.

The harbour district has always been a city-within-a-city, populated by tough and rough sailors and fishermen of all nations and races, many of them dealing in petty piracy on the side. They are a lifeblood of the city, it's only link with the outside world. Risk their wrath, and Londin starves: not of wheat and lamb, which is brought from the surrounding countryside, but of anything the nobles *really* care about — the Frankish cloth, silver and ivory trinkets from Gaul, Iberian wine, exotic slaves from the eastern forests and, just as, if not more, important — news from the relatives and trading partners in Armorica and beyond. Aware of their prominence, the sailors guard their independence fiercely. Wortimer would need a good reason to disturb their peace — and if I don't want to provide him with one, I need to stay out of sight.

I creak the hut's door open. Outside, a midday lull descends on the piers. It's a hot, sunny day, and although nobody here ever takes a real break, the work and bustle slows down to a lazy crawl, as if everyone got caught in syrup.

A new vessel bumps up to the wharf nearest to me, a fisherman's single-sail boat, heaving with silver bounty. In the noon haze which mutes all sounds, the fisherman and his apprentice make the only noise, unloading the nets into barrels. By the types of fish he's caught, I recognise he must be plying the murky straits of Tamesa's mouth, between the reed-grown islands and the briny marshes — exactly where I need to be. I reach for the knife strapped to my thigh. It will have to be enough; I've left my *seax* and spear with Fastidius at Caesar's Market.

I leap out and dash the hundred or so yards separating me from the fishing boat. In the silence, my feet stomping on the pier boards make a terrible racket in my ears, but I reach the vessel unnoticed — until I jump onto the boat, pulling the old fisherman down with me onto the deck.

I press the knife to his throat and my hand to his mouth. "Tell him to calm down and be quiet," I say, glancing to the young apprentice. The fisherman nods at me, then at the boy, with panicked eyes. The apprentice drops the oar he's been holding over my head and steps back.

"I will take my hand off your mouth now. One sound and you're dead."

He nods again.

"You will sail again, right now," I tell him. "Leave the fish and the boy here."

"Sail… Where to?"

"To the marshes where you got those eels from," I say.

"The winds have changed — it would take the rest of the day…"

"Then you'd better hurry up!"

"Hey there! What's going on?" a voice calls out. "Why are you letting those fish rot on the pier?"

It's a harbour guard, not one of Wortimer's men — I've been hiding here for so long, I recognise them by the sound of their voice now — but I can't take the risk. I order the fisherman to sit up and squeeze myself under his bench, covering myself under the netting. I press the knife to his groin through the boards. "Not a word," I hiss.

"I — I need to go back to the marshes," the fisherman stutters. "I forgot my nets…"

I can almost hear the guard's eyebrows rise. I could punch that old man just for how foolish his excuse sounds.

"He forgot something else," the young apprentice adds, with a forced chuckle. "On the Scad Creek, if you know what I mean."

"Oh — oh!" the guard laughs. "I see. Don't worry, I won't tell your Totia anything. Off you go, before the *net* goes away."

"What's on the Scad Creek?" I ask, as the apprentice boy pushes the boat out into the river.

"What do you think?" the old fisherman replies, gruffly. "Whores."

Beadda's fingers twitch. "Is Beaddingatun safe?"

The Iutes arrived at Caesar's Market while I was gone, eager to move on to meet their families, and dismayed to learn there was no easy way to cross the Tamesa now that all roads to and from the capital were locked to them.

"I don't know. Postumus has had no news from Ariminum since the coup. Those of the Iutes who fled the city were headed to Cantiaca — it's likely the others have joined them."

I take another gulp of the inn's ale, then another, until there's nothing left in the big mug. It is as stale, bland and muddy as it always was, but after a day of wandering through the stinking Kelmer marshes around Caesar's Market, it tastes like the drink of the gods.

For a brief moment, I remember the old fisherman, and wonder if he got back home safely. Once we sailed out of sight of Londin's Wall, I told him who I was and why I needed to capture his boat — and that once the *Dux* was returned to his rightful throne, I would seek him out and reward him for his help; but I doubt if he believed me.

I notice the smell of rotten fish lingering around the table, and then realise it must be coming from me. It's a good sign — at least my sense of smell is returning, along with my thirst and hunger.

Fastidius slams the table with his open palm and turns to Beadda. "We need to act quickly if we want to save your people — and the city. Ambrosius's Legion won't be here for a couple of weeks yet, but time is short."

"What do you propose?" Beadda sits up. "My men are at your service, Father."

It's the first time I have noticed how much respect Fastidius has gained in the eyes of the Iutish chief. Before the battle at the beach, the *Hiréd* treated him like they treat all priests, clerks and other members of that useless, weak caste the Britons are so inexplicably fond of. They never dared to openly taunt him the way they would Paulinus, but only because he was my friend and kin. Leading them to victory over the Picts turned him from a meek cleric into a warchief; now *he* is the one of whom they sing songs and write poems — and I am merely his companion.

But this time he sits silent, ponderous, lost in thought, and I fear this task might be too much for either of us. I don't care what anyone else sees in him, I know deep down he's just a boy, with only a year or two of life experience more than I have. He's got the book learning, which helped him devise strategies, and he got fortunate with the traitor's confession; but he's no general, no *Drihten* — no miracle-maker. All we have at our disposal are our wits and twenty *Hiréd*. Forget Londin — it wouldn't even be enough to raid a hillfort…

"If only we could lure Wortimer out of the city," I say. "Trap him outside the walls, on the road, the way Aelle ambushed our father…"

Fastidius looks up. "Yes." His eyes gleam. "Of course. Beadda, how fast can you get in contact with your *Drihten*?"

The chieftain calculates. "If we can find an easy crossing of the Tamesa, two days each way."

"I don't know this stretch of the river at all," says Fastidius. "It could be marshes all the way to the sea."

"Did somebody mention the sea?"

Dene, the exiled merchant, wobbles up to our table. His breath stinks of ale, wine and vomit, but his gaze is surprisingly clear.

"How much have you heard?" asks Fastidius, his eyes narrowed in distrust.

"Enough to know you could use my help. I have a boat here in Caesar's Market. A fast one. It can take two men down the Kelmer River, to the salt flats by the sea."

"That's the wrong way," says Fastidius, the only one with some grasp of local geography. "We need to get across the Tamesa."

"You *need* to reach Reculbium, where the Iutes are. Trust me, it's faster by the sea. I made that trip many times, when I was looking after my oyster farms. If the tides are good, you'll be on the Cantish shore in a day."

Fastidius and I look at each other. I can't vouch for Dene — I haven't seen him often enough at the court; he always seemed more busy with his oyster farms and saltworks than with affairs of state. But if he was Wortimer's spy, he would have betrayed us already...

"What do you want in exchange for your help?" asks Fastidius.

The merchant gasps in pretend affront, then grins. "All I want is peace of mind; to be left alone to my own devices. We all know what life is like under Ambrosius. If he's really the one behind this coup — if he is Wortimer's mentor... There will be more taxes, tolls, more courts. Not good for business."

Fastidius scowls. Taxes was the one part of Ambrosius's regime we both thought was sensible. Londin's treasury is badly in need of replenishing; there's no money even for basic needs: street repairs, cleaning the gutters, dredging the harbour... I now understand why *Dux* Wortigern could never implement new tolls — not until people as rich and powerful as the oyster farmer held sway in his Council.

"You'll have your peace of mind," I say, despite my better judgement. "As soon as the rightful *Dux* is restored to power."

All four of us shake our hands on the deal, though Beadda seems confused as to what it is that he's agreeing to.

"Excellent. Let me show you the boat. It's the finest in all of Trinowauntia, I assure you."

The small, sleek boat, propelled by eight oarsmen and a broad red sail, is even faster than the oyster farmer promised. On a good wind and friendly tide, we round the Othona Cape and take a giant leap across the mouth of the Tamesa evading Cantish patrols, before delivering me and Beadda — Fastidius remained with the *Hiréd* to coordinate the rest of the plan — at a narrow beach a mile from Reculbium, an old Roman fortress on Cantiaca's northern shore, where *Comes* Worangon has recently granted the Iutes a swathe of desolate, windswept heath.

The Iutes have wasted no time in establishing their new settlement. There's frantic activity all around us. They're setting up temporary huts and tents, digging the pits for their pit-houses, hauling in timber for walls and wheat straw for thatch from deeper inland. An entire town is about to grow on the dunes in the shadow of the striped Roman wall, if one can call a chaotic jumble of huts and lean-tos a *town*.

As we near the walls of Reculbium, some of the Iutes recognise Beadda and rush back to the fort with the news of our arrival. By the time we reach the gaping hole in the wall, grown over with gorse, which is all that's left of the fort's western gate, there's already a small crowd awaiting our arrival.

Rhedwyn stands among them, in drab, mud-splattered working clothes, her hair tied tight and grey with dust, her face smeared with charcoal. I rush to her; she hesitates at first, shy of her uncouth disposition, but once she sees I don't mind, she reaches out to embrace me and bursts in tears.

"Ash! They said you were dead."

"Who did?"

"Wortimer's men. They told us the Picts slaughtered you all."

"They could never stand against Beadda's warriors!" I laugh, but inside I feel a shiver. How did Wortimer's lies get even here, so fast? How many people in Wortigern's domain chose to believe them?

I prolong the embrace, and my hands wander to caress Rhedwyn's back. She stirs, but doesn't pull away, even as I go lower. Her breath quickens by my ear. For a moment I forget all about politics, war, and the world around us.

Beadda's hand on my shoulder brings me back. "Come, boy. The *Drihten* awaits us."

CHAPTER VIII
THE LAY OF HENGIST

There is no Hall yet in Reculbium; a ruin of the legionnaires' bath house, roofed with thatch and animal hides thrown over some wooden beams serves as the *Drihten's* temporary abode.

Beadda tells the story of battle to Hengist's household, all gathered under the makeshift roof by a blazing bonfire; it's his glory to boast about, and besides, he's still much more skilled with the Saxon tongue than I am, and this is a tale that requires a poet's talent to do it justice.

He is almost as fine a storyteller as he is a warlord. He keeps the audience tense as he describes the preparation for battle and our march through the swamps. Hoots and cheers erupt in response to our initial victory by the boats. The demise of Odo's lancers is greeted with a loud groan, reflecting the respect the Gauls have earned among the Iutes over the years; Fastidius is given most of the credit for the ultimate victory, and rightly so; his arrival in the battle cart is described in terms reserved to demi-gods. "He may *look* like a weak priest of the Roman God," says Beadda, "but that day he was more like Donar, descending from *Ansegeard* to save us." I chuckle, imagining what Fastidius would have thought of that comparison.

As for myself, I'm just glad to hear my name mentioned once or twice, in the repeated lists of warriors, as Ash of the Anglian *aesc* — I haven't done much to earn more attention, other than get myself almost killed by a flying stone. Every time Beadda speaks my name, Rhedwyn, who's been sitting beside me all evening, squeezes my hand. I haven't presented her with the necklace yet; this will have to wait until we're finished with the official business. I feel it lying heavy in the leather bag at my belt.

It is now *Drihten* Hengist's time to speak. He, too, has a story of victorious battle with the Picts to tell, more for my benefit than his people, most of whom have witnessed the fighting at Tanet; but he rushes through it, eager to move on to more pressing, current matters. It appears Wortimer's rule has already begun to affect those living on the borders of his domain.

"He's been pulling all fighting men from the borders into the city," the *Drihten* says. "The land is unsafe again. The Saxon bandits have returned to Andreda Forest — and this time, it's not a mere rumour. They've already struck near Orpeddingatun."

"Aelle's back?" I exclaim. This, of all news, is the worst. Has he reneged on our deal, seeing the situation change in Londin?

Hengist nods. "For now, he seems to harass the Britons more than us. We've sent some warriors to guard the villages in your absence. But they won't hold long if the Saxons come in full force. I do not understand why the new *Dux* is letting this happen."

"That's simple — he wants to destroy you all."

They all turn to me, waiting for me to explain the meaning of my words. I repeat hastily what Fastidius has learned in Londin about Wortimer's destructive plans.

"The more Saxons and Iutes bleed each other out, the better," I finish.

"But the Britons will suffer from this conflict too," one of the Iute elders opposes.

"Only the serfs in the villages," I reply. "And to Wortimer, their lives are worth no more than yours."

I'm surprised at their surprise, before I remember: these people have not lived and breathed Londin's politics the way I have done for the last couple of years. They don't know Wortimer like I do; they may have heard rumours of his behaviour from their brethren in the Forum, but would've dismissed it as just more local politics. They respected Wortigern, they knew and valued Catigern, and expected Wortimer to continue his father's legacy, even if he did come to power through a lawless coup.

In the long silence that follows, Hengist sits up, resting his hands on his knees. "We can't hope to win against both Wortimer and Aelle, not while they're hiding behind their walls of stones and trees. And when those soldiers from the West reach Londin…" He does not finish, instead he stares at his elders and beyond them, at the makeshift shanty town outside; the Iutes may be numerous, but beyond the *Hiréd* few would be able to defend themselves against a regular army, trained in Roman ways and experienced against barbarians.

"We will fight to the death," says one of the elders. "Take as many of them with us as we can."

"We could've stayed in the Old Country for this," replies another, shaking his head. "Maybe it would have been better if we had."

"We will neither die nor flee," says Hengist. "We struggled for too long to gain even this meagre foothold." He pauses. I can see how it pains him — a warchief, used to leading people into battle and glory — to speak the next words:

"I will plead for mercy and hope we can strike some kind of a deal. If not with Wortimer, then maybe with those other Britons young Ash spoke of. They sound easier to reason with."

"We may not have to do any of those things," I say. "We — I mean, Father Fastidius — has come up with a plan how to stop Wortimer for good."

Seeing how quickly mention of Fastidius's name brings a gleam of hope to their eyes, I feel a pang I haven't felt in a long time. I explain Fastidius's design, to frowns and gasps of disbelief — but I know the gasps would be louder if I presented it under my name.

Hengist scratches his chest under the tunic.

"We are not ready," he says. "And what if we fail? We'd risk becoming outlaws, like those forest Saxons."

"You can't fail, the plan is perfect," I bluff, counting on Fastidius's newly built reputation. "And if you help bring Wortigern back to his throne, he'd reward you all greatly," I bluff again.

"How would I explain it to my people? All we ever wanted was to live peacefully among these Britons. Now you want us to challenge them openly?"

"Can you not just order your men into battle?" I ask, with genuine surprise.

"I'm not a tyrant, like your Roman Imperators," Hengist explains. "I'm just a *Drihten*, subject to the will of the *witan*. I'd have to convince all free men in the tribe before we'd decide on something as important as this."

"First, we'd need a cause for war," says one of his elders. "A change of ruler in Londin is not enough, not even one known for his dislike of Iutes — "

"*Hatred* of Iutes," I interject.

" — so you say. All we have now is one Roman's word against another. How do we even know this Fastidius is telling the truth?"

A concerned silence falls on the Hall, followed by engaged whispers. I fidget. This is something Fastidius did not prepare me for; we hadn't foreseen Hengist would need to convince his men to go into battle, even a pretend one. But of course, the *Drihten* has to think about the welfare of his own people before meddling in the politics of the Britons. Failing to defeat Wortimer would bring them nothing but more misery, maybe even a total ruin. The Iutes have nowhere else to go from Cantiaca — they don't have enough ships to take everyone to a new home even if they wished to, and all the land roads pass through hostile territory.

I feel Rhedwyn's hand slip from mine. She stands up. All eyes turn to her.

"I will be your cause, uncle," she says.

Hengist looks her in the eyes. "What do you mean?"

"I may be a maiden yet, but I'm no fool. I have seen how this *wealh* looked at me when I was at the palace." Her cheeks grow red, not with shyness, but with excitement of speaking at the great Hall moot. "*Dux* Wortigern knew this too, when he sent me home as soon as trouble began." She takes a deep breath and swallows loudly. "Let him know that I'll be going to visit our villages, down the coast stone road. He will not be able to resist."

The *Drihten* guffaws. "Don't be ridiculous, child. It's far too dangerous."

"I'm not a child anymore, uncle. I'll be sixteen this year, as old as some of your warriors."

This gives him pause; I grab her hand. "You'll get yourself killed!" I whisper. "Let the elders think of something."

"It would certainly rouse people's wrath, especially in Eobba's household," one elder notes. "They would join you in the clamour for war. With Eobba, you'll have a majority in the *witan*."

Hengist nods.

"You cannot be serious," I oppose. "She's your only remaining family! And what if something else happens to her — what if she's attacked by Aelle?"

"He wouldn't dare," the *Drihten* scowls. "Not on the coast road." He scratches his beard. "You make us all ashamed with your bravery, Rhedwyn, but we will try to find another way." He then dismisses us all, leaving only his elders and Beadda with him. "I will make a decision tomorrow. You must be in need of rest, Ash. Rhedwyn, please show our guest where he can sleep."

She takes me to the north-eastern corner of the fort. The cliff here, battered by the storms, has crumbled into the sea, taking a portion of the wall with it and leaving this section open to the elements. The soil on top of the cliff is thin and hard, so the Iutes can't dig their pit-houses here; instead, they've raised a cluster of huts made with rubble from the fallen walls, for use of the *Drihten*'s guests. The huts remind me of the cells in which the Tanet monks live, which I'm guessing were the original inspiration for these unusual buildings.

Rhedwyn shows me in. There's a bedding of sheepskins on the floor, a small clay basin beside it and a tallow candle on a wobbly stool. With the candle yet unlit, the only light falls in through the low entrance, and the inside of the hut is shrouded in shadow. The hut is tiny; we're so close to each other I can smell the lye soap on her hair. She's no longer covered in grime and soot — she's washed herself for the moot, and put on the emerald dress, the one from my dreams.

"Would you really go to Londin, if the *Drihten* ordered you to?" I ask, as I light the candle to take a better look at her.

"It was my idea," she replies. "Of course I would."

"Wortimer is a dangerous man."

"I'm not afraid of him," she says, her eyes gleaming defiantly. "He's a slimy snake."

"A snake that can bite. It would take a few days for your uncle to come to your rescue. Who knows what Wortimer would do to you in those few days."

"I would bite off his thing if he tried anything."

She snaps her teeth and grins. I chuckle in surprise. This isn't the quiet, reserved Rhedwyn I know from the palace; being back with her kin, working hard on the settlement, has changed her beyond recognition. She almost makes *me* feel embarrassed.

"I…" I stutter. "I brought something for you. From the North."

I reach into the bag at my waist. The necklace shimmers in the faint flame of the candle and casts a dancing cascade of flickers on the soot-blackened wall.

"Oh, Ash!" She puts her hand to her mouth. "It's so beautiful…!"

"Do you think so?"

I'm relieved she likes it; I knew the heavy golden buttons and the silver intricate chain were worth a lot, but I have no experience assessing the beauty of such jewellery.

"It's too much," she says. "I can't accept it."

"Nonsense. Beadda's *Hiréd* is bringing a chest full of plunder. Soon all their women will be parading around in such things."

I bite my tongue too late; I have diminished the value of my gift by mentioning the other treasure. But she doesn't seem to notice. She admires the gold, as it flows and shimmers in her fingers.

"It's too much," she whispers again, but her voice lacks conviction.

"Turn around," I say. "Let me see it on you."

I put the necklace on her and close the clasp. My touch raises goosebumps on her bare skin. On an impulse, I lean in and kiss her neck softly. She reaches back and holds my head down for a heartbeat, before stepping away and turning back.

She's smaller and shorter than the woman for whom the necklace was designed. It hangs low and heavy between her breasts, bordered on each side by her braids, as golden as the five pendants. The metal jingles with each breath, each rise and fall of her chest. I reach to touch it, and my fingers brush the thin green cloth underneath. She doesn't flinch; she stares at me in a challenge.

Overwhelmed by desire, I push her to the wall and kiss her; she replies with a passion that takes my breath. I draw the necklace out of the way and pull the top of her dress from her shoulders, to reveal that which until now I only imagined. Her skin is pale pink, but it quickly turns red-hot.

"I love you," I hear myself say between kisses, the words easy to say now that she's under me, her fingers in my hair, her tongue in my mouth. She moans in reply and tightens her embrace, but when I reach under the green dress, she pushes my hand away.

"Not today," she says.

The moment is gone. Still blushing, she pushes me away, pulls up her dress and runs out of the hut. It's fine. I've been with enough girls to know what's going on. I can wait a few days. For her, I can wait a lifetime.

By midday the next day, the *Drihten* announces his decision. The elders have agreed, partly, to Rhedwyn's plan; but they have added an alteration.

"We won't let him take you," he tells the girl. "Just being attacked will be enough to provoke the Iutes' wrath."

"You assume you'll have a choice," I say. I'm devastated by this turn of events — I spent the night hoping all of Hengist's elders would come up with a better strategy than a sixteen-year-old girl. "You can't know with how strong a force Wortimer will come for Rhedwyn."

"We will send the riders ahead. If there's any sign of trouble, we'll send her back."

"Riders?"

Hengist beckons at somebody behind me. Odo moves into the light, holding on to the reins of his stallion.

"We arrived at Dorowern yesterday," he says, "but the *Comes* wouldn't even meet with me. I'm an embarrassment to him now, with most of my men gone and no plunder to show for it. I had nowhere else to go."

"The *Decurion* of the White Horse is always welcome among the Iutes," says Hengist.

"How much of the plan have you heard?" I ask.

"More than I needed to. In truth, Beadda asked me for assistance when I arrived, and I agreed without knowing any details. I couldn't possibly refuse a brother in arms."

He pats the chief of the *Hiréd* on the broad shoulder and they both grin.

"It's settled then," says the *Drihten*. "Rhedwyn, my girl, make ready for the journey, and …" His gaze falls on the necklace on her chest. "What is this?"

"A gift, uncle," she answers, sheepishly. I now see her shyness is an act before the *Drihten* and his court, just as it was in the palace.

Hengist's eyes turn to me, but he says nothing. "Don't flash it on the road," he tells her. "Leave it in my treasure chest for safe-keeping."

"Yes, uncle. Who is going with me?"

"Take whoever you want from women and servants. I will choose the warriors to accompany you myself."

I step forward, with my hand on the hilt of my sword. "I would go."

"You should rest, son. You've done enough."

"I would go, *Drihten*," I repeat, with emphasis.

Hengist frowns, smooths his moustache in thought, then looks around the Hall. His eyes pose the question. The elders, one by one, stare first at me, then at Rhedwyn, and then, slowly and in silence, all of them nod.

With every day we move closer to Londin, I grow more anxious. Two days after leaving Reculbium we pass Robriwis, the once-mighty, now ruined, fortress at the mouth of River Medu, the same river on the shores of which we first fought with Aelle's band. I find myself unable to sleep, my heart constricted, my mouth dry. Not even before the battle at the beach have I been so nervous; but there, I had nothing to lose except my own foolish life. This time, it's Rhedwyn who's at risk.

We don't get to spend much time alone together. She's always surrounded by guards and the old women from her retinue, for security. In the shadows of Robriwis' walls we meet for an hour under the pretence of continuing the reading lessons, and we spend most of that hour in each other's thirsty embrace, but it's hardly enough to satiate my desire… or to diminish my worries.

It is not only her safety that I'm anxious about. Though her passion burns no colder than mine, my restless mind invents questions and doubts. When I confess my love to her, her replies are moans and sighs, not words. What if, like the Anglian girl in the Iken wood, what she seeks in me is not myself, but a connection to the greater, brighter, richer world I inhabit and represent? Nobody who caught a glimpse of life in Londin could ever want to return to the squalor of the Iutish villages, of that I'm sure — what if she's only using me to get closer to it all?

And would I really mind it if she did — as long as that meant I could be close to her…?

"Why do you always pretend?" I ask her as we return to the camp.

"Pretend?"

"You were this shy, gracious, sweet girl at Wortigern's court, and even before your uncle's elders — but when we're on our own, you're bold and forthright, like any other shieldmaiden."

She tilts her head to the side. "Oh? And which one do *you* prefer?"

"Whichever is the real you."

She laughs. "Good response."

"You haven't answered."

She shrugs. "I was raised an orphan among men. I have learned to behave in whatever manner they expect me to. It's easier that way."

"I'd never have guessed that was what the *Drihten* and the elders wanted from you."

"You'd be surprised," she says, and I sense a bitterness I rarely hear in her voice. "The Iute men are not like those Angles you've seen. They *fear* women in power — they'd never let one become as strong as that *Comes*, Una. How many shieldmaidens have you seen in Beadda's *Hiréd*?"

She's asked me to tell the story of the war with the Picts so many times now, she must have learned it by heart. Now I can see what made her so curious. I admit, there were a lot less women accompanying Beadda into battle than there were in Angenwit's army — though I chose to believe it was because the raid took the Iutes far away from their children and harvest, and somebody had to stay in the village to take care of both.

"The Geat maidens go into war still with their children inside them," she says. "And a man can mow the wheat just as well as a woman."

"This is not how things are in Rome," I reply. "Or in Britannia. There are no women on the Council — it would be barbaric."

"Then I'd rather stay barbaric than be civilised!"

"And was I the same?" I ask, recalling the innocent charm which drew me to her when I first saw her. "Were you playing with me as well?"

"In the beginning," she admits. "I was told you were a Iute, so I treated you like I would one of my uncle's warriors." She remembers something and laughs. "And you *did* fall for it."

I can feel my cheeks burn hot, though it's a cold and wet night here at the coast.

"What made you change your mind?"

She sneezes and wipes her nose with her fist.

"The amphitheatre."

What does it mean?

"Something good came of Wortimer's games, then," I say.

Her lips narrow to a thin, furious line. "Don't mention this snake's name in my presence. I hope when we defeat him, my uncle will splay him from side to side."

"I… I don't think this will be possible."

"Why not?" She frowns.

"He *is* the *Dux's* only son," I explain. "We're fighting to bring Wortigern back to power in Londin, but once we do, he will let his son return to the court with only some diminished privileges."

This stops her in her tracks. "You mean to tell me that no matter what we do, Wortimer will one day rightfully rule this land?"

"There's no other way." I throw up my hands. "Wortimer is the heir — the Council decided so long ago. But Wortigern is strong, and has many years in him yet," I try to cheer her up. "Enough for the Iutes to prepare for whatever comes."

"There isn't time enough in the world for us to prepare for Wortimer," she says. There is murder in her eyes; her fists clench and unclench. The hatred in her voice takes me aback. "Sooner or later, we will have to fight him — and *kill* him."

On the fourth day, we reach the long village sprawled on all sides of that great crossroad south of the Londin Bridge, where the east-west highway meets the stone road to New Port. My anxiety reaches its climax. If Wortimer wants to steal Rhedwyn from us, this is the best time and place for it; we're only a few hours away from the capital, in the heart of his domain. Yet we still haven't heard anything from Odo's riders, sent in vanguard a day ahead of us. Has the gossip not reached the palace in time? We've been careful to spread enough rumours of the Iutish "princess" travelling to check on her kindred's safety with just a small retinue of servants and warriors. What if Wortimer decided Rhedwyn was not worth his effort after all, not even as a hostage…?

I hear a horse coming to a sudden halt outside. A moment later, Odo bursts into the inn.

"They're coming," he announces. "I've been outwitted."

"What do you mean? How far are they?"

"Almost here. They cut off the roads from the south and east," he replies.

"What do we do? Go back to Robriwis?"

"No, we'll be too out in the open there." He looks out the inn's southern window. "We need to go into the peat lake."

I know the place he means. I've seen it many times, marching up and down the southern road from Londin: a vast sea of loose peat, stretching several miles each way, so dense and damp even the Romans could not traverse it, and had to bend their great stone road in a wide arc around it.

"Nobody ever comes out of there," I say.

"That's just what the robbers and runaway slaves would want you to believe. There's always a way out."

I rush up to Rhedwyn's room. She emerges calm and composed, already in her travel clothes, as if she was expecting trouble.

"You, take all but three guards with you and go down the southern road as bait," she orders the youngest women of her retinue. "Don't go down without a fight. Make me proud."

The women accept the command without protest and shuffle outside; the older ones stay at the inn, too frail to take part in any subterfuge, while Rhedwyn and I follow Odo and the three remaining Iutish warriors out the back.

We follow the narrow cattle path out of the village, and reach the peat-cutters track, the only way into the inner marsh. The foul smell coming from the hissing mud makes us all nauseous. Although it's nothing compared to the great swamps we've passed through in the land of the Ikens, without a guide I'm loath to enter deeper into the marsh.

"They'll guess we're here, sooner or later," I say, "we can't hide forever."

Rhedwyn says nothing. She already looks wretched; her tunic and dress are caked with sticky peat, her arms are covered in scratches from the branches of the creepy black trees she grabs onto to help herself move forward.

"We have to get to the other side," says Odo. "Back to the eastern road, past the blockade."

But he doesn't sound confident. He's never been here either; his service for *Comes* Worangon never requiring him to venture so far away from his Cantish vineyards. The Iutes aren't of any help, either. I'm the only one who knows where we are in relation to the main roads, and even this only vaguely.

We skirt the edges of the deepest marsh, heading east. The track is narrow, winding, ducking and weaving through grass islands and low tree clumps; if it wasn't for the setting sun lighting up the sky behind us, we'd be hopelessly lost already. I'm aware we have to get out of here before dusk, or else we'll be trapped for the night. We'd never dare risking the marshes in the dark.

"Did you hear that?" says Rhedwyn.

I stop. Yes, I hear it. Shouting, calling, from ahead and behind. These aren't peat-cutters.

"Search parties," says Odo. "We should get off this path."

I look to my right, where the swamp bubbles and dribbles; there are no tracks here, only sand spits linking small patches of grass. One wrong step and we'll be sucked into the marsh.

"It's too dangerous."

"It's dangerous to stay here."

An arrow buzzes past my head. I duck, pulling Rhedwyn down with me.

"A stray," Odo says. "They can't see us clearly yet."

The shouting grows louder and more frequent. Reluctantly, I take a step off the path and onto a sand spit. It holds firm. I make another step, and this time, the sand gives way and my foot sinks into the mud. Rhedwyn clutches at my arm.

"It's no use," I say.

Some armed men, bearing Wortimer's armbands, leap out on us from the bushes. I draw the *seax*. With the Iutes and Odo there's five of us against four of them — six, counting Rhedwyn, who refuses my attempt to push her to the back and stands to my left holding a small single-edged dagger. Seeing they're outnumbered and outmatched, Wortimer's men turn tail. One falls with a throwing axe in his back, Odo catches up to the other and slashes him with his cavalry sword, but the other two retreat, calling for their comrades.

We run the other way, still keeping to the path, and emerge onto the shore of a muddy stream. A dozen militiamen bar our way across. Our three Iutes charge forward; they don't fight as well as the *Hiréd*, but they are fuelled by desperation and devotion to Rhedwyn and her uncle — and Wortimer's men are a poor match to their training. Still the enemy comes, in greater numbers, threatening to overwhelm and encircle the unfortunate Iutes and cut us off from any hope of escape.

Odo and I race around the fighting, with Rhedwyn in tow; as she leaps over what seems to be a slain militiaman, he reaches and grabs her by the ankle. She trips; he starts climbing up her leg. She stabs him in the hand, then kicks his face with the free foot until he lets her go. I help her up and we splash across the stream, only to find more of Wortimer's troops heading our way. *Where did they all come from?*

"Go east," says Odo. "I'll hold them here."

It's a valiant offer, but a pointless one — I spot a couple of archers among the militia, their bows drawn and aimed at me and Rhedwyn. The others surround us from the south and west, cutting off the only route of escape. Rhedwyn stands between me and Odo, a bloodied dagger in her hand. She is a Iute maiden, after all; death in battle would be better than any other fate Wortimer may have in place for her.

A bolt whistles through the air; an unmistakable sound — no other weapon in Britannia sounds like it. The bolt lands in one of the archers' necks. His comrade turns in panic, only to have his chest pierced with another missile.

The scrub behind the militia erupts with howls; some twenty men burst out, waving clubs, hatchets and an occasional *seax*. They make short work of the surprised militiamen on both sides of the stream — though not short enough to save the three brave Iutes. Their leader appears last.

As he approaches, he winds up the chain on his weapon and slides two new bolts into the box on the top.

Aelle.

"Come quickly," he says. "There are more coming. I don't want them to track us down."

"Come — with you?" I scoff. "No, thanks. We're going back to Cantiaca."

"You'll never make it on your own. I'll take you through the woods."

"Why should I trust you?"

"Do you have a choice?"

"Is this…?" Rhedwyn doesn't finish the question.

I nod. "Aelle, the chief of Andreda's bandits."

Her eyes widen, her grip tightens on the grip of her dagger. But then we hear more shouts and calls coming from the swamp, and from the road. One of Aelle's warriors runs up and urges him to hurry back.

"Last chance," says Aelle. "Would you rather face me, or Wortimer?"

"I fear he's right," says Odo. "We'll be safer in the forest."

The calls grow nearer. I look to Rhedwyn. She nods, her lips narrow.

"Fine," I say. "But if you try anything …" I wave my *seax* in his face.

He grins and hoots, beckoning his men from the other side of the stream.

CHAPTER IX
THE LAY OF HLOD

The Iutes of Beaddingatun call the forest which sprawls the chalk ridges between Londin and their villages the Great North Wood. It is not the same dark, dense, wild tangle as Andreda, but it's big enough to lose any pursuit between the borders of the peat lake and Aelle's temporary camp, set up on a stretch of isolated heathland by an ancient dead oak.

"So the rumours *were* true," I say, when we finally sit down and catch our breaths by the fire. "You did come back to the forest."

"I came back *because* of the rumours," he replies. "And because of Wortimer. With him in power, I figured our deal was off."

"Perhaps — but it's not yet certain he'll stay in power."

"We'll see about that when your *Drihten's* little mad scheme succeeds."

"How did you know about the scheme?" I ask. "And how did you know we might need help?"

"We have ears in Hengist's Hall," he replies. He reaches into a pot of tar and proceeds to grease the mechanism of his weapon. "We know all about what goes on there."

This surprises me less than it should. There were a number of Iutes in Aelle's army, who returned to Tanet after the Battle of Saffron Valley. It seems a few of them still keep in touch with their fellow Saxons.

"It's *we* now? You mean you and your father? Doesn't he have enough on his plate in the South, fighting other chieftains? I'd think he couldn't spare any of his warriors to send our way."

"I see you, too, know a little of what goes on beyond your borders," Aelle grins. "We no longer need to rely on just my father's warriors. Now that Wortimer's in charge, the Saxons and Iutes have been flocking under my banner from all over the place. The camps in Andreda have grown even greater than you remember."

"Is that why you've helped us?" Rhedwyn asks. "To spite Wortimer?"

She's balancing the dagger blade on her knees, all tense and ready to pounce at the slightest sign of the threat.

Aelle scowls. "It makes no difference to me or my father who rules Londin — as long as they leave us alone in the South. But the Britons are stronger when united, and Wortimer is making friends with that other warlord from the West —"

"Ambrosius," I offer.

"That's the one. My father says if they join forces we won't be able to keep them away for long."

Odo's been silent for now, having no quarrel of his own with Aelle, but this stirs him. "Stand against Wortimer? Is that really what the *Comes* of the Regins is planning?"

Aelle laughs. "You mean Catuar? He's a weak old fool. He'll do whatever the Saxons tell him to do."

"Then it's your father who rules the Regins now?"

"It's not that simple yet." The boy shrugs. "What you've heard is correct — there is still much disagreement among the Saxons. Some warlords would rather hold complete dominion over their own pitiful scraps of land than acknowledge my father's supremacy and join the greater cause. Others still — a diminishing few — remain foolishly loyal to the *wealas*..." His face turns in a false grin. "Besides, we'd rather leave the administration of the *pagus* to Catuar and his Council. We're warriors, not clerks!" He shakes his weapon. "We'd rather count heads than coins."

Aelle's story confirms some of the rumours that have been reaching Wortigern's court lately; though the Southern *pagus* was still represented at the palace by *Comes* Catuar's *legate*, the merchants and travellers often raised complaints about having to deal with the Saxons rather than Briton officials in their day-to-day matters.

"But why are you *here*?" I ask. "What does your father gain from you raiding the Briton hamlets on the borderlands, or from you helping us escape? What's his plan?"

"Please," Aelle says, putting away the weapon. He picks up a bolt and starts to sharpen it on the stone. I sense the questioning makes him uncomfortable, as if he himself wasn't sure of all the answers. "I'm not here to discuss my father's politics. This is between him, Catuar, and the other warlords. It's enough that he wants me to help you — and for that, we first need to get you all back to Reculbium in time, or none of this will matter."

"In time? In time for what?"

"For the battle, of course," says Aelle, licking the bolt's freshly sharpened head.

Rushing from hill to dean, from glade to forest, from marsh to heath, we follow Aelle down the wood cutters' paths and boar tracks that form the invisible highway across Andreda that only his men know, ever eastwards; I recognise some of the paths from my time in Aelle's service, or at least I think I do. We move faster than I remember — our party is smaller than a raiding war band, and we can take narrow shortcuts through the denser parts of the wood. Aelle urges us on without regard to our condition. I can see Rhedwyn is exhausted, but she's saying nothing, so none of us men dare to raise any complaints, either.

At last, the woods part, and we stand on the high shore of the Medu River, not far from the ford where Aelle and I first met.

"You'll find a friendly village and horses across the river," says Aelle. "I cannot cross the border — not yet."

I watch the boy disappear back into the woods, not yet a friend, but no longer an enemy, still unsure what to make of him and his plans, whatever they may be.

There is a great crowd of angry men and women gathered around Hengist's Hall at Reculbium, awaiting our arrival. The women take Rhedwyn, who's nearly fainting from exertion, and disappear with her into the healing huts, while Hengist invites me and Odo under the thatch of the ruined bath house.

"We know what happened," he says, raising his hand before either of us speaks. "We had a messenger from Andreda last night who told us the whole story."

"Then you also know Aelle's back to his old tricks."

"Yes — but we will have to deal with him later. For now, we have a vote to win. The *witan* is called for tomorrow."

"Isn't this a little hasty?" asks Odo, whose knowledge of Iutish tribal politics is far superior to mine.

"You've seen the people outside. They've been coming since yesterday, from Tanet and the other settlements. They've all heard the news of Wortimer's assault on their beloved Rhedwyn."

"I bet you made sure of that," I say. His response is a wry smile.

"Will you have enough votes?" asks Odo.

"With the way that crowd is raging, I pity anyone who dares to vote against the war. Not only did Wortimer try to kidnap their princess, his men slew her servants and warriors. Justice must be served."

He notices the change in our faces as he speaks of the slain servants. "You — you didn't know?"

"How many?" I ask, quietly. During our journey to Londin, I developed something of a selfish aversion for the young women in our company, for the way they prevented me from being alone with Rhedwyn — but I knew they were only performing their duty; and seeing them obey their mistress without a word of complaint as she sent them to their doom made me greatly appreciate their devotion. I was hoping that at least some of them would survive and return safely to Tanet, but the *Drihten*'s shaking head tells me that hope is lost.

"He even got to the ones you left behind," he says. "Gods know what harm he thought a couple of old, toothless women would cause him. Wortimer's wrath was so great at how you've outsmarted him, he displayed the heads of his captives on stakes at the Bridge, as a challenge to us."

Odo bangs his fist on the table, sending the plates and cups flying. "He wants us to march on Londin, and bleed out against its walls!"

"No," I say. "Remember, even this is all part of Fastidius's strategy. We must trust my brother's intellect. We are going to win this, I'm certain of it, if we only stick to the plan."

"Well said, Ash," Hengist booms. "The victory will be ours! Now go, you must be needing a rest after what you've been through. Don't forget to come to the *witan* tomorrow. You will witness a rare moment indeed — a Iute *fyrd* resolving to march to a war!"

A few days after the *witan* votes unanimously for assembling the *fyrd* — a gathering of all adults able and willing to bear arms — under Hengist's command, I spot a frown deepen on the *Drihten's* face. Yet another half a dozen warriors appears before the makeshift Hall to volunteer their services; these ones are all one family, led by Hlod, their bearded patriarch. After staring at him for a while, I recognise with astonishment the old Iute I saved from Wortimer's mob in the Forum, almost two years ago. He's no longer the refuse-rooting beggar I remember; he is a warlord now, the only one of his clan armed with a sword and wearing a pair of old leather greaves, while the others carry spears and small shields. Hengist nods with a badly concealed sigh and points them to the western side of the fort, where the rest of the *fyrd* is setting up camp.

"What's wrong?" I ask. "This should be more than enough to take on Wortimer's cohort in the field."

With Hengist's permission, I have been sitting at his right hand during these proceedings, a position I'm uneasy with; it is where a chieftain's son normally would sit, where Catigern sat with Wortigern when he was still alive. But my father was Master Pascent, not a Iute warlord, and my place is at the court in Londin, not in the mead hall in Reculbium… There must be some in Hengist's household who, rightly, believe they deserve this seat more than I do. For now, they keep quiet — it is not wise to question the warchief when the *fyrd* has gathered.

What might Hengist's sudden fondness for me mean? A way to get closer to Londin's inner politics? I am Wortigern's Councillor, after all, even in exile. Or is there something more to it — something related to that strange, formal manner with which the elders accepted me as Rhedwyn's travel companion…

It's Rhedwyn who should be sitting here, instead of me, I think. *She's your flesh and blood — and she's smarter and braver than most of your Elders.*

"I know, boy," Hengist says. "But what after that? Once these men taste victory, how will I stop them from more fighting?"

"Won't it be enough to get vengeance on Wortimer?"

"This is not why they're here." He shakes his head. "Many are, yes, the ones who heard the story on the day you came back, or at the *witan*… But those who arrive now only want to join the *fyrd* to take part in the glory of a battle, no matter the reason. It's been too long." He rubs the pommel of his sword — it is a fine weapon, its hilt studded with jewels and inlaid with gold. "We may not be warlike like Saxons or Angles — but we still like to fight. To win."

"What about those Picts you fought on Tanet? Or the sea raiders?"

He scowls. "We pushed them all back into the sea with little effort. It only served to whet our appetites. As did hearing all those songs of your battles in Andreda and in the North." He looks to the east, where the sea shore disappears in a blue gloom. "I hoped we could leave our warlike ways behind in the Old Country, forge a new life of peace — but it wasn't to be. The warriors' blood runs hot again, and it will not cool easily. Who will we fight once we defeat Wortimer?"

If we defeat Wortimer, I want to correct, but I bite my tongue and wave for the guard to let the next group of the recruits in.

In the end, we have to order half of the volunteers to stay behind, in reserve. We don't want to frighten Wortimer into locking himself behind the city gates — we want him to think he stands a fighting chance. The *Drihten* selects two hundred of the best volunteers to accompany the thirty-strong core of trained warriors, and we march out in a long, slow column, down the coastal highway.

It's not just an unruly warband on a raid — it's a procession; the *Drihten* and his elders are accompanied by a monk from the Tanet monastery, who carries with him a small chest with Iutish demands written on parchment in the Imperial tongue, and sealed with Martinus's seal. The Iutes demand that Wortimer apologises to Rhedwyn, that he pays *wergild* for the men and women slain in the attack, and that he grants more land to the Iutes as compensation.

This is another of Fastidius's ideas, a way to pin the blame for the coming battle on Wortimer. It's obvious that he'll never accept Hengist's demands; but it will be the *Drihten* who will show himself as the one reaching out for peace, a truly Christian gesture from a pagan lord.

As we near the Medu, the forward patrols return with news that the old Roman fortress at Robriwis still stands empty.

"What kind of fool is this Wortimer?" muses Hengist, smoothing his moustache. "A dozen men on those walls would hold us for a week."

"Maybe he thinks it would make him seem weak," I say. "His father never saw the need to man those walls, even against the sea raiders."

"Or he's just too arrogant to think us a threat," says Odo.

"Wodan is with us," says Hengist. "If it's like this all the way to Londin, we will reach it in no time." He looks ahead. "This is a good place to camp for the night," he says, pointing to a meadow on the outskirts of a small town nestled in the shadow of the fortress.

I know this spot well — it's where Rhedwyn and I shared our "reading lessons" not long ago. The memory stings my heart and my loins. She is not with us today; Hengist forbade her from joining the march: "One risky escapade is enough. No need to tempt the gods twice."

The people of the small town, having fled at our approach, return warily in the morning and, seeing we haven't plundered their empty homes, send out a delegation of nobles to check why we have come in such a great force, and so far from Tanet. Hengist sends me out to greet them.

"The Iutes are not our enemies," I tell the delegates. "All they want is justice. *Dux* Wortimer attacked the family of their chieftain, unprovoked. Any of you would do the same."

"You say '*our*'," one of them replies, "and you say '*they*', but aren't you a Iute yourself?"

He steps forward and attempts to stare me down. Most of these people have never seen a Iute, even though we're still in Cantish territory. But the richest of them must have been guests at Worangon's and Wortigern's courts many times. I search for familiar faces in the group, but don't spot any that I could put a name to.

I stare back at the first one. This is no time for self-doubt. "I am Fraxinus of Ariminum, son of Pascent, brother of Father Fastidius of Saint Paul's," I say. "I am as much a Briton as you are."

This seems to calm him and the others down. They murmur among each other. "Why are they here?" they ask. "Are they leaving soon?"

"They are leaving tomorrow," I reply first, to ease their worries. "And are headed for Londin, to demand an apology from Wortimer."

My explanation is met with guffaws of laughter and disbelief. "An *apology* from Wortimer? The man never said sorry to anyone in his life!"

"Nevertheless, they will be firm in their request."

"He'll have their heads off!"

I step back and invite the nobles to examine the camp sprawled under the fortress walls, and assess the size of the Iutish *fyrd*. Some, I notice by the scars on their hands and military belts at their waists, are veterans from the days of Rome. They must realise we stand a good chance of destroying Wortimer's militia in the field — if we manage to make him leave the safety of the capital's Wall.

The delegates huddle together again, and then their leader leans forward and speaks to me in a quiet voice:

"What would they do if they got what they wanted from Wortimer?"

"They would return to Reculbium, to their wives and children, satisfied," I say, and then add, as that's clearly what worries him: "They will not harm anyone in this town, of that I assure you. However…" I look to the camp and an impish thought occurs to me. Leaving the town with nothing would seem *too* noble, too suspicious.

"… they *have* grown hungry and thirsty on the way…"

"Oh, of course!" His face brightens in relief. This is a situation he's familiar with, an army on the march demanding provisions. "I understand. Say no more."

The nobles rush out and a few hours later return with carts of more food and ale than we can eat.

We put some of it away for the victory feast.

I realise, with some surprise, I'm in no mood for another battle. I've had enough blood and glory in the North to last me a lifetime. Now, I'm perfectly happy to let the others earn their share — I would much rather be back in Reculbium, romping in the sheepskins with Rhedwyn, than here in these midge-infested marshes, sharpening my *seax* against a smooth stone fallen off the ruined wall of some Roman watchtower.

This is not how a Iute warrior would think. For them, there seems to be no such thing as *too much* fighting. They may have been peaceful peasants, talented craftsmen or romantic poets back on Tanet, but once they became part of a *fyrd*, everything changed. War and death is all they sing about, what they write their poems about, all they live and train for, all they dream of; there are no heroes other than warriors, no greater ambition than to die in battle, or win enough plunder and glory to be immortalised by a *scop's* song. And now, at long last, they may have a chance to fulfil those dreams.

Our patrols inform us that Wortimer, having finally gathered the courage to march out against us, has set up his defences on the western shore of the River Crei, near a place the Romans called, unimaginatively, the New Market. Once, this used to be a thriving station town on the road to Dorowern, serving as a market place for the *villas* settled along the meandering, brackish rivers of this damp, low-lying, land; now, with so many of the properties abandoned and the trade diminished to a phlegmatic trickle, it has been reduced to a hamlet clustered around a couple of inns and the rubble of an old Roman bridge, serving merely as a marker for the ford.

It is at this ford that we will be trying to force our way through the Briton army. It would have been better for us to meet in the open field, but not even Wortimer — or rather, whoever is really in command of his forces — is foolish enough to try this.

As our *fyrd* prepares for the battle, I entertain myself imagining the arguments at Wortimer's court preceding his departure. Leaving the walls of Londin is madness: he could hold out in the city for weeks, waiting for reinforcements from Ambrosius. In four centuries since the Iken War, no enemy has breached its walls, and it is highly unlikely our handful of armed farmers, with no siege weapons or even boats to cross the Tamesa with, could do them any harm.

But Fastidius guessed Wortimer's character right. We both knew how brash and arrogant he was, and how little regard he had for the "barbarians". Fastidius's role in the entire plan was to play on this very arrogance. As soon as the news of the Iute *fyrd* reached Londin, using their connections in the city, Fastidius, Deneus and Postumus started spreading gossip and rumour to counter Wortimer's own web of deceit; they diminished the strength of the Iute army, they accused him of relying too much on Ambrosius's soldiers — a charge obvious to anyone who saw where things in the city were going — and finally, they goaded him into leaving Londin, reminding him that shutting himself within its walls was just the kind of calm and measured — and cowardly — response to the crisis his *father* would have chosen. Nothing roused Wortimer's anger more than comparing him unfavourably to the *Dux*.

Judging from the messages I received from Caesar's Market, the task was easier than we expected. The Councillors may have sworn loyalty to the new *Dux* under threat of force, but once they sensed blood, they quickly returned to their old ways. Some of the courtiers picked up on our warmongering and started spreading it themselves, seeing a chance of ridding themselves of the young usurper, or at least weakening him through humiliation in battle, and thus strengthening their own position. Soon all of Londin was buzzing; the crowd demanded action, the townsfolk wanted to see pagan blood flow down the Tamesa.

It was all too much for Wortimer. Trapped between his own ambition and courtly intrigue, he made the only decision he saw possible. He would meet the Iute band head on, and show the people of Britannia that the pagans could still be defeated by Christian arms, with or without Ambrosius's help.

And he doesn't seem to be starting badly at it, either. Since dawn, his soldiers have been preparing to meet the *fyrd* on the western shore of the ford. There are some veterans among this rag-tag band, who help set up a decent imitation of a *fulcum* shield wall along the high bank. I recognise some of them from the battle at the beach — their loyalties bound to the seat of the *Dux*, rather than the person sitting on it.

Archers are set on either of the shield wall's flanks, and behind it, deeper in the back, a second line of defence, made of older, better trained militiamen. There is tactical thought in all this that I know was not born in Wortimer's mind. I suspect who is the real strategist today: just like at Saffron Valley, it must be *propraetor* Brutus, the commander of Wortimer's cohort.

I observe it all with growing doubt. Our warriors will need to wade across the ford, and climb the high shore, all under arrow fire, and though we outnumber Wortimer's forces, the outcome of the battle is far from certain.

We are all pagans here, about to fight a Christian host; other than Aelle's attack on the forest church, I have never taken part in a battle with such clearly defined sides, not at Saffron Valley, not at the Iken beach. According to everything I've been taught in my youth, this is not a fight we, demon worshippers, can win. But the Iutes believe otherwise.

All through the night, they have been making sacrifices to Donar, their God of War, just as the opposite shore shone with candlelight and rang out with psalms. What if, at the end of the day, it all comes down to which god is stronger? Which one rewards his followers with more victories? What if we chose the wrong god — what if *I* chose a wrong one? The memory of sorrowful, sombre Christ staring down at me from the mosaic at Saint Paul's fills me with greater awe and dread than the visions of Wotan and Donar I've had at the pagan ceremonies. But visions and mosaics alone can't win wars… *can they?*

And if the outcome of the battle is to be decided only by the quality of men on either side, can we truly depend on our superiority? The Iute *fyrd* is a great unknown. Never in a generation has there been such a host of Iutes, from all clans and families, gathered under one chieftain. Will they heed the orders — will they fight in formation, or will they just rush headlong, to be slaughtered like the barbarians the Britons believe them to be?

And what of our commanders? I know nothing of Hengist's prowess as a general; I don't even know if he's gained his position through his skill in battle, or through his cunning and talent in tribal politics. The songs I've heard sung about him at the feasts told of how he led men to fight in Frisia and the land of Danes, but those were skirmishes between barbarian clans, not a war with a Roman-trained army. We've put all our trust in Fastidius's tactical brilliance, but he's barely more than a boy; he may have read all the wise books, and come up with successful tactics against the Picts — but Brutus might well be his equal, if not better. He's got far more experience and training than Fastidius. He's already shown he knows what he's doing, by setting up the cohort in a strategically advantageous position, and in an advanced formation… This isn't just a band of roughs we're facing today. I look to Hengist — he watches the preparations on the other side with a furrowed brow, stroking his chin absentmindedly. This is not a good sign; he must be just as worried about our prospects as I am.

His eyes meet mine, and he nods.

"It's time."

I leave his side and sneak away, along the reeds and brambles which grow thick on this side of the Crei. Behind me, the *fyrd* bursts into a war song and moves out, two hundred and thirty men determined to win or die. But I don't look back. I race half a mile upstream, until I reach a bend in the river, where the current slows down and the stream grows wide and shallow enough for me to wade across. The water is crystal clear as I pass, the chalk sand glistening like silver at the bottom; I can't hear the sounds of battle anymore, or any human noise at all, only the wood sparrows chirping in the old oak tree and sheep bleating in the distance; I stop midstream, and I'm struck by the silence ringing in my ears. For a moment, I feel like nothing we humans concern ourselves with matters: the battle, the politics, the intrigues, the glory… Only the beauty of this empty, immaculate land, of its green meadows, its winding streams under the azure sky, its birds, singing in the bushes, unaware of the slaughter happening so near…

Then I remember why I came here, and climb out the other side, wet as an otter.

CHAPTER X
THE LAY OF HAESTA

The sound of the *fyrd* mass smashing against the Briton shield wall is like that of a rolling thunderclap, the sound of lightning striking a great oak, hewing it in twain. Every man in the Iutish army is driven by only one desire: to kill an enemy in battle, or otherwise to die slain himself; either of which will grant him the seat at Wodan's feast table.

The Iutes push, bite, tear and hack for a time, before the horn calls them away from the shields. Many can't heed its beckon: they lie in the Crei, lifeless, their blood staining the river pink. They've made no dent in Wortimer's line. The horn sounds again, and again the Iutes strike, a wave of limbs and blades gnawing at the cliff of shields.

Beadda grunts. He takes one last glance at his *Hiréd.* Those who returned from the war with the Picts ferried across the Tamesa in secret a few days before, to meet with fresh recruits, sent from Tanet to replenish their numbers after the recent losses; there are new, young, green faces among the twenty; some of them not much older than myself. They are the best trained and equipped warriors in Hengist's army, but without the battle experience of those who they came to replace, all their training may yet prove for nothing.

In the morning, they all forded the Crei far downstream, out of sight — we hope — of Wortimer's spies. This is one ruse that was not part of Fastidius's plan; he's too far away, still in Caesar's Market, to manage such minute details of the battle. Odo, ever the cavalry officer, was the one who came up with the flanking manoeuvre — and I, the only one knowing this part of Wortigern's domain well enough, proposed the hiding spot, a thick clump of gnarled yews on a hill that drew my attention when we were travelling this way with Rhedwyn. To my surprise, Hengist trusted me enough not only to choose the location on which depended the entire outcome of the battle, but also to deliver the signal to attack. I'm hoping I can repay this trust today.

Beadda raises his sword, and we sprint out of the yews. Five hundred feet of uneven, sloping pasture separates us from the rear of Wortimer's army, and it's the longest five hundred feet in my life, as we run across the meadow, first in silence, then, as the henbane soars through the Iute veins, raising as fierce a battle cry as our throats can muster, to terrify and confuse the unexpecting enemy. We spread out. We must strike fear into their hearts before they realise how few of us there are. They must believe themselves trapped between two hordes of bloodthirsty barbarians. They must think the battle is lost before it begins in earnest…

I search for Wortimer, knowing he'd be here, in the rear of his forces, hiding behind his men, rather than in the fray at the river side, but I can't find him. Instead, I spot a tall officer, wearing an old, tattered red cloak with a purple trim, and a plumed legionnaire's helmet. I can't see his face yet, but I'm certain it's Brutus. He's one of the first to notice the approaching *Hiréd*. He shouts an order at the men nearest to him and rallies them to his side. Most are plain militia, like the ones fighting on the riverbank, but I see a few more veterans among them, all wearing the eagle armbands signifying their allegiance. They gather around him in a half-circle, spears forward, ready to face the enemy.

I call on Beadda, trying to draw his attention to the threat on his flank, but it's too late — the *Hiréd*, drunk on henbane wine, ignore me and their commander. They charge ahead, aiming for a rearguard, defending the approach to the riverbank. They sweep the Britons before them in a flurry of blood and hacked-off limbs. I hit a few fleeing enemies at random, but once again I'm too slow to keep up with the main assault of the frenzied Iutes. The rearguard falls quickly aside, opening the way to the backs of those fighting on the shore.

Just then, Brutus leads his men to an attack from the flank. Its sudden force catches the Iutes unawares. The militiamen are not supposed to fight with such fierceness and skill. The *Hiréd* waver — those in front of the charge are still hacking away at the Briton rearguard, the others turn to face the new threat. A gap appears in their ranks which, I'm sure, the commander as experienced as Brutus is bound to exploit.

I slow down and pull away from the brawl. I wipe blood off my *seax* and sheathe it; instead, I weigh the spear in my hand. The shaft is new, a length of good Cantiac ash re-forged by a Iutish blacksmith at Reculbium to fit my height and heft, but the blade is still the same trusty Anglian leaf, created for me by old Weland.

Fifty feet. Not a problem in training, but this isn't training; this is the heat of the battle. Arrows and slingshots whizz around my head, my palm is slippery with sweat. I can't get any closer or the archers will get me… But I can't miss. Killing random Briton militiamen will not get my name into the song of this battle — I will never surpass the Iute warriors' prowess in hand-to-hand combat; but this might just get me there. This is my chance at glory, this is my chance to repay the trust Hengist put in me — and to earn

Rhedwyn's admiration and, perhaps, love. I feel the same rush that drives all Iutes on the field heat up my veins, even though I haven't drunk the henbane. In that one moment, everything around me slows down. My breath grows steady and my grip on the shaft tightens.

I take aim and let the dart fly. It slips from my hand and misses my intended target, striking the Briton commander on the left shoulder instead of his chest. He falters. For a second I fear it's not enough, as he raises his right arm to give another order. Then he falls mid-shout and disappears from my sight.

I let out a roar of triumph, but there's no one there to hear it.

An arm clad in purple cloth reaches for the spear. Wortimer rips it out of the commander's body. The officer moans and stirs, waking from shock, reaches to stem the bleeding in his shoulder. Wortimer ignores him. He studies the Anglian blade, then looks up to search for me on the battlefield.

He orders his remaining bodyguards to join the battle, which by now has moved further upstream. The counterattack faltered without Brutus's command, and now the battle has turned into a chaotic, splashing brawl in the middle of the Crei current, with the Briton line pushed off the high bank and into the water, where they became trapped between the *fyrd* and the *Hiréd*. Their defeat is not yet inevitable — a skilled captain could still turn it around. But Wortimer no longer cares about the battle, and his soldiers look for his guidance in vain. His attention is focused solely on me. He shortens the distance between us in purposeful steps. I draw my *seax* and throw the sheath into the grass. He does the same with his Roman *spatha*, and stops just out of sword range.

"So, you've decided to add murder to the list of your crimes," he says. "I'm afraid you've failed in this, too."

"He is an enemy commander."

"Brutus is a Roman officer," he snarls. "A Christian. He was your Master's companion at arms, a centurion in Wortigern's palace guard. A loyal servant of the Council. I knew you'd eventually choose to stand against us. Once a Saxon…"

"I'm a Briton, just like you," I interrupt him. "Loyal to *Dux* Wortigern, whom you betrayed."

He sneers, sensing the lack of confidence in my voice. *Am I?* Few of Wortigern's loyalists have joined our cause; most preferred enduring a Briton usurper — or, at best, working to undermine him from within — over openly siding with the barbarians. There are no Britons fighting on the side of the Iutes, other than myself and Fastidius; I know Fastidius is doing this because of his devotion to me, his last remaining kin — and because he truly believes Wortimer would be a bad *Dux* if allowed an unchecked rule. But why am *I* here…?

"The old man had it coming. He's grown weak and senile in his old age. He started fraternising with your pagans. Giving land to barbarians? Making a Iute into a Councillor?" He scoffs. "What an abomination! All true Romans knew he had to go, and there was only one man in Londin brave enough to do it."

The speed with which Wortimer spits out these accusations betrays how much these woes must have been gnawing on him. Though there is nothing surprising about his hatred of the Saxons and Iutes, I'm intrigued to learn that my presence at Wortigern's court was so high on the list of reasons that spurred him into taking action against his father. Did my position help him rally the other Councillors around him? I never noticed any other courtiers sharing Wortimer's loathing, but perhaps I just didn't know how to look…

"Your *true Romans* have just been handed their sorry bottoms by the Iutes," I note, sourly.

He looks over his shoulder. The battle in the stream is nearing its end. One by one, his militiamen break away from the line and flee into the muddy fields. The flanks still hold, protected by the archers, but once the centre falls, they, too, will have to save themselves or face annihilation.

Wortimer turns back, his face red with shame and fury. "Enough talk," he says. "Let's finish this once and for all. There'll be no one to save you this time."

He adopts the ancient Roman stance, just like in the amphitheatre, holding the sword high by his head, the purple cloak wrapped around his left arm in place of the shield. But if he thinks I'll give him a formal duel, he's got another think coming.

"I don't need saving from you!" I cry and, mid-word, I lunge forward and down, avoiding his thrust by a hair's breadth. I grab him around the waist and bring him to the ground as his blade tears through my right shoulder — skin, muscle and tendon. He drops his sword and it flies out of his reach. He launches a barrage of punches, each blow landing squarely at my stomach and liver, a mark of a well-trained pugilist. We wrestle some more before I disentangle myself from his grabbing arms. I raise the *seax* in both hands and aim at his neck. He flails his hand and a ringed fist reaches my nose. Blinded with pain I stab down, but miss; the blade of my sword sinks into wet clay with a squelch. He grabs me by the neck and chokes me.

"You… even… fight… like a barbarian," he seethes through clenched teeth. "Without honour…"

"You know nothing about honour!"

I hit at the inside of his elbows and tear his hands from my throat. Scrambling up, I knee him in the groin. I roll away, slashing blindly. The tip of my sword cuts through flesh. Wortimer howls and throws sand in my face. I slash again, this time the blade whistles in the air.

A javelin flutters through the air and tears the ground between us. I rub the sand from my eyes just in time to see Brutus help Wortimer up from the ground. They both limp away, leaving a bloody trail in the mud, to join their men fleeing across the flat meadow.

Hengist forbids us from rushing straight after the panicked militiamen. The Iutes may have emerged victorious, but they are exhausted from the day of heavy fighting. If Wortimer — or rather, Brutus — has left any troops in reserve between Crei and Londin, we would be easy prey in our current state.

The *fyrd* climbs the tall bank and halts there to rest, to count our dead and tend to the wounded. I wrap my cut shoulder with a piece of torn cloth. I see Beadda approach me, holding half of the broken shaft of my *aesc.*

"There's a good amount of blood on the blade," he says. "A fine shot."

I consider telling him of having felled the enemy commander with it, but with no witnesses, it would seem like a baseless boast. Instead, I just mumble thanks as I reach for the weapon. I realise the injustice of fate; nobody will ever know what I did in this battle. All my glory is between me and the gods, watching from their heavenly halls.

"The edge is still sharp," Beadda says. "All you need is a new length of ash wood."

"I think I've finally outgrown it."

While we wait for our reserves to pull up from Reculbium, a small band of warriors gathers on the road around a young clan leader, who's riding a handsome bay pony. Judging by their bloodstained tunics and heavily notched blades, they took part in the heaviest of fighting, though they seem mostly unharmed and eager to keep fighting.

"What's going on?" I ask Beadda.

"They say they will march after the Britons whether the *Drihten* orders them to or not," he replies with a glower.

"We're tired of waiting," the young clan leader cries. "We're letting the Britons get away!"

"You've had enough glory for one day, Haesta," says Beadda. He comes up to the pony and holds on to the reins. "If Hengist says we stay, we stay."

"Hengist is a coward!"

"Hengist fought battles before you were born, boy."

"Then maybe it's time he let someone else do the fighting!"

Haesta kicks the flanks of his pony, and the beast rears, tearing the reins out of Beadda's hands. He rides westwards, followed by what has now become more than twenty young warriors.

"Let them go," says Hengist. "They'll never learn otherwise."

"Who is he?" I ask.

"A cousin of mine," replies Hengist. "His father fought with me in Frisia, arrived on the same boat as I did. Brashness of youth." He shakes his head. "Everywhere the same problem."

I remember the name now: he was the young warrior seeking support to topple Hengist's rule earlier in the summer. Is he one of those who resented my rise at Hengist's side? Have I now, inadvertently, caused a rift at *two* courts?

No, it's not about me, I realise as Haesta disappears beyond the horizon. It's about what I am. I can't think of anything I have done that deserves any of the power and privilege I was given, neither by Wortigern, nor by Hengist —

other than being a Iute raised into a Briton family of some merit. It is a mere accident of fate that's turned me into a useful pawn in their politics.

At midnight, Haesta returns, without a pony, and with only a handful of the young warriors. He goes back to his tent without a word, but we gather enough from his companions to know that the *Drihten* was proven right: a reserve unit of city guards and Wall sentries intercepted them just a mile up the road from our camp.

"We fought long and hard," one of the youths boasts. "And in the end, we sent them fleeing back to Londin."

"But you lost so many that you couldn't continue the pursuit," grunts Beadda.

"If the entire *fyrd* was with us, we'd have prevailed with ease."

"And then we would get slaughtered at the next ambush. Go to your tent and have a good rest. You're not going anywhere tomorrow. We'll conquer Londin without you."

"But — "

"Go!" Beadda snarls. I don't think I've ever seen him so angry. Like any good commander, he hates seeing young lives lost needlessly.

In the morning, we are joined not only by the reserves from Reculbium, but by Fastidius and Dene, coming by boat from Caesar's Market. Along the way, they picked up crucial news: Wortimer, who at first settled in a fortified camp halfway between us and Londin to face us again in the open field, changed his mind at dawn, left his troops under Brutus's command — and with a handful of his closest courtiers is now rushing towards Londin.

"You must reach the city before them," says the *Drihten*. "We will lay siege to Brutus's camp, to hold them back."

Only Odo's cavalry horses can hope to catch up to Wortimer. Fastidius and I mount up alongside him and we canter onwards as fast as our skills allow — the beasts themselves could run even faster under a good rider, but I can barely hold onto the reins as it is. Soon we reach another Briton barricade; I tighten my grip and clench my thighs, and with half-closed eyes I let my horse do what it wills, hoping it's smarter than its rider. Following Odo's cue, the horse leaps over the fences and the spears of the defenders. As its hooves hit the ground on the other side, I almost fall off. Odo slows down to hold me up and help me back into the saddle, and we charge on again, followed by feeble whooshes of arrows let out by Brutus's confused archers.

Despite our neck-breaking pace, I fear there's little chance for us to catch up to Wortimer. As we slow down to a quick trot to let the horses catch some breath, I make the calculations in my head. There's thirteen miles between Crei and the Bridge; it will take us at least two hours to cover that distance, if we don't want to kill our mounts — and ourselves. If Wortimer set out at dawn, even on foot, it couldn't have taken him more than four hours to reach the city gates…

Nobody stops us from entering the Bridge. The checkpoints are empty, the guards having either been pressed into Wortimer's army, or abandoned their posts in fear of the approaching Iute horde. The silence is disturbing; the Bridge, always a rushing torrent of men and beasts of burden, has never been this quiet. It's as if the city has been stricken by a plague.

I rub my eyes, glued together from lack of sleep. From a distance, I can see that we're too late. The gates of Londin are closed shut, the *ballistae* armed and aimed — but not at us; the tips of their death-dealing bolts point at a small group of men huddled in the shadow of the Wall: Wortimer and his loyal courtiers.

Wortimer sees us, grabs a sword from one of his courtiers — his own *spatha* still lying in the trampled grass on the banks of the Crei — and turns against us, his back to the gate. I dismount and move forward, drawing my *seax* at him.

"Give up, Wortimer," I say. "All your men are slain or scattered. You've lost."

The courtiers try to stop him, but he shoves them away and charges at me with a wordless growl, fiercer and more desperate than the day before. His assault falters as his injured leg gives out and I manage a dodge. He pivots with a wild roar, in time to parry my blow. He presses on, blade against blade. My shoulder explodes with pain — the wound he gave me yesterday is deeper than I thought. I make three steps backwards, parrying all the time, until my back hits against the rail. My sword arm grows numb. There's madness in Wortimer's eyes which fuels his strength like henbane wine. The grinding blades inch ever nearer to my face with each blow. I glance to my left — Beadda and Odo are nearing me with spears in their hands, but are wary of the *ballistae* staring at them menacingly from the Wall.

"Stop this insanity, Wortimer!"

I look up to find the source of the voice: it's *Dux* Wortigern, standing atop the gatehouse in full regalia, the jewel-studded diadem gleaming brightly on his head, surrounded by a remnant of the palace guards. Next to him stands Postumus and a few other loyal courtiers.

"Shut up, Father!" Wortimer cries back. There is a dramatic change in him when he sees the *Dux*. His eyes darken, his face contorts in a grimace of conflicting emotions — fear, shame, anger, remorse… His entire body shrinks, slouches. "Why do you *always* have to side with that slaveling over me?"

"You have so much to learn yet, son. You are not ready."

Wortimer bites his lips. For a moment his pressing onslaught on me slackens. I shove with all my remaining strength and push him away — just enough for Beadda to grab him from behind in a tight, unclenching grip. Wortimer's sword slips from his hand and clangs on the bridge boards.

"Come back home," Wortigern pleads, not like a ruler to a mutinous subject, but like a concerned father to a wayward son. "There is plenty we need to talk about."

James Calbraith

PART 2: 447 AD

CHAPTER XI
THE LAY OF CLODIO

Slow, heavy petals fall quietly on the rotting heads stuck on the spears at the entrance to the Bridge.

In the old Iute country, I was told, it often snowed all through the winter; here, it is a rare sight, even in the middle of January. The petals melt before they hit the wooden boards, leaving only a slick, slippery layer of not-quite-ice. The snow smothers everything in a dozy silence. Even the usual crowd moving back and forth along the Bridge slows down to stare at the spectacle in awed stillness — and there isn't much that can make these people stand and watch.

They certainly pay no attention to the impaled heads; not anymore. By now, months after the coup's failure, the elements and the carrion crows have reduced the sad remnants of Wortimer's closest loyalists to little more than bare skulls, with scraps of flesh and patches of hair still holding the same way the courtiers clung on to Wortimer to the very end, even after the disaster at the Crei.

The old *Dux* has been more thorough and ruthless than his son in the purge, proving himself, even in this, the more effective ruler. Nearly a third of the Council has been removed from Londin, and not just to their *villas* in the outskirts, but banned from Wortigern's domain altogether, their property confiscated to refill the city coffers, empty after the costly few weeks of Wortimer's rule.

The harsh measures provoked a show of outrage and condemnation from Bishop Fatalis — but neither he nor anyone else could do anything to stop Wortigern's revenge. With the Iute *fyrd* at its southern gates, and Ambrosius's legionnaires at its western borders, Londin was terrified into submission. If anything, Wortimer's untimely coup helped his father grasp the reins of power stronger than ever before.

I pass under the spiked heads and through the armed checkpoint. The guards nod me through. They know me well — I'm one of the few Iutes still tolerated in the city. The townsfolk, whatever their loyalty to Wortimer, took badly the defeat at the River Crei. They never thought of the Iutes as a threat before — they either loathed them or pitied them as refugees; but the battle has changed all that. Many families lost their best in that river; fifty of Wortimer's cohort, young sons of noble pedigree, perished in the cold current. Between the battles with the Iutes and the Picts, Wortigern's veteran guard have been all but vanquished. The Iutes are no longer welcome within the city walls; they are a terror to be feared, like all the other barbarians.

The mood is different in the countryside. I am returning from the Yule feasts in Beaddingatun. Far from Londin's problems, the *Hiréd* and their families have been celebrating a year of bounty and glory, of fine harvest and great victories, over Picts and Britons. They drank mead in memory of the fallen, and winter ale to cheer the births of a multitude of plump newborns, whose giggles and gurgles rang out throughout the village — a sound rarely heard in the streets of Londin. They sacrificed pigs and ducks to the gods to ensure the next year will be as fruitful as the last, and they shared their salted meats, cheeses and breads with the people of Saffron Valley, and the labourers of Ariminum, who have by now grown used to coming over to take part in the pagan festivities before their own, Christian feasts of Lord's Birth and Epiphany. The Yule celebrations stirred in them a memory of their own pagan rituals, which the eldest in the village may have still remembered from their childhood. It was only the watchful eye of Paulinus, observing the festivities from his stone church across the graveyard, that prevented them from fully immersing themselves in the rites.

As I sat among the mirthful men of the Iute settlement, I felt a peace which I haven't felt in a long time. These people were as close to a family as I could hope for, with the exception of Fastidius and Paulinus. They were my kin, my tribe; I fought beside them, shared their glory; I mourned and cheered with them. I hadn't realised when I started longing for this settled, familiar life, away from the bustle of the city and the intrigues of the courtly politics. Is this what made Master Pascent move to Ariminum, to abandon his place at the Council in exchange for the simple pleasures of the countryside?

The odd longing passes as soon as I enter the city gates. I am not old enough to settle in a country *villa* just yet. Londin is my home as much as Ariminum, if not more. What is Ariminum, but an empty ruin, grown over with vine, a memory of something that no longer exists? Londin is here to stay; its mad crowds will be forever rushing about the broad avenues, hither and thither, seemingly aimless but always purposeful. I may be just a tiny cog in this ever-spinning Archimedean machine, but *what* a machine it is! Isn't it better to be a small cog here, than a great mill stone in some desolate hamlet?

As I stride down Cardo Street towards my rooms at the Bull's Head, I choose not to see the glances of fear and distrust thrown towards me by the passing townsfolk. It's only temporary, I tell myself. Soon they will forget why they didn't like the fair-hairs in the first place, and the Iutes and Saxons will return. Life in Londin moves too fast for anyone to dwell on past grudges for long.

The palace gardens feel more empty and quieter than they ever have before. Not only are there fewer courtiers, but also fewer guards — many have perished in the battle at the Crei Ford, and many more vanished after the defeat, fearing Wortigern's retribution.

One of those banished was the last of the *Praetorium's* gardeners. In his absence, the unkempt vines have overgrown the cracked ruins of the pond, the grass turned dull yellow in the summer, and then grey and dead through the cold days, weeds choked the flowers. At least the starlings and sparrows enjoyed the unfettered vegetation while it was there, but it's winter now and all fled away to the coast.

There's no reason for anyone to come down to the gardens anymore. I'm only here today to remind myself of the times spent with Rhedwyn. I haven't seen her in a long time — too long. Her uncle keeps her away from Londin, and I can't blame him — the city's no longer safe for her, or any of her kin.

I sense a presence in the garden. It's Wortimer, standing on the other side of the pond, looking forlornly at the Tamesa, upstream, towards the setting sun. Somewhere out there, on Wortigern's western border, a powerful Briton army once stood, waiting for the turn of events in Londin, waiting to hear that the city gates were open, the population subdued, and they were welcome to march in support of the new regime. It never happened. In the end, all that Ambrosius could send were missives assuring Wortigern of his peaceful intentions and congratulating the *Dux* on his successful reinstatement. The army, claiming to only have been gathered to defend the border region from any disturbance following the coup, returned to the West, joined by the guards who served in the city in Wortimer's employ. That was the final, bitter act of Wortimer's coup, his ultimate, utter defeat: not even those he looked up to and depended on the most wished to have anything to do with his endeavour. Ambrosius was far too shrewd a politician to associate himself with a failure.

He turns — our eyes meet. I don't expect him to speak. There's nothing either of us could say to one another. He has grown to accept, grudgingly, my continued presence at the court —and I have consented to the surprising leniency of his punishment. Or perhaps it was not surprising after all. He is still Wortigern's only son and heir; as I told Rhedwyn, one day he *will* rule this city rightfully — and there will be nothing anyone will be able to do to prevent it. The *Dux* could only have humiliated him so much for what many saw as simply hastening the fate.

He was suspended from the Council. The command of his militia — what was left of it — was taken from him. And, as a final insult, given the office of city sewers to command for a year; but that was all. By Epiphany, he returned to the Council table. It was easy to forget the coup had ever taken place.

"I hear you'll be visiting my former property in the spring," he says. His voice is colder than the winter breeze flowing from the river.

This was to be the most painful of Wortimer's punishments. Yielding to the Iute law, Wortigern ordered him to pay the *wergild* for Hengist's slain men out of his own purse — and, when that wasn't enough, with his own land. Thus, the Iutes have gained another patch of land to settle, on the west bank of Medu, across the river from Robriwis. In exchange, they are obliged to man the old fortress and guard the old Roman ford.

"Your father sends me as peace envoy to the Iutes," I reply. "Somebody needs to clean up the mess you've started."

He scowls. "I'm well aware of that."

"So what do you want from me?"

His face smooths out, almost mellows. But his eyes stay narrow and cruel. "Why can't you just stay there?" he says, seeping poisonous honey from his lips. "Wouldn't you be better off living among your own kind — now that they no longer live like the animals they are?"

I run my fingers through my hair to stop my fist from clenching. I will not let myself be provoked. My position at the court is tenuous as it is; only the loyalty shown during the coup prevented me from being expunged with the rest of the Iutes. Wortimer still has enough secretive supporters in the palace to have me thrown out at the smallest sign of mutiny, and with Fastidius and the Bishop out of the city on a diplomatic mission, I would have no one to defend me.

"Let's not go through this again," I say with a trained sigh.

He stares at me, gauging my reaction.

"You will *never* be like me," he seethes, sounding as if he's finishing some other conversation he's had with someone else.

Seeing he won't get anywhere further with me tonight, he moves back towards the palace. As he limps past me, he pats me on the shoulder — right on the scar from the wound he give me. I grit my teeth not to hiss with pain. "Be careful on the road, *Fraxinus*," he says, mockingly pronouncing my Roman name, "the bandits may be gone, but it's still a dangerous route at this time of year."

The waters of the Crei are calm and ice-cold as they wash under the belly of my horse. This far from the city's stoves and furnaces, it's still the heart of winter, even though we're deep into Lent; patches of snow scattered in the fields shroud the bitter, frozen earth. Across the ford, south of the Roman road, rises a low mound topped with a stone cross. The Briton casualties from the battle are buried there: those whose families didn't pay to have them exhumed and brought to the yard by the Cathedral. A bit further, on the opposite side of the road, stands a second mound, higher and elongated, with no markings. This is the Iute grave.

"Is there nobody left to take care of the Briton dead?" remarks one of the emissaries, accompanying me to the *Drihten's* court to formalise the handing over of Wortimer's property. He glances at the Iute mound with disgust. There are fresh garlands of flowers scattered on its slopes, and the remains of sacrificial beasts in a pit at the bottom, gnawed on by the crows, are no more than a few days old.

"It's a long way from the nearest village," I say.

"It's even longer from the Iute territory," he replies, "and yet, they manage to come here."

He's right: it takes us a couple of hours to reach the outskirts of the new Iute settlement. If it can be called that at all. Built on top of — and in the midst of — an old serf hamlet, it's larger than any of the Iute villages in the South. The homes are built in a mixture of styles — there's the old Briton wattle roundhouse, here a new Saxon timber wall, and between them a Roman brick, gathered from some nearby ruin and shaped into a semblance of a house. I hear just as many, if not more, voices speaking the native Briton speech, in all its many varieties, as Iutish. The people are a mixture of races, too, almost as much as in Londin.

Overlooking all this stew of peoples is the white wreck of an empty *Domus*, jutting out like a broken tooth from a nearby hill. It's not a recent ruin — rather, it seems Wortimer never bothered to maintain it after taking over the *villa* from whoever owned it previously, and simply let it fall apart. I know now where the brick and stone for the village had come from.

I have never seen the Iutes live side-by-side with the Britons like this. Even in Beaddingatun, none of the Saffron Valley folk decided to live permanently among their neighbours. I can see some of the emissaries observe this intermixing with dread. For them, it's a nightmare, this mixing of blood, faith and custom. It's what Wortimer has always warned them about — that one day, it will become impossible to tell a Briton from a Saxon or a Iute, a Roman from a Barbarian, a Christian from a Pagan. But for me, this is a dream come true, the dream I shared with Aelle on the eve of the battle at Saffron Valley.

We reach the Medu River and ferry across its murky waters, towards the Roman fort, its ramparts now manned by a crew of Iutes. A brand-new timber hall, its wood still fresh and damp, stands within the walls of the keep. I lead my horse to the stable and notice the dapple coat ponies of Rhedwyn's retinue are already here.

"You look like an Empress," I note, admiring her new appearance. Her brow is adorned with a delicate band woven of thin silver and golden foil, clasping a wimple of sheer white cloth. She's clad in a tunic of fine Frankish cloth, a gift from Clodio's court, and on her breast lies the necklace from the Pictish hoard.

She laughs. "An Empress of a village." She takes off the wimple and the headband and puts them on the table. She unlaces the top of her tunic, but stops there; we are under the watchful eye of a couple of old women sitting on the other side of the room. Their purpose here is not clear to me yet, but they are doing a good job of unnerving me with their grumpy stares.

"So, are you in charge of this place now?" I ask. "Has Hengist made you the *Gesith*?"

"Me? In charge?" She rolls her eyes. "Remember what I told you about Iutes and their women? Beormund is in charge of the fortress and overall defences — " Beormund, once the chief of the warband that hunted the Pict raiders, won himself great glory by slaying three Britons at the Crei, and was now one of the most prominent warriors in Hengist's tribe. " — but other than that, nobody gets to rule these people. They're mostly Britons anyway, so the only authority they would recognise would be in Londin."

"Where did they all come from? When we passed here with the *fyrd*, there was barely anyone living this side of the river."

As I speak, I realise that whatever Britons still lived along the old Roman road, would've run and hidden from the approaching pagan army anyway.

"Some are serfs of Wortimer, who've always been here. Others moved from Robriwis. A large group arrived in early winter from Cantiaca."

"Why would they leave Cantiaca?" I ask, remembering the lush, fertile hills of the eastern *pagus*.

"They say they no longer feel safe there. Can't say I blame them. Odo's cavalry is not there to protect them. And here, they get to rule themselves, without the *villa* owners lording over them. There are even some runaway slaves."

"I imagine their masters were not happy about it."

"They're welcome to try and get them back."

She grins and reaches for the meat plate. I notice the muscles on her arms under the silk tunic have bulked up in the way they could only have through weapons training. There is nothing left of the fay, shy girl I once knew. It only makes me want her more.

I chuckle, watching her devour a leg of mutton. "Do they not have meat in the South?"

"They slaughtered all their good animals for Yule feast. Now all they're left with are the fish."

She has just returned from a mission to the Regins. Now that the Iutes are no longer beggars confined to a muddy island, Hengist has decided it's time to dabble a little in diplomacy of his own, and not just by receiving emissaries — and who better to send to shower the neighbouring leaders with gifts and flatteries than a princess?

It is one of my tasks as the Councillor to discover what Rhedwyn has found out in the South. In the aftermath of the crisis in Londin, Wortigern's grasp on the four tribes, always tenuous, has slipped altogether. And while a promptly dispatched mission to the North, led by Fastidius and Bishop Fatalis, secured the renewed allegiance of Elasio and his Cadwallons, and Worangon's Cants and Peredur's Trinowaunts were too weakened by the war to resist for long, the *Comes* of the Regins, Catuar, has posted armed guards on his border and refused summons from the court. We have had no real news from New Port since then, other than what rumours the merchants and travellers brought us. No official delegate from Londin ever got as far south as Rhedwyn did.

"Is it true what they say?" I ask. "That Catuar no longer rules in the South?"

"It's just like Aelle told us in the forest — the Saxons are letting him be the figurehead and sign all the edicts with his seal, and deal with the day-to-day bureaucracy. But it's Pefen and the other *Drihtens* on the *witan* who control him."

"And have you seen Pefen himself — or Aelle?"

"There were no Saxon lords in New Port — they stay away from the city, to keep up the pretence of Briton rule. I was offered a journey around the countryside, to see some of the Saxon villages, but I excused myself with a headache and exhaustion... I am just a frail princess, after all," she adds with a coy, pretend smile, then turns serious. "I was glad to leave that place as soon as I could."

"How so?"

"All the time I was there, I sensed they resented my presence. Catuar and his elders all smiled politely when I talked to them, but as soon as they thought I looked away, their faces would turn sour. Others did not even bother to hide their disgust. It was worse than when I was in Londin. There, at least, I was a curiosity, but the Regins just seemed to hate me for no reason."

She shakes her head.

"They hate us because they fear us," I say. "Or rather, the Saxons — but the Britons could never tell the difference between us and them. Did Catuar say why he won't accept any messengers from Londin? Or why the Saxons wouldn't let him answer?"

"I couldn't ask too many questions — I was just there to present gifts from my uncle and introduce myself to Catuar's Council."

"And awe them with your beauty, no doubt," I add. She drops her head and blushes in a studied manner, but soon recovers with a beaming grin. I hear one of the old women in the corner clear her throat.

"Who are *they*?" I ask quietly.

She shakes her head. "Some great aunts of mine. My uncle has them follow me around on this journey and watch over. Now that I'm his official representative, he wants me to *behave* properly. Especially when I'm around handsome lads like you," she adds with a wink.

"And they are with you all the time?"

She lowers her voice to a barely audible whisper. "Not when I'm taking my bath."

"You've grown pudgy," she says with a giggle.

Rhedwyn's right. I have been neglecting my training through winter. I have been telling myself that it's because I was too busy with the court duties, but that's only half of the truth. I've had enough of warfare after the events of the previous year. So many of those who perished in the battles with the Picts and Wortimer's band were people I knew — not friends, maybe, I had very few of those in Londin, but familiar faces from the palace, the city or the Iute settlements. As the war went on, I was able to suppress the weariness, with increasing difficulty. But once peace settled back in, it returned. For weeks the sight of a bloodied blade would make me nauseous. Every time I tried to pick up a sword or a spear, the faces of the dead flashed before my eyes and their dying groans filled my ears.

I can't say any of that to Rhedwyn; I'm certain she'd mock me. Instead I laugh nervously. She's got a good look of my body — as I have of hers; we are both covered with sweat from the herbs-infused steam and the passion we just shared on the straw floor of the bath house. We dare not do anything that would bring the attention of the servant girl, bribed to let me take her place, waiting just outside the wicker door — but it's enough to satiate the first hunger of our bodies.

This is a village bath, built for and by the Briton peasants, which they agreed to share with the Iute newcomers — just a thatched hut, with a wooden tub for one dug into the floor and filled with water boiled on the stove in the corner. Rhedwyn had never seen a functioning Roman bath and as I help her wash her hair I entertain her briefly with the stories from my childhood at Ariminum.

"I've always felt there were so many wonderful things I've missed out on," she says.

"I grew up in the ruins of ancient glory," I reply. "Surrounded by memories of the Empire."

"But at least you got to experience some of it. All I remember from my childhood is mud, cold and hunger."

I feel a pang of guilt — I have always complained about the conditions in which I grew up, but in truth, the fate that threw me overboard spared me the woeful life Rhedwyn and her kin experienced at the same time. I kiss her to hide my shame.

"It's all better now, though," I say. "You're safe here, away from the Tanet mud and the dark sea."

"Why won't you stay here with us, Ash?" she asks all of a sudden. "With me?"

"I — I need to deliver the missives to *Comes* Worangon. It's important news about Wortimer and Rome…"

She scoffs. "You know what I mean. Once you're done with your work. We are your people. This could be your village. Your *home*."

"Somebody else asked me that question a few days ago," I say evasively.

She reaches out to caress my face with a soapy hand. "An Empress needs an Imperator, doesn't she?"

Is she — is she *proposing* to me?

"What would your uncle say to that?"

"I'm sure he'd be delighted. I heard him say you're like a son he's never had."

"Have you told him about us?"

"Not yet. I wanted to know how *you* felt about it at first."

I fall silent. She grows annoyed. It's clear she did not expect me to hesitate — she must not be used to men saying "no" to her.

"Is it because we don't live in houses of stone? Because we don't keep slaves? Because we don't worship your Roman God?"

How can I tell her the truth? That coming to live among the pagans would prove Wortimer was right? That it would mean cutting myself from my past as a Briton — as a

Roman? Yes, I have grown to feel proud of my Iute blood — but I've rarely *felt* Iutish. My father was Master Pascent. Fastidius is my brother. The home I grew up in was a Roman *villa*; I spent my adolescence and adulthood in a Roman palace, among the ruins of a Roman city, surrounded by Britons. Is an accident of birth enough to scratch all of that out? Does the colour of my hair and eyes matter more than my entire life until now?

"I don't know if I'd feel at home here …" I try to explain. "I'm not really — "

"Not really a Iute?"

"Not really a countryside person," I turn it into a joke, but it's futile. She turns away.

"I think you'd better put your clothes on now," she says. "Before the attendant returns."

"We gain one village with each battle we win for you… At this rate, in a hundred years we will take it all!"

Warchief Hengist's jest — translated by me into Imperial tongue — does not land well with the Briton emissaries. To them, the threat is all too real; ill-tidings reached Londin just before our departure.

"It would be good of you not to talk of conquest, *Drihten*," remarks one of the emissaries. "It is no time for such levity. They say pagans have crossed the Rhenum again, and flooded Rome's dominion in Gaul — what's left of it."

"Bacauds have risen in Armorica once again," adds another, "and Franks have been settling on Roman land uninvited. At this rate, Rome itself will be threatened."

"It happened before," says the third, oldest of the courtiers. "And it will happen again." A visible shiver passes through the delegation. The memory of the past chaos, of the war and destruction which engulfed Britannia only a generation ago is still fresh in their minds as if it happened yesterday; the terror, the rebellion, the civil war, it all started with news of Rome's sacking by a barbarian army, brought to Londin by panicked ship crews, fleeing the city's destruction. Ever since then, the townsfolk and the nobles alike have lived in fear of the same happening in Londin.

"We have heard this news also," replies Hengist. "It's a short journey from Reculbium to Frankia. I received an embassy from Clodio of the Franks no more than two weeks ago."

This provokes further murmurs. Accepting foreign embassies is a prerogative of a ruler, not of some tribal chieftain allowed to dwell on somebody's land. This Clodio, whoever he is, should have requested an audience with Wortigern, instead of sending a messenger to Hengist. The shadow of pagan conspiracy again mars our negotiation. Hengist notices he has said too much.

"I assure you, you will never have anything to fear from us," he says. "Look around you! How few we are compared to the Britons, or even the Saxons in the South? How feeble are our forces against the might of Londin's Wall? We only asked for more land so that we could be better equipped to protect you from danger."

He's trying to flatter them with these comparisons, but I can see all this talk of forces and walls only makes the Britons more uncomfortable.

"Your villages are spread like a choke collar all around the city," murmurs one of the courtiers. "And now you've got hold of a fortress that could cut us off from Cantiaca for good. What guarantee can you give us that you will not ally with the Saxons against us? Or the Picts — or those Franks from across the sea?"

Hengist rubs his chin. "I was hoping we could return to our previous arrangement."

The emissaries look at each other.

"I'm not sure one hostage would be enough this time," says the oldest of them, and I realise he means Rhedwyn. Is Rhedwyn going to come back to Londin, then?

"A dozen of our most noble sons and daughters," replies Hengist. "Young enough not to threaten anyone. And my cousin, Haesta."

They murmur and argue among themselves in hushed voices, until eventually, they all nod in agreement. I wish I could tell them about Haesta — but I don't want to say anything that could jeopardise the negotiation. I see what Hengist is trying to do — getting himself rid of the rash youths under Haesta's command, who must be as much of a nuisance to him as Wortimer's roughs were to the *Dux*.

None of this matters to me. Sending Rhedwyn back to Londin would solve one of my problems; I wouldn't have to choose between living with her in a Iutish village and in the capital with other Britons… for a while, at least.

"I will have one condition of my own," Hengist adds, while the emissaries continue discussing the new terms. "Considering everything that happened, I would request that my niece, while she lives in Londin, remained under personal protection of one of your Councillors."

He looks straight at me as he speaks.

"I don't think this will be a problem," says the oldest of the delegates.

"But Wortimer — " interjects another, quietly enough so that only our side can hear him.

"Let the *Dux* deal with his son's rampaging loins," snarls the first one. "By all the saints, we've just had one war with these people, and we barely scraped it through. We can't risk another just so the boy can quench his thirst in a Iute wench's goblet."

He turns back to the *Drihten* and, also glancing towards me, says:

"Peace among honest men pleases the Lord. I'm certain the *Dux* will agree to your terms."

CHAPTER XII
THE LAY OF CATUAR

Old Peredur of the Trinowaunts is, as always, the first to arrive, on the morning of the fifth day after Pascha. The Augustan Highway, down which he comes bobbing in a bronze-plated carriage with a couple of wretched Pictish thralls in tow, is still decorated with flowers and white linen banners left over from Easter celebrations. This has been the first public feast thrown in the city since the Pictish invasion and the coup; even some Iute and Saxon traders were allowed into the city for the occasion, and mingled freely with the crowds of the revellers — all blissfully unaware, or choosing not to be concerned, with the disturbing news coming from the Continent.

The carriages of Worangon and Catuar drive up in front of the palace the next day, one after another; it's been a long time since the latter was last seen in Londin, and I've almost forgotten what he looks like. He is short, bald, with a belly protruding under the robes; his hands are red and sweaty, but there is still enough muscle rippling over all this to remind everyone this man was once an officer in the Legions — if the old military belt and shoulder pin weren't enough. His eyes are swift, and he draws an overall sharper figure than that of Worangon. Wortigern had to use the last of his authority to persuade him to come to this Council, even going as far as ordering the city guards to march up to the border posts of the Regins, in a show of force. They both knew it was a bluff — the *Dux* could not afford another war

— but it was signal enough that Wortigern was not about to tolerate any more defiance from the rebellious *pagus*.

The unfortunate *Comes* of the Cants looks just like I saw him when delivering the summons to Dorowern, a couple of days after leaving Rhedwyn's village: shrivelled, bent, aged by the events of the past year. He supports himself on the shoulders of one of his bodyguards: they are Iutes, and they greet me with a whoop, recognising me from the battle at the Crei Ford. A troop of Saxons also accompanied Catuar, but they were stopped at the city gates, where they remain, gawping at the mighty Wall and the Bridge with their mouths wide open.

Elasio of the Cadwallons appears in the evening, riding his chariot, which brings out a small crowd of onlookers curious of the odd vehicle. His attire and appearance is as striking as the day we met on the crossroads, though he's chosen to dress halfway between the Roman and Briton way, and brought a handful of Briton warriors with him, rather than his *Gewisse* guard. His beard is trimmed, his hair tied on his back, a red cloak and tunic conceal the coat of mail. A gold diadem rests on his head and on his chest hangs a thick silver cross. Without knowing anything about the two, anyone might think that Elasio is the *Dux* and Wortigern, in his plain purple-lined robe, is his subject come to pay the tribute.

It could be taken as a challenge to Wortigern's power, but he chooses to ignore it; until the other chieftains repeat their pledges of allegiance — and it's not certain that they will, especially Catuar — his position is not yet strong enough to make demands. Besides, there are more urgent matters to discuss. Chief among them: the letter to Rome.

It was found hidden in a pile of documents prepared for burning by Wortimer's loyalists. The copy of a parchment sent by the usurper to a certain Aetius, who bears the lofty titles of the Imperator's Protector, *Vir Magnificus* and Supreme Commander of Rome's Legions in Gaul. In all the commotion of recent events it was easy to forget there was still a world beyond Britannia's shores, or that what happened on the Continent, much less in faraway Rome, could ever have any noticeable impact on our lives again. Our merchants do trade with the Franks, our nobles travel to Armorica when they grow weary of life, and there are still Saxon boats appearing off the eastern shores from time to time, but this has been the limit of our interaction with the lands beyond the seas for a while now. What possessed Wortimer to write to this "Aetius", and who is this man who calls himself the Supreme Commander, anyway?

The mention of Aetius's name stirs unease among the Councillors and the nobles. Clearly, they've heard of him before, though none expected to have to care about the man ever again — but to me, he remains a mystery. I didn't even know there were any Roman Legions left in Gaul to command; judging by the speed with which the pagan hordes of the Franks, Goths and Alamanns were pouring over the Rhenum, I presumed all land between Armorica and Italia was already lost. Has there been a resurgence of Roman power any of us failed to notice? And if Aetius is leading his Legions through Gaul — how far away is he from Britannia's shores?

It doesn't escape my attention that Wortigern and the Council are far more concerned with the possibility of an approaching Roman Legion, than they were with the pagan invasion. Yes, there was some effort made to strengthen the coastal defences — part of which was the Iute settlement at

Robriwis — but only the mention of Aetius made the four *Comites* finally decide to get off their backsides and travel all the way to the capital to discuss the threat he posed. I'm sure I can't be the only one in the Council who notices this paradox, but mentioning it out loud could be misconstrued as supporting Wortimer's disgraced faction, and nobody dares to do that — not yet.

Of the four, Worangon and Catuar are the best positioned to know what's going on across the sea, and are asked to report, but first, the letter itself is read out aloud, to Wortimer's shame. His face reddens as the reading progresses, until by the end he resembles an angry beetroot:

"…the barbarians drive us to the sea, the sea drives us to the barbarians; between these two means of death, we are either killed or drowned."

"This sounds more like something Ambrosius would say," Fastidius says quietly. He's been sent to the feast as the Bishop's representative, as he's been many times over these past few months. He is now a Vicar General at the Cathedral, and is broadly assumed to succeed the Bishop himself — provided he restrains himself from engaging in any military adventures in the future.

"I don't believe for a second Wortimer wrote it himself," I agree. "And I doubt anyone else here does. Do you think this plot went all the way to Rome? That Ambrosius and Wortimer coordinated with this *Aetius*?"

"If they did, the Legions would be here by now. At the very least we'd have heard the response… But, let's hear what Catuar has to say about it."

The *Comes* of the Regins stands up heavily. He looks first to Wortimer and stares at him uncomfortably long. There is no love lost between the two, though not knowing their history it's hard for me to discern the reason.

"First of all, yes, the Aetius in question is the same one who suppressed the Bacauds in Armorica ten years ago," he says. "As some of you remember, we feared he would cross the sea and bring us back under the Empire's yoke."

"It was a dark time," says Wortigern, brooding.

"Fortunately, he was distracted by more rebellions in Hispania and South Gaul, and he's been busy dealing with those until now. As far as I can tell, he's still fighting somewhere in Hispania."

"Then he's not coming for us?" asks one of the courtiers nervously.

"Not in person, no. But his Legions *are* nearby. There's a *legate's* camp in Augusta Suessionum. The Romans made peace with the Huns, and are busy pushing back at the Franks' last warring season. With their eastern flank safe, there won't be a better moment to strike at us than now."

Wortigern nods and the *Comes* sits down among hushed murmurs. Rome — sending Legions? He may have as well said an army of dragons has woken up and is flying on Londin. Rome is a myth, a legend, a tale from another generation. It's been nearly forty years since the Council of Britons voted to abandon the Empire, and the Empire never expressed any desire to return the stray sheep to the fold.

"Do we have no spies on the Continent?" somebody asks. "Must we rely on gossip and the testimony of passing merchants?"

"If you're willing to sponsor a network of spies, Caratacus, you're more than welcome," snaps Wortigern. "Though it might do us better if you simply wrote to your rich cousins in Armorica for news."

"I have friends and relatives in Frankia," says *Comes* Worangon. "Rome *is* coming — but not for us. Not at first. Clodio, the Frankish king, is preparing to cross the *limes* in great numbers. Until then, Aetius is bound to be kept busy."

"Clodio?" Wortigern looks to me. "The one who's such friends with the Iute *Drihten*?"

"I wouldn't say *friends*…" I reply. "They've merely exchanged diplomatic pleasantries."

"Hengist wouldn't be planning on sending him some of his men for this… adventure?"

"I know nothing about that. He barely has enough warriors to fulfil his obligations to you, my lord *Dux*."

"Then it appears this… *groan* of yours was premature." Wortigern waves the parchment in his son's face. "Why did you write it, really? Who helped you?"

Wortimer reddens. "It is what it is, Father. There is no subterfuge here, that much I swear. Whether Aetius decides to come or not, it is his own choice." He shrugs. "I don't know why you're making such a fuss about it."

The *Dux* raises his eyes to the ceiling. "Oh, if only Catigern was still alive…" He turns his gaze to us. "It looks, then, that the danger, if coming at all, is still some time away. This gives us time to prepare ourselves."

Elasio scoffs. "You mean ask the Saxons and Iutes to prepare themselves. We all know how little of your troops are left after last year's calamities."

"This is a threat greater than any Pictish raid," says Wortigern. "I'm sure the nobles will agree to spare some of their wealth to keep us from Rome's embrace."

"I'll believe it when I see it," replies Elasio, shaking his braids.

Wortigern leans towards him with a penetrating gaze. "This is serious. I'm counting on *all* of you to provide the men and supplies for this campaign."

"Don't count on us," says Elasio with defiance. "The Ikens and the Coriadaws are still too much of a threat."

"Is it the Ikens you worry about," interjects Catuar, "or that your *Gewisse* will not fight where there's no plunder to take? From what we've heard about the war with Drust, we'd be better off asking the Ikens themselves for help."

Elasio's fist slams the table. "I will not stand such slander! I lost some of my best men on that beach. At least *I* still rule my land, and my *socii* are not running around the woods terrorising the peasants and merchants."

"This is just a foul rumour. Pefen's loyalty is paramount."

"Is it paramount enough to make him fight the Romans for us?" asks Wortigern.

Catuar wrangles his fingers, seeking an answer that would not anger Wortigern further.

"I vouch for the Iutes," I interject, to relieve him from his squirming. "They will always heed our call." It should be Worangon saying that, but it's plain to everyone he holds no control over Hengist's tribe and the hamlets they've settled. Right now, it falls to me represent these people — *my* people — in the Council.

"Well said. And will you vouch for your Saxons, Catuar?"

"They have sworn to protect the shores of Regins, *Dux*. From any enemy."

"I will need more than that," presses Wortigern. "Will they fight Rome if we tell them to?"

I stand up. I can see Fastidius's bewildered stare on me; his hand reaches out to hold me back, but stops inches from the hem of my tunic, as his curiosity wins over caution.

"I will go talk to the Saxons," I say. "They know me — I know them. If I can't persuade them, no one can."

I'm not quite sure why I said it, but somehow, amidst Catuar's meaningless ahm-ing and err-ing, I saw my chance — a chance to show why I deserved to be at this table, to prove myself something more than a mere pawn in Wortigern's play. I know the Regin *Comes* has no power over his Saxons — even if he promised something today, there's no way he could fulfil that promise. Pefen and Aelle have no conflict with Rome, and neither would they be interested in joining an alliance of the *wealas*, something they fear the most. They need to be convinced that heeding Wortigern's call would be to their advantage — and I think I already have an idea of how to do it.

Wortigern looks at Catuar with a raised eyebrow. "You would agree to this?"

"He can't stop me," I say, emboldened by the attention the Council is paying me. "He has no more authority over who gets to enter his borders than I have over the bed bugs crawling on my sheets at the Bull's Head."

A smattering of snickers spreads throughout the hall. Catuar turns dark red and is ready to burst, when Wortigern silences him with a stiff gesture. "Don't get *too* angry with the boy, Catuar. We've all heard the rumours from the South. If your word still holds sway over the Saxons, surely there is no harm in him going over to visit his distant kin. If not…"

He ends with a shrug that says everything he really thinks of Catuar's chances at persuading Pefen to do anything. Not bothering to wait for Catuar's indignant response, he turns to the last *Comes*, Elasio.

"I trust that you will provide us with as much assistance as you're able to."

"That much I can promise."

"Just remember: when Londin falls, your land will be next, and not even Albanus will save you from Aetius's Legions."

A twisted smirk appears on Elasio's face. "We'll see about that."

"The *Dux* agreed to my idea rather eagerly," I note to Fastidius as we leave the palace.

"This surprises you?"

"Shouldn't it? I expected more resistance. I expected him to let Catuar explain himself first."

"Wortigern is not one to cling to old ways when they're clearly failing him. He knows Catuar doesn't mean anything in his own *pagus* anymore. If he continues to support him, the South is as good as lost to Londin — and then others might see it as encouragement to demand more power for themselves."

"This *does* surprise me. So he'd be fine with the Saxons taking over?"

"If they pledge allegiance to him, why not?" He shrugs. "The *Dux* never cared much for blood ties. Don't forget, he himself is a stranger in Londin — born in Gaul, his father hailing from western Britannia…"

"It looks like a lot more depends on the success of my mission than I thought."

"Don't worry about it too much, the *Dux* always has more than one plan ready. Where you fail, there will be others."

He pats me on the shoulder, as we cross the palace's courtyard and into the street, and notices his words do little to reassure me.

"Anyway," he adds, in a comforting voice, "I'm sure he's more concerned about Elasio than about Catuar these days. If those skirmishes with the Ikens turn into an all-out war… It might mean the end of Wortigern's power in the North."

"How so?"

"Londin won't be able to send any meaningful help to the Cadwallons — Wortigern admitted as much himself. And that would be just the excuse Elasio needs to drop any pretence of allegiance. I've made some inquiries while up North, and I'm sure it was Elasio himself who started provoking the Ikens. Our victory over the Picts helped placate them for a while — but it will not last long."

"And what about this 'Albanus' the *Dux* spoke of?"

Fastidius makes the sign of the cross at the name. "*Saint* Albanus," he corrects me. "Or so some believe. It's an old story. I'm surprised Wortigern raised it today — maybe he knows something I don't know…"

"How old?"

"It started with a visit from Germanus, twenty years ago. It was he who set up a chapel for Albanus's worship up in Werlam."

Having recently returned from Elasio's capital city, Fastidius is the best informed about the situation in the land of Cadwallons — but even without this knowledge, he's got an advantage over me. A long time ago, even before I came to question my faith altogether, I lost any interest in the numerous saints produced by the Church on a seemingly weekly basis, whose only virtues appeared to be increasingly elaborate ways of dying. They were no match to the tales of heroes and demi-gods from the myths and legends of the pagan age.

Fastidius's scowl tells me it's not a story he enjoys telling.

"Nobody had heard of this *Albanus* before Germanus's arrival," he says, having explained first that Germanus was a high-ranking Bishop who came to Britannia from Gaul when we were still children, to deliver news of condemnation and death of the philosopher Pelagius. Needless to say, neither the news nor the messenger were welcomed in Londin, where most of the clergy and the faithful still believed Pelagius to be a great and holy man.

"Condemnation…" I repeat and remember the words from Pelagius's treaties learned in my youth. What did the Church in Rome find so offensive in them?

"He taught that the rituals of the Church were gratuitous and unnecessary for one's salvation, if you remember," Fastidius explains. "But if that were true, what was the need for the Church at all? This could never stand."

"The heresy Riotham spoke of."

Fastidius nods. "Ambrosius soon embraced the new ruling, but Wortigern would not denounce the man he saw as his mentor and teacher. Did you know they all met with Pelagius, back in Gaul, when he was fleeing Rome? Wortigern, Paulinus and Pascent?"

"Yes, I remember."

"It drove an even deeper wedge between us and Ambrosius. A wedge any enemy would have been keen to exploit."

We reach the crossroads with Cardo Street and wait for a gap in the traffic heading for the market before moving on.

"Germanus needed something tangible to convince Britons of the power of the Roman Church, so he went to Werlam and 'found' the remains of some martyr he claimed to be called Albanus," he continues. The purported miracles of the holy bones did more to sway the faithful in the direction of the righteous doctrine than any of Germanus's lectures. For a while, it seemed the teachings of Pelagius would be all but forgotten.

"Having a recognised saint in his capital would make Elasio more powerful than Wortigern," I say and nod towards the passing wagons. "The common folk care more about miracles than doctrinal disputes."

"That's what the palace was afraid of," Fastidius confirms. "But then another war came to Gaul, as usual, and Germanus had to return to his flock before his work in Britannia was done. We got cut off from Rome for good, and between one thing and another, the conflict subdued. Bishop Fatalis has been striving to strike a balance between the two factions ever since."

"And do people still worship this Albanus?"

"Only in Elasio's domain, and even that reluctantly, from what I've seen."

We start climbing the Cathedral hill; the edifice blocks out the morning sun, a solid reminder of the Church's hold over the city and its people.

"How are *they* settling in?" I ask.

"Better than could be expected, all things considered," replies Fastidius.

The twelve youths — six boys and six girls — sent by Hengist as hostages, have been allocated dwellings in the Cathedral precinct, under the watchful eye of the Bishop and Fastidius. Rhedwyn also lives nearby, she and her retinue granted an entire wing of one of the confiscated *villas* in the shadow of the Cathedral hills, rather than a room at the *Praetorium.* Nobody wants to risk her getting too close to Wortimer this time.

"Will you baptise them?"

"Only if they ask," he replies. "They *are* curious children. The Bishop allowed them to come to the Mass, if they can behave themselves."

"They will have never seen anything like this back on Tanet. They'll be as amazed as I was the first time I saw a Mass."

He chuckles. "Great is God's glory."

As I stare at the lime-washed walls and marble pillars of the only new Roman-style building constructed in a generation, a strange thought strikes me.

"Everyone fears the return of Rome," I note, pointing at the sculptures of Imperator Constantine and his sons adorning the corner of the Cathedral, pillaged no doubt from some official building of the old administration, "but it hasn't really gone anywhere, has it?"

Fastidius smiles mysteriously. "You've noticed it too, huh? Try not to think about it too much. Nobody else does."

We embrace and part ways as my brother enters the Cathedral to report on the Council's decisions to the Bishop, and I reluctantly make my way back to the *Praetorium*. I glance towards the half-plundered *villa* that is Rhedwyn's new abode with a heavy heart. I would much rather spend this night beyond its overgrown hedge than in the cold audience halls of Wortigern's palace. But my presence is required in the audience hall. The four *Comites* are about to pronounce their pledges of allegiance to the *Dux* and the entire Council of Britannia Maxima. I can't wait to see their squirming faces as they do so.

CHAPTER XIII
THE LAY OF PEFEN

A mangy, grey, feral dog bares its teeth and growls at me. I stoop to pick up a stone and the dog, guessing my intention, runs away with a whimper.

I take a look at the stone. It's a strange-looking, veiny chunk of pink, pure marble, too small to be used for a wall. On closer inspection, it turns out to be a remnant of a finger, its details eroded almost beyond recognition, except for a faded out signet ring. It's twice the natural size — it must have once belonged to a great statue set up on the side of the old Roman road. I can only read three faint letters on the signet: CAR… Whoever it belonged to — a triumphant general? A visiting Imperator? A forgotten god? — can no longer point at the ghosts of passing crowds.

I have seen my share of Roman towns past their glory — half-ruined, half-dismantled, turned into villages of timber houses — but not one as thoroughly abandoned as this one. It was once called New Market of the Regins, then simply Regentium; now it's a nameless ruin. There are no wooden huts raised on the old concrete foundations, no new narrow alleyways and fences disturbing the old street grid; no one quarries what remained of the amphitheatre and the city baths, nobody picks at the mighty city walls to get out the quality facing stone. Even the columns of the old pagan temple — dedicated, judging by the faded markings, to Neptune and Minerva — still stand, overgrown with vine and moss, never rebuilt into a Christian church.

I can only guess at what made the Regins abandon their capital and move to New Port. It couldn't have been the sea raiders — the new seat of the *Comes* is much more exposed to the attacks of the pirates; was it the blocking of trade routes along the Gaulish coast? New Port and other harbours to the east are better suited to serve the short-distance trade between Britannia and Armorica or the land of Franks than the grand harbours to the south of Regentium. Or was it that New Port was just that little closer to Londin, along a straight, short, well-defended road cutting through the narrowest part of Andreda Forest? Whatever the true reason, it all seems to me a part of this narrowing of the world that I have witnessed in the North, among the Ikens and the Cadwallons. Regentium made sense as a capital of an outward-looking province, a small part of a greater Empire that spanned the entire known world. But for a main town of a tribal land, focused on local politics and dwindling trade with only the closest neighbours, New Port, where Catuar has built for himself a tiny *villa* only a fraction of the size of the old palace of the Regin Council, was more than sufficient.

Not that this entire region is abandoned and uninhabited. It would be pointless — and dangerous — for me to come here if it was. There's a small inn on the outskirts of the town, to accommodate other travellers as lost in these parts as myself. A few fields are still being tilled by serfs sheltering in huts by the forest's edge. There are fishing villages still scattered along the meandering coast, among the ruined wharves of the Great Havens. There is even a Iutish hamlet here — where the boats sent out from Tanet to seek out a more welcoming coast landed a generation ago, only to find more mud and disease-ridden swamp they've been trying to drain ever since. But I am not here to visit either of those.

Ten miles north from the vine-grown ruin of Regentium, in a valley shrouded in the shadows of the southern edge of Andreda, a clan of Saxon mercenaries have made their abode. I learned about it from the Southern merchants I interrogated back at Londin, just before I left on my mission. The Saxons here, according to the rumours, are no friends of Pefen and Aelle; their fortified village withstood several attacks by Pefen's forces over the past few years, and the mercenaries, by all accounts, remain steadfastly loyal to Catuar and the remnants of Regin Council at New Port, even if that means fighting their own Saxon brethren.

There are more such villages between Regentium and Pefen's territory around Anderitum, most of them in the western part of Catuar's domain, but this one is the largest and the oldest of them all. Whoever rules this band of mercenaries, has made himself the chief adversary of Pefen's quest to unite the Saxon tribes.

I look forward to meeting him in the flesh.

"Pefen likes to *think* of himself as a *bretwealda*," says Hrodha, using a Saxon word the meaning of which I am not yet clear on. "He commands the greatest warband, and holds the greatest fortress on the Saxon Shore. But when it's time to tell Catuar and the Council what to do, he needs to wait for the *witan* of all clans to gather and make a decision, just like everyone else."

Hrodha's village has no Hall — we meet in his house, only slightly bigger than the others in the settlement; it's clear that the priority of the mercenary band lies not in the objects and buildings of prestige and status, but in protection and defence. The village is accessible only from the south-east — in all other directions, it is guarded by steep sides of a narrow, wooded valley. Across the southern approach stands a ditch and an earthen wall, with a single wooden watchtower looking over the valley, towards Regentium, almost all the way to the sea.

The Saxon huts are not the only buildings in the valley. Along the road from Regentium, I passed the remains of two *villas*, both smaller than Ariminum, and long abandoned; the third one, on the eastern slope, though half-ruined, is still inhabited by some Briton family. The Saxon village appears to have been settled on what once must have been their land, in an arrangement similar to that between Beadda and Master Pascent.

"I don't remember," Hrodha replies, when I ask him about it. "This village was here before my time. But the *wealas* of the *Domus* have always been our friends. We guard them from the bandits, and they bring us news and exotic goods from New Port."

He dabs at a tin platter of cold meats with bored expression. I notice that his silver and goblets are of poor craftsmanship, cheap and likely locally made wares — but the sword at his side and the brooch clasping his cloak are as fine as any I've seen on a pagan lord.

"I don't know what Pefen's problem is," he continues. He strokes the back of his bald head and grimaces. "The *wealas* treat us well. No warrior of mine has ever been a slave. And there's always an opportunity for glory and plunder in their service."

"Has the *witan* ever openly defied him?"

He laughs. "Oh, plenty of times! The other clans know all too well how dangerous it would be to give the man too much power. He thinks we're not aware of what he's plotting in Andreda with that imp of his."

"And what *is* he plotting?"

Like all Saxons, he is as quick to turn serious as he is to laugh. "This does not concern you. It's a matter between the clans."

He rolls a slice of meat into a ball and pops it into his mouth.

"We remain loyal," he adds. "We have no quarrel with the *wealas*. And there are more of us than Pefen thinks. Tell your *Dux* we will deal with him when the time comes."

The mighty fortress at Anderitum is now manned by the very same Saxons against whom it was originally constructed. There are too few of them to man the entire length of the immense, crumbling wall, almost comically vast for its intended purpose — instead, the guards are clustered around wooden watchtowers raised in the corners on top of the Roman foundations, an earthen embankment extending the perimeter in a defensive ring, and under a timber roof shielding the ancient gatehouse, of which twin turrets only one still stands, like a gaping, toothless skull.

The new embankment, spanning both sides of the causeway, guards the fortress from the side which the Romans neglected in their time, choosing instead to focus their efforts on protecting the harbour from sea raiders. It's proof that to Pefen and his army, the real enemy comes not from the sea, but from the land — his fellow Saxons.

The guards at the embankment nod us through. Not just because they know their chieftain is expecting me — I've made sure my journey from Londin was well advertised and promoted as if it was an official embassy, although I have not been granted any privileges by the *Dux*, nor do I bear any gifts to the Saxon chieftain — but because they recognise my guide, a boy from New Port who led me here through the network of narrow causeways winding through the surrounding marshes.

He is a typical New Portian, in that in his veins flows the blood of all the peoples who've ever passed through the harbour city. He is part Briton and part Saxon, part Frank and part Armorican, there's even a dash of a Syrian centurion, if the family memory — which he shared with me in detail along the way — is to be believed. He is the living proof that some Saxons at least have always dwelled in the South, before they came in greater numbers as mercenaries: they passed through as merchants or travelling craftsmen, settled as serfs or fishermen, hired themselves out as bodyguards, or got themselves captured as slaves. But there were always a few of them, mingled among the native majority, and they were never united — not the way Pefen set out to unite them, into a single force, able to challenge Briton rule.

As we pass through the embankment and the fortress gate, I try to spot whether the warriors manning the barricades come from different clans, but I see no totems or other markings, except an ubiquitous banner of a white *seax* painted on woad-dyed cloth, a clear sign to all who would bother to make the arduous journey from New Port that *here live the Saxons; the people of the sword.*

The resemblance is strong. Pefen is an older, wiser, taller and more battle-scarred version of his son. He has the same square jaw, the same long, golden locks, and a similar scar-mark of diagonal dots, only his runs along both cheeks. The only feature Aelle seems to have inherited from his mother — if it is she who's standing beside the *Drihten* — are the deep blue eyes, where Pefen's are watery green.

We meet not in Pefen's Great Hall — a majestic building nestled in the south-eastern corner of the fortress, with its back to the ancient wall, and a painted gable carved into dragon heads — but outside, on the outskirts of the small hamlet that grew around it. The settlement is surprisingly small for what has supposedly been Pefen's base of operations for the past twenty years. It occupies maybe one quarter of the entire space bound by the Roman wall, extending eastwards towards a single-pier harbour at the bottom of a low cliff. It's not only smaller than the several bustling Saxon villages I passed along the coast, between New Port and the great white cliffs; it's even smaller than the Iute villages in the North. I'm sure there isn't enough space here to house the number of warriors that man the ramparts and the embankment. Where does Pefen's army *live*?

"Whatever it is you've come to tell me, you'd better hurry, boy," he says, with his back towards me. He is saddling his war pony, and his wife is helping to strap his saddle bags. Five other men are preparing to ride out with him wherever it is he's going; one of them is Offa, Aelle's one-time bodyguard. He gives me a blank nod of recognition when he sees me, but there is no malice in his eyes.

I have marched from New Port for half a day, across marshes and tall, wooded hills. I am tired and I am hungry. Pefen knew I was coming, and yet he chose this day to leave on some errand; I will not let him make a mockery of me and my mission.

I step closer to him. Offa's hand moves to the axe, but Pefen stops him.

"I bring word from my lord *Dux* Wortigern of Londin, the commander of Britannia's armies, to whom your *Comes* swears allegiance," I say in my most commanding voice. "You *will* hear out what I have to say."

Pefen smirks. He turns to face me with an amused smile.

"Aelle warned me about you. Ash, is it?"

"My name is Fraxinus, and I would prefer to continue this conversation in your Hall."

He stares at me for a while; I stare back. I must look up a little to meet his gaze — he is taller than most Saxons I know. I stand tall, but he must see I'm holding back from slumping and swaying after the long journey. My left leg trembles, and the scar on my arm, from the duel with Wortimer, is blazing up as it tends to do when I'm weary.

He looks to his men and rolls his eyes. "Fine. Flaed, give the boy some bread and cheese," he tells his wife, "And last year's mead — the good one." He turns back to me. "You have half an hour to feed and rest. If you want to talk, you need to ride with us."

I nod. At least the man knows how to compromise.

"Somebody find him another horse!" Pefen cries. "The rest of you, go back to your wives for one last cuddle," he adds, to a roar of bawdy laughter.

"You must know how little I care for Catuar and whomever he swears allegiance to," says Pefen. "Why would you bring him up?"

"You still take his money," I note. "And live on his land."

We ride single file across the narrow marsh causeways, Pefen in front, me just behind him, so we have to shout our responses over each other's backs.

"I haven't taken pay from Catuar in years," Pefen scoffs. "And we've earned our land in his service. He's welcome to take it back, if he so wishes."

He looks over his shoulder and flashes his teeth in the same mischievous grin I recognise from Aelle.

"I am not here to settle your arguments with the *Comes*," I say. "But to bring a proposal from Wortigern."

"A *proposal*?" Pefen slows down and turns around again. "You mean Wortigern would talk to me over Catuar's head?"

I now have his attention. I reach for the mead skin at my side and take a deliberately long sip.

"Tell me, chieftain, how goes your plan of uniting the Saxon tribes?" I ask. "How many clans have you gathered under your sword banner?"

"This is not knowledge I would share with a *wealh* courtier," he replies, grumpily.

It's fine. I come prepared.

"You know I've been to Regentium before coming here," I say. "And to Weorth's place — and at Angenmaer's village."

He scoffs, but I can hear in his voice that the news has not left him unperturbed.

"Whatever it is you need, these cowards cannot give it to you. They can only hide behind their walls for so long before I pick them out, one by one."

"What I — what my lord *Dux* — needs, is loyalty. And arms that can bear swords."

"Then you've come to the wrong place. You should've stayed at Regentium."

"You haven't heard yet what we have to offer."

"There is nothing I need from the *wealas* that I can't take myself."

I kick my pony's sides. The causeway here is just wide enough for us to ride side-by-side. We are heading north-east, towards the wooded hills and slag fields of Andreda, along the brackish marsh edging a shallow, silted sea. The wind smells of salt and mud.

"You can't take the entire *pagus* by yourself."

I see his chin tense up.

"Nonsense," he says.

"Wortigern has no use for a *Comes* who's under the pagan heel. He'd much rather do business directly with the heel itself."

"He would make *me* a *Comes*? A barbarian?"

"Rome is gone. We are all barbarians now. Look at me — I'm a Councillor in Londin, yet in my veins there is not a drop of Briton blood. And if I play my cards right, even I could be a *Comes* one day."

He raises his hand, and the cavalcade stops.

"This is about the Roman Legion at Suessionum, isn't it?" he asks.

"You know about them?"

"*Everyone* knows about them, boy. They have all the Goths and Franks in Gaul shaking in their breeches. They say the Roman commander has never lost a battle — even in an ambush."

"And now he's coming here," I say.

"Is this confirmed?" He frowns.

"Reasonably," I lie. "He could be here in a matter of weeks."

He pinches his lower lip between his thumb and index finger.

“I have no quarrel with the Romans,” he says. “The Saxons weren’t the ones who threw them out.”

“Do you think they will let everything stay as it is, once they’re back? They’ll put their own in charge. Wortimer…”

“What about Wortimer?”

I lower my voice. “We think it’s Wortimer who asked them for help.”

But this revelation has the opposite effect to what I intended. “Then they already have friends on the island. And you expect me to stand against them? If I welcome them, they might reward me. If I fight them, and lose, they will destroy me. I know Rome’s wrath.” There’s a painful glint in his eyes, and I remember Aelle telling me his father fought against Romans in the service of Franks, and against Franks in the service of Romans… He knows the Legions better than anyone on the island, with the exception of Wortigern and his veterans.

“But if you fight them and win?”

“Win, against Aetius? Win where the Franks and the Goths failed?” He shakes his head. “I’m not too keen on the odds of that.”

His recalcitrance surprises me. I expected him to lunge at this chance. He *is* a Saxon warlord — even in loss, there is glory, even in death, a victory. But he’s as cunning and cautious as a Briton. I can see now how he’s managed to gain such a following… But also, why he hasn’t yet triumphed over the remaining clans. There is such a thing as being *too* cautious in war…

"Think about what that would mean for your position in the *witan* — " I start, but he waves me away.

"Enough. I need to think about it. Let's move on — unless you want to go back to Anderitum, now that you've spoken your piece."

I look back at the winding causeway. There's no way I would be able to make my way back to the fortress alone — and it's already getting dark.

"Where *are* we going, anyway?" I ask.

"Haven't you guessed yet? We're going to meet with my son and his *Hiréd*." He chuckles. "I imagine you two will have a lot to talk about."

The marshes turn into low mounds, then into taller hills, pocked with heath and beech wood, the edges of the great forest beyond. We halt at the bottom of one such hill, in a broad gap cutting through a tall, sharp ridge of chalk downs. To the south is the sea of reeds and swampy islets, to the north — the dark, ominous line of Andreda, shimmering in the hot, humid wind. There are boulders and crumbling setts sticking randomly out of the path, but if the Romans ever deemed this pass useful for building a road, they must have abandoned that idea centuries ago.

"We should be much further north," remarks one of Pefen's companions, looking towards the forest, black now in the falling night.

"We've lost no more than an hour," Pefen dismisses his worries. "We'll make it up tomorrow."

Offa approaches the Saxon chieftain and whispers something in his ear. Pefen turns to me with a suspicious glower.

"Were you being followed?"

"Through these marshes?" I shrug. "I could've been followed by a Legion and wouldn't have noticed."

"At least you're honest." He nods. He whispers an order back to Offa, and the silent axeman mounts up and departs north, towards the forest, now only a slightly darker line in the darkness that surrounds us.

He orders our remaining four to set up camp, but stay vigilant — and armed at all times. We light up a small fire and sit around it in such a way that each of us can observe a different direction for incoming threat.

"I assume you've promised the same thing to the other chieftains," says Pefen. He tears into an apple-sized globe of smoked ewe's cheese and gives me one half of it.

"I promised various things to various men." I see no reason to keep these a secret from him — sooner or later, he'd find out from his agents in the other households. "Hrodha will fight simply to prove his loyalty, and to keep his deal with the *wealas*," I say, though I omit the part where I sweetened the deal by showing the Saxon warlord an almost brand-new golden coin I brought from Wortigern's treasury, with a promise of there being plenty more of those where that came from. It was a lie: the coin was a gift from one of the courtiers wishing to prove his loyalty after Wortimer's coup; how he obtained it, was anyone's guess — but there was only one such coin in all of Londin.

"Weorth wants more land, and nearer the coast," I continue. "Angenmaer simply asked for better weapons and armour, from the Angles — he was greatly impressed with my spear."

"Fools." Pefen shakes his head. "Not a shred of ambition in any of them."

"I have left the ambitious one for last."

"You spoke to Bucge, then."

"Bucge wants us to get rid of *you*."

He chuckles. "Of course she does. Should you even be telling me this?"

"I respectfully declined."

"Did you, now." He chews on the cheese. It's rubbery and stale, and smells of a sheep barn. "How did she take it?"

"She understood it wasn't something we wanted to involve ourselves with." Eventually. After a lot of yelling and spitting. "But she *is* your greatest rival in the *witan*, and we will have to reward her accordingly for her service."

I put a chunk of bread on a stick and hold it over the campfire, and in the crackling silence that follows, I try once again to sort out in my mind the nauseating assortment of the Saxon clans, tribes, households and chieftains with which I had to familiarise myself over the past few weeks. It was, perhaps, the most gruelling and thankless task I've ever undertaken in the *Dux's* service. My brain is filled with names and locations of which I had no idea just a month ago, and which I hope to forget a month since. Some of these men hold sway only over their small villages, others, like Bucge, control swathes of territory, long patchworks of land, weaving like salamanders between what is left of the Briton *villas* in the hills and along the coast either side of New Port. But all of them — even Bucge — agreed that none of the other chieftains commanded a *fyrd* as great and as fierce in battle as that of Pefen's.

"We *are* building this army, chieftain," I say. "With your help or without it, it will be the greatest this island has seen in a generation."

"A rag-tag rabble of mercenaries and militia roughs. It still won't be enough against Aetius and his eagles."

"It might make us seem unpalatable. Make them move on to an easier prey."

There's the lip-pinch again.

"There is something else you haven't mentioned yet."

"I… don't think there is?"

"Now that the Franks hold the approaches to the northern ports in Gaul, there is only one good place for the Roman fleet to land: Anderitum. This is why you *really* need my help."

In truth, I had no idea. I was concerned only with getting the Saxon warriors on our side, as per Wortigern's demand — I never gave a thought to where and how the Roman Legions might arrive on the island. I don't know the coasts of the Narrow Sea as well as the Southerners; I don't even know if Pefen's right in his assessment — but he seems as certain of his words as he is taken aback by my surprise.

"*You* may not have known," he says. "But your *Dux* must be aware of this."

"If he is, he hasn't shared this knowledge with me."

"Perhaps you were not the only one sent to negotiate with me," he says, somewhat mysteriously; it resonates with something Fastidius told me when I was leaving Londin. But before I have time to ask what he meant by that, the forest around us spews forth a band of silent warriors, clad in darkness and mail.

There are nine of them, all armed with good *seaxes*. One of Pefen's men, who had the misfortune to sit with his back to the attackers, falls at once, pierced through the kidneys. He wrestles his attacker down to the ground with him. Pefen grabs a burning log from the fire and waves it before him, keeping three of the enemies at bay. Dodging a blow, I roll over to my bedding where I keep the Anglian spear, swirl it in my hand and throw without aiming. In this close a brawl, it's enough for the leaf-shaped blade to slice through a thigh of the assailant nearest to me.

Another one leaps at me from the left. I parry, barely; my sword hand wobbles. I step back, trip and fall, inches from the campfire. I grab a handful of hot ash and throw it in my foe's face; we both scream in pain. I slash at his leg. My blade chips on bone. He staggers, and I finish him off with a two-handed blow across the side.

I drop the sword from my burning hand and gasp for air. I crawl a few feet away from the fire and glance to my right. Of Pefen's remaining warriors, one is assaulted by two men, and pushed back, bleeding from several wounds. Pefen himself is injured, but one of his attackers lies dead. Furthest from me, the third of Pefen's Saxons grabs his foe by the neck and thrusts the *seax* through his stomach — only to be himself slashed in the back by another enemy, appearing out of nowhere behind him.

I scramble up and rush to Pefen's aid, but one of the men he's fighting with spots me and whirls his sword at me with a great force, like an axe. With a crash of metal on metal and a shower of sparks, my *seax* flies away. The returning sword whizzes inches from my face. I lunge to hook him and pin him to the ground, but he stands firm like an oak tree. He bashes at my shoulder with the pommel, until I drop to my knees. I leap away and reach for the last weapon in my arsenal, the *pugio* in my boot sheath, but I can no longer hold it firmly enough and the blade slips from my hand, leaving only a scratch across the enemy's arm.

The enemy kicks me away and turns around just in time to block Pefen's incoming slash. As I lie in the dust, I sense an approaching vibration in my back. I roll over to see what's coming. A charging pony rushes past me; Offa's axe flies over my head and into the back of the man I just fought. A fountain of blood blinds me for a second, and when I wipe it from my eyes, I see another enemy fall, with a black bolt in his chest.

Pefen raises the sword over his head and drops it down on the head of the last foe still standing before him. The last of the attackers has just dispatched a third of Pefen's men, but seeing he's now outnumbered, drops his weapon and launches into a desperate run. I find my spear in the mess of mangled limbs. Offa turns his pony around. I hear the twang of string and the whistle of a flying bolt passing me as I release my missile. The leaf-shaped blade, the black bolt and Offa's axe all strike the runaway at the same time, turning him into a heap of shattered flesh and spurting blood.

It's too late to help two of Pefen's warriors, but the third one still moves. More of Aelle's men appear, rushing to help us with our injuries.

"Careful," Pefen says. "There may be more hiding in the woods."

By the light of a blazing log, he leans over one of the fallen.

"I know this man," he says, pointing. "He's one of Bucge's." He turns to me sharply and presses a point of his *seax* to my neck. "You led them here."

"I didn't! I had no idea!"

"Then how come you've survived while three of my best men were slain?"

"Providence?"

He punches me in the face and orders the others to hold on to me.

"Father, wait."

Aelle kneels down by another of the dead foes — the one I scratched on the shoulder with my dagger. He tears off the rest of the tunic sleeve.

"What is it?" Pefen asks.

"See for yourself."

In the light of the torch, a golden shimmer glints around the dead man's arm. A bronze armband — marked with a letter V.

"What does it mean?" Pefen demands with a frown.

"It means Wortigern is not the only one gathering an army to welcome Aetius," I reply.

CHAPTER XIV
THE LAY OF HRODHA

A sea of tents and campfires stretches as far as the eye can see along the broad pebble beach. This is what a thousand-strong army looks like; restless, waiting. They're all here — the loyal Saxon clans, the Iute *Hiréd*, town militias, old Briton veterans, those of Wortimer's cohort who were forgiven their part in the coup and renewed their vows of allegiance to Wortigern. There's even a small detachment of Angles and Ikens, sent by Una in gratitude for the victory at the beach.

The largest single contingent of them all is that of the pagan mercenaries from Frankia and further afield, lured not only by money and plunder, but by the prospect of fighting Aetius again. The very mention of the Roman commander's name brings their blood to the boil. Not long ago, his Legions destroyed the army of King Clodio and forced him to pay tribute to Rome. And now, if the reports are true, they are poised across the sea, waiting for a good tide to strike at our island. Wortigern, the very last of his treasure to pay them an advance on their fee — the rest of it they were promised to receive from their share of plunder, if there is a battle. I can only hope the *Dux* has a plan for what to do with the mercenaries if Aetius decides *not* to come after all…

But perhaps just as important as who *is* present on the beach, is who hasn't shown up to the gathering. Elasio sent only a token force of archers, to minimally fulfil his obligations — and excused himself from coming with them, due to a sudden illness of his only son. And, crucially, Pefen's

Saxon army remains hidden behind the walls of Anderitum, watching us from a distance, warily, both guarding and blocking our eastern flank.

Pefen was right; the coast of Anderitum is the best and most likely place for Aetius's legion to land. With the fortress in allied hands, even this "rag-tag band of mercenaries and roughs," as Pefen called it, might stand a chance at holding back the invasion. Without it, all of our effort is just for show. Even the most cautious estimates of Armorican merchants and Frankish spies put Aetius's force in Gaul at four times as big as ours. I doubt he'd even bother sending his entire army against us — not while there are still Franks and Goths to deal with to his North, and an ominous rumour of the Huns riding again from the East — but whatever he'll send will be likely more than enough to deal with Wortigern's band, if we can't convince Pefen to join us…

At night, the beach gains a certain beauty, as the myriad campfires blaze up along the waterfront. But with each passing week there are fewer of those lights, as the nights grow warmer — and the fuel grows scarcer.

I go into the dunes for a night's piss. As I lace up my breeches, I sense a presence. I reach for the dagger. Aelle comes out into the light, his right hand raised in greeting, his left, cautiously, on the hilt of his sword.

"I didn't expect you this far from your woods. What are you doing here?"

The last time I saw him, he was leaving Anderitum in a huff. The disagreement he had with his father over how to deal with Wortigern's demands turned into a loud quarrel. I had never seen Aelle so angry before — not even when he lost the Battle of Saffron Valley.

In the end, we both failed to convince Pefen to join Wortigern's new army, though my failure was not treated as such in Londin, since I have managed to secure a substantial contingent of other Saxon clans in exchange. Only the *Dux* and a few of his courtiers most familiar with the situation in the South knew the potential impact of Pefen's decision.

"I've come to try once again to talk some sense into my father," he replies. "And to check on your forage parties. They have been ravaging Andreda all along the Downs. It's become hard to even catch squirrels."

I know he's not exaggerating. The multitude of men we've gathered has come with its own set of problems. The warriors need shelter, and sustenance; many have brought or built their own tents and huts, but others, especially the Frankish mercenaries, have to be accommodated at Wortigern's expense. Food is another matter — not only have the foragers brought doom to the game of the Andreda Forest, they've been trampling the adjacent countryside, leaving barren fields and orchards of the nearby *villas*, to the rising groans of the Regin landowners.

"You've come to complain about it to Wortigern?"

"No, I just wanted to talk to *you*."

He sits down, cross-legged, on the sand and gestures for me to join him.

"What about?"

He doesn't answer outright. Instead, he nods at the flickering campfires. "This can't last long," he says.

"No, I suppose not."

"My father has friends across the sea. He says the Romans are not coming."

"That's not what the *Dux*'s spies report."

"I don't know who's right. What I do know is that sooner or later, with or without the Romans' help, your *Dux* will run out of money. And then food."

I know how right he is — and that irritates me. I do not wish to be reminded of our predicament. Aetius doesn't need to attack us — he just has to wait us out. With all his immediate enemies defeated, and the wealth of all Gaul at his disposal, he can sustain himself until winter if he so wishes; meanwhile, we'll be forced to disband our army in a matter of weeks — and deal with the mercenaries, one way or another. Was this the Roman plan all along? Was this Wortimer's plan? He is not here — he's been sent, with the small army he's started building again from the ruin of his cohort, to the Cantish coast, to patrol another possible landing site near Rutubi; but he could be back here within days, to take advantage of the chaos that would no doubt erupt once the situation worsens.

"They will be looking for someone to blame for this failure," Aelle adds. "And they will turn against us. All of us. It'll be the end of your little fairytale. No more peaceful Iute villages. No more cordial *wealh* friends."

"We've beaten Wortimer once. We'll beat him again."

"It won't be just Wortimer this time. All *wealas* hate us, and fear us — and envy us. We are virile, strong, fertile, fearless." He shakes his fist, and his eyes gleam in the starlight. "My father says that to every child born in the Briton villages, our women give birth to two. And *they* know this, too."

"Why are you telling me all of this?"

He laughs, which makes me even angrier. "Because — you're one of us, and that's what they'll see when the time comes! You're not even one of those mongrels from the villages in the Downs. You're pure-blooded. They'll never let you live once the fighting starts for good."

The fighting?

"You're wrong," I say. "I have *seen* it, Aelle. Iutes and Britons, living together, side-by-side. Not in the cities — but in the villages. In Saffron Valley, and up on the north coast, by the Robriwis Fortress. These common, simple folk will not join your war. There is no fear or hatred in any of them."

"That's because the Iutes are still weak," he replies. "But note, if the *wealas* may live freely among the Iutes, why not the other way around? Why has Wortigern banished your people from Londin? You know they are rattled by your rising power."

I say nothing. These thoughts are not alien to me, but they make me too uncomfortable to dwell on them for long.

"And it's getting worse here," he continues. "You'd have seen it if you only had your eyes open. Why do you think my father keeps us in those old ruins, instead of moving to a palace in New Port?"

"It's a good defensive position," I say. "And these are dangerous times."

"We don't need an old heap of rubble to defend ourselves," he scoffs. "You must have noticed how we're hiding the real number of our warriors. Scattered among the clifftop villages, and in the forest bands, so that there are never more than a handful at one time at Anderitum."

"I did wonder about that."

"Everyone else does the same, even those loyal to their Briton masters. We may control Catuar and his courtiers, but we can't make them *like* us."

"You've hardly been out of sight in Andreda." Suddenly it strikes me. "Is that what you were making ready for? A war with the Britons?"

He nods. "We've been hard at work. We've fortified the entire northern frontier. Reinforced the old hillforts. Built up supplies. Dug up the forest roads, filled them with traps. If it comes to the worst, we can hold out there for months, maybe longer."

"What about Catuar and the Regins? Don't they get to have a say in anything?"

"Once we cut them off from Londin, the *wealas* here will fold like a lean-to in a storm. They have depended on our arms so long, they've forgotten how to fight."

The scope and audacity of what he's taking about leaves me breathless. Here we are, preparing to defend against the Roman Legions, and all the while Pefen's Saxons have already been making plans to defeat and conquer an entire Briton *pagus*.

"So that's why your father didn't care about Wortigern's offer," I say. "He will take the Regins on his own terms."

"That is what he believes."

A curious turn of phrase, which reminds me how angry Aelle was with his father. "But you're not certain."

"There is still the *witan* to consider — and many would vote against my father's plans just to spite him… He should've accepted your *Dux's* offer. It would've made things easier." He shrugs. "It is what it is." He stops. "I should not be telling you any of this."

"You don't trust me?"

"You still believe you might become one of them."

"Your secret is safe with me."

He stands up. "I need you to swear it."

"I swear."

"Properly. Swear an *ath* before the gods."

I stand as well. I have no qualms about humouring him; it seems a trivial matter to me. But as I speak the words of the *ath* I once learned from Fulco, my tongue feels heavy. I call upon Wodan and Donar to assist me in fulfilling the promise, and suddenly, here, under the starry sky, with the clear breeze blowing from the open sea, I feel as if they are with us, watching — and judging.

Aelle smiles, knowingly. He's felt that, too.

"You *are* one of us," he says. "I have to go now. But remember what I told you about tonight. If — when — the *wealas* turn against us, go look for us in the woods, when you've got the chance. We'll be waiting."

"I'm sure it won't be necessary," I say.

The breeze feels somehow a lot colder than before.

Every time a sail appears over the horizon, every time a merchant boat or a patrol *ceol* brings news of strange ships plying the waters of the Narrow Sea, every time the tides and winds change in our direction, the camp stirs in anxious alarm. It's no different this time: a dot at first, it grows into a large vessel, a double-rowed *liburna* with a large striped sail. It's only a single ship, but it's soon clear it's heading straight for us, rather than any of the more friendly harbours east or west of the beach.

I rush down the dunes where Odo and the other commanders have already gathered. "What does it mean?" I ask. "Why only one ship?"

"An emissary, no doubt," replies Odo. "Looks like Aetius wishes to negotiate."

The Gaul was put in command of Clodio's mercenaries, since he speaks the tongue of the Franks and knows their customs. He's let his black, lustrous hair grow long again, and bound it with a silver band; he looks like a pagan chieftain, and the mercenaries like it, as much as they like anything in this unfamiliar land.

The wind is weak, the tide unfriendly, and the ship moves painfully slow. By the time it reaches the beach, the entire camp has gathered at the sea edge to observe the mysterious visitor. *Dux* Wortigern is here too, with his Councillors. There is a mark on the sail, not of the Imperial Eagle, but of two golden keys and a cross in a circle. The pagans among the mercenary warriors murmur and throw magic gestures towards it. At long last, the ship reaches the remains of a Roman merchant pier and grinds to halt on a sandbank.

Two men disembark and wade towards us, their white robes, soaked in the sea, flapping in the wind. The one in front is ancient, wrinkled, white-haired but not balding; he supports himself on a crooked staff. His vestment is lined with gold, and his headgear is studded with gems. I hear Wortigern mumble a curse word as the old man comes close enough to be recognised.

The old man stands straight and bold before the *Dux*, then stares around the beach, searching for something — or rather, some*one*.

"Where is Wortimer, your son?" he asks. There is no age in his voice — it is booming, resounding, as if we were standing inside a Cathedral and not on a windswept beach. My spine tingles. "I was hoping to speak with him."

"He's not here," the *Dux* replies, simply. "I am still the ruler of Britannia, Germanus, though I know how it must pain you. You will speak to me, or go back where you came from."

The *Dux* and the two newcomers stand silent long enough to make everyone start feeling uncomfortable. The wind whistles through the fist-sized gaps in the wall of a half-crumbled clifftop palace which Wortigern has made his temporary headquarters, and tears at the clerics' flowing robes. I've now had time to remember Fastidius telling me about this Germanus and his previous mission to Britannia — if it is the same man. He looks old enough: faint tufts of silver hair peek from under his tall hat; sweat flows down his brow, furrowed with wrinkles like a freshly ploughed field; his left eye is clouded white, and his hand, clenched tightly on the shepherd's staff, trembles. But his right eye is as bright and piercing as it must have been in his youth.

"Why have you returned?" Wortigern asks, at last.

"I have heard dreadful rumours, and needed to make sure they were true," replies Germanus. "I've heard you have allied yourself with pagans against Christians. I've heard the barbarians were stealing land and threatening the cities and the villages, while you did nothing. And, worst of all, I've heard that the heresy is just as strong as it was when I left."

"Then you weren't sent here by Aetius?"

"Aetius?" He reels in theatrical surprise. "Aetius is in Italia, strengthening Rome's borders against the Huns. Why would he send me here?"

Wortigern's jaws clench. He can't call the Bishop a liar — that would be a blasphemy of the highest order.

"What about his Legion in Suessionum?"

"The troops are there to protect the harbours of northern Gaul from barbarians," says Germanus. He looks around. "I wish others would have done the same, instead of allying themselves with the pagans."

This is too much for the *Dux*. He steps forward and straightens himself, until he towers over the age-bent Bishop. "Let me remind you that it was *Rome* that abandoned Britannia first!" he booms. Spittle from his mouth lands on the Bishop's headgear. "We were left to our own devices — without the Legions, without the silver! What were we supposed to do — pray the sea raiders away?"

"Better to die a Christian than to live as a pagan-lover," retorts the Bishop's companion. I've heard this term before — used by Wortimer and his roughs against me. Have they picked it up from their Roman contacts?

Germanus raises his hand. "Patience, Severus," he says. "These people are not martyr material. And the *Dux* is right. We have neglected the needs of this forlorn province for too long. This is why we are here, after all."

"And what do you plan to do about it?"

The Bishop raises his arms and eyes to heaven. "Pray, my lord *Dux*. Pray."

"I have my own Bishop to pray for me."

"A heretic's prayer will not reach the ears of the Lord."

Before Wortigern can answer, a rumbling, growling noise rises outside the palace, like a rolling sea in a storm. A messenger bursts through the door, bowing in apology.

"What is it?" the *Dux* snarls. "Can't you see we're busy?"

"It's the Franks, lord *Dux*," says the messenger.

"What about them?"

"They've heard the rumours… That there will be no battle — no plunder… They want to be paid now, so they can go home before summer."

Wortigern waves, impatiently. "Send for the Saxons. The loyal ones, what's their names… Hrodha and Bucge. They will make short work of the Franks."

The rumbling noise outside grows nearer, and turns into an angry murmur of a roused crowd. It can't be just the Franks in the throng — other mercenaries must have gathered with them by now.

"My lord…" The messenger scratches his neck nervously. "Hrodha has… joined the Franks."

"And here I thought you were one of the loyal ones," I say.

Hrodha snickers. He slurps a hot spoonful of a thin meat stew and licks his lips. The tip of his tongue runs along the greying moustache.

"I am as loyal as I always was," he replies. "But every loyalty has its price." He scoffs and pushes away the bowl with disgust. "Look at this slop. This isn't the food a tribe chieftain should be eating at this time of year. There's barely any meat left in the woods. And if we miss the harvest, this same thing will happen in my village. I can't allow that."

"This isn't the deal we've made."

"The deal is over if the Romans aren't coming." He coughs. The air in the tiny hut is stale and heavy, filled with smoke from the small stove where the stew pot slowly simmers. I don't know what happened to the owners of the cottage — or of any other hut in the small cliff-side village; either they fled before the gathering army, or they decided to move away when the foragers started commandeering the produce from their fields and gardens.

"We don't know yet for certain that they're not coming."

"I've heard what the old priest said."

How? Only a few Councillors witnessed the conversations between Germanus and Wortigern, yet the news reached the army camp before they even stopped talking. Some of the crew on Germanus's ship must have been quick in spreading the rumour as soon as the galley reached the beach.

"He may not have been telling the truth."

"I thought your priests were not allowed to lie."

I have no convincing answer. Wortigern and the others readily accepted Germanus's words. Nobody thought to question his pronouncements; nobody thought it possible that he may be misleading us. The *Dux* and the Council were so convinced he was telling the truth, they have already started making secret arrangements for their return to Londin as soon as the mutinous mercenaries have been dealt with.

"I have been a mercenary all my life — I know how this is supposed to work," says Hrodha. "You always count on most of us dying in battle, and then share the spoils between those who survive. But there will be no battle — and there will be no spoils. So — " He shrugs. "There's no reason for us to be here anymore. Just pay us what you owe for the time we've all wasted, and we'll be on our way."

"And if we don't — then what? You would fight us?"

"The Franks will." He nods outside. In another cramped hut, Wortigern is talking to the leader of the Frankish mercenaries. It is unlikely that he will change their minds. Hrodha is clearly aware of that. "They don't care for your politics or diplomacy. They have nothing to go back home for. The came here for a fight, and they will get it one way or the other."

"Then help us stop them. You will be paid, as soon as the army is disbanded."

"Paid with what?" He scoffs. "Show us more of those gold coins you flashed the last time we talked."

He's called my bluff; I don't know what other arguments to use. I have appealed to his loyalty, to his honour and to his greed, all have failed. And, in truth, I understand where he's coming from. Without the threat of Aetius, there's no reason for any of us to be here on this wind-battered coast.

"If you know we have no money, why fight? You can't plunder an empty chest."

"My people expect me to at least try. Besides, there's always *some* money hidden somewhere with you *wealas*. When you're squeezed, you bleed silver."

I like that this man doesn't call me a Saxon in Briton service — he's been among Britons long enough to know how to look beyond appearances. It's a refreshing change from how I'm treated by the likes of Aelle or Wortimer. I wish I could help him solve his dilemma without violence — but I can't think of anything.

"I'll tell you why you can't find an answer, boy," Hrodha says, correctly guessing the reason for my silence. "It's because there isn't one. You haven't been sent here to talk — but to delay."

He stands up from the wobbly, three-legged table and comes up to the window. He smiles. "I can see Wortigern preparing his positions on the hills from here. The Franks will soon realise this, too." He takes a glance at my face. "You didn't know! That's why you played your part so convincingly!"

I shrug. It wouldn't be the first time the *Dux* used me like this. I was only ever privy to his plans as far as it was necessary for me to fulfil my roles in them. "I've said my piece," I say. "I still believe there's no need to shed blood over this."

"It's up to your *Dux*." He takes another glance out the window. "And by the looks of it, he's made his choice — or a choice was made for him."

Wortigern bursts out of the hut opposite, crashing the remnants of a wicker door. His officers follow after him in a hurry, towards the line of dunes.

"You'd better go, boy," says Hrodha. "Unless you want to stay and fight with us."

"What news of Hrodha?" asks Wortigern.

"His heart isn't in this," I reply. "But he feels he needs to show he's serious. This is more about honour than silver for him."

Our conversation is deceitfully calm. Before us, on the broad, brackish plain below the dune ridge, the Franks are setting up in rigid formations. Although our position holds the high ground, and makes use of the fortifications of fascine and shallow ditches prepared to repel the Roman invasion, the outcome of the coming battle is far from certain. The Franks are battle hardened professional soldiers. Half of our force is made up of tribal militiamen, who've never seen war before. The mood in the camp is jittery — the only thing that stems a panic is Wortigern's stoic poise.

"The Franks don't care about honour," he says. "Only money. But that doesn't mean they'll fight with any less resolve."

He summons an officer. "Ride down to Hrodha. Be discrete. Make him the offer we talked about."

As the horse slides down the dune, Wortigern's gaze turns with envy to the east, where the jagged walls of

Anderitum rise over the marsh on a spur of chalk. He says nothing, but I know what he's thinking. If only we had control of Pefen's fortress, we would fear neither the mercenaries, nor the invading Legion… But the gates of the fortress remain steadfastly shut, and Pefen's guards stand silently on the outer embankments, watching our predicament with studied disinterest.

The first attack comes at dawn and the fighting continues sporadically throughout the day, in waves of relentless, wearying assaults, but with few casualties on either side. The Franks are keen to show they mean business, but do not care for bleeding themselves against our defence — and we're not keen on dying in defence of Wortigern's empty treasury. At the end of the day there are only a few bodies left on either side of the front line.

"If only we had one more cohort of reserves, we could take the fight to the enemy," says Oda. "Should we not call for Wortimer?"

"He'll never get here in time," replies Wortigern. I know there's a different reason for him not wanting his son here — this is just the kind of situation Wortimer would exploit to gain more power. "We'll have to make do with what we have."

The unfortunate Gaul looks wretched. On the day of the mutiny, he barely escaped the Franks, who wanted to take him hostage. And since the battle started, he and his men have been forced to fight on foot, their horses useless in a pitched defence, a sad fate for any cavalryman.

"What would you do if you had enough men?" I ask.

"That's easy. I would strike at those boats — " He points to the anchorage where the Frankish ships are lapped by the gentle waves of a high tide. A bit further out into the sea reddens the striped sail of Germanus's ship, like a floating fortress. The Bishop and his retinue retreated there in the morning to await the resolution of the conflict — unperturbed by the mercenaries. "This would leave them without any means of escape or returning home."

"Wouldn't this just anger them more?"

"I want them to be angry. I want them to lose patience and throw themselves at us — and then realise they have nowhere to go, that they're at our mercy… But, why waste time talking of that which can never be? Better prepare yourself for what is inevitable," he adds, gloomily.

We lose more men overnight, not from the fighting, but from desertions. Most of Wortigern's courtiers have already disappeared, fleeing as far as their carriages could take them at the first sign of trouble, down the only road North. They wouldn't even stay at New Port — they know full well that the wrath of the Franks, once released, can easily sweep all along the coast, with no one left to stop them. Worse still, one of the lesser Saxon clans marches off in the morning; not enough to make a dent in our ranks, but dealing a severe blow to everyone's morale.

"There is good news, too," reports the officer sent out to speak to Hrodha. "The Saxon stood aside the entire day, just as agreed."

"It won't last long. We have nothing else to give him. And now the Franks will think I *do* have money to give away."

"Then we better deal with them soon," I say. "Before we lose any more of our army to fear."

This time, the Franks strike in earnest. They, too, are running out of time. We've cut them off from foraging land and most of the supplies gathered for war with Aetius. They are in a hostile, unfamiliar territory, and can only count on themselves; no Briton fisherman will sell them fish, no Saxon butcher will provide them with meat. If we could hold out for a day or two, they should run out of food and their situation would get desperate. But if they manage to break through on our sides, where the dune ridge disappears into the low marsh, and take control of the old Roman road, it is us who would be cut off…

At noon, the line breaks on our left, weakest, wing. The Franks punch through the frail defences of Trinowaunt militia and proceed to roll up our flank until Odo's men, at last able to ride their chargers into battle, stop their progress and push the enemy back down the dune. A lull of several hours follows, while the Franks lick their wounds — but as the sun sets, they strike once more, with renewed vigour.

I have not taken part in the fighting until now — as one of Wortigern's courtiers, I was merely observing the battle from the tallest hilltop in the centre of the camp. But when the line buckles under another Frankish charge, I can wait no longer. I grasp my *aesc* and a round buckler and rush into the brawl. I take the place of a fallen Briton, block a spear thrust and push back. My blade lands in a Frank's body with a squelch.

"Take heart, men!" I cry. "Beat them back, in the name of Christ!"

I see no effect of my rallying call. The Briton line wobbles again. Another man falls beside me. An order comes down from the centre: pull back, towards the camp. A trained army would have no problem executing this order — we are still holding tight, and the camp defences are no more than a hundred feet away. But these militiamen, who until a few months ago were ploughing their fields and fixing holes in the roofs of their huts, know nothing about the art of war, of manoeuvres and tactical planning. To them the signal to retreat is a signal to a rout. One by one at first, then in groups, the Britons tear away from the frontline, leaving gaps too big for the loyal Saxons and Iutes to fill. I hack to my left and right, trying to stop the Franks from pushing through the holes that suddenly appear at each of my sides. I feel my spear blade slide against mail and bone, blood spilling down the shaft, making my grip slippery. An axe blow splits my shield in two; I throw it away and slash with both hands.

Through the noise of battle and cries of the fallen I hear an odd sound. I can't identify it at first — it is at once mournful and jubilant, a piercing, prolonged howl of some great wounded animal… Then I recognise it: the battle horns of a Saxon warband.

The thrust on our line grows weaker. The rout is halted, though not yet reversed. I kick and push through, to see what caused the Franks' hesitation. All around me, the Saxons and Iutes do the same.

The first thing I see is smoke. A dozen black pillars, rising high into the air from the direction of the Frankish anchorage. I look to the east. The gates of Anderitum are thrown open.

The battle horns announce the arrival of Pefen's host. Silver-speared and clad in mail, they stand between the burning boats and the Frankish rear. Not yet attacking, just presenting their strength to the confused mercenaries.

The battle turns in a blink of an eye. Wortigern and Odo lead a charge from the centre, pushing the Franks down the dune. It takes a while before the ripple of the counterattack reaches the wings. By then, the mercenaries are in full retreat. Before we can launch into pursuit, the *Dux* calls us to halt. There's no point losing more men in the hunt — trapped between the two armies, the Franks might yet bite back, like cornered badgers. Instead, we let them go back to their beach tents and, just as the last rays of the setting sun disappear beyond the dark sea and the smouldering boats, we return to our hilltop camp to count the dead and tend to the wounded.

"Was this your doing?" asks Wortigern. He hisses, as the camp physician tightens a bandage on his arm. The *Dux* has been fighting in the middle of the fray all through the day and added a new grid of scars to his already impressive collection.

"I cannot take all the credit," I reply. "But, I may have helped…"

At night, after the first day of fighting, I made my way across the network of marsh paths, towards Anderitum. The Franks didn't think to put up any patrols between us and the fortress, no doubt assured by their Saxon allies that Pefen wasn't planning to march to our help.

"You again?" By a stroke of fortune, the guard at the fortress gate recognised me. "The *Drihten* sleeps. Come back in the morning."

"Have you not seen what's been happening today?" I called back. "Go wake your lord — if he's really asleep, and I don't believe that for a minute, and tell him *Dux* Wortigern wants to talk to him."

"I'll tell him *you* wish to talk. I don't see no *Dux* here."

The Saxon *Drihten*, as it turns out, not only wasn't asleep — he was waiting for me in his Hall.

"You should have come sooner."

"I thought you didn't want to talk to us."

He scowled. "That was before the two priests arrived. Before we got news from the Continent."

"What's changed?"

"The balance of power has shifted — you know it, too, otherwise you wouldn't have come."

"You mean, you wouldn't have risked a fight with the Roman Legion — but you'll have a crack at a bunch of Franks."

"You make me sound like a coward."

"Or a shrewd leader."

He rolled his eyes. "Does Wortigern know you're here, boy?"

"He doesn't."

"Then your promises are worthless."

"You don't need my promises. You don't need to ask anymore. You can just take whatever you want."

"And you think I need *you* to tell me this? I expect you've come here with some hare-brained scheme how to save Wortigern's army and earn his eternal gratitude."

"It's not my scheme — it's Odo the Gaul's."

I could see a change in his eyes when I said it. Odo's fame has reached even here, to the Saxon coast — was it Aelle who brought the tales of the Gaulish *decurion* here? Pefen looked at me the same way the Iutes looked at me when I told them I was bringing a battle plan devised by Fastidius. What would it take for anyone to listen to *my* plan for once?

"I expect I'll hear from Pefen soon," says Wortigern after I tell him of my nightly escapade.

"He hasn't sent anyone yet?"

"He knows we're not going anywhere… The Franks are far from defeated yet — and I still have that damned Bishop to deal with."

"Germanus! I almost forgot about him."

Wortigern sighs and puts his face in his hands. "I wish we could all forget about him, son."

CHAPTER XV
THE LAY OF SEVERUS

The crowd gathered at the ruined temple at the crossroad to listen to Germanus far outnumbers what is left of Wortigern's meagre forces.

It took us weeks to gather an army ready to face Aetius and his Legion. It dispersed within days. First to leave were the Franks; most of them have accepted the *Dux's* bargain, content only with symbolic payment for the time they spent on Anderitum's beach and a free crossing back home, on ships supplied by relieved New Port merchants. With the Franks gone, one way or another — and I suspected many to have vanished into Andreda, instead of dutifully sailing away to the Continent — the Saxons themselves have begun to rumble, and Wortigern had no choice but to dismiss even the most loyal of them. By then, there was little point in staying on the coast. Had the Romans changed their minds and decided to land, the force that remained wouldn't even be enough to slow them down. Elasio's archers and Una's Angles simply disappeared one morning, without a word, and soon even the tribal militiamen began to roll up their tents, leaving as they came, village by village, until all that was left were the ever faithful Iutes, Wortigern's own Londin regiment — and Pefen, now the victorious master of the battlefield and, by the sight of things, of the entire *pagus*.

Aelle's father was right: the balance of power has shifted there, on Anderitum beach. Hrodha, miscalculating his rebellion, was left with nothing, weakened and humiliated, no longer a threat to Pefen's domination in the *witan*. Other

Saxon warlords lost warriors in battle and gained no plunder to show for it. Wortigern's silver barely covered the cost of their expedition. For a moment, it seemed as if the *Dux* had yet another mutiny on his hands… Until the woods behind our backs came to life, as Aelle returned to the beach with a hundred fresh warriors, to support his father's bid for power. In the end, Pefen needed nothing from Wortigern, except a promise of respecting the vote of the w*itan*, when it would eventually gather — and a small chest of silver, "for the effort".

It was, at last, time for us to heed Germanus's urging. There was nothing else for us to do but pack up and accompany him back to the capital.

This is now the third Mass the Bishop has conducted since we left. The first one was in the garden of Catuar's small palace in New Port. The gardens overlooked the city from a high cliff, and a great crowd had gathered underneath to witness the unusual spectacle. But the New Portians are a practical race of merchants, sailors and trade clerks, and they were not easily swayed by Germanus's high tales of saints and martyrs, of heretics and devils; only a handful of new followers joined us on the road back to Londin, and most of them beggars and other assorted marauders, hoping to catch a trickle off the Bishop's silver platters.

Things changed once we entered the countryside. The humble village folk flocked to our procession in their dozens. This time, their interest was genuine. These were natives, Briton serfs, left to tend to themselves by their city-dwelling masters; they had no shrines, no priests ever stopped by on their way down the Roman highway; if there was no urgent need, once a year they would travel to Londin for confession and prayer. Pagan Saxons encroached on their land, expanding from the coast inwards in numerous settlements, showing an alternative to the old faith that was fresh and vibrant. But the Britons of the valleys remained as fervent believers as they had been in the days of Rebellion. To have a Bishop not merely pass through their land, but to pause and perform a Mass especially for them, was by far the greatest event in their meagre lives — at least of those who didn't remember Germanus's *previous* visit.

The news of the Bishop's march spread quickly throughout the *pagus*. By the time we reach the crossroads that mark the northern border of the Regins, the crowd counts in hundreds, some of them having walked for days, from all over Catuar's dominion — maybe even further, braving the bad roads, forest bandits, and wild beasts. Others are here, too, those who follow such crowds, regardless of their purpose: wandering vendors, cutpurses, pleasure-givers and pleasure seekers, and various assorted gawpers. They transform what once was a quiet, solemn place of reflection into a loud, chaotic marketplace. In religious fervour, their feet, bare or clad in wicker and bark, trample the eroded stones and rotten timber of the ancient shrine into dirt; the pile of pebbles, once marking the graves of Fulco's fallen comrades, has vanished in the mud. The last standing column of the temple falls over, unable to withstand the multitude thronging around it. Somebody dies, crushed underneath the marble; few notice. The mangled body is taken away along with the remains of the pillar, to make way for Germanus's field altar.

Wortigern observes all of this with badly hidden disgust. The situation has been out of his control from the moment Germanus's ship landed on Anderitum beach. The battle with Rome was lost — without a single javelin thrown. Now, he can't even count on his barbarian allies to ensure our safety.

The Saxons and the Iutes have to stand back from the ceremony, as the crowd's angry murmurs at their presence threatens to grow into an outright riot. I see now where Aelle's reluctance towards an alliance with the *wealas* was coming from. The Saxons may be in control of Catuar and his Council — now more so than ever — and they may be on good terms with the merchants whose caravans they protect and with the landlords whose properties they guard — but they are not welcomed in the valleys and the villages of the Briton serfs.

Germanus commands the mob like a general. He chooses several of the most literate men and appoints them as his heralds, translating his message from the high Imperial speech into the Vulgar Tongue. He splits the crowd into two more manageable divisions, and leaves the larger in the care of Severus. It is a clever ruse: even though the selection was, as far as I can tell, random, those chosen to follow Germanus's footsteps instantly feel elevated, selected for some greater purpose, and raise an even greater clamour when the Bishop steps onto a makeshift rostrum, set up in the centre of the old ruin.

"He's not going to say anything new," Wortigern says. "Whatever it is he's really come for, he's waiting with it until we reach Londin."

"And what do you think it is he wants from us — from you?"

The question, which lingers on all our minds, is posed by Fastidius, sent from Londin to welcome Germanus and report on his mission. But the Bishop, so far, has refused to find the time to meet with anyone other than the representatives of the common folk, and the purpose of his visit — except, ostensibly, to reignite the flame of True Faith in the Briton hearts — remains as mysterious as it had ever been.

"A submission of some sort," replies the *Dux* with a heavy shrug. "You are a church man, you tell me. Doesn't Fatalis know anything about this?"

"We weren't informed of this visit, so no. I'm even surprised to see Germanus still alive — a year ago we heard he was gravely ill, and dying. We offered prayers for him at the Cathedral."

"Another miracle of our Lord, no doubt," scoffs Wortigern, to Fastidius's grimace. "Still, what can one man do?"

"A lot, if that man is Germanus," says Fastidius. "Just look at the size of that crowd. And he's hardly alone here… Have you seen your son lately?"

"Wortimer is trampling the beaches in Cantiaca. I forbade him to return to Londin until this blows over."

"He doesn't need to come to Londin to conspire with your enemies."

Wortimer scowls. "Don't you think I know that? I did all I could. At least in the city we will be on our home territory. Hopefully this will balance the things out a little."

There is more bad news waiting for us at Saffron Valley, the final stop on the Bishop's itinerary before the capital.

"The Bishop wants to use the new church for the Mass," announces one of the "heralds" of Germanus. "But the heretic has barricaded himself inside and threatens to burn the place down."

For a moment, I don't know what he means — new church? The heretic? — before both Fastidius and I realise he must mean the stone church at Ariminum — and Paulinus.

We decide it's best if I ride alone to the *villa*, since I'm the last person with whom Paulinus managed to keep good relations. He might regard Fastidius as the agent of Germanus — and he wouldn't talk to anyone else.

The church is as unfinished as the last time I saw it, and without the workers milling about it looks desolate and abandoned. I bash at the bronze door.

"Go away," Paulinus yells from inside. "I'm not going to let Pelagius be denounced inside my church!"

"It's me," I say. "I'm alone."

I wait until I hear furniture moved away. The door creaks open by an inch. I push my way inside. The dark interior reeks of ale and old wine. The beams of light poking through the holes in the incomplete roof remind me of the *villa's* old bath house and, for a split second, Eadgith's young nakedness flashes before my eyes.

"I've heard what happened," I say, covering my nose from the stench.

“If you’re here to convince me to let that bastard use my chapel, you’re wasting your time. I’d rather give it to those pagans in the village for their orgies.”

“Is that wise? He *is* an envoy from Rome. And a Bishop. Even Wortigern doesn’t think to stand against him — next Sunday, Germanus is going to celebrate the Mass at Saint Paul’s.”

“Wortigern is a politician and a warrior, not a man of God. He doesn’t have the luxury of doing what he thinks is right.”

“And what do you think he should have done?”

“Lock the city gates. Have him wait in the cold and dark.” He repeats the same question that’s been bothering Wortigern: “He’s just one man, what can he do?”

“It’s too late for that. He’s gathered enough followers to storm the walls by now.”

Paulinus picks up one of several clay flasks from the floor, sees it empty and throws it away with disgust.

“Does anyone know why he’s come this time?” he asks. “Has he said anything yet?”

I admit the truth — we are all in darkness. All we know, from the spies Wortigern sent out to Gaul after the Bishop’s arrival, is that the Roman Legion still stands, waiting, across the Narrow Sea — but it is, just as Germanus said, without its commander. Is Rome simply playing for time until Aetius’s return from Italia? Is this all just a giant ruse? We can’t possibly guess.

"How much do you know about his last visit?" asks Paulinus.

"I've heard about Albanus," I say.

He nods. "He's going to pull off another trick like that this time, mark my words." He rubs his chin. "Saint Paul's is as good a place for it as any. I'm sure Wortigern and Fatalis both know it, but, as you say, it's too late now."

"What can we do?"

He shakes his head. "Nothing. Just watch and wait your turn. It's all in God's hands now — but Devil take me if I make it easy for him to do what he wants. Let him preach from a hilltop, like our Lord himself. I'll sooner burn this place down than let him in." He finds at last a flask with some liquid still in it, and exclaims in joy. He raises it to his lips, trips and falls.

I pick him up from the floor. "Let me take you back to the *villa*," I say. "Nobody's burning anything tonight. I'll let the Bishop know of your decision. I'm sure he'll understand."

The tufts of grass peeking from under the setts on the Cathedral hill are scorched straw-white by the summer sun. The rust-blazed hedges provide little shade, and as I wipe a layer of oily sweat from my forehead, I regret not taking a hat. At long last, I turn north, just before the Cathedral gates, and enter the shadowy maze of newly built wooden huts. These simple, dome-roofed dwellings, similar to the hermit cells in the monastery at Tanet, and surrounded by a wicker fence, have been constructed to accommodate the twelve Iute "hostages" sent by Hengist as his part of the bargain with Wortigern.

There are more than just these twelve men and women now living in the neighbourhood. To gain Hengist's assistance against Aetius, Wortigern eased the restrictions on Iutes and Saxons living in the city. Ever since then, a small, cautious trickle of newcomers has flowed through the Bridge Gate. Some of them settled here, around the twelve cells, others returned to the camp in the northern corner of the Forum, beginning to eke out a semblance of as normal existence as was possible in these uncertain times.

A man in warrior's garb stops me at the wicker gate: it's Haesta, Hengist's cousin and nominal leader of the community.

"What are you doing here?" he asks, brusquely. "Shouldn't you be on the coast?"

"I'm here to see Rhedwyn," I reply. "Out of my way."

"Rhedwyn is under my protection." He puts a hand to my chest. He bears no arms — none of the hostages do — but the look on his face tells me he's willing to fight me with his bare hands, if need be.

"Since when?"

"Since you decided to wander off with the *wealas* army, like the little Roman lapdog that you are."

I reach for the *seax* with one hand, and grab his wrist with the other. For a moment, we measure each other in silence. "I have no quarrel with you," I say, at last. "I bring warning. Let me pass."

"Haesta!"

Rhedwyn emerges from her abode — not a hermit's hut, but a fine Roman house, or a remnant of one, attached to the Cathedral's northern wall. She paces towards us impatiently.

"I told you, I can protect myself well enough," she says. "Leave us alone."

"Yes, my lady," replies Haesta, red-faced and downcast. He gives me one last suspicious glance before wandering off.

"Will I have to fight him off too, to get you?" I ask, only half-joking, once we stop kissing.

"Are you jealous of Haesta?" She chuckles. "No, you have nothing to worry about. He's not interested in me — I don't think there's any woman he's interested in… He just takes his role here very seriously, that's all." Her voice trails off. "Why *are* you here? What was that about a warning?"

"You must tell all your kin in the city to hide somewhere for a few days," I tell her. "Maybe a week."

"Why?"

"Have you heard nothing of what's been happening outside?"

"All I know is that there's a lot of commotion at the Cathedral — I saw your brother leave in a hurry a few days ago, and Bishop Fatalis hasn't left his offices in a week — not even for the Sunday Mass…"

I tell her of Germanus's arrival and march through the *pagus* of the Regins as we return to her house — what was once a dining room and a couple of adjacent chambers of some rich *Domus*, of which most has been cleared to make place for the Cathedral. A surprising amount of the old decoration has been retained — there are shards of mosaic on the floor, curtains and carpets hang around on the stone, and a remnant of a large mural on the wall once facing a garden, now an open space filled with the hermit huts, showing some scene from an ancient myth.

Once we're safely inside the house, I tell her of the confrontation at Ariminum, where Beadda's Iutes stood side-by-side with the *villa*'s servants, roused by Paulinus, to stop Germanus from forcing his way into the church. It was a strangely uplifting sight, the pagans and the Christians standing together, around the whitewashed church, too few to stop the Bishop's followers from trampling the cemetery and the wheat fields around the village, but determined enough to make the mob pause in their tracks.

"Paulinus may be a bad neighbour, but he's *our* neighbour," Beadda told me. "We don't know anything about this new priest, other than that he doesn't like Saxons. Still, if your *Dux* wants us to let him pass, he only has to say so."

But Wortigern remained silent, content with merely observing the developing situation, and ostensibly not taking any side in the conflict; though I couldn't help but wonder if Beadda's determined resistance wasn't all a part of the *Dux's* plan, to test the Bishop's resolve before our arrival in Londin.

As the tension grew throughout the day, it seemed as if the mob would at any moment rush at the handful of defenders and tear them limb from limb in pious frenzy — until, at last, as the sun drew to the horizon, Germanus changed his mind and announced he would conduct the ceremony under the open sky on Woad Hill, in imitation of the Lord's sermon — just as Paulinus predicted.

"The Bishop appeared magnanimous at first," I continue the story, "but the next day, he confronted Wortigern and demanded an expulsion of *all* the men of Saxon and Iute blood from the capital while he's here. Even the baptised, even the citizens. He didn't say anything about hostages or slaves, but it's clear he wants you *all* gone."

"And the *Dux* agreed to it?"

She is as shocked as I was when I first heard Wortigern's decision. The expulsion, even before the *Dux's* approval, was first pronounced on the outskirts of Beaddingatun, to the stunned Iutes and villages of Saffron Valley. Germanus's newly appointed heralds were soon seen rushing up and down the network of the Roman highways, making sure the demand reached anywhere the Iutes and Saxons had settled, including the villages where their kin have lived for generations.

Even those of Wortigern's own courtiers who supported the earlier expulsions were astonished by the severity of the demand. The new order included some of their own kin, business partners and servants… They were placated only when Wortigern assured them that the measure was temporary, until the Bishop's visit was over.

"It is for the Devil worshippers' own good," the Bishop's heralds explained — ignoring the fact that most of those to be expelled this time were already baptised, or even born into Christian families. "They would not be able to withstand being in the radiant presence of his Holy Person."

"The *Dux* doesn't want to bother the guards with executing the order in its fullness," I tell Rhedwyn. "There's not enough of them, in the first place. Trying to enforce the Bishop's demands would only cause unnecessary confusion and chaos in the streets — and there's been enough of it as it is. So if the Iutes just hold their heads down until the Bishop's gone, I'm certain everything will work out fine."

"You're not certain at all. I can see it in your eyes. What if that Bishop of yours *never* leaves?"

"It's only for a little while," I plead. "This is a difficult time for all of us."

"Difficult time?" She scoffs. "You're so fortunate not to know what it's like to be a real Iute. Expelled, invited, expelled again, accused of all sorts of things, banished, beaten, trapped forever on a filthy, squalid island... Maybe Aelle was right," she says, recalling the many times we've discussed my conversation with the Saxon. "Maybe we *can't* live side-by-side with the *wealas*. Maybe it will have to be us or them."

I take her hand and stroke it softly in silence, as I often do when I run out of arguments. She sighs. "I suppose it's not your fault. You're only a messenger."

I wince at the accusation in her voice — but, was there anything I could've done? Could I have convinced the *Dux* where none of his Briton courtiers did? If I pressed any harder, the faint protection I'm given by my status and friendship with Wortigern and Fastidius might come apart, and I would be threatened with expulsion myself. At least this way, I might be able to help anyone still left in the city — or so I'm telling myself…

"It looks like we don't have much choice — again," she says. "I will send Haesta with the news." She looks around the room absentmindedly. "And what are you going to do today?"

"I need to go back to the *Praetorium*," I reply. "There's a lot to prepare for Wortigern's and Germanus's entry into the city."

From beyond the wall comes a deep snoring — one of the old women who guard Rhedwyn must have fallen asleep in an adjacent chamber. A mischievous smile appears on Rhedwyn's lips.

"Let me show you something I discovered here a few days ago," she says.

She takes me by the hand and leads me to a swathe of red curtain shrouding most of the eastern wall. She unveils it to present an ancient, faded mural. I stare at its faint lines and splodges of paint until I grasp what it's showing: a satyr and two nymphs, frolicking naked among olive trees. All three are rendered by the artist with great attention to detail, as far as I can perceive through the dust and time; it's rendered in the same style as the illustrations in the *Elephantis*, the book of passions I once found in Master Pascent's study.

"I have been staring at this a lot lately," she whispers, and runs her fingers up and down my arm. "I didn't know the *wealas* made such things."

"Nobody knows how to paint like this," I say, equally quietly. "Not anymore."

I feel a stirring in my loins.

"Do you *really* have to go back so soon?" she asks and bites on my ear.

She is shrouded in the fuzzy afterglow of our love. We are both spent, the remains of our passion slowly evaporating in the summer heat. She has only recently begun to allow me inside her, and the excitement of it still makes me finish early, as if I was an inexperienced youth. We have been as quiet as we could, not to awaken the old crone behind the wall — but now Rhedwyn, too weak to resist any longer, lets out hoarse moans as I suckle at her nipple like a baby.

"Have you learned this from your little Anglian lover?" she asks.

I freeze. My hand hovers over her other breast, hesitantly.

"I've heard all about it from Beadda," she chuckles. "Or did you think nobody noticed you two disappearing into that forest?"

"You — you don't mind?"

"Why should I? We haven't been sworn to each other. I know very well what men are up to on war raids."

I release myself from her embrace and pull away. Is this all I am to her? A love toy?

"Oh, don't sulk," she says, annoyed. "I hate it when you sulk."

"Have you lain with others, too, then?"

"There's nobody here I'd want, other than yourself."

"Is this all that's stopping you?"

"You're jealous of my imaginary lovers, when I let you sleep around with real flesh and blood women?"

She laughs and reaches for my manhood. I should turn away in a huff, but I long for her touch too much and let her caress me, trying to keep an unamused face.

"You know I love you," I say.

"I know you keep saying it when we make love," she replies.

"Why won't you believe me? Is it because you can't love me back?"

She leans over to kiss me. I pull away, but she pulls me back.

"That's not an answer," I gasp when I finally wrestle out from the kiss. She giggles, then turns serious again.

"Why don't you have a wife yet?" she asks.

It is a blunt question, but a fair one. Other than Fastidius, all the men my age I know are already married.

"I don't think any *wealh* woman would want a Iute for a husband." It's a lie — I have received a few offers from various daughters of Londin's nobles — and Rhedwyn is too wise to fall for it.

"Don't be silly. You're a Councillor at Wortigern's court. You own a prosperous *villa.* You're virile enough — if a bit hasty," she adds with a sly smile.

She's not saying it outright, but I know she's skirting around the same topic we've argued on before. If I love Rhedwyn so much, why won't I marry her? Hengist would agree in an instant — it would be a prestigious match for his family, and he must know by now how I feel about his niece.

Except, she would have to be baptised, and accepted into the Church, or I would lose all I have. Would Hengist agree to that? Wedding a pagan woman, in the current climate, would be disastrous. Wortigern would have to disavow me. He might even take Ariminum from me.

But I would be with Rhedwyn, and it should make everything else meaningless, so none of this is reason enough to hesitate with the marriage proposal.

How can I tell her what I'm really worried about? How can I admit I'm afraid of angering the gods, or tempting the Fate, whoever or whatever is responsible for the path chosen for me in my life?

I'm afraid to lose her like I lost Eadgith. What if the same happens now — what if I am cursed by my choices again? Who knows what consequences I would bring by angering Wortigern or Germanus — not just upon myself, but on Rhedwyn, and all the Iutes? What if we were separated, what if I never saw her again?

I know she would not take me seriously if I told her this. It sounds like a made-up excuse even to me. But I can't help it that every time I think of us eloping together to some Iute village, I see the miserable face of Master Pascent and the furious scowl of Paulinus, telling me how disappointed they, and their God, are with me…

She doesn't deserve this. She doesn't deserve *me.*

The snoring behind the wall ends abruptly in a fit of cough. The old crone has woken up.

"I should go," I say, hastily picking up my clothes.

"You know, one day you will have to choose who you want to be," she says, with no hint of humour in her voice.

"I want to be myself," I reply, but she's in no mood for jokes. I lean to kiss her goodbye. "I really do love you, Rhedwyn."

"Then start showing it," she says, presenting me with a cheek, rather than her lips. "Before it's too late."

CHAPTER XVI
THE LAY OF GERMANUS

"Give me your clothes," I order the kitchen slave. "And hide yourself somewhere for the next couple of days."

It is sheer fortune that the slave boy running errands between the rooms and the kitchen at the Bull's Head is a Saxon, roughly my age and size, and that all I need to look like him to an untrained eye is to smudge my face with kitchen grease, shear my hair with a blunt knife and put on the drab, grimy, lard-stained tunic that is his only garment.

When Elasio, *Comes* of the Cadwallons, upon arriving to Londin on the same day Germanus and his horde marched into the city, settled himself at the Bull's Head inn — the same one that I lived in — I didn't make much of it at first. There were only a few inns in the city large enough to lodge a *Comes* and his retinue, and though normally it would have been more proper for Elasio to stay at one of the guest rooms in the *Praetorium*, or a suburban palace of one of his friends, there is nothing normal or proper about the situation in the capital, and in the overwhelming chaos few even notice the unusual choice of Elasio's accommodation.

It is only after I remark to Fastidius how Elasio and I have passed each other at the inn's common room, without him showing any hint of recognition, that it occurs to both of us what an opportunity this provides us.

"He's moved to the inn to be away from Wortigern's spying ears," says Fastidius. "No doubt he's come here to plot something with Germanus."

"And I can sneak around him unnoticed."

"Are you sure he doesn't know who you are? There are so few of your kin left in the city — and none as well-known as yourself."

"I must have looked as wretched and tired as a slave when we met," I say. "Elasio doesn't strike me as one who pays attention to the faces of those he deems lesser than himself."

"It *would* be useful to know what his plans are," admits Fastidius. "There are few men more dangerous to Wortigern's position than Elasio. But what if he finds you out?"

"I can defend myself," I boast. "And if that doesn't work out, I know this city better than some Northerner. Don't worry, I can take care of myself. I just need to find a way to get closer to him and his retinue…"

And so I found myself sneaking into Elasio's quarters with a platter of bread and cheese and a pitcher of ale, moving deliberately slowly and clumsily about the room so that I can hear the most of his conversation with his guest: Severus, Germanus's younger companion.

"Wortigern knows his hold on the *pagi* is tenuous," Elasio explains to the Bishop. "The Regins are practically independent — or rather, subject to the Saxons. The other two are too weak and afraid to resist us. It would only take the slightest of pushes for his rule to crumble."

"You must understand, we do not seek to control the land," answers Severus. "All His Holy Eminence is interested in is salvation of souls."

"Naturally," Elasio nods. "But somebody will need to fill the void left after the heretic's fall. If you let Britannia fail, it will be lost not only to Rome, but to the Church. Chaos is the Devil's playground."

"And what of his son? It was he who called us here, after all."

"Wortimer is ambitious, but foolish. He tried it once already, and it ended in a disaster. By all means, let him take over after his father again. He will not last a month. The people of Londin will be glad to welcome anyone in his place, as long as they have the Church's blessing."

"You will have our support, son," Severus says with a fatherly inflection. "We know you have always been the most faithful and respectful of the true teachings. Speaking of which — " His eyes fall on Elasio's travel chest. " — have you brought it?"

The *Comes* opens his chest and reaches into it — but before he takes out what's inside, he spots me, hovering in the corner with the empty tray.

"What are you still doing here, boy?" he hollers. "Get the hell back into the kitchen! Do you even understand me?"

I mumble something apologetic in Iutish and, bowing, retreat slowly towards the exit.

"We should've got rid of the slaves, too," murmurs Elasio. "Even their very presence tempts the weak astray."

"All in its own time," says Severus.

As Elasio leans over the chest, with his back to me, I stop at the door for a few more seconds — long enough to see him raise, with great reverence, a box, about a foot long, covered in white silk and embroidered with the letter '*A*' and a cross in golden thread.

Severus makes the sign of a cross and raises his eyes to heaven. "Blessed be those who die in the Lord," he whispers in pious awe, "for they will live again."

Has he really come all this way just for another sermon?

We wait under the cavernous vault of Londin's Cathedral, in the stuffy, frankincense-infused darkness. The pillars of light from the lantern windows underneath the vaulted roof set the robes of the nobles and courtiers in front ablaze, and shroud the rich merchants and landlords at the back in a grey, doom-laden shadow; from the courtyard and further outside comes a sound as if of rolling sea billows: it's the murmuring of an immeasurable crowd, city and country folk alike, enduring an early summer heatwave to hear the message from Rome — a word from God.

Fastidius stands beside me, resplendent in Vicar General's robes, and nervous; I can see it in the twitchiness of his gestures, in the subtle movement of his jaw, betrayed in the grinding teeth; in the inadvertent scratching of his cheek and the top of his hand.

He's not the only one anxious. From the *Dux* to Londin's Bishop, we all want whatever Germanus has prepared to be over with already. Not even Fatalis is privy to the secret. Though of the same official rank as Germanus, he is quickly sidelined by the older and more experienced guests. Germanus has access to the Pope's ear and seal, which means a lot more in the complex hierarchy of the Church, even as far away from Rome as Britannia.

"Then I was right," I say when Fastidius explains this to me. "We thought we got rid of the Imperators, but they were only replaced by the Popes."

"It's Aetius and his Legions that grant him authority, not the Pope," replies Fastidius.

"I don't see either of them here. Only a crowd so great they could take over the city if Germanus ordered them to."

The murmurs calm down, as Bishop Fatalis climbs the three steps to the canopy shielding the altar, to celebrate the ritual part of the Mass. Germanus stands by his side, listening to Fatalis's Latin, and wincing whenever the celebrant stumbles upon a word. Fatalis, too, is nervous. Sweat trickles from under the golden headgear. The Mass finishes sooner than usual. We sing a quick hymn and then the Bishops switch places. Germanus gestures at the altar boys. They bring him a thick tome, a large candle, and a box of intricately carved ivory.

"That's the box," I whisper to Fastidius. There's little doubt as to what the box contains, and the fact that Germanus chose to bring it out at the start of his sermon makes everyone still a little more nervous than they already were. In the silence, my whisper carries far, and everyone turns to me, including Elasio, who stands in the second row. The *Comes* of the Cadwallons looks at me with a mocking half-smirk. Did he recognise me after all, back at the inn?

Germanus's commanding gaze renders the hall silent once again. He opens the book seemingly at random and, not looking at its pages, begins his speech.

"Where there is Light, there is Darkness," he booms. "Forty years ago, this island, once a bright, young child of the Church, succumbed to the Darkness. The Darkness of rebellion. The Darkness of heresy."

Fastidius groans and rolls his eyes. Fatalis reddens.

"When I last came here," Germanus continues, "I hoped to stamp out the heresy of mortal free will for good — but Satan, in fate's guise, intervened and my work was not finished. And yet God is infinitely greater than Satan, and saw it fit, in his wisdom, that I would live long enough to return to this blessed island, and to respond to your groans."

He picks up a sheet of parchment from among the book's pages, and though it's too far to see, we are to understand this is a copy of Wortimer's letter.

"It is not only your sons who wrote to me, Britons. Your *Bishops* wrote to me also — though, I notice, not yourself, Father Fatalis."

The Bishop of Londin squirms and cowers under his accusing gaze.

I look to Fastidius for explanation. "It must have been the Bishops of Ebrauc and Lindocoln," he whispers. "I heard Riotham went there after Wortimer's coup — I did wonder why..."

"As soon as the dire news reached me, I knew I had to return," Germanus continues. "I asked the legate at Augusta Suessionum to lend me the fastest of his ships, and I prayed for good winds to bring me here in haste. But most of all, I prayed for the letter to be false. An exaggeration. Could it really be, I wondered, that the Pelagian heresy is not only not extinct, but flourishing within the walls of this holy city? Could it really be that you've invited *heathens* into your midst? That the demons are worshipped in your villages openly, as in the old days? Beasts and men are sacrificed to the old gods, as if our Lord Jesus Christ had died in vain?"

There is a noticeable stir now in the front ranks. It is one thing to attack the way we pray and worship; it's for the priests and Bishops to decide among themselves what is right and what is wrong, before explaining it to the faithful. But Germanus's sermon is now moving to politics, siding openly with Wortimer and threatening to reignite last year's bloody conflict.

"As you have abandoned Rome, so you have abandoned God," he continues. "And the evil fruit of this decision rots everywhere outside this edifice." He raises his arm. "Your fields lie barren; your walls have crumbled; your treasury is empty; you have to rely on barbarians to defend you from other barbarians."

"Steady on, it's not *that* bad," I hear somebody whisper behind me.

"And worst of all, even your sons and daughters are turning to paganism, and choose heathens to lie with instead of good Christians!"

He points an accusing finger at the crowd, and though I know he can't possibly see me, I feel as if his eyes are on me. But this last remark is aimed not just at me, but at the loyalists in the Cathedral and the crowd outside. They are mostly young men, and they are all acutely aware of what the women of Londin think of the tall, strong, fair-haired warriors from across the sea. This one bites the hardest.

"But fear no more. You will live in Darkness no longer, for I bring you the Light of our Lord — " At this, an altar boy lights the tall candle. " — and word of True Faith," he adds, putting his hand on the book. "And the Power of the Saints, as represented by these miraculous bones of Albanus, gifted to me yesterday by this humblest of God's servants, Elasio."

Elasio bows low, beaming.

"With these before me, and with the power of Rome and the Church behind me, I implore you, *Dux* Wortigern, revert from your mistaken ways. Abandon the misguided doctrine of Pelagius, banish the heathens, and return to Rome's fold as all Christians should!"

"Rome and Church as one," whispers Fastidius. "It's just as you said."

"Wortigern will never agree to this," I whisper back.

"It's either that or facing Aetius..."

Germanus pauses, as if waiting for an answer, but no answer is forthcoming. He smiles wryly and repeats the summons.

"It is not for me to decide, Bishop," Wortigern replies at last. "I shall call the Council and address your demands."

"Council? Demands?" Germanus scoffs. "Are you not the leader of your people?"

"We're not barbarians, Bishop. I am no tyrant. We have rules and laws, just like in Rome."

"The only law you should follow is the divine law! Your very *soul*, and the souls of all your subjects are under threat. The longer you dawdle, the closer you are to hell."

Wortigern hesitates. His resolve falters under Germanus's lightning gaze.

"My lord Bishop, I must — "

"Never!" a man cries out in the crowd. He jumps out at the altar brandishing a sharp *seax*. "We will never surrender to Rome's yoke again!"

"Who's that?" I ask, unable to see the man clearly over the sea of heads.

"No idea," replies Fastidius, his voice trembling. "Never seen him before."

The man leaps forth, pushes away the altar boy and plunges his *seax* into the Bishop's chest. Blood stains the vestment. Wortigern's guards rush to apprehend the assailant and wrestle him to the ground.

A great, woeful cry fills the Cathedral, but it's stifled a moment later by an even greater wail coming from outside, when the heralds inform the congregation what's happened. The crowd heaves. The rushing of sea waves grows into a raging storm.

"There will be a riot," I hear Wortigern cry. "Guards, to the door! We have to get out of here before we're trapped. Ash, to me!"

I push through to the *Dux*; Fastidius follows close by.

"The Iutes, are they in position?"

"Yes, *Dux*."

On Wortigern's orders, a dozen Iute warriors have been hiding among the congregation until now, in secret defiance of Germanus's demands. They now rush to us with their weapons drawn, awaiting my command.

"Have them clear the way to the bottom of the hill," Wortigern instructs. "Join up with Beadda's men — they're waiting at the Bridge. And look out for Elasio, he will…"

The Cathedral gate bursts open. The guards try to stop the crowd rushing in, but it's like trying to stop the flood with bare hands. Wortigern and the other nobles run to the sacristy door, led by Bishop Fatalis. I scan the walls for another way out — there are windows over the altar to which

I could climb over the wooden canopy. I point it out to Fastidius, he nods, and we hurry in that direction.

Rhedwyn. All the other Iute hostages have hidden themselves among the abandoned houses in the western part of the city, just as I asked them to, but Rhedwyn remained in her house next to the Cathedral's walls, believing herself protected by her high status. Now, with the furious crowd surrounding the temple, her life might be in danger. I must get to her as quickly as —

"Halt!" a voice booms. "Behold, the power of God!"

The might of the call stops all of us in our tracks. I turn back to the altar to see Germanus stand up, leaning against his companions, blood still soaking through his vestments. But the paleness on his face retreats, the strength returns to his limbs. He's holding the box of bones in his right hand — it seems to be glowing from within with a mysterious light.

"A miracle!" he announces. "A true miracle! Albanus brought me back to life!"

The call is repeated by the acolytes, then by heralds, and then by the crowd of commoners. They all fall to their knees in the face of the wonder. Reluctantly, the nobles follow their example, their heads lowered before the triumphant Bishop. I wait until only Wortigern remains. He looks around, notices me standing by the canopy with one leg on the timber beam, and smiles.

"Wortigern!" Germanus addresses the *Dux* directly. "Your foul plot has failed. The Lord himself intervened to thwart your devilry. You have all witnessed the miracle of

Albanus. *Now* will you repent your sins and return to the flock?"

"What plot? I've never seen this man before in my life," replies Wortigern.

"My lord!" the assassin wails. "I only did what you ordered me to!"

"Your servant's words betray your satanic intentions, *Dux*. Repent!"

The crowd raises their voices in the repeated cry. "Repent! Repent!" Wortigern's face turns wine red. His knees begin to crumble. Germanus looks around triumphantly and spots me.

"You, half-heathen! Kneel down before the miracle of God!" he booms.

I drop to the floor and stare at the black marble floor. The multitude of the voices crying "Repent!" rings in my ears, echoing from the Cathedral's walls, rumbling in my head. Tears well up in my eyes. I cannot comprehend what's going on; I don't know what is happening between Germanus and Wortigern. Who's the assassin? Was he sent by the *Dux* — or by one of the nobles, in a show of misguided loyalty? And what about the miracle — did the God of the Romans really bring the Bishop back to life? Is this the light of divine favour shining inside the box — or just a candle hidden within?

Something glints by my left knee. It's the assassin's knife. He must have thrown it away in the commotion. I pick it up without thinking. There is no blood on it — and the third of the blade is snapped off cleanly at the tip.

"Repent! Repent!"

The *Dux* kneels and opens a trembling mouth. I raise the *seax* closer to my eyes. It's not easy to see in the dim half-darkness of the Cathedral, but as I run my finger along the snapped edge, I become certain.

"My lord," I cry. Wortigern turns to me, and I slide the knife along the floor to him. He studies it for a moment, then realises the truth. He stands up from his knees.

"Just as I thought — it's a trick!"

"How dare you — " Elasio stands before him, but Wortigern pushes him aside and raises the blade to the light.

"This is a theatre knife, made to break off. And I bet that's pig's blood on your vestment. This is no miracle. This is fraud, plain and simple!"

We all expect Germanus to burst in anger — but instead he shakes his head sadly. The light inside the reliquary grows dim.

"I see the Adversary has already taken over your heart. You would even refuse to believe the testimony of your own eyes. So be it. I have given you one last chance — you chose not to take it." He steps over to the altar and raises his hands. "In the name of God the All Powerful, Father, Son, and Holy Ghost..."

"No — stop him!" shouts Fastidius, but everyone just looks at him in confusion. He and Bishop Fatalis are the only ones who realise what's going on. Germanus might be a fraud but he's still a Bishop, and a representative of Rome. Even

Wortigern sees no harm in letting him finish whatever ritual he is performing; it can't possibly be any worse than what's already occurred in the Cathedral. I look to the crowd at the door — the heralds stopped translating the high Roman speech into their common tongue, and they're having a hard time following the unfolding events.

"...by the Blessed Peter and of all the saints, I deprive you, Wortigern son of Vitalinus, and all who aid and abet you, of the Communion of the Body and Blood of Our Lord." Germanus speaks quickly, foregoing his usual stentorious manner. "I separate you from other Christians and exclude you from the Church in Heaven and on Earth."

He leans forward heavily on the pedestal. "I lay an anathema upon you, Wortigern! You are condemned to the Eternal Fire! By my command, your soul and body will be delivered unto Satan. So be it!"

"So be it!" repeat Germanus's acolytes — and the crowd behind us, goaded by the heralds, though they know not why. The Bishop slams his book shut, and his acolytes throw down the candles around them and stamp their flames out.

Silence and darkness fall upon the Cathedral. Germanus and his retinue storm down the aisle — followed closely by Elasio and his Cadwallon nobles. The crowd parts piously to let them all outside. Their murmurs rise again, threatening to erupt into another riot — but for now, everyone is mostly mystified by what has just happened.

"Fatalis, Fastidius!" Wortigern calls. "Explain."

"I feared this would happen. We've been excommunicated," says Fastidius, his face pale like a funeral shroud. "You and all those who serve you."

"Excommunicated?"

"The harshest of punishments," adds Fatalis. "Reserved only to the worst heretics and enemies of God. You are to be shunned by all Christians. I… I can no longer even talk to you, *Dux*." He turns his back to Wortigern and gestures at Fastidius to do the same. "Now please, leave, before all of Londin suffers the same fate."

PART 3: 449 AD

CHAPTER XVII
THE LAY OF POSTUMUS

The echo of my sneeze reverberates throughout the cold, empty, unlit corridor.

I stumble in the dark. I'm still unfamiliar with the road back to my chamber from the latrines. I was forced to move here, to the eastern wing of the *Praetorium*, after the innkeeper at the Bull's Head refused to serve me anymore. "You must understand, Councillor," he said, all in apologetic bows, "how bad it is for my business to host someone like you. The guests are afraid your… unique situation will affect all of them."

He wasn't the only one in the city struggling to find the correct way to deal with Bishop Germanus's strange pronouncement. It took a couple of weeks for most cityfolk to even register what really happened at the Mass. Wild rumours persisted — many still believed for days that Germanus was dead, slain by the *Dux* himself or one of his Iute allies. The excommunication order, once distributed throughout Wortigern's domain, was confusing and unfamiliar. What was the punishment for associating with the *Dux* and his Council? Who would execute this punishment? Were slaves and servants released from their duties — and if so, what were they supposed to do with themselves in their newly found freedom? And most importantly — and mysteriously — was the *Dux's* soul really damned for eternity?

I pass more empty rooms on my way back. One by one, as the effects of the anathema began to sting, Wortigern's courtiers fled not only the palace, but the city — moving north, to Elasio's court at Werlam. There, bathed in the holy light beaming from Albanus's miraculous bones, the *Comes* of the Cadwallons raised a new stone chapel to house the relics, and a new dwelling to house Bishop Germanus and his acolytes after they stormed out of the Cathedral, declaring it a den of devilry. With all this activity, Werlam, already one of the largest cities of Britannia, is dangerously close to overshadowing Londin — and as its prestige grows, so does the fame of its ruler.

There is one light still shining from under the door: Wortimer's room. He received a dispensation; the Bishop hopes he will influence his father to change his mind and repent; but Wortimer doesn't seem interested: neither in this, nor in running the city in his father's place on a daily basis — not until he can officially claim the seat of the *Dux*. Instead, he lets those of us who are still left on the Council stew in our own juices and observe with mocking indifference as we struggle to control the city against the odds. The result, predictably, is total chaos.

The capital outside is as cold and dark at night as the *Praetorium*. There's no one left to keep either of them heated or lighted. No merchant is willing to sell us enough fuel. The townsfolk are forced to burn their furniture — and they have to do it themselves. The slaves and servants may have been just as confused about what excommunication really meant as everyone else, but they soon grasped that it meant *freedom* — if they were lucky enough to have masters who decided to weather the storm in the city. Most of these slaves fled to the countryside or hired themselves out to new masters in Werlam; the few who stayed did so only because they had nowhere else to go. Only a handful remained to serve Wortigern and his family out of loyalty.

It is one of those last few loyal servants who finds me in the corridor. He puts up a torch to my face. "Your presence is requested, Councillor Fraxinus," he croaks.

"At this time of night? Tell the *Dux* I'll be in the audience hall in a minute."

"Not the hall — you are needed at the Bridge Gate."

"The *Bridge Gate*?" I frown. "Do you know what's happened?"

"I do not, Councillor. All I know is I've been sent to bring vicar Fastidius, too, from the Cathedral. If you will excuse me…"

He brushes past me and hurries towards the courtyard, leaving me in the darkness again.

I don't know what I expected to see at the gate, but it certainly wasn't this: all twelve Iute hostages, led by Haesta, and with Rhedwyn in tow, in her green tunic, facing a handful of city guards, barring their way across the Bridge. The Iutes are unarmed, other than with sticks and stones, except Haesta, who found somewhere an old, rusty Briton sword. The guards wield spears, but are hesitant to use them; they pull back when Haesta steps forward with force.

"What's happening?" I ask him. The guards look at me with uncertainty. Some of them must recognise me — I've passed through this gate enough times to know every guard by name — but they can't be sure if I've come to thwart the Iutes, or to help them. "Did Hengist break the treaty?"

"I haven't heard anything from Hengist, and I don't care," replies Haesta. "There's nothing for us here. We're going home. Now, tell these men to let us pass, if they don't want a fight — if you still have any authority over them."

"A *fight?*" I look him over, doubtfully. The remaining hostages are mere children — the eldest is a sixteen-year-old girl. They look famished and miserable, but their faces are glowing and their eyes are burning. Still, it would be sticks and fists against spears, and no amount of spirit would change the outcome of that battle.

I turn to the guards. "What are your orders?"

"We… we don't know," replies their sergeant. "The *Dux* told us to halt them, and then disappeared somewhere — "

"Wortigern was here?"

"Yes, but — he's been excommu-… excommuni-…"

"We don't know if we should follow his orders," the other guard interjects. "Or yours, for that matter."

"If it was up to me, I'd let them go," says another. "I don't know why we need their lot in the city, anyway."

"Quiet, fool," the sergeant shuts him up. "We need them here so the Iutes don't rise against us again."

Rhedwyn comes up to me. She puts a hand on my chest. I take a deep breath. I am desperate to touch her under that green tunic. If only we were alone now… This is the first time she has let me get near her since our quarrel before Germanus's Mass. All this time, she has remained cold and distant, waiting for me to make the first move — waiting for me to choose her over my privileged Roman life…

"Do you see now, Ash?" she says. "This is what they think of us. We've had enough."

With Germanus gone from the city, the Iutes of Londin no longer need to hide — and the hostages are free to return to their cells; but other than that, their position hasn't improved. The Bishop's heralds joined forces with Wortimer's roughs in spreading their message of hate and fear against all Iutes and Saxons. With Wortigern's protection weakened, the twelve Iutes became prisoners in their new homes, unable to walk the streets openly for fear of being pelted with dung and tile shards wherever they went. Only the fear of Hengist's retribution kept the roughs from overrunning the Cathedral compound. I cannot blame them for wanting to leave the city for good.

"Tell them to let us go," she says. "Before the *Dux* returns."

Where *is* Wortigern, anyway? Where did he need to go that was more important than this — and why did he call for me to handle this debacle? He knows I have no more authority over the city guards than he does. One word from him would sort everything out…

This must be a test of my loyalties, I decide. He's sent me here to see which side I would choose when left to my own devices. If I let the hostages go, my career at the court is over. I would need to go with them, back to Tanet. Has he been looking for a pretext to remove me from the Council?

"It's time to choose," Haesta says, as if reading my thoughts. "Are you a Iute, or a *wealh*?"

That's easy for you to say. I grind my teeth, furious at Haesta. I can see why Hengist wanted to rid himself of the impetuous youth. My choice would've been far easier if this was only about my and Rhedwyn's, and nobody else's, future. But bringing the hostages into the mix complicates everything. There's still a risk that with the hostages gone, the war with the Iutes might erupt again. Not because of Hengist — of that I am sure — but because of the fear unleashed by their disappearance. The hostages were always just a way to placate the Londin folk, to make them think they controlled the situation. With them gone, the Britons might be convinced towards a pre-emptive strike against the Iute villages. I have no doubt Wortimer would be quick to use this opportunity to divert everyone's attention from the chaos and confusion permeating the capital.

And I could do nothing to stop him. Forced to hide away in some remote settlement in Cantiaca; no influence at the court, no contact with the loyal Councillors, cut off even from Fastidius… It would be so much worse than during Wortimer's earlier coup. No, I cannot allow this. I am still of use in the city — I am still of use to Wortigern, now more than ever, since I'm not as affected by the anathema's terrible curse as his Christian supporters.

"I… can't let you go," I say. "Not without the *Dux's* permission."

"Ash!" The accusation in Rhedwyn's voice stings like a spear thrust. She slaps me in the face. Haesta raises his rusty sword against me and the guards. I reach for the *seax* at my waist.

"Don't do this, Haesta," I warn him. "You're all going to get hurt — or worse."

"Now I can see you're just a *wealh*," he replies. "A Iute would know it's better to die fighting than to live like a slave."

I hear the two men run from the direction of the Cathedral before I see them, emerging from the Wall's shadow: Wortigern and Fastidius. They appear in the nick of time — or have they been waiting there all this time…? Fastidius, ever the peacekeeper, stands between me and Haesta. I can see a few of the hostages step back, either out of fear or respect for the priest. Wortigern towers over the sergeant of the guards, the sheer power of his stare forcing the soldier to succumb to the *Dux's* authority, anathema or no anathema. The spears in the guards' hands hold firm. There is no doubt now that they will let no one cross the Bridge without a fight.

"Out of my way, priest," Haesta snarls.

"Peace, son," Fastidius pleas. "Return to your homes. All will be fine, as God is my witness."

"I am not your son," Haesta retorts. "And your God of Peace doesn't impress us — it never has, right, lads?" He addresses the hostages behind him, and they reply with a subdued murmur of agreement — some, I notice, less enthusiastically than the others. "Step aside, if you don't want to get hurt."

"Please, make him stop," I say to Rhedwyn. There's no point arguing with Haesta anymore; the boy has a death wish, I can see it in his eyes. Once he's drawn a blade, he will not rest until it's bloodied.

"Why should I?" she replies, mockingly.

"Think of your people. If anything happens to any of you, your uncle will have no choice but to seek retribution. There will be more fighting, more death. Londin is like a bundle of straw soaked in oil — a single spark is enough for it to burst into flame. Is this really what you want?"

"Anything is better than going back there," she says.

"It will change. Fastidius and I will make sure you're safe from now on."

"You knew what was happening. You haven't done anything. Why should we trust you now? Why should we trust *any* of you?"

I take her hand in mine. "Because I give you my word. I will take care of you from now on."

Her lips narrow. There is no gentleness in her eyes as she takes my hand away. "Haesta, put down the sword," she says. "This has all been a bad idea."

"Don't tell me you trust this… *wealh*!" Haesta spits out.

"I don't," she says, looking me straight in the eyes. "But he's right. There's no point starting a war over us."

Haesta throws down the blade — it lands in a plume of rust. It wouldn't have held even against a wooden stick. The hostages slump and turn around, resigned to their fate. I feel Wortigern's hand on my shoulder — he was right behind me all this time.

"You did well, Fraxinus."

I struggle to contain tears.

There are few of us left at the long Council table — too few. Only the most loyal of Wortigern's allies remain with him: the veterans of the Gaul wars, his oldest companions, who've been with him through the worst — and a handful of Londin nobles who decided to join him in this strange spiritual exile, hoping for a quick solution to the conflict, old Postumus among them.

Wortimer is here, too. He would not pass an opportunity to gloat over his defeated father. He sits back with his legs on the table, playing with the fruit knife, with a lingering smile on his face.

"And now, the bones of Saint Albanus have cured his son," the *Dux* says, mockingly. "I bet it was just a cold."

"I didn't know his son was ill," says one of the nobles.

"I didn't even know he had a son," replies another.

"Shows how much you know, Nemmonius," the *Dux* scoffs. He reaches for the silver jug — there are no servants left to do it for him — pours the last drop of the wine into his goblet, then throws it on the floor. The jug spins with a whistling clank.

"That was the last of the Burdigalan," he grunts.

"Wine is the least of our problems," replies the *praefectus* of the granaries. "The harvest has passed, and the wheat is wilting in the fields. The grain stocks will run out long before the winter at this rate."

"The Gauls will not sell us any more," complains another nobleman. "They've been ordered not to by their bishops."

"What about the pagans?" asks Wortigern. "The Saxons shouldn't care about the Church's edicts."

"They're gouging us dry," replies the *praefectus*. "They know how bad our situation is."

"Last night the last of my serfs fled North," adds one of the veterans. "Even though I had one of them whipped the week before for attempting to do the same. All I have left are my slaves — and they're awful workhands."

"Even the slaves are no longer bound to obey us," says the *praefectus*, "but I'll be damned if I let them run away."

"We're all damned anyway," says Postumus, and spits a half-chewed piece of gristle from a badly cooked haunch of some grey meat.

The others murmur in agreement. It's a tale they all share. The anathema is a terrible curse to the loyal noblemen: it leaves them with no trade, no workforce, and no revenue.

"You will all be compensated generously once this is all over," Wortigern says and waves a hand dismissively. He puts on a brave face, but it's clear to all he's as rattled as everyone else.

"And when *will* it be over?" asks the grumpy veteran. "How long can we keep this up?"

"Well, what would you want me to do?" the *Dux* erupts. "You know this is about a lot more than grovelling before Germanus and his friends in the North. Shall I surrender to Aetius without a single spear throw, and bring back the Roman yoke? The Roman taxes, the Roman Magistrates to bleed you dry? Roman press gangs coming for your sons? Because if that's what you want — and God help me, I wish you would — I will have the carriage ready by evening prayers!"

"Maybe it's better to pay taxes and live, than to starve and go to Hell," whispers one of the courtiers, but the others promptly silence him. If they wished to surrender to Rome's bullying, they would've ordered the *Dux* to do so a long time ago.

I did not understand this at first, even after all my years at the court. Shortly after the excommunication scandal erupted, I confronted Wortigern in his throne room. It was a moment of startling honesty for both of us. In this dire moment, we could no longer afford wasting time on decorum and deception.

"What's so bad about going back to Rome?" I asked. "Is it just because you fear punishment for your usurpation?"

The *Dux* scoffed. "Usurpation? The Governor's seat was empty when I entered the *Praetorium.* Those who wanted it weren't strong enough; those who were strong enough did not want it. All they did was vote this way and that until they almost voted themselves into oblivion. Just about the only thing they could agree on was that they needed a strong man to help them against the rebels. And still they shirk from any responsibility! Only my son has enough ambition to wish to take my place." He brushed his hair from his forehead. "No, I don't fear Rome, Germanus or the Pope. If I thought it'd make a difference, I'd give Britannia back to them tomorrow."

"Then why not?"

He looked to the ceiling, then down again. A hole in the roof, unfixed for weeks, was letting in a jagged ray of sunshine. It danced on the floor, covered half with a remnant of a mosaic and half with a straw blanket shrouding a broken pavement.

"Forty years ago, when the Legions left," he answered at last, "the Britons understood something about Rome. It didn't want to rule them as equal — it no longer had the resources for it. What it wanted was to drain them for its wars. Take their gold and their young men and shore up the defences on the Rhenum and in the Alps, guard Gaul and Italy from the barbarians, Britannia be damned."

"What if it's no longer like that?" I protested. "What if Aetius is going to bring back the Empire of old? What if Britannia is left out of it?"

"Ah, bring back the Empire…" the *Dux* replied wistfully. "You younglings can't even imagine what it was like. To live in houses that weren't ruins, to have hot water to bathe every day, to drink wine that didn't taste of vinegar, eat food that tasted of foreign spices, not just of the swill the pigs muck about in…"

"I'm not that young," I reminded him. "I remember the baths at Ariminum when they still worked. And the feasts."

"Yes, yes." He waved his hand with impatience. "The point is, I would love nothing more than to bring it all back. But it's not happening. Did Germanus promise us anything in return for allegiance? Was he open to negotiations? No, he only had threats and insults. Why? Because he has nothing to offer. Why doesn't Aetius invade yet, instead sending that fraudulent priest? Because he can't afford it — it would leave his flanks open to the Franks and the Goths. He's struggling to keep Gaul as it is. No, they don't want us to be part of their new Empire… They just want to use us to help them save themselves, what's left of them. Mark my words. Sooner or later, Germanus will have to admit what they really came here for."

"And what if you're wrong, *Dux?* What if all that is needed to bring back the glory of Rome is Britannia's renewed allegiance?"

He gave me a wry smile. "Then we're *all* doomed, boy."

"We could start by getting rid of the barbarians, as Germanus demands," remarks a man sitting closest to Wortimer. He casts me a sly look. "That might placate the Empire somewhat."

"Banish the pagans, you say? Get rid of your bodyguards, your blacksmiths, your craftsmen?" Wortigern mocks him. "And then what — send off your flaxen-haired wives and daughters? I know all about your… predilection, Nemmonius. Don't think I wouldn't make sure your mistresses would be the first to go."

The Councillor falls silent, red-faced. Wortigern now points to Fatalis. The Bishop sits at the opposite end of the table, as far away as possible, as if we were all stricken with a plague. He's come here in disguise, after repeated summons from the palace turned to desperate pleas. Fastidius sits beside him, with parchment and stylus ready to jot down any decisions made.

"Aren't you a Bishop, too? I am your *Dux* — I command you to reverse this."

"I'm afraid I have no such power, my lord. Germanus speaks for the Pope. Only he can reverse the decision."

"Blood and guts, Fatalis, this is all your fault. Why didn't you warn me this could happen? We all knew he didn't just come here to preach."

"Excommunication is a tool used against the gravest, most unrepentant of heretics, lord," the Bishop replies, twitching. "I didn't expect the Church to use it as a weapon against secular rulers."

"There was the precedent of Imperator Theodosius," remarks Fastidius.

"What is it, boy?" Wortigern leans forward.

"Some sixty years ago, Imperator Theodosius ordered his soldiers to massacre the population of some small city in the East. The Bishop of Mediolanum excommunicated him for this atrocity."

A grim silence falls briefly, interrupted by Fatalis. "But that was different. It was a clear crime and a clear punishment, and nothing else came from it. It's only a footnote in canonical history now."

"There is no difference in the law," objects Fastidius. "On that, all books and treatises are clear."

"I expect the Imperator had the Bishop's head on a stake the next day?" I ask.

"No, lord. He repented before the Council of all of Italia's Bishops in Mediolanum."

All are taken aback by the revelation. If not even an Imperator is free from the heavy justice of the Church, what chance is there for a mere *Dux*? But in their astonishment, they fail to notice what seems to me an obvious solution to the crisis. I wait to see if anyone else spots it, but they all sit in stunned silence. I look to Fastidius, but even he doesn't say anything. Can nobody see it?

I raise my hand. "Could we not get a Council like that set up in Londin?"

Wortigern looks at me, then at the Bishop, then his face lights up. "The boy has a point," he says.

“It’s a thought,” says Fastidius, nodding, somewhat surprised that I came up with the idea instead of him. “It would take every Bishop in Britannia.”

“A Council of all Britannia?” Fatalis gasps. “We haven’t had one since the days of Maximus!”

“We’ve never had an excommunication, either. Doesn’t mean it can’t be done.”

“It would take weeks to organise… The cost alone… and how would you convince them to come all the way here — from Ebrauc, from Lindocoln?” Fatalis shakes his head. “Even if you do, what about Lucius of Corin? He won’t do anything without Ambrosius’s say-so.”

But Wortigern’s not listening. I can almost see the ropes and pulleys turn in his head. He is thinking of a plan — a complex plan. His eyes fall on me, then on Fastidius. The corners of his lips rise in a smile.

“Don’t worry about Ambrosius. I know just how to tickle his chin.” He claps his hand at the servants. “Goat skin! Four sheets! And plenty of ink!”

CHAPTER XVIII
THE LAY OF MASUNA

The land here is flat, damp and bland, and excruciatingly dull. The skies, with layers of clouds torn apart by the autumn gale, present more interest to the eye than the ground. A circle of red kites follows us like crows after a butcher's wagon; their unnerving shrills raise the hair on my neck. The chalk hills tantalisingly appear to the north or south from time to time, promising some respite from the dreary expanse of heathland, pockmarked here and there with sparse, thin wood, but it's only a trap for the tired mind, pulling the weary traveller unwittingly off the stone road into the treacherous swamp on either side. Where the swamp and heaths end, there are fields, endless swathes of wheat and barley, but who owns them, I cannot say — the *villas*, few as they are, are hidden from sight by box tree hedges and juniper groves, and we have neither time nor inclination to go out of our way to pay them a visit. A fallen pillar or a broken arch here and there mark where the ancients deemed it suitable to build a roadside shrine or shelter, but it is all gone now, ground into dust and ash by time and the unstoppable wind, howling mercilessly across the plain.

We stop overnight in a memory of a town on an island in the middle of the Tamesa. The Romans linked the island with the river's muddy shores with two stone bridges, which gave the town its name. The bridges still stand, but are so cracked and full of holes, that those of us who don't travel by horse or wagon, prefer to traverse the sprawling marshland by a ferryman's boat. The ferryman also owns the only *mansio* still standing in what once must have been a town of a few hundred souls, but is now reduced to a village of a couple dozen mud huts and lean-tos. Their inhabitants come out in the morning and watch us pass in weary silence. There is not a spark of thrill in their eyes at what must surely be one of the most exciting events in their dreary, everyday existence. It's difficult to tell whether their indifference stems from the fact that they know we all bear the harsh punishment of the Church that makes us nigh untouchable, or that they simply greet all newcomers with the same blank, grey faces.

"There was a time when passing of the Governor's procession meant something in these parts," grunts Wortigern. "I bet they were more enthusiastic when Riotham came through here."

Beyond the river, the hills rise at last, slightly, and the woods grow thick as we pick up the pace. But then the road turns away from the hills again and back onto the plain, which is now sand and mud, as we near another slow, lazy, muddy riverbank, this time crossed by a ford, though judging by the amount of rubble in the stream, a stone bridge must have once stood here, too. Here we are met by a small troop of warriors led by a short, wiry man, whose dark bronze skin testifies to the distance his ancestors must have travelled to settle in this remote part of the world. I remember having seen him a few times at the Council.

"Hail, Wortigern!" he calls to us. The *Dux* climbs down from his horse and the two meet in the midst of the ford. They exchange a few formalities, and then the procession moves slowly onward. The road is better maintained from here on, with fewer holes and patches of grass showing between the flagstones.

"Who's that?" asks Beadda.

"Masuna, *Comes* of the Atrebs," I reply. "His is the border territory between us and Ambrosius."

"And what is his allegiance?"

"That depends on whose armies are closer to his borders."

Beadda nods, satisfied with this explanation.

His band of *Hiréd* is guarding the rear of the procession, which includes six of the Iute hostages, riding ponies behind an unmarked one-horse carriage. The carriage has only a single passenger, her radiant face peeking at times through a small window, hidden behind a veil of dark cloth and silence: Rhedwyn.

Quite why Wortigern insisted on her, and the hostages, accompanying us, nobody's quite certain. Fastidius believes — or rather, hopes — that Wortigern plans to baptise them, and in this way ingratiate himself before Germanus and the other Bishops; but I doubt Hengist would ever agree to something like that, even for a promise of more land for his tribesmen; and without Hengist's approval, the hostages would never be released for a journey as long and dangerous as ours. Beadda, at least, is not aware of any such designs towards himself and his men.

I could always ask Rhedwyn — she, at least, should have some idea of why she's being made to travel all this way. But we haven't spoken a word since the Bridge, and I'm not certain if asking "why are you here, anyway?" is the best way to start a conversation after so long a pause.

By dusk we reach Callew, the capital of the Atrebs. The town, sprawling atop a risen promontory, is substantial and handsome, surrounded by a strong seven-sided wall. Shielded from pirates or sea raiders by its distance from the coast, and sitting cosily halfway on the main highway between Londin and the West, it has retained some of its ancient wealth. Heaps of glass-making spoils rise to the east, around a glass plant that, remarkably, appears still to be working, belching grey smoke high into the air. I assume Ambrosius and his court must be the ones who can still afford to buy its produce, since I haven't seen any new glass in Londin in years.

Though even here, the decline is clearly visible. The amphitheatre rising to our right has been reduced by quarrying to little more than a sunken hillock; the dense grid of streets is only partially filled with still-standing houses — and only those nearest the central plaza still have intact walls of stone. Still, it is among the most populous and rich settlements outside London I've ever seen.

There is only one gate in the eastern wall, but four roads lead out to the west, and by each there's a coaching house; all are still open and as near to bustling with patrons as any establishment can be these days. Wortigern is invited to rest in the *Comes's* "palace" — a richly decorated *tepidarium* of the town's otherwise ruined bath house — but the rest of us need to settle for a coaching house near the westernmost gate. I approach Rhedwyn's carriage to help her out — but I'm bounced aside by Wortimer.

I did not expect to see him here. Last I heard, he was in the North, having volunteered to deliver summons to the Council to Elasio and Germanus. I hoped he wouldn't be joining us until we all gathered at Sorbiodun, where the Council was to be held. And now here he is, haughtier than ever, in a shiny new mail coat of a *Gewisse* pattern, and with a long, slender sword at his side, a strange new type that looks to be halfway between the Roman *spatha* and a *seax*. Whatever he did in Werlam to obtain such rewards, must have had something to do with him switching his allegiances from his father to Elasio. One thing Wortimer could never have been accused of was unwavering loyalty…

He scoffs at me without a word and turns to Rhedwyn. She hesitates, seeing his outstretched arm. Impatient, he almost yanks her out of the carriage and laughs as she trips into his arms. Two Iutes stand by my side to defend their princess, but Wortimer's new guards — *Gewisse* spearmen, rather than his usual militiamen — bar our way forward until she and Wortimer are out of our earshot. He says something to her, and she reels away in horror, but he laughs again and holds her hand in a tight grip.

The next morning, the *Comes* of the Atrebs invites us all to a hunt in honour of the *Dux*. The nearest decent wood is some five miles to the west, on the slopes of a low ridge of chalk downs, and so we all have to leave at dawn to reach it in time for the chase. Rhedwyn stays at the coaching house with other women; in the commotion of preparations for the hasty departure, I sneak past Wortimer's guards and knock on the door of her room.

"It's me, Ash," I spit out the words in a hurry, "are you alright? Did he hurt you?"

The long silence makes me sweat with anxiety.

"Talk to me, Rhedwyn. Why are you still angry? Have I not kept my promise?"

For the past two months, I have been paying out of my own purse for guards to be stationed around the Cathedral compound, and to accompany the hostages whenever they moved through the city. It wasn't cheap — I had to sell some of Master Pascent's ancient art and silver from the *villa.* But it was the only way to ensure the safety of the young Iutes, given no guards were taking orders from either me or Wortigern anymore.

And in all this time, I have not heard a single word of gratitude from any of the hostages. Haesta continued to give me dagger-sharp stares whenever we passed on the street. Rhedwyn would not see me. The only way I could get any news from the Iute compound was through Fastidius, who took over the duty of looking after the hostages' daily needs.

"I'm fine," she replies at last. "He didn't touch me." Her voice is muffled by the door, but loud enough for me to hear her distress. She must have been crying only moments ago.

"What did he want from you?"

"He said that… He said I will soon be his — that his father promised him as much."

"He's lying," I say. "Wortigern would never do something like this — he depends too much on your uncle's warriors."

I try to sound earnest, but my voice lacks conviction. A pagan princess, forcefully baptised *and* wedded in Roman fashion? Not even Elasio could boast such a feat. This might indeed be enough evidence of Wortigern's Christian credentials to sway the gathered Bishops…

"None of this would have happened if you'd let us through on that bridge."

"Whatever happens, I promise we'll get out of this together," I blurt out without thinking.

"And then — what?"

"We'll do whatever you want. We'll go wherever you tell us to."

"I hope you mean it this time — " she says and pauses.

This gives me a brief moment to reflect. What else *could* I have said? The urgency has given me a rare clarity of thought. I can't hold my decision off any longer — I can't pretend I even *have* a choice. For all I know, it might already be too late for it to even matter — but I can't allow myself to believe this. There must be a way to save Rhedwyn from whatever fate Wortigern and his son have planned for her; this time, I will not let my curse destroy another innocent life.

"I do," I say, between the beats of my heart.

Another long silence.

"I have to go. Any moment now, the *Gewisse* will return…"

"It's fine. If he tries anything, I still have my hidden dagger," she says, and sniffles.

"Wortimer's coming with us to the hunt, so you'll at least be safe for the rest of the day. I'll come see you when it's all over."

"I wish I could go to that hunt with you," she says. "I do feel like killing something."

I grin, hearing a rare smile in her voice. "I will shoot a deer for you," I promise. "If they even have deer in these mangy forests."

I hear the guards approaching up the stairs, whisper a quick goodbye and get away out the small window at the back of the corridor.

By the time I make my way down to the stables, the beasts of the nobles have all been made ready for the hunt; the horses stand in dignified silence, in resplendent tack of fine leather, and stare with indignation at the hounds baying at their feet. The Britons are as proud of their hunting hounds as they are of their children. Even the Romans appreciated their value and imported them to their mansions throughout the Empire. But that was a long time ago. Now, no matter how proud of their lineage the Callew breeders are, their dogs no longer are the fine, pure blood specimens they once were.

"Mongrels all," says one of the passing Londin courtiers; I can't tell if he's looking at the dogs or at me and the Iute warriors beside me. Only Beadda is invited to the hunt; the others are made to stay in a camp outside the town walls in our absence. The locals, isolated from the coast, rarely see a fair-hair here and are more than wary of an entire troop of them sauntering freely down the Roman-cobbled streets. It is almost refreshing to feel a straightforward fear emanating from the locals I pass, rather than the loathing and disgust, badly hidden under the sycophantic pretence of respect I get in Londin. Beadda is merely bemused. He's been used to such treatment for far longer than I have.

The *Dux* nods at us to ride closer. Our ship ponies appear comically short next to his great white steed. *Comes* Masuna's pony, however, is only slightly bigger than our mounts: a local breed raised on the grim moors of the South.

We start off on a slow trot, following the beaters, towards the black line of hills to the north. Wortimer rides in the rear with a disinterested scowl. I imagine he'd rather stay back in town, with Rhedwyn — but his father doesn't want to lose sight of his ever-scheming son so close to the border with Ambrosius.

"I'm grateful for you giving us this welcome," Wortigern says to the *Comes*. "I wasn't sure anyone in Britannia would wish to even talk to me anymore."

Masuna nods with a sly smile. "The Atrebs are squeezed between the great powers of this island. We live off commerce and transit. We can't afford to choose sides."

The *Dux* chuckles. "Your shrewdness serves your people well. I did not expect it from one coming from such a warlike race."

"It's true my forefathers arrived here from the land of Maurs, but now there's more Briton merchant blood in my veins than that of the desert warriors."

"I hope you're not *all* merchant yet. We do have a stag to catch."

Masuna reaches for the short hunting spear on his back and shakes it in the air.

"Oh, I will make my ancestors proud today, God willing!"

I have a similar spear shaft at my saddle, but topped with the leaf-shaped blade of my old Anglian *aesc*. Chipped in the battle at the Crei Ford and blunted beyond hope of recovery on a Frank I killed at Anderitum, it will no longer pierce armour, only skin and hide. Old Weland died before I could ask him to re-forge the blade back into a weapon of war, and I did not want to risk spoiling the master's work by giving it to a smith of lesser skill. Out of sentiment, I shafted it on a thicker and shorter ash pole, attached boar flanges behind the blade and kept it for the odd big game hunt, such as the one ahead of us today.

I had few opportunities to hunt during my time in Londin. I took part in some foraging parties organised by the Iutes while we waited on Anderitum's shore, and I went a couple of times on the annual boar hunt at Beaddingatun — but I was little more than a visitor there, watching Beadda's warriors exercise their prowess against the beasts which roamed the edges of Andreda. I struggle to remember if I've killed an animal since I left Aelle's bandit army — certainly nothing greater than a hare. For a moment, I wonder if I will be of any use in today's hunt, but then I remind myself that the chances of even seeing a worthy animal in the local woods must be slim.

We reach the edge of a forest of slender beeches and ivy-smothered box trees, which the Atrebs call the Berroc. A chalk escarpment rises dull grey and oppressive beyond it, a wall of ashen-hued rock that binds Masuna's land from the north-west. Rumour has it that the summer heat forced a royal stag down from the forests at the crest into the humid river valleys below. We pause atop a bald grassy knoll and dismount in the shadow of the beeches. The slaves proceed with setting up a look-out point, while we let the beaters and the hounds do their work and bring the game to us.

"What if I forced you to choose a side?" asks Wortigern. He gives me a glance and I feel sick in my mouth at the reminder of him having forced me to make the same choice not so long ago. He doesn't yet know that last night I changed my mind and have chosen to stay with Rhedwyn — no matter what happens on this trip.

I have had more time to consider my decision since the brief exchange at the inn. Now that my heart has cooled down, I'm even more certain of it. I was fooling myself into thinking I can have the best of both worlds, forever. I can't hesitate any longer — I can't lose her to Wortimer. Even if it means leaving my Londin home, abandoning Ariminum and everything I know, and moving to some Iute village, I will do it — and I will announce my decision as soon as we return to the capital. I can only hope it's not too late by then…

Masuna rubs his chafed thighs. A slave runs up with a pitcher of cool water.

"I would feel most uncomfortable, *Dux*," the *Comes* replies, wiping his mouth. "Almost unbearably so."

"Don't forget who helped your father when the Rebellion threatened your borders. By the Treaty of Sorbiodun, your land still falls under Londin's command."

The *Comes* smiles. "I'm sure you don't need reminding we've paid off this debt with interest, whenever your treasury ran empty," he says. "We are, naturally, closer to Londin than to Corin, both by road and by politics — and at any other time, I would not hesitate to support your claim. But, things have changed. There's more than two sides at play now."

"That turbulent Bishop." Wortigern clenches his teeth.

"Him as well," Masuna replies enigmatically. Before the *Dux* can inquire further, we hear the baying of hounds and the hooting of bugles close in on our camp.

We climb to the top of the knoll and position ourselves in the hide, disguised with leaves and branches to resemble a large shrub. A heath-spattered meadow, enclosed in three directions, spreads further northwards, and it is there that we expect the game to appear. We all step back, letting the *Dux* take the best point. Beadda strings a bow — he alone takes the hunt seriously, choosing arrows over javelins. I glance back to Wortimer — he hasn't even drawn a weapon yet.

The hounds are nearing from our left. I strain to peer into the light-dappled darkness among the trees. For too long, there is nothing. The spear shaft in my hand turns wet with sweat. Black spots dance in front of my eyes. Finally, I see it, a faint reddish shape. The others spot it too. We wait, motionless, except Beadda, nocking an arrow in total silence. Even the hounds fall quiet, brought to heel by their handlers, satisfied there is nowhere for the deer to go from here but towards us.

The stag leaps out onto the heath and stops, blinded by the sun. I gasp. I have never seen a beast as magnificent as this, not in the sparse forests of Ariminum, not even in the depths of Andreda. From what ancient legend has it sprung? It's at least nine feet tall. Its antlers are like gleaming trees, topped with sharp knives, now fatigued and covered with torn greenery. A great beard-like cloak flows down its neck, giving it an appearance of a stately elder. I hear some of the Atreb nobles behind me whisper a pious prayer to a Briton god of the forests. It is fitting: the stag looks like a deity come down among mortals.

It notices our horses, then makes a few steps towards the hilltop, and gazes up, assessing the hide's disguise. For a brief moment, I feel it's looking straight at me. Then it changes its mind and darts to the side.

With a grunt, the *Dux* heaves the spear. It scratches the stag's back and bounces into the forest, splashing a thin red trail. A split second later, *Comes* Masuna and I let loose our short-shafted missiles. Beadda's bow twangs next to my ear.

The stag stumbles, and sways under its heavy crown of antlers, then scrambles back up and leaps again into the forest, dragging the spear shafts behind it just as the first hounds appear on the meadow. We jump out of the hide and rush downhill to where the servants already prepared our mounts.

"A bag of silver for whoever brings me the head!" shouts Wortigern.

It's easy to follow the panicked stag — it tears a broad path through the dense wood, marked with blood splatters on the tree trunks and brush leaves. In the harsh terrain, our ponies charge ahead of the tall horses. I slow down only to pick up my red-tipped spear that the stag tore off against a tree trunk — it did not penetrate deep enough to stay in through the pursuit.

The trail swerves northwards, and the reason soon becomes apparent, as the ground angles down and turns muddy. A stag as great as our quarry does not survive that long without having some tricks up its sleeve. The forest opens onto a river. The banks, grown with weeping willows dipping their boughs in the water, are steep, but low, and the current hemmed between them is not much wider than the Loudborne. I spur the pony to wade through, but notice Beadda halt at the edge. He nods back towards our superiors, who only now reach the riverbank. He's right — it would be unseemly to cross the river ahead of the *Dux* and the *Comes*.

The *Dux* splashes into the stream, but the *Comes* hesitates on the brink.

"What's wrong, Masuna?" cries Wortigern.

"It's… been a while since I crossed this stream, that's all," Masuna replies with a nervous smile.

The *Dux* looks to the far side. "It is still the land of the Atrebs, isn't it?"

"Yes, but perhaps we are getting too close to Elasio's border…"

"Nonsense. It doesn't start until way beyond the ridge. Unless there's something you're not telling me?"

Masuna grits his teeth and spurs his horse to splash into the river, passing the *Dux* and emerging first on the other side.

The trail meanders through the sparse wood. Men have passed through here recently; a couple of large pines have been cut down and taken away, and a row of willows has been freshly coppiced. The hoofprints grow deeper and more laborious: the stag is losing its strength, stumbling and swaying. We dismount now, and follow the track on foot.

Beadda sniffs and frowns. "Smoke," he says. "Ahead of us."

Carefully, we tread on, until we enter a large clearing. There's a village here, not unlike the one where old Weland lived, with its sunken huts and a few wooden homes, surrounded by tarring pits. A smouldering ruin of the largest house stands in the centre, the embers still crackling. No other sound disturbs the silence.

I hold the spear forth, the others draw their swords. The stag, its bloody trail lost on the trampled ground of the village, is forgotten. I glance to Masuna. There is no surprise on his face, only tense concern. Beadda moves to investigate the sunken huts, while the rest of us approach the burnt-out ruin. I'm the first to spot a dead body, sprawled on a blackened timber.

There are more of them, a dozen or so, some inside the house, burned and suffocated, others around it, slain with weapons. Women, children and old men — no warriors among them. All of them Saxon. I now recognise the faint shape of the ruin — a small Saxon hall, a miniature version of the mead halls of the Iute and Anglian chiefs.

"What is the meaning of this?" asks Wortigern, breaking the morbid silence. "You have Saxons in your land, Masuna?"

"They're *Gewisse*," says Beadda. He's emerged from one of the huts carrying a withered body of an old, white-bearded man, clad in a long, thin tunic and a cloak. He lays it carefully on the ground. "This one was not slain — he was being prepared for burial." He points to the mangled brooch holding the old man's cloak, marked with a spiral pattern. "The *Gewisse* we fought with at the beach wore brooches like these. Ask the ones in Wortimer's guard, they'll confirm it."

"How can you be sure?" I ask, incredulous at him remembering such detail.

"You learn to have an eye for these things when a brooch or a pin is your entire treasure," he replies, grimly. "Besides, there is more of their craft inside. Whoever did this, did not come as a thief."

"No," says Wortigern. "After all, stealing is a sin."

I follow his gaze to see a great cross of two young beech trunks tied together, standing on the edge of the clearing, its foot splattered with blood. On a wooden board nailed to the cross I note a scratched mark in the shape of two keys and a crossed circle — the seal of Germanus.

"You must know what happened here," the *Dux* turns to Masuna. "Explain."

But before the hapless-looking *Comes* can reply, I hear a loud grunt in the trees, followed by the beating of hooves on soft ground. I turn just in time to see the royal stag, charging straight at us. Its lowered antlers gleam like a cascade of spear blades.

Beadda leaps towards it with his sword, but the beast storms past him — so great and fast, that it throws the Iute to the ground merely by brushing him with its bloodied flank. In the corner of my eye I spot Masuna dive for safety. Only me and my *aesc* stands between *Dux* Wortigern, armed with just a cavalry sword, and five hundred pounds of furiously galloping, steaming deer flesh.

I let the instinct and the gods guide my arms. It all happens in the blink of an eye, between the two beats of the stag's heart, each marked by a spurt of blood out of the torn spear wound in its side. I throw myself forward, without hope of stopping the beast. The last sounds I hear are the squelch of the spear blade penetrating the hide and the shriek, gurgling grunt of agony coming from the stag's throat. The last thing I see is its bearded, fur-trimmed front, tumbling at me, through me, and over me.

CHAPTER XIX
THE LAY OF KERN

Pain attacks my body from head to toe, in a number and variety of ways too great for me to count. Hot needles pierce my left shoulder. A hungry wolf gnaws at my shins. A blacksmith's hammer pummels my head. My stomach churns from the heavy, pungent smell of the ointments with which my bandages are soaked, mixed with blood. The only part of my body that does not ache — indeed, produces no sensation at all — is the right arm.

Through the buzzing and ringing in my ears, I hear Beadda's voice.

"Congratulations," he says, "you now have more scars than the most battle hardened of my men."

I make out his silhouette through teary eyes, leaning against the frame of a door.

"The *Dux* — "

"Unharmed. The gods have protected him through you." He points at something outside my field of view. "There's more than this sack of silver waiting for you back in Londinium, I bet."

"I don't need Wortigern's silver," I say. The strength is seeping back into my bones. My body doesn't feel as mangled as I feared. If only I could move my right hand… "I want to speak to him."

"He's not here," replies Beadda. "He departed to Sorbiodun as soon as the hunting feast was over. They might even be there already by now. You and I are the only ones left in Callew."

"Rhedwyn…?"

"She's with them, as are all my *Hiréd*."

I try to raise myself, and the room spins.

"Woah, there, son." Beadda rushes to my aid. "There's no need to hurry. The Council will manage without you."

"You don't understand. I must speak to Wortigern…"

The sheet drops from the bed, revealing my right side. My arm is crushed and twisted as if in a vice. It's wrapped in a bandage stained black and blue, stinking to high heaven — and is completely numb.

"It bore the brunt of the entire stag falling on you," says Beadda. "The *Comes's* physicians looked after it as best as they could, but they're not sure it can be saved. They say you need to rest a few days."

"I don't have time for this — I need to get to Rhedwyn."

"The princess is safe. You need to rest."

"She's not safe with Wortimer around."

I tell him what Rhedwyn told me. He turns serious, but shakes his head in disbelief. "Hengist would've told me if he'd planned something like this."

"Maybe the *Drihten* doesn't know about it, either."

"That would mean war."

"Better a war with the Iutes than one with Elasio — and the Church. You've no idea how desperate Wortigern has become."

Beadda rubs his cheek in thought.

"I'll see if I can find us a carriage," he says at last. "You're in no shape to ride."

As the wheels of the hay wagon, the only vehicle Beadda could procure at short notice, rattle on the worn-out flagstones of the Callew Highway, I'm pondering what to ask of the *Dux* when I reach him. I can only hope that he will find time to talk to me at all. The Council must be well under way by now. I cannot demand or threaten him to change his mind; if he did decide to baptise Rhedwyn and give her to Wortimer, he must have considered the full consequences of such a deed — and accepted them. All I can do is plead my cause.

The pain and fever are making it difficult to think. The burning grows with each mile away from Callew, and now my entire right side is on fire. I drink jugfuls of weak ale, and pints of herbal brews prepared for me by Masuna's physicians, and all this serves only to stem the spread of the aches, to contain them around the shoulder and chest. With each bump in the road, the pain bursts anew, as if a red-hot spear was thrust into my side. I'm beginning to wonder if it really was a good idea to come here after all…

In fevered dream I see the scenes from the hunt played out over again and again in my mind. The charging stag. Masuna, leaping away. Beadda's arrows. The pony chase. The burnt-out village. The charred *Gewisse* corpses.

I have enough time to think about what we saw in the forest to make an educated guess at what happened. The *Gewisse* must have been refugees from Elasio's *pagus.* Germanus no doubt convinced him to expel the pagans just as he had in Londin. With nowhere else to go, the Saxon women and children fled to Masuna's territory, where he allowed them to settle in secret, deep in the forest… But even that wasn't enough for Germanus. Without their men to defend them, they were an easy prey to some marauding band of roughs, stricken by pious fury, eager to bathe themselves in the communion wine of pagan blood.

I wonder about the *Gewisse* in Wortimer's guard. Do they know what happened to their kin? Do they serve Elasio because they've been told their families have been taken hostage, rather than expelled? How many such refugee villages are there, scattered throughout the wild forests — and how many more have endeavoured to travel even further, perhaps towards Andreda, that eternal refuge for the dispossessed?

The bitter irony of their fate is not lost on me. The *Gewisse* arrived in these lands maybe ten years before the Iutes, and like the Iutes, they sought here a safe haven from the onslaught of war across the sea. Those slain children would have been the first, at most the second generation born in Britannia. And now, another war they didn't care about found them here — and destroyed them before they grew old enough to raise a sword.

I hear Beadda's voice through the haze of pain. "This looks like the place."

I raise myself on the elbow to look over the cart's side. We've reached a small hill overlooking the floodplain of a wide-spilling, meandering river. Its crest is bound with the remains of an ancient wall, reinforced with Roman earthwork, forming a double ring of impressive proportions — but the settlement within is only a memory of what the wall once protected. The houses are sparse and poor, built of wattle and thatch in the manner the Britons have been building their dwellings since before the Romans came. A small church rises over the ramparts, standing on the foundation of a Roman temple dedicated to some forgotten god.

A further grid of streets can still be traced on the side of the hill descending towards the river, but all that remains of the old suburb is a couple of inns and a few shops serving those travelling along the Roman highway. Across the river, a sharp chunk of a *villa*'s corner stands like an accusing fist aiming at the heavens.

Sorbiodun. It doesn't seem like much now — but it's the history of the place that made Wortigern propose it as a place worthy of the great Council of Bishops of all Britannia. Both the hillfort and the road itself are older than Rome. The river here forms the original border between the two Roman provinces of Maxima and Prima — and it is a border even now, after the treaty that ended the bloody civil war between those who pined for the olden days of Rome, and those who thought they no longer needed the Imperial power… Perhaps most importantly, it is much closer to Corin, Ambrosius's capital, than Londin — and it is, after all, Ambrosius's support that Wortigern will need to seek to win the Bishops over to his side.

The cart passes through a city of tents and huts sprawled on the floodplain to accommodate the great mass of retinues, courtiers, servants and hangers-on that accompany those who've arrived to the Council. A large barn is raised on stone stilts to the east, to hold the supplies needed for the many days of feasting and negotiating that is to follow; nearer the river, straddling a newly dug canal, stands a thatched roof bath house, no doubt built for Ambrosius and his court, used to old style luxuries; but both of these structures are dwarfed by the immense timber construction being built in the centre of the floodplain, a circular enclosure, half as large as Londin's old amphitheatre.

I rise higher to scan the crowds for some familiar faces, when the cart jumps on a bump in the road. I hit the side board with my shoulder and the pain explosion knocks me out for good.

When I awake, it's already dark. Somebody enters the tent. I scramble to light up the lamp, but my visitor reaches it sooner.

"I haven't yet thanked you for saving me, Fraxinus."

Wortigern holds the lamp high. It gives his face a pallid, ghostly glow.

"It was my duty, my lord, as your servant."

"And yet, no other servant stood between me and that stag's antlers."

He puts the lamp back on the table.

"You should have stayed in Callew. That arm doesn't look good."

"I had to know."

"Know what?"

"What you plan to do with Rhedwyn."

He sits down and wipes his face. A slight twitch in his left eye is all that shows how tired he is.

"I don't know anymore. I thought… I thought converting the Iutes, through her, would be enough to placate Germanus and Rome, but after what I saw in that village… There is a viciousness in what they're doing that I hadn't accounted for."

He looks up. "But, you probably didn't know — "

"I've guessed enough. Germanus and his roughs will not rest until they rid this island of the pagans and bring it back into the Church's fold. It's only a matter of time before they strike at the Iutes and Saxons."

Wortigern nods. "I should never have underestimated that accursed Bishop. You say 'Germanus's roughs' — but when that ship landed on Anderitum beach, there were only two of them. Now he's got enough of an army to replace Elasio's *Gewisse*."

"Where did he get the money for all the soldiers?"

"He doesn't need money. They are all volunteers. They flock to him from all over the island, to the new church he's built in Werlam, to the miraculous bones of Albanus he's parading around every Sunday…"

"An army of volunteers is not enough to take Londin. Or even defeat Saxons."

"That's not his plan." He shakes his head. "It's all about showing another way. Proving that Britons can defend themselves on their own again, if motivated enough. Without the pagans, without the barbarians, without Rome even — and with pious Elasio at the helm instead of me. And I can see it working. It's all everyone here is talking about. Wortimer, especially — "

He sees me wince. It's another bite of pain, forcing me to shuffle to my other side, but the *Dux* interprets it differently.

"Does mentioning my son's name pain you so much? I guess you're not the only one."

"It's not that, it's…" I remember what I *really* wanted to ask of him. "Is the baptism all you want from Rhedwyn?"

His eyes narrow. "Is that what made you come all this way, in your state? The fear that I'd give her to my son?"

"That's what he told her."

He scoffs. "The boy is a fantasist. After everything he's done, why would I reward him like that? And risk the wrath of the only allies I have left?" He scratches the side of his head. "He must have found out what I was planning for the Council…"

"And what is it?"

He stands up. "This is not the time to discuss this. Rest assured, the girl is safe." He pauses at the tent's door. "I'll ask her if she wants to see you."

My next visitor is not Rhedwyn — but it's someone I'm almost as glad to see as her.

"Fastidius!" I exclaim. "I thought you stayed in Londin!"

"I came with Fatalis," he replies. "We could not be seen accompanying the *Dux*, as I'm sure you understand. But I can't stay long — I'll be going back to the capital as soon as everything is set up." He looks me over with worry. "I've heard about what happened, but didn't imagine it was so bad…"

"It only looks terrible, really," I feint. I make an attempt at rising from my bedding. "Can you help me out?" I ask. "I haven't seen the sky in days. I don't even know where we are…"

Fastidius covers his concern with a smile. "You'll be glad to see how close your tent is to the main event."

Biting my lower lip to stifle the moan, I lean against his arm and limp outside. He's right — my tent is positioned on the outer rim of Wortigern's encampment, a stone's throw away from the wooden enclosure. The construction's fringe is now decorated with banners of various tribal chiefs and other magnates fluttering in the summer breeze. The same banners top the great tents set up around the structure, around each of which a cluster of smaller tents and huts marks the camp of the followers of each of the guests.

Four of the banners rise the highest of all, in four corners of the auditorium. All four symbols incorporate a cross and a set of keys, and I recognise one of them as the banner of Fatalis; it's easy to guess the other three must belong to the remaining great provincial Bishops.

"From here to the Aelian Wall, the church is still set up along the ancient ways, regardless of what else may be happening around it," Fastidius reminds me, noticing how I study the banners. "Five capitals of five old Roman provinces — and a Bishop's seat in each of them."

"This must be the Bishop of Corin," I say, pointing to the cluster of tents nearest to the river, clinging to the edge of a mud flat, as if afraid to stray too far away from Ambrosius's land. The banner is an Imperial Eagle, wings spread wide, in gold and silver thread.

"Ambrosius is with him," Fastidius adds with a nod. "But not Riotham — they left him to deal with some border insurgency in the West."

"Those two by the marshes — Lindocoln, and…?" I point to a banner with the design of a stylised stone tower.

"Docca of Lugwall, in the farthest North."

The word stirs in me a strange yearning, though I've rarely even heard it mentioned in Londin. A city so distant, it's more a legend than a real place, reputedly overlooking the ancient Aelian Wall separating us from the Picts. The following of the Bishop of Lugwall is the smallest of all, a mere dozen tents of undyed cloth.

"You never told me there was a Bishop that far north," I say.

"His was the last seat set up by the Romans before they left," replies Fastidius. "And the first to be overrun by the barbarians. From what I've gathered, Docca is a Bishop in name only — his flock, a band of exiles, settled in Corin under Ambrosius's protection."

"So Ambrosius always has two votes instead of one."

"At the least."

I take a wider look around the field. "You mentioned *five* provinces…"

"Donatus of Ebrauc arrived yesterday, but hasn't set up his camp yet," he replies. He nods towards the edge of the forest, where a company of labourers finish raising a cluster of unmarked tents.

"What took him so long? The Council is about to start."

"He passed through the *pagus* of the Cadwallons, to meet with Germanus and Elasio along the way."

"No awards for guessing whose side he's on, then."

"I'm not sure," he replies with a slight shrug. "He said his *Dux* is now Drust of the Hundred Victories, and he has no allegiance to anyone but the Pope. Certainly not anyone here in the South."

"Drust the Pict?"

"The same," Fastidius nods. "It seems his power has spread south of the Aelian Wall after all, despite our best efforts."

"What does that mean for Wortigern?"

"Nobody knows. But any uncertainty works for us, rather than Germanus. It's no use convincing Ambrosius and his allies — but without Donatus we'd at least have a stalemate — " He stops and stares at me. "You've turned green. I think we'd better go back."

"No, I'm fine." I gasp and my body bends forward. "It's nothing, I just — "

The world spins and the sky wraps around me with a loud thud.

I drift in and out of fevered sleep. Sometimes it's dark outside; sometimes I'm wakened by birdsong or the patter of rain on the canvas. Sometimes an unfamiliar face leans over me, forcing my eyes open and shining an oil lamp into them. I hear snippets of conversations, from which I gather the passing of time and the events around me. One of the unfamiliar faces is an herbalist from the town on the hill, changing my bandages and poultices. The other is a physician of Roman learning. They both agree my condition is deteriorating, but I can't hear them coming up with any solutions; whether they discuss it when I'm not awake, or whether they don't think I can be helped, I can't be sure.

When she comes in, at first I think it's just another dream. Rain moistens her dark-green, thick woollen cape. She throws down the hood and leans over me. I spot a grimace just before she pulls back. I'm a stinking, aching mess by now.

"Hasn't anyone been looking after you?" she asks, her sky-blue eyes wide open more in shock than concern. "You look like you're dying."

"An herbalist comes every few days," I reply, weakly. "I'm fine, don't worry about me. What of you — how do you fare at the Council?"

I know I should be out there with her, and with my lord *Dux*, making notes and witty remarks, and acting as a counter to Wortimer. But I can hardly get up from bed, and so it's down to Rhedwyn to represent the Iutes' side at the Council meetings — and to observe the proceedings before relaying them to me on my sick bed.

"I don't do much." She runs her hand down her face. "They have me sit at the back, as some kind of decoration. I can barely understand what anyone's saying."

"Your Imperial has got a lot better this year."

"It's not my Imperial that's bad, it's theirs. Those Northerners speak with some odd accents."

"You're doing great." I reach out to caress her, hiding the pain it's causing me. I can sense the fever coming to overwhelm me from the extremities of my body. She does not pull away — instead, she leans her cheek against my hand, as she used to before our quarrels.

"Has Wortimer been bothering you again?"

"Not since we arrived here… He's been spending more time with Ambrosius than with his father."

"He's plotting again… But if this means you're safe… Wortigern told me he never planned to marry you off to him — that it was all just his fantasy."

"And what about you?" she asks, a sudden cold snap in her voice. "Was your promise also just a fantasy?"

"No," I reply firmly. "If anything, I only grew stronger in my resolve. Facing death has helped me see things more clearly. If… *when* I get out of this… Everything will change."

I feel an oncoming coughing fit, but I hold it in, not knowing how exhausted it will make me. Sometimes I cough so much, I faint… and this conversation is too important for me to miss its conclusion due to something so trivial.

"I want to marry you," I say.

"Even if it means you would need to abandon everything you know? That you would have to return with me to the Iute lands?"

"None of this matters anymore."

She flashes a radiant smile. "You may *not* have to sacrifice anything, after all."

For a moment, I can't remember what she means.

"The baptism! You've agreed to it?"

"I thought it would make things easier for you — for us… And for my uncle," she adds, hastily.

"What about… you know… the gods?"

She shrugs. "Our gods are not as jealous as your Roman ones. They will understand."

I feel a strange anxiety when she says it. I know what Fastidius would have to say about this — or Paulinus; baptism is not a thing to take lightly, it is not a trick with which to gain divine favour, not a simple switching of allegiance from one master to another. I still remember the way my body and soul were filled with divine light as I entered the bathing pool. The God of Rome demands more than just loyalty — he demands devotion…

"Have you — have you started learning yet?"

"Learning?" She tilts her head. The question only confirms my doubts — nobody explained to her what baptism truly means before she made her decision. It was never going to be Wortigern, for whom so much depends on her performing the rite of her own volition, and who wouldn't dare risking her changing her mind on the matter… And I'm not sure it should be up to me, either.

"There is much to learn before the ritual — the prayers, the catechism… Didn't the *Dux* tell you anything? Or Bishop Fatalis?"

"Nobody talks to me here. Wortigern just sits in the wooden circle, silent, grim, with Wortimer at his right hand, listening to the clerics and the nobles arguing about…" She searches for the right word. "…Church matters. There's a lot going on here that has nothing to do with Wortigern or Germanus."

"This was to be expected. A Council like this happens once a generation, if that. They'd have a lot to discuss other than the recent — "

The cough I was holding in erupts through my teeth with a bloody splutter. By the time it's over, I'm too fatigued to speak. Rhedwyn puts the pitcher of water to my lips. She touches my forehead.

"Ash, you're all burning!"

I croak a mumbling reply. Darkness quickly approaches from the corners of my vision until it covers everything in the, by now, all too familiar, damp, hot shroud.

The darkness is still there when I open my eyes, hazy and grey. Then, as the world forms around me again, I take in scattered flickering flames to the sides and pin pricks of stars above.

I lie on a damp blanket in a shallow hole in the ground, and for a moment I'm struck by deep, animal panic: I'm to be buried alive. Then a shadow extinguishes the stars over me.

"You're awake."

I breathe out in relief. It's Beadda. He leans in to touch my shoulder — or, rather, the tight bundle of foul-smelling wrappings bound around it. They smell of heady herbs, oils and, faintly, of dung.

There's another odour, wafting its way into my hole, of smoke from burning wet leaves and grass. I hear crackling of twigs in the flame. Sparks fly into the sky, merging with the stars.

"What's going on? Where am I?"

"Don't move," says Beadda. "You'll be fine."

There's a tinge of unease in his voice which does little to calm me. He disappears and for a long while, nothing else happens, until I hear another voice, further away, muffled. It starts a slow, gravely chant in a tongue that sounds at once ancient and familiar. The ground around me shakes from stomping of heavy feet, too heavy for a human. A low bellow and rattling of a chain confirms it: somewhere nearby a large bullock is growing restless.

The flame grows and illuminates my immediate surroundings. I see a portal of three giant straight stones standing over my head, ancient and moss-grown, silent and imposing. A heavy, blue smoke crawls on the ground and oozes into my shallow pit. It whispers in my nostrils and scratches at my eyes, forcing streams of tears to flow down the sides of my face.

The chanting grows louder and nearer, as do the hoof steps. I recognise some words now, spoken in a manner that sounds at once ancient and timeless, though it's been decades since I last heard them. It's a tongue that's kindred to the mumbles spoken by the Old Man and the Old Woman back at Ariminum, the tongue of the old people who once lived here before the Romans came. There are words of healing and of prayer, of invoking gods of the trees and rivers. But there are older words, too, words as old as the rocks of

Britannia itself, words that sound as if they had been spoken by people who put up the giant stones above my head, words that send shivers through me as I peer past the smoke-filled darkness and into the stars.

The smoke and the herbs are beginning to work their magic on me. The flames turn bright and full of colours, the edges of the stones grow sharp and shimmering. I'm starting to hear other things now, things that aren't there, voices trickling like a babbling brook, whispers, moans. Wisps of light and specks of dust swirl into my vision.

The bullock moos again and I sense it move towards me. Wet dirt trickles from the walls of my pit. A new shadow appears in the smoke; at first I take it for another animal, but then I see it's a man wearing a stag's head on his shoulders. It's this mask that muffles his voice. He wears a white robe and holds a sickle in his hand, glinting golden in the flame. He tugs onto something and the bullock comes into my view, as white as the man's robe. I have seen enough such rituals to know what's going to happen next.

The horned man throws some twigs at me. I raise one up to the light — it's dried mistletoe. He then pours cold water over me, and as I splurt and cough, he, with a swift, sharp flash of the sickle, cuts the bullock's throat. I close my eyes and feel the warm, steaming blood splatter all over me. Through the beast's gurgling howls, the horned man speaks clearly, in words I can now understand:

Gods of this land, ancient powers, I call upon you in this hour of need

Wake up! Take this newcomer as one of your own!

I call upon you, Nod, may your healing waters flow through him

I call upon you, Taran, may your thunder grant him strength

And I call upon you, Kern, the Horned One,

You who care for the hunter and the hunted,

Deem this boy worthy of your gentle mercy

Take him through the threshold of Death and bring him back to Life!

The smoke and blood tear into my throat and I start to cough. The swirls of light and shadow blur all I see. My shoulder flares up, and I realise I haven't been feeling any pain until now, but the wonder is brief as the agony spreads through my body in a violent spasm.

The horned man kneels down and reaches into the pit. He lifts up my head. Through tears and flames I see more of these giant stone portals around us, all set up in a great circle, the size of an amphitheatre. There are more people between the stones, watching me, blurred, unrecognisable silhouettes. The horned man puts a narrow-necked pitcher to my lips and forces me to drink a thick brew. I spill and spit most of it, and what gets in my throat is bitter and burning. The lights swirl faster and brighter; the smoke grows darker and denser. The horned man speaks again, his hands raised to heaven, and I can barely hear him through the crying voices and the howling of wind and rain ringing in my ears, out of nowhere.

The sickness is a treatment

The poison is a remedy

To live, you must die

To be born again, you must perish

The circle turns.

He puts his hand on my eyes and pushes me back into the bottom of the pit. But there is no bottom. The earth opens and swallows me whole.

A narrow ship in a storm. Black, wrathful clouds in the sky…

I have seen this vision so many times. I know exactly what's going to happen next. A strong arm will grasp the blankets I'm bundled in. The boat will heave. The grip will slip.

It's much clearer than I've ever remembered it. Everything is sharp, as if seen by an adult, rather than a frightened child. I see the faces around me in great detail. I remember the names I thought long lost in the dull mist of time. I see my father, Eobba, the chief of the boat, at my side, struggling with the oar and cursing at the wind. My mother, Osthrid, her hair still gleaming bright gold even in the grey midst of the storm, wails and prays over the screaming bundle in her arms. The bundle is my sister. I don't know what to call her yet, there was no time to name her as we boarded the three *ceols* to escape the encroaching war. But I know her eyes, bright blue, like the sky reflecting in a bowl of mountain water. Everyone says she'll grow up into an unearthly beauty.

The war is a fainter still memory. Only now, looking from this, familiar, past to an even more distant time, can I recall any of it. The riders in strange helmets, appearing in twos and threes over the horizon, out of bow range, to take stock of our villages. The refugees flooding with tales of death and plunder. The marauders, left over from the battles that our neighbours lost, sneaking in for a bit of pillage, only to meet their end by my father's and his brothers' swords. The red light blazing over the eastern sky at night, ever nearer.

How could I have forgotten all of that? It is my legacy, my people's heirloom. I am the son of a chieftain. One day I will lead the clan into battle, beside my two uncles, to avenge our refuge, to defeat the invaders who forced us into this woeful exile. But first, we need to reach the new lands, find a safe haven, build up our strength.

I know what's coming next, and I dread it at first, but then I accept it. The child that I am in this memory calms down. Such is the fate — what has happened, cannot be undone. The lightning bolt strikes. The prow leaps upwards. The hull planks tear apart with a scream of mangled wood, the ship breaks, falls, rolls, the depths open before me.

Wodan appears the same as he always has, grey-haired, hooded, one-eyed. I cannot tell whether his appearance in the vision is a memory of a dream, or a dream of a memory… but I sense a difference in how I see him this time. He is no longer only a shapeless vision. He is here, with me, the same way he was with me in the basement of the chapel at Ariminum, when Fulco sacrificed the wild pig — when I lost my rune stone… I reach to my neck — the rune stone is still there in this vision. It feels hot to touch.

"You belong to me, Aeric, son of Eobba," Wodan speaks, thunderous like a Bishop at a sermon. "My blood flows in your veins, through your fathers and your fathers' fathers. Your fate is mine to command."

"You told me my destiny was my own," I protest. "That no god had power over me."

His laugh is like the roaring of a storm. "Did no one ever tell you, boy — Gods lie!"

With a ripple and a splash, the hooded face disappears. I hear my father desperately call my name through the raging storm, the name he gave me three years earlier, before Wodan and Donar, the first letter of which he's carved himself into the rune stone at my neck:

Aeric!

His grasping hands disappear in the spray as the impassive ocean takes me away into the black oblivion.

"Where did you find that masked man?" I ask.

We are heading back to the camp at Sorbiodun in the same carriage that brought me there from Callew, but we're following a different, winding dirt road across an empty, ancient landscape. Outside, I spot a cluster of barrow mounds, then another. A lonely standing stone teeters, tilted, in a barren field. Wind sweeps up dust like an army of wraiths. The sun is dimmed by grey clouds, but I see enough of it to tell we're heading due south.

I don't remember much from the previous day. I woke up, dazed and groggy after the ritual, in some small, damp tent, then was carried into the carriage by Beadda and another Iute, where I slowly regained my senses.

"He came to Wortigern the night you fell unconscious," explains Beadda. "Saying his gods told him his services would be needed there. We thought he was one of Ambrosius's men from the West, but nobody in their camp knew anyone like him. He said he was a *Drui*, a wise man of the *Wealh*, a seer and a healer."

"And you believed him, just like that?"

"We were desperate. There was nothing else we could do. We tried all the doctors first," he says, grave-faced. "Then the priests. They were no help."

"Doctors and priests? How long was I out?"

"Ten days." He looks to the sky. "In the end, it was even too late to cut the arm off to save you. The black burning had spread all over your side."

I find his words hard to believe. I feel no pain anywhere in my body now, except for a slight tingling and itching along the scars. My right arm is still bandaged, but moves freely. The fever is gone. I feel as healthy as ever.

As Beadda proceeds to describe the man's mysterious appearance, his white robe, grey hair, dark eyes and a short, scruffy beard, all of which he hid under the deer mask when he started his ritual, I'm reminded of a particular brief passage from Tacitus's writings on the conquest of Britannia. I read it many times in Paulinus's study, fascinated with its wild depictions of the furious, torch-bearing, black-clad women, and of savage men casting curses at the Roman army. The term Tacitus used for these men, a term taken, if I recall correctly from Caesar's earlier work on the Gaulish War, was *druides*… Could the horned man have been one of them? I thought Rome destroyed them all, a long time ago…

"The place of the ritual…" I start.

"I have never seen one like it," Beadda is eager to answer, as if he'd waited for a chance to talk about it with someone. "A circle of stones twice as tall as a man, in the middle of a flat empty plain… It was like one of your Roman temples, but greater and with no roof or walls, only those immense pillars."

Your Roman temples? I frown. A bump in the road makes us both jump. I hit the wall of the carriage with my arm and the pain returns, for a brief moment, but it's nothing compared to what it would have been before.

Was it really a miracle of the *druides* magic? Paulinus would say it was either the Devil's trick, or, more likely, a skill of a native healer, more familiar with local herbs than the doctors from faraway Londin. Why would the gods — or demons, for that matter — need poultices and ointments to do their work?

"He had us dig up a grave of some ancient warrior," Beadda continues, "and put you there, with all those herbs and flowers and ointments he'd prepared in the meantime. He said the dead warrior's spirit would guide you through the healing."

"All this without ever telling you where he'd come from?"

"*I come from the past*, he said," Beadda recalls. "He told us he was the last of his kind in this land, that all others ventured West and North, beyond Rome's borders. He used to pray for the gods to call on him to follow his brethren, but they told him to stay and wait for a chance to prove himself."

I look out the window and gaze at the ageless land. There's a mist coming from over the dark wood on the horizon. A murder of crows lands in an old grain field, long barren, searching for worms. There are secrets hidden here, I can sense them, and so does, by the confused look on his face, Beadda.

I have sensed the presence of the gods in Fulco's rituals, and in the Saxon ceremonies. I have felt the awe of the Roman God in the gold-glinting, incense-filled dark vaults at Saint Paul's. But I have never before witnessed a true miracle, and this whole story sounds like a miracle straight from the lives of the saints, from the appearance of a mysterious stranger to the wondrous healing of my wounds. It would be easy to assume that that's exactly what it was, but I remain sceptical. If the old, forgotten Gods of Britannia do still live here among the standing stones, why would they choose *me* to show their power, after all the centuries of silence?

The carriage slows down and climbs up a ramp which links the old road to the Roman highway. Sorbiodun's fortified hilltop, and the Council's sea of tents, are no more than a mile away. From their direction, a small group of horsemen rides out to meet us, bearing Wortigern's colours.

CHAPTER XX
THE LAY OF DONATUS

The herbalist from Sorbiodun insists that I wash my wounds, now that I can walk on my own, so I head for the thatch-roofed bath house by the river. Supporting myself on a servant's shoulder, I descend into the lead-lined pit filled with steaming hot water. I hold my bandaged arm over the edge. The heat works wonders, permeating my bones and sore muscles, a well needed respite after the days of pain. I drift off in bliss.

Someone else enters the bath house — a stocky, corpulent man, with a scar across a bulbous stomach and a mass of muscles bulging on his chest and shoulders. As he slides into the water, all other guests leave the room without a word. I rise to leave, too, but the man nods me to stay.

"Please," he says, forcefully. "I'm not *that* fat yet. There's more than enough space for the two of us here."

I force a smile and rest my back against the bath's edge.

"So, you're the boy healed by the pagan magic, aren't you?" the man asks.

"I don't know about the magic, but yes, I am the one. And you are?"

The man chuckles. The fat on his belly wobbles, but the muscles remain in place. He is an ex-soldier, of that I have no doubt. Is he one of Ambrosius's noblemen?

"I am Donatus of Ebrauc," he replies. "You may have heard of me."

"Your Holiness!" I try to bow, but I only slip on the lead floor and splash about. "I didn't know…"

"Calm yourself. I'm only a Bishop. I know you're used to being in esteemed company — Councillor Fraxinus."

How does he know so much about me?

"I thought you were a soldier," I say.

He looks down at the scar. "You mean this? Yes, I did my share of fighting in my younger years. The North is a rough place."

"In the Roman army?"

"I was a chaplain at the Wall — at Aelian Bridge, while there was still a garrison there… When the Pict raiding parties came, it was every man to himself," he muses and scratches the scar with a sigh.

"And now a Pict king rules over your land."

"You mean old Drust?" He nods, sagely. He moves his loaf-sized hands with surprising grace, to mix the cold and hot water around him. "He's a good ruler — the best thing that's happened to us since the Romans left. But remember, he's only in charge of his subjects in *this* world — I'm responsible for what happens to them in the next."

"And how's that working out for you?"

He chuckles again. "As well as anything in these troubling times. I have my share of pagans and heretics to deal with. Some coming from across the sea — others from across the Wall…"

"So it's true what I've heard — you have Saxons in the North."

"Not as many as here, certainly — and those that do come, settle peacefully on the empty land in the moors and the valleys…" He gives me a questioning look. "Though their numbers have begun to grow worryingly in recent months."

"Fleeing Germanus's edicts and Elasio's warriors," I say.

"It would seem so. They do tell some terrible tales." He stretches his arms and back. "Wench, bring us some cold ale!" He shouts. A moment later, a girl appears with a pitcher and two mugs.

"Little good comes of Rome meddling in our affairs," he says, after quenching his thirst.

"You do not support the anathema?"

"Germanus has been away from this island for too long," he replies. "He hasn't seen how much it's changed since his last visit. He doesn't understand the need for a certain… balance that we all need to strive for."

"What kind of balance?"

"You strike me as a clever man, Fraxinus. Can you imagine what Drust of Hundred Victories would do if he found out I can lay an anathema on him for any transgression?"

"He would beg your forgiveness?"

He smiles. "Try again."

"Is he not a Christian, then? Is he not baptised?"

"Ah, yes…" He gulps some more ale. "I remember Ninian — the man who baptised Drust and his army… A great man, a holy man, did more to spread the word of the Lord than any before him. He studied under Martinus in Rome… But he was naïve in certain matters. He truly believed his baptism transformed all who undertook it."

"It is what a true baptism does," I say, somewhat taken aback by his scepticism.

"To those who already grew up in the light of the Lord, perhaps," he says with a nod, "but Drust was raised in the cold, pagan North… For him, the True Faith is just a tool. A tool he needed to expand south of the Aelian Wall — to earn respect of the Briton lords — to gain support of the Church and to recruit Christians into his army…"

"And he would discard this tool as soon as he no longer deemed it useful," I guess. "Or felt threatened by it."

"It is quite a predicament, young Fraxinus. Drust is not one of your Southern lords. There are enough pagans, or former pagans, in his army, for him not to fear Rome's distant touch."

Why would you be telling me all of this?

"Then you would vote against Germanus in the Council?"

There is a mystery in his smile. "That is between me and the Lord." He reaches for the pitcher, but it is empty — he drank it all himself, without even noticing.

"The water is getting cold," he says. "It's best for either of us not to dwell here for too long, Councillor."

"Yours is the only good news I've heard all week," Wortigern tells me.

He holds up a bottle made of thin glass, filled with ruby red wine, pours some into a jewelled goblet and takes a sip. He winces, but the grimace is not one of distaste, but jealousy.

"Ambrosius brought me this flask," he says. "Tarraconian. It's the best damn wine I've tasted in years."

"Then why are you so mad?"

"Do you know how much it cost to bring wine like this from Hispania? And in a glass bottle. Glass! The vessel itself is worth more than all the jewels on this cup. I'm a *Dux* of Londin, and I could never afford such riches. Even if I could, the Council would raise havoc, suspecting I swindled what paltry tax they pay."

"Maybe it was a gift…"

"Oh, you bet it was. A gift from Germanus, or Aetius, or some other Roman official conspiring to get rid of me and bring Britannia back into the fold." He wipes his mouth and stares out the tent door, into the distance. "They still think it can be done — the Empire's return. They think *I'm* the only one who stands in their way. And why not? They've bought off everyone else."

"What if they're right? The Empire has been through worse. What if there's another Constantine…"

He scoffs, wearily. The bags under his eyes are the colour of the wine in his goblet. His hair is dishevelled, and with more wisps of grey than I remember. He's tapping his left knee with his fingers.

"Rome is never going back. Not how they imagine it, at least. Sure, Aetius can hold the barbarians at spear's length as long as he's alive, and then maybe some other brilliant commander will come in his place…" He raises his hand, as if grasping for something. "But the spark is gone. Their world is a ruin. All they can do is defend what they have left, and try to desperately win back some of what they've lost, but with each generation they lose more than they pry back, until there's nothing but moss-covered stones and mad men roaming in the wilderness, crying for a past they no longer remember."

"Then why do you care for them so?" I ask. "Why do you insist on clinging to their remnants?"

He looks up at me, unsure. I don't think he expected me to answer his tirade — it was a monologue aimed at no audience, and requiring no response. "What do you mean?"

Once, I would never have found the courage to speak like this — but I have faced death twice in a matter of weeks, and lived through it, and I feel like all my fear has been burned out by the fire in my wound.

I don't know if this was Bishop Donatus's intention when he told me of his troubles in the North — but I now see with rare clarity how his dilemma might provide the solution to Wortigern's. And I'm sure he does, too. I can see his eyes staring with furious envy at the goblet's rim, decorated with emerald crosses, and at the silver crucifix that stands on my table, a gift from Bishop Fatalis to aid my recovery — and I can almost hear his thoughts. But he's been alone with these thoughts for too long; there is nobody around him with whom he could share his most secret ideas… I doubt he'd even dare to admit them to himself.

"Look around you, *Dux*. Five provincial Bishops have come from five provincial capitals to decide the fate of this country, as if they replaced the Governors of old," I say. "And they look for guidance to the Pope in Rome, as if he was the Imperator. Rome never left. It just disguised itself as the Church, and uses the faith instead of the army to keep us under its heel."

"The Bishops have no say in the running of the provinces. Their power is only over the souls of their flock."

"But Germanus showed them how to wield this power like a hammer," I reply. "Look at how they're making us grovel. How can you say you rule your province, if you need to ask the Bishops for forgiveness? And what about the others? Who rules Flavia? Who rules Secunda? Why are there no *Duces* or *Comites* here other than yourself and Ambrosius? Have they no interest in a matter of such importance to any lay ruler in Britannia — or are they too afraid of their Bishops to object?"

He's taken aback by my sudden outburst, but there's a hint of a smile lingering on his lips.

"Now do you see my problem?" he says. "They set the rules. I have to play by them. They dig up some old bones and make up miracles, and then we all have to bend our knee to them. Don't look so surprised — I spoke to your brother, I know there was never any Albanus. It's all a fairy tale. But now we all have to pretend we believe it."

"The Iutes don't. The Saxons don't. The *Gewisse* only do because their families have been taken hostage. The Picts beyond the Aelian Wall couldn't give less of a damn."

He stands up and picks up the silver crucifix. He looks at it for a long time in silence, deep in thought. I sense a change in him. Gone is the weariness, the all-consuming envy.

"I see what's happened to you," he says at last. "You think you have witnessed a true miracle. Your arm, which none of our doctors and priests could save, returned to full health, overnight. And by whose power?" He waves the crucifix around in dismay. I resist telling him that parts of my right arm and side are now beginning to ache again, under the tight, oil-darkened bandages. "The pagan gods, which we've shunned. Maybe you're right. What if we were wrong, and the barbarians were right? The Iutes, the Franks, even the Picts — all grow strong and virile within Rome's borders, while we talk of Christ and forgiveness — and grow weak. Our walls, of stone and faith…"

He pauses for breath, and I realise what's going on. His eyes pan across the room, staring into the distance, as if at an unseen audience. He's *rehearsing*. He's playing a new speech in his head, one that might replace the one he's had prepared for the Council, and testing if it has a desired effect. Just like the speech with which he started our conversation, I am not its intended target, merely a receptacle for its rhetoric.

His gaze falls on me and he stirs as if he'd only just seen me.

"Don't mind me," he says, patting me gently on the bandaged arm. I hide a wince. "It's just the ranting of an old man, frustrated by how many around him wish him harm. *You* don't wish me harm, do you?" He reveals his teeth in a broader, even more terrifying smile, before I can answer. "No, of course not, Ash. You're one of the few I can trust in this den of snakes. Go back to sleep. The demons may have cured you, but you still need the rest."

I stutter, my lips suddenly parched. "Y-yes, sire." He nods, puts the crucifix absentmindedly back on the table and picks up the half-empty bottle of wine before leaving the tent — but leaves the goblet on the floor; in its finely polished rim I glance the laughing face of the one-eyed god.

The embrace of Rhedwyn's arms is soft, long and warm. She's hurting my shoulder, but I dare not flinch, not wanting to worry her again. I haven't yet peeked under the bandages to see if the healing power of the *Drui's* miracle still holds. I don't know if I want it to. For if the healing was not the miracle the horned man purported it to be, then neither could the vision induced by the mistletoe smoke…

I haven't yet told anyone about the vision. What would be the point? There is nobody alive who could confirm or deny what I saw. For all I know, it could've been just a feverish nightmare, another delirious vision sent by demons to torment me. It didn't feel like it, though. It felt true… More true than any dream I've ever had.

Reluctantly, I slip away and slide back onto the bed, feigning weariness. She sits next to me, her head on my shoulder, her breath in my ear.

"It was awesome to behold," she speaks in a half-gasp, half-whisper. "To think there was still such power in this land! I thought the Roman priests destroyed it all."

"Everyone did," I reply, then I notice what she just said. "Wait, were you there, too?"

She nods. "All who worried about you were there. The *Dux*, the Iutes, some courtiers — even Ambrosius sent a representative."

"*Ambrosius?* He'd never condone this display of pagan idolatry."

"He sent a priest to pray the devils did not take your soul." She giggles. "Looks like that's all their Roman God is good for."

I scowl, by reflex. I find her light-hearted blasphemy troubling. But even more troubling is the news that Wortigern organised my healing ritual into some sort of display for the delegates to the Council — and would not tell me about it afterwards. No wonder Donatus recognised me — he may even have been present at the ritual himself. I've seen such things organised too often at the court in Londin to know the gathering of the nobles at the stone circle was no accident.

She leans in for a kiss, but I pull away. The vision returns, as clear and vivid as the night before.

"What's wrong, Ash?"

I can't stand to look into her eyes, open wide and gleaming like two polished sapphires.

"My — my head still hurts a little, must be a side effect of the healing process."

There's no point asking her again about her family. It would only confuse her needlessly, and there's nothing new she could add. If Hengist and Horsa decided to withhold any information from her, they must have had their reasons. And if they hadn't, then, well, it was all just a dream, a bad dream…

"Aeric," I whisper, inadvertently.

"What's that?"

"Nothing." I smile weakly.

"I thought you said *Aeric*," she says and chuckles. "But of course, you couldn't — "

"I couldn't what?" I ask, my voice a bit too sharp. She startles for a second, then composes herself.

"When I was a child…" she starts. "There were children my age on Tanet, but none in my uncle's household. Sometimes I'd get lonely at night, and I'd imagine a friend to talk to. A boy my age — no, maybe a little older… I'd name him *Aeric.*" She laughs. "I suppose he'd look a bit like you now. Maybe that's why I like you."

She mistakes my stunned silence for disapproval. "It's silly, I know. I've never told anyone about this before."

"It's not silly at all." I pull her closer, but stop short of kissing her. "Thank you for sharing it with me."

We sit like this for a while. I dare not speak, fearing I'd start blubbing. I don't recognise all the emotions that tear through me right now. Revulsion mixes with anger, sadness is marred by the fear of the sin we have inadvertently committed. I'm close to tears and I don't want her to see it. She seems so content in my arms.

Hengist *must* have known about this. As soon as we get back to Londin I will need to ask him about this Aeric, son of Eobba — no matter the consequences.

Rhedwyn's fingers slide down my back and into my breeches. My body is not repulsed; it doesn't care what the truth is. I can excuse myself with the headache for now, but how much longer can I keep up the charade before she starts to suspect something?

At night, somebody changes my bandages. They no longer wrap my entire side, but line the shoulder and arm, up to the wrist, in a thin, fragrant layer. I can move my hand freely now — as much as the pain allows. I'm still hiding the discomfort. I do not wish to spoil the joy my miraculous recovery seems to bring Rhedwyn, Beadda, and all others who wish me well. Besides, it does feel immeasurably better than before the night ritual, so I tell myself that the healing must simply be taking more time than I expected.

The crowds gather around the great timber enclosure. It is the last day of the Council. The Bishops are about to declare their final verdict. There is little doubt as to what it will be. Although there may be a few dissident voices — notable among them, Fatalis and the eternally grumpy Donatus of Ebrauc — Wortigern has clearly failed to convince the majority of the gathered clerics and delegates of his innocence. He will need to make a decision today; most likely, he already has: whether to plea for the forgiveness and mercy of Rome, or remain, stubborn, excommunicated, an outcast in the eyes of the Lord and the people of Britannia.

As I follow the solemn, queuing procession to the enclosure, I spot Wortimer and Ambrosius at the entrance, surrounded by some of their retinue. They talk and laugh like old friends, making no effort to conceal their amity. I retreat deeper into the crowd and sneak closer to hear their conversation. Wortimer spots something and falls silent. I follow his gaze to see Rhedwyn, entering the arena with Beadda at her side and the six young hostages in tow, all wearing the white baptismal robes. Wortimer's face turns that peculiar mixture of lust and viciousness with which he always meets the Iute princess, but there is something else there now, too, a tinge of… regret?

"You'll have to forget the girl, Wortimer," says Ambrosius. "I will not tolerate my daughter being second in your affections."

"Not even as a slave?"

"Control your loins, boy. A greater reward awaits you."

The crowd pushes me forward and I miss out the rest of the conversation, but what I've heard is enough to launch my thoughts racing. A daughter…? A reward? What arrangement is it that they are so keen to discuss in the open? I'm so baffled I almost forget to feel relieved at the news Rhedwyn might be safe from Wortimer's advances for good. I don't even care what the price for this could be.

Then I remember what I've just learned about her — about us. *This is even more important if she's your sister*, I tell myself, but it's useless. There is a black hole at the back of my mind where I resolved to keep the secret for the time being, while matters of state are being decided around me. It is like a sore tooth — the more I try not to think about it, the more I prod it with my dark thoughts, but it produces no solution, only pain. I did not speak to Rhedwyn again after her last visit, excusing myself with being busy preparing for the final vote. I do not know how I would share the truth with her — I don't even know that I should. She need never know. If she doesn't know of the sin, it cannot harm her. Perhaps I should simply disappear from her life.

Perhaps I should disappear from *everyone's* lives.

Drowning in my own sorrow I don't notice when the crowd spits me out into the timber enclosure. The construction is now finished, and I see it's a distant echo of a Roman amphitheatre, a mockery of an auditorium, but with barely a hint of an arena — instead, there's just enough space in the middle for a small podium, shielded from the sun by a cloth canopy spread on four posters.

There's already a speaker there, a bald priest addressing the crowd that's still finding their places on the rough wooden benches. I can't hear him through the noise, I don't think anybody can, though I spot a small group of similarly old and bald priests sitting in the lowest circle, listening intently. It feels like we've intruded on some theological debate. The preacher pauses, looks up, as if noticing for the first time the dozens gathered in the enclosure, and finishes up his speech with a rhetorical flourish that gets lost in the breeze. The remaining old priests hastily retreat from their seats as the five Bishops and their retinue move in to take their place at the foot of the podium.

Lucius, the Bishop of Corin, is the first to step up. He bangs his crooked cane on the floor. The noise reverberates and spreads a blanket of hushes around the audience. At last, everyone is seated and quiet. The final day of the Council begins.

Three hours into the proceedings, the only thing that stops me from dozing off is a desperate need to take a piss. Everyone else in the audience is just as bored and tired. The Bishops have been presenting their individual opinions in long, solemn sermons. All save Fatalis have so far condemned Wortigern and voted for sustaining the anathema. Donatus, sitting in the last row, high above the arena, refuses to speak until it is time to cast the final vote.

"It is more than just the stubborn insistence on following the absurd Pelagian heresy that angers us, though this, of course, makes the Mother Church's heart ache the most," says the last speaker, Severus. He arrived from Werlam last night to represent his mentor and, by extension, Rome. Rumour has it that Germanus himself has grown too ill to travel such a long distance — despite the healing powers of the sacred relics. Severus's voice is shaky, wobbly. His ranking is lower than the Metropolitan Bishops, and from what I've heard he's understood to have been promised Fatalis's position once Wortigern and all who follow him have been dealt with. The conflict of interest is obvious to the point of absurd, but there isn't anyone brave or stupid enough to point it out.

"It is his friendship with pagans," he continues. "And it is his refusal to subject himself to Rome's judgement — despite the proof of God's will in the many miracles of Albanus! When this great city, the very heart of civilisation itself is threatened, once again, he sides with the same barbarians who invade her borders. God in his wisdom and mercy has put his chief representative in Rome — and it is the duty of every Christian soldier to march to her protection, rather than welcome her enemies into your homes and villages!"

It is a thunderous speech, but it ends in resounding silence. In his fervour, in his desire to ingratiate himself with Germanus and his Roman masters, Severus went too far. This is exactly what Wortigern predicted before we left Londin. A call to arms in defence of Rome is too much for the gathered nobles to accept. Even those on Ambrosius's side stir uneasy, though they, as everyone else, say nothing. Donatus was right: Germanus has been away from Britannia for too long. He's lost touch with the will of its people — and with the patience of its rulers. I seek out the Bishop of Ebrauc. He notices me and shakes his head with a despondent grimace.

A spinning gust of wind breaks the silence and picks up sand and sawdust around the podium in a whirlwind. As the dust settles, Wortigern rises heavily from his seat, his face grim. He hasn't shaved for a few days, and he's kept his hair shaggy and unkempt, giving him a deliberately weary, haggard look. For the first time since the Council started, he wears the jewel-studded diadem, the insignia of Britannia's Governor, on his head: a clear challenge to Ambrosius. He crosses the arena and stares at Severus until the priest retreats from the podium, like a frightened dog.

"These people you call pagans," he starts, his voice bellowing with a slight croak at the back of the throat. "These people you call barbarians. They have lived among us longer than anyone can remember. They are our neighbours. They are our friends. And, yes, some are even family." He looks to me. So does everyone else. I shift in my seat. "And who invited them here in the first place?" He raises an accusing finger in the direction of Ambrosius's retinue, where Severus hid himself from Wortigern's wrath. "Rome! You brought them here as your *socii*, just like you did in Hispania and Gaul! They were good enough when you needed them to fight your wars, but now that you feel strong again, you would throw them away like a broken spear. Just like you threw *us* away, thirty years ago."

There's an amused scowl on Ambrosius's face, as if he didn't believe the sincerity of Wortigern's speech.

"You speak to us of Christian duty," the *Dux* continues. "You speak to us of saints and miracles. But your saints are some old bones dug up from the ground, and your miracles are theatrical props. Let me tell you about a *true* miracle, one that you've all been witnesses to."

He nods at me and gestures me to come down and join him at the podium. I hesitate. He smiles invitingly, but there's menace in his eyes. I know better than to ignore his summons for the second time.

"This boy was born a pagan. One of those Iute refugees you all scorn so much. He grew up, as Bishop Fatalis can attest, into a decent, Godfearing Christian, a warrior and, I'd venture, somewhat of a scholar. I treat him as I would a son." Here, a glance at Wortimer, who only scoffs. "Some of you have come to know him too, while he has been here. And yet, when death arrived to take him from us, where was the God of Rome? Where was Christ's help that we all prayed for so?"

At this, the Bishops are beginning to rise up. They already suspect where this is going, and they're not about to let it pass without protest, but Wortigern only raises his voice louder over the murmur.

"You all saw it, with your own eyes! The pagan gods came and healed this boy's arm, when no doctor or priest of Rome could help him!"

He's shaking me by the injured shoulder and I do all I can not to cry out in pain. The murmur rises into a rumble.

"It was the work of the demons, not gods!" booms the Bishop of Corin. "Beware what you speak of next, blasphemer!" shouts another.

Even Ambrosius stands up, at last stirred into action. "Tread carefully, Wortigern," he warns. "There's no need for any of this hysteria. Remember our deal."

"Ah, yes, the *deal*." Wortigern throws his head back in a bitter laughter. "I know all about the *deals* you and your son have been making. A deal with the pagan *Gewisse*, who still serve in Elasio's armies, even though their families are being slaughtered in the name of Christ."

Ambrosius's face turns dark red, but he stays silent. Among the chaos, I catch a glimpse of Wortimer, looking back and forth between him and his father. Abruptly, he stands up and leaves, nodding at his Briton retinue to follow. His *Gewisse* bodyguards remain in place, baffled, not certain if they've understood Wortigern's words correctly.

Wortigern leans forward and lowers his voice for effect. "And another deal you've made — with *me*, a blasphemous heretic. Your daughter and my son, a union of the families, and me abdicating in their favour, in exchange for your Bishop's vote against the anathema. This is how much your *God* is worth to you. This is how much you care about the Pope's pronouncements. This isn't about faith — this was always just about *power*. It's all lies, a game of light and shadow."

He grabs my shoulder again. "This boy is all the proof I need of the power of pagan gods. Denounce Pelagius? No, I will not denounce him. He was a good man, but only a man. Instead, I denounce Christ himself!"

The rumble turns into a roar. At Wortigern's subtle signal, Beadda and his warriors rush to surround us, their long knives, hidden in their boots until now, drawn. Rhedwyn is among them, her face crumpled in fear and shock. Even the six hostages have joined us, revealing mail under their white robes. The sight of naked blades induces panic in the audience — nobody else thought to come armed to the proceedings. The clerics and minor officials are already trickling out the entrance, not willing to wait to see how the conflict is resolved.

"Devil take you and all who stand with you!" cries the Bishop of Corin, followed by the rest of the Council. Even

Fatalis joins him in the denunciation; still, Donatus remains silent, smiling mysteriously. The courtiers from Londin stand divided, wavering. Wortigern calls at them.

"It's time to choose — be slaves of Rome again, or stand proud and alone. Do not fear their curses, they have no power over you. The Gods of the Saxons and Britons of old will protect you, like they protected Ash!"

I want to cry out, to protest; I don't want to be used like this, I don't want to be a pawn in the *Dux*'s game. I understand everything now — all of this must have been planned by Wortigern not long after the hunting accident, maybe even before. This is why he had all those nobles and priests attend the ceremony at the stone circle. The horned man was likely his invention, too. He knew I would provide him with a motive — did he expect I would be the one who would *goad* him into it?

Except… the ritual *was* a miracle. My arm *did* get better. How could Wortigern have known it would work? Could it have been a true miracle, even if it was planned beforehand?

The solution to this mystery must wait. I notice Rhedwyn's face turn pale. Wortigern holds her wrist in a tight grip, and glares at me. It's a clear threat. *Obey me.* Even in this terrible moment, I can't help but admire his audacity. We're surrounded by Beadda and his Iutes, the only defence against the chaos outside — and still he dares to threaten Rhedwyn's safety? I feel I should call his bluff, but I'm paralysed by the sheer dauntless force of his spirit. How can I defy him — how could anyone? He's a leader who's just turned his people against Rome, against the Church, against God — and not as some mad impulse, but as a cold, calculated, long prepared decision. I sense that only now do I fully understand how he came to rule Londin and the better half of Britannia. I am powerless against such will.

I turn back towards the raging crowd. The group of Londin delegates has split almost in half. I'm surprised it's even that many. Wortigern must have been sounding them out in preparation for his move.

"Out," commands Wortigern. The Iutes press forward, clearing the way with the backs of their swords. The *Dux* pushes me and Rhedwyn to the front, the loyal courtiers follow at the back. The curses of the Bishops still ringing in my ears, I emerge onto the tent-spattered floodplain outside and see Wortimer and about twenty of his men, armed with clubs and sticks, lined up in front of us, barring our way; his *Gewisse* bodyguards, I notice, are no longer with him.

"Not now, son," Wortigern says, tiredly. "I'll deal with you some other time."

The Iutes make short work of the enemy and we're free to pass. Nobody's seriously harmed; the stand was a symbolic one, to show Wortimer's resolve before his ally Ambrosius. I look around, but I can't spot the Governor of the West or his retinue anywhere nearby. The enclosure is emptying fast, only the Bishops remain inside to discuss the unexpected development. Before I lose sight of the arena, I catch a glimpse of Fatalis, red-faced and shrunken in the face of the others' wrath.

We reach our encampment. Wortigern's warriors and the remaining Iutes have already prepared a makeshift defensive perimeter. There are more men here than before, some I don't recognise. They look and sound like locals, Britons; their accent is coarse and similar to that of the horned man. I have no time to ponder this discovery. Wortigern shoves me and Rhedwyn into his tent. Beadda stands guard outside.

"Right. Now let's have those bandages off of you before you *really* get hurt," he says.

Dumbstruck, I let one of the servants remove the thin wrappings from my side and shoulder. It is the first time I have seen my wounds since leaving Callew. They look different than I remembered. The deepest cuts are well stitched with sheep's gut sutures, and covered in week-old scabs. The itching and pain I felt are coming not from the injuries, but from the bruises and bedsores spreading all over my side and shoulder. Nothing I see is life-threatening, but nothing looks as if it had been miraculously healed.

"Don't be a child, Ash," says Wortigern. "Haven't you realised yet? You were fine all along. Well, maybe not fine, but the Callew surgeons did a decent enough job, you just needed to rest. I had my herbalist feign the effects of wound fever on you. Do you understand now?"

I don't think I do. I stare at Rhedwyn — she stares back at me, as shocked as I am. Then it was *all* for show? There was no miracle? But… the vision… *Aeric*…

"Get dressed now," the *Dux* commands. He hands me a bundle of clothes which are far more elegant and elaborate than the ones I have on me. There's another, similar bundle waiting for Rhedwyn, a dress of white silk trimmed with green and gold, and a headband of wrought silver. "Now that we no longer need a priest, I can perform the ceremony myself. We'll do it all properly once we're back in Londin, but I'm not sure when — "

"Ceremony?" I interrupt him. "What ceremony?"

He blinks and puts his palm to his forehead. "Haven't I told you yet? Too many things on my head…" He turns to Rhedwyn, takes her hand and mine and holds them together. "The Handfasting, as your people call it. I promised Hengist you two would be wedded, to seal the alliance. All you have to do is to exchange the oaths, here and now, on my authority."

He notices my hesitation and, for the first time today, it's his turn to be stumped.

"Isn't this what you've always wanted?"

CHAPTER XXI
THE LAY OF RHEDWYN

The *Dux* is pacing back and forth, wringing his hands behind his back. There's only enough room in the tent for him to make three broad steps before he has to turn around.

"This is bad," he says quietly. Beadda is still outside, keeping watch, and neither of us wants him to know what we just talked about. Rhedwyn was sent to her tent with the white silk dress. "How far did things get between the two of you before you found this out?"

"Too far."

He winces in disgust. "She's not expecting, is she? Things would get really complicated if she were."

"I — I don't think so. I don't know."

He shakes his head. "I can't deal with this right now. As tough as this is on you two, I have a bigger problem to deal with. Damn it all! I've made all the arrangements with her uncle, everything was agreed upon, everything was proceeding as planned. She was to be the peace-weaver between us and the Iutes. This was what you two were born for!"

I didn't want to tell him. I didn't want to tell anyone. I was hoping there was a way I could take the secret with me to the grave. But Wortigern's plans depended too much on my and Rhedwyn's betrothal, and he forced the confession out of me after long prodding. A formal alliance between him and the Iutes was to be sealed by this marriage — a marriage with the *son* of a *Dux*, as Wortigern announced, to my astonishment. The adoption letters were already laid with the registrar in Londin, waiting for his seal.

He seemed incredulous at first when I told him about the vision. For him, the *Drui's* ritual was just a farce, a piece of theatre, with no real meaning or effect. But just like myself earlier, mentioning Rhedwyn's imagined friend made him realise there may have been some truth in the dream — at least enough to put the plans for the wedding aside until we can know more for certain.

I was right to fear the cruel fate. Once again, it played with my future. Once again, the bliss that was within my grasp, was taken away from me; this time, it seemed, for good. What gods have I angered for them to curse me so? Was it Christ's revenge for forsaking Him — or Wodan's trickery?

Your fate is mine.

"I need those Iute warriors at my bidding, otherwise all is lost," Wortigern says. "I will have to marry her to *somebody* in the family."

"Not Wortimer," I say, aghast.

"I wouldn't give him the satisfaction," he replies with scorn. "And he would never keep to any deal I've made. Besides, he's already promised to Gweyn, Ambrosius's daughter. He may be a fool most times, but even he knows that's a better match than any pagan girl."

"Ambrosius would honour this engagement, even after today?"

Wortigern nods. "*Especially* after today. Don't think for a moment they're not going after us, together. We'll have to reach Londin before them. But first we need to sort *this* mess out."

"What about Fastidius?" I propose, though I already know the answer.

"Your brother is devoted to his God. I doubt he'll even want to talk to me once he learns what I've done." He pauses. "It will have to be me."

"*You*?"

He shrugs. "And why not? I have no wife, since my dear Sevira perished. I may be old, but I'm not infirm. It's only a political marriage, anyway." He scratches his beard. "Yes, it's making more and more sense, I can see it now… I should've proposed it in the first place, but I yielded to your young love. Now that you're out of the way…"

"You can't — " I rise towards him, but the protest dies in my throat. I have no right to oppose him. If she *is* my sister, then… I can only wish her happiness. He's right, her marrying a *Dux* is worth more to her, to her uncle, and her entire tribe than some foundling boy.

"What if I'm wrong," I whisper. "What if it *was* just a dream…?"

"We'll go ahead with the arrangements when we're back in Londin, whether it's you or me that gets to keep her hand.

You'd better keep all this to yourself until we reach Hengist. He's the only one who can solve this mystery."

"What about Rhedwyn? What should I tell *her*? She's measuring the dress as we speak…"

Wortigern stops his pacing and puts his hand on my shoulder. In this moment, more than ever before, he reminds me of Pascent — and of Paulinus, before he succumbed to the drink. "You know her better than anyone alive, Ash. I trust you'll know how to deal with her."

Seeing her in that dress and tiara, I feel like my heart is about to burst in two. She's never looked more beautiful.

"Did you know about any of this?" I ask, playing for time.

"I found out only yesterday that my uncle was planning to marry me off. I saw messengers going back and forth between the *Dux* and the Iutes, so I suspected something was going on, but I'd never have guessed it would be like this…"

She's smiling, radiant. She doesn't suspect anything. "We need to hurry," she says. "I can't wait for us to utter the vows. We'll have a great Iutish wedding when we're back home."

She throws her arms around me and leans to kiss me. I push her away.

"What's wrong, Ash?"

"I… I cannot do this, Rhedwyn."

This takes her aback. She pulls away, her eyes narrow. "What — what joke is this?"

"It's no joke." My lips shake, and I think I'm about to vomit. "I — I cannot tell you why."

"Did Wortigern put you up to this?" She keeps retreating from me, until she reaches the wall of the tent. "Is this another trick of his?"

"It is no trick. I wish I could explain, but… You have to believe me. This wedding cannot go through — not with me, at any rate."

"Have you spawned a bastard with some *wealh* bitch? Is that it? Is her father chasing you?"

"No, it's nothing like that, I swear…"

"Then what the fuck is *wrong* with you?" she cries. "How many times are you going to change your mind about this? This is your only chance — *our* only chance at happiness! What possible reason would you have to refuse me?"

I stand silent. Would it be better if I told her the truth? The world sways around me.

She sits down on the bed. "You promised," she says quietly. "You promised we'd be together, forever. You promised you'd protect me from Wortimer."

"You *will* be safe from him," I say. "This I can still promise."

"Why would I believe you? You've been lying all this time. You never had the intention to marry me. You've been playing me all this time, just to get into my… into *me*."

She reaches for a cup on the small table and throws it at me. I duck, the cup bounces off the tent's wall and hits the floor with an anticlimactic clank. She moans and hides her face in her hands. She's not crying — just sits there, silent, unmoving. Sweat trickles down my back. I don't know what else to do.

"Leave me alone," she says. Her voice is colder than the Northern wind.

I open my mouth, but I have nothing else to say.

"Go!" she cries, with a tremble of hysterics. "Go to Hell. I have no need for a *little boy* who can't make up his mind."

I reach for the door, and turn around at the entrance. "Wortigern…" I swallow. "Wortigern wants us to march out to Londin as soon as possible."

"I understand," she replies after a long pause. "I'll make myself ready."

She tears the silver tiara from her head and throws it to the floor.

We march all day in silence, our ranks increased by a dozen *Gewisse* from Wortimer's guard, who joined us upon learning of Elasio's betrayal, preferring to cast their lot with fellow Saxons than with the deceitful *wealas*. By sunset we reach the walls of Callew. I don't know what pact Wortigern has made with Masuna — I can only guess he promised to help him deal with the Elasio's roughs violating his borders — but the gates open wide before us, and close shut after us, shielding us from any pursuing armies for the night.

Not that we've seen any. The watchmen left scattered between Sorbiodun and Callew report no troops on the move. It seems Ambrosius and Wortimer are still figuring out how to react to the recent events. Or perhaps Wortigern has been too rash, too quick to imagine threats where there aren't any… What if he's made the wrong decision? What if he's doomed us all? Now that I'm no longer overwhelmed by his presence and have time to think, the doubt is creeping in. Doubt — and fear.

I fear for my soul. I am smothered in sin. I have fought, and killed, Christians in battles at the side of a pagan army. I have committed a deadly sin with Rhedwyn, and now I follow a blasphemer. If the God of Rome is real, I am damned for eternity. And if he isn't, then the gods of the Iutes must have cursed me instead. Whoever it was, a god or a demon, has laid traps throughout my life — and I fell into every single one of them.

As I look back, I see everything around me turn to dust. My story starts with a murder — a cruel death of the old man in the bowels of the bath house. The original sin that marked me for life; a sin that I have never confessed to Paulinus or any other priest, never asked for forgiveness. If that wasn't enough to damn my soul, I soon sealed my fate with a sin of disobedience: rising against my Master and foster-father, wounding Fastidius, causing grief to all who loved me, irrevocably destroying the happiness of Eadgith and her family, all for my own selfish purpose. I turned to pagan gods, but they brought me no respite; instead, they mocked me and drove a wedge between me and the last family I had: Fastidius.

But I have another family, I remember. As Aeric, son of Eobba, I have an uncle in Hengist, and further relations back in the Iute villages of Cantiaca. And… I have a sister.

I haven't talked to Rhedwyn since last night. She's been locked up in her carriage, guarded by Beadda's warriors, and now she's shut in a room somewhere in Masuna's palace, refusing to speak to anyone. I don't even know what I would say if she did agree to see me. Is there any way for us to move forward from where we are now? For her to acknowledge the reality, for us to be siblings, instead of lovers, as we should always have been? Is there a way to wash off the filth of what we've done? Not before gods, but before ourselves, in our own souls, in our own minds…

It sounds impossible. I might convince myself, in time, to learn to think of her as a sibling, but my body has its own ideas. I dream of her nakedness, of my fingers running down her spine, clasping her breasts, her mouth on me, taking me in… I wake up covered in the oily sweat of shame and guilt.

I wonder if Wortigern already told her about his new plan. I doubt she'd care — I doubt she'd care about anything right now. I find it difficult to care myself. I'm overwhelmed with emotion as it is. Life holds no meaning for me beyond fear and shame. I cannot live with Rhedwyn — and I cannot live *without* her.

In the darkness, I reach for the *seax*. The blade is freshly sharpened, gleaming in the moonlight. It's still the same blade, forged by the old smith Weland in the dark forest of Andreda, all those years ago. It has tasted so much blood since then. Would it be eager to taste mine?

With a trembling hand, I put it away. I don't know which god awaits me on the other side, Christ or Wodan — and I'm not ready to face either.

There's chaos around the wagons when I come down in the morning; men running around, shouting, the robes of the Britons flapping about, the Iutes grimly silent, gathered in small groups around the square. I instinctively reach for my sword. Are we being attacked? I look to the walls and the gate in search of a breach, but the commotion is focused around the *Comes*'s palace and the Forum, rather than at the ramparts. I don't see anybody else brandishing weapons.

I find Wortigern in the eye of this storm, red-faced and bulgy-eyed. He spots me, too, and strides towards me. He grabs me by the collar.

"By all the gods, boy!" His spittle showers my face. "This is all your fault."

"What's — gnnh…" I muster through choking.

"Rhedwyn's gone. She left the city at dawn and disappeared."

He lets me go and pushes away. I hit the dirt.

"How is it my fault?"

"Have you told her what you told me?"

"No, of course not. She only knows the wedding's off — not *why*. I don't understand why she'd want to run off because of that."

"She must have decided we were tricking her into something again. You broke her trust one time too often — now she won't trust anyone. She wouldn't even tell Beadda she was running away." He rubs his forehead. "I thought I told you to sort this out!"

"And how was I supposed to do that?" I cry. "I'd like to see you cope any better with what's happened. I barely lived through the night myself, if you must know."

"Hush, you arse!" He picks me up and puts his hand to his mouth. "Do you want everyone to wonder what we're talking about?"

He calms down a little and runs his hand through his hair. "I'm sorry. I can't even guess how distressed you must be. I promise we'll find a way for you two to deal with this… mess once we're in Londin."

I don't believe it's possible even for Wortigern to find a way out, but I appreciate the offer.

"In the meantime, I had to tell Beadda something — I told him you two had a lovers' quarrel, which is not far off from the truth, from what you tell me. We need to find her before she hurts herself. Where could she have gone?"

"I have no idea. I doubt she would know herself. She doesn't know this land. Have you sent out search parties yet?"

"Of course I have. And they'll find her eventually — she's a girl, not a roe deer. But we need to find her before she hurts herself."

"Which gate did she go through?"

He points to the west — it's the nearest gate from the Forum, and one through which the main road from Londin to Corin passes. I run outside and look around, trying to put myself in Rhedwyn's mind. She can't have gone far — she was still wearing the night dress when the guard at the gate saw her. She'd be confused and dejected, in anguish, but not afraid — she'd be more at home in the wild than in the stone Roman city. The metalled highway turns south-west. To the west spread the fields of wheat and barley. To the north, a morning mist rises over the marshes, shrouding the forested hills that border Masuna's land, where we went hunting, and beyond it — the land of the Cadwallons.

"Did she speak to Wortimer's *Gewisse* before disappearing?" I ask the *Dux*.

"She did — how did you know?"

"She would be asking them about the refugee villages in the forest. She wouldn't trust Beadda's *Hiréd*, but she would still seek help from someone of our own kin rather than the *wealas*."

"One of the tracking parties went that way," says Wortigern. "Take my horse. You'll catch up to them at the river ford."

I find one of the trackers at the river's edge: a small, grim Briton in a felt cloth cap. He's crouching on the clay bank, chewing on a sage leaf. A bunch of white cloth gleams in his mud-grimed hands.

"What's this?" I ask, my heart sinking.

"We found these scraps on the thorns all along the way," he says. "She must be half-naked by now."

I curse myself for the lusty image my mind throws before me. "Where are the others?"

"I sent them both sides of the river. But if I was her, I'd go west."

"Why?"

"More mud, less scrub. Easier to run, easier to lose pursuit."

I thank him, ride across the river — and go east. Rhedwyn wouldn't choose *easy*. She's far too clever for that.

I leave the horse where the thicket grows thickest and proceed on foot. The thorns tear into my skin and clothes. I accept the pain with gratitude, a minuscule punishment for all my transgressions. The ground grows slippery, and I trip a few times. Bloodied and battered, I reach a narrow bend in the river, where the stream quickens into a white rushing rapid. There's nowhere else to go — the brambles are impassable.

A dreary thought strikes me. Could Rhedwyn have guessed the real reason for calling our wedding off? The last time we talked before leaving Sorbiodun, we spoke of Aeric, and of her imagined childhood friend… What if she remembered more since then? What if she, too, knows now what I know — or suspects, at least? Is this what drove her to flee into this wilderness?

I find another tracker here, studying the footprints in the mud. Several white and green threads hang from the thorns above his head, bloodied.

He hears me and turns around. "Who are you?" he asks, reaching for a knife in his boot.

"I'm with Wortigern," I reply. "I'm the girl's betrothed. What do you see?"

He relaxes and points to the mud bank. "She slipped into the water here, but she must have scrambled back. A body would get stuck among those boulders downstream."

I don't like him talking about Rhedwyn's *body*. I'm sure she's still alive and well, somewhere.

"Who did you think I was?" I ask.

"There's somebody else here. Two men at least, also following the girl."

"Maybe more trackers from Callew?"

He shakes his head, doubtfully. "They're not from around here."

Maybe the Iutes have sent their own hunters, I suggest. He shrugs. "Maybe — but then why would she be running away from *them* in such panic?"

Panic? My blood runs cold.

"You've got gauntlets?" he asks. Seeing my confusion, he waves his hand dismissively. He puts on thick felt gloves. He wades into the rushing stream and waddles on, holding onto the brambles with the gloved hand. He moves at a snail's pace around the slick boulders until he disappears behind the river bend.

I hear him cry out in triumph, then see him emerge against the current. His hat's gone, taken by the current. He waves at me, but there's no way I can reach him where he is.

Before the tracker can reach me to explain his find, I hear hooves splashing on wet clay, on the other side of the river. I recognise the horseman as one of Masuna's men.

"Are you the one they call Ash?" he cries over the rushing water. "You're needed back at Callew."

"Have they found Rhedwyn?"

But the rider only shrugs and turns back.

There's a new carriage at the courtyard of Masuna's palace, marked with the insignia of Saint Paul's. A banner of truce hangs from the carriage door. Everyone except for servants and guards is already inside — I can hear their agitated voices as I dismount at the entrance.

I rush inside, hoping to see Rhedwyn alive and safe, but I see only Bishop Fatalis. He's alone, standing in the middle of the hall, leaning on his crooked staff. Everyone falls silent when I enter.

"What's going on?"

"They have the princess," says Beadda. "Wortimer and Ambrosius. Or so the priest claims."

"It's true," says Fatalis, "I swear by the Holy Cross." He presents some scraps of white, green-trimmed cloth, but the others are not convinced — I have more of these in my bag, brought from the marsh.

"He's right," I say. "We found the place where they caught her, by the rapids." This was what the tracker wanted to show me. From the sight of the footprints he could tell Rhedwyn was captured without a struggle by the two strange men.

"What do you want in exchange for her?" asks Wortigern. He stands opposite the Bishop with his arms firmly crossed.

"Only that you come with me to negotiate with your son and *Dux* Ambrosius."

"*Negotiate?*" scoffs Wortigern. "Negotiate what? If you mean *surrender*, no girl is worth…"

"Perhaps… Perhaps we may come to some sort of arrangement," the Bishop replies. His grip on the crooked staff tightens. "We believe there is still some good left in your soul, a place for Christ's mercy. *Dux* Ambrosius loathes bloodshed. He still remembers the Rebellion you and your father helped to put down."

"They're playing for time," I say. "They're setting up their army for an assault as we speak, no doubt."

"They do not!" the Bishop protests. "You have my word as a man of cloth. I am here on the authority of not just *Dux* Ambrosius, but the Church's. There must be a way out of this that doesn't involve any more Britons slaughtering other Britons."

To my surprise, Wortigern seems to seriously consider the Bishop's proposal.

"You speak only of Ambrosius," I say, "but what of Wortimer? He will have no qualms about shedding Briton blood."

"Wortimer is a loyal ally to Ambrosius, he will listen to the *Dux*."

"He wouldn't listen to his own father," says Wortigern under his breath. "The boy's blood runs hot, and he heeds no master. But if you and Ambrosius vouch for my safety, I will go — if only to check that Rhedwyn's unharmed."

"My lord!" I and a couple of other courtiers step forward in protest. As much as I want to see Rhedwyn back, this is all too obvious of a trap. Only the day before we were an army of foolhardy rebels on the run — now we're willing to negotiate with our pursuers… Has Wortigern lost all of his will to fight overnight?

I glean signs of weariness in his face. Maybe he, too, understood he was too rushed and made a mistake. Or maybe it's something else — maybe my revelation forced him to rethink his original plan altogether. Maybe he's come up with a new scheme — one that he hasn't yet had a chance to share with anyone else. These… *negotiations* would give him a chance to back out, and try a different approach…

The *Dux* raises his hand to silence us. "I presume you have some conditions."

Fatalis wipes sweat from his brow and nods. "The meeting is to be at sunset at the old farmstead five miles west from here. You may take one guard with you, and however many slaves you think necessary, within reason."

"We will be armed," says Wortigern. "I'm not an idiot."

"Very well," replies Fatalis. "Though I swear on Christ's Wounds that no harm will come to you," he adds hastily, making the sign of the cross.

"Will the princess be there?"

"Yes."

Wortigern rubs his chin. He looks at his courtiers, then Beadda, then me.

"*Gesith* Beadda, will you accompany me to this meeting?" he asks, still looking at me rather than the Iute.

"It would be my honour."

Wortigern points at me, and turns to the others. "Ere I return, young Fraxinus here will be your commander. Do whatever he tells you to."

The western gate creaks and slams shut after the *Dux*, Beadda and a couple of slaves, depart to the place of the parlay. Moments later, the same creaking and shutting sound comes from the three other corners of the walls: the city locks down for the night. And, perhaps, for good.

"This isn't like him," says a weary old voice. Postumus stands behind me, leaning on a walking stick. I haven't spoken to him much at Sorbiodun — he, like other loyal nobles in Wortigern's retinue, was too busy with the Council to find time for idle discussions.

"I've never seen him like this. Something's happened." He looks at me and points his walking stick at me. "You know what happened, young Fraxinus."

"I… I do not!"

"He's only spoken to a few people since Sorbiodun. It couldn't have been me or Beadda. What did you tell him?"

"Why do you think anyone told him anything? Maybe he simply realised his plan was flawed."

"Hmm." He shakes his head. "When he stood in that enclosure, I saw his spirit ablaze as it hasn't since the Rebellion. There was no hesitation. He knew exactly what needed to be done. He would not throw all of this away for some Iutish princess."

"Perhaps he trusts Ambrosius. He is, by all accounts, an honourable man. And Fatalis swore…"

"Wortigern wouldn't trust this lot with a wiping sponge." He shakes his head again and turns to return to the palace. "Make sure you look to our defences, boy. This is not an end to the surprises, I bet."

I order the Iutes and the *Gewisse* to man the ramparts alongside Masuna's watchmen. I know little of siege warfare, and Callew is not my city to defend, but it's the least I can do. The Iutes I speak to all feel uneasy. They also never had to defend a city wall before — their villages and towns had only wooden palisades and shallow ditches for perimeters. Callew was only supposed to be a stopover, not a place where we would be forced to make a stand — and without two of our best generals to guide us.

"They won't have any *machinae*," I tell them. "Only bows and arrows, and some ladders robbed from the farmsteads. We're not facing Ambrosius's standing army, just the bodyguard he's come with to the Council, and Wortimer's bunch of roughs. They won't have the heart or supplies for a long fight."

In truth, I don't know what to expect. I never had the chance to inspect the troops Ambrosius brought with him back at Sorbiodun — and it's likely he's had more warriors waiting somewhere nearby in case things turned violent at the Council.

I'm full of fear, and I don't mind it. I let the dread wash over me; it douses the flames of guilt. The Iutes must sense this fear and, somehow, it calms them down more than my words: they feel better knowing that I'm not some cocksure youth, but a cautious commander. I may have a death wish for myself, but I wouldn't want any of them to die needlessly.

I have less confidence in the rest of the troops manning the walls and the gates. Alongside the Iutes and the *Gewisse*, we have some guards and veterans from Wortigern's retinue, and a few dozen armed slaves belonging to the loyal Councillors. Masuna has no army of his own, and barely enough soldiers to protect his city from an occasional attack of bandits or brigands. Either way, they're under the *Comes's* orders, and I can't expect them to hold their ground against fellow Britons.

I make sure at least two watchmen are posted at each of the gatehouses and the corner watchtowers and check that the gates themselves are locked shut, and go to bed.

I can't sleep. I toss and turn in the bed, thinking of Rhedwyn. I pass in and out of waking dreams of her naked body; an angry, bearded god — can't tell if it's Wodan, the God-Father of Rome, Jupiter, or some other deity — scowls at me from the heavy grey clouds, lightning bolts shooting from his eyes. A hooded figure in the mist shakes its staff at me. The silver-wrought gates of Heaven shut before me, and when I turn around, so do the doors to the song-filled Mead Hall. I am alone, in a fiery darkness.

I wake up to the sound of swords clashing in the hallway. Flames dancing outside flash on the walls of the room through the open window. I reach for the *seax* and wait as the noise grows nearer. The door breaks open. One of the Iutes, his face and shoulder bloodied, tumbles into the room.

"Betrayed!" he cries.

I help him up and deflect a spear leaping at me from the darkness. I pull at the shaft and impale the enemy on my sword. Looking over his shoulder I see the hallway filled with men, carrying torches and primitive weapons — clubs, hatchets, chains — all coming towards us.

"What happened?"

"Masuna's men opened the gates," says the Iute. "And joined the attackers. We've been slaughtered!"

"*Wortimer.*" I hiss, spotting his shadowy silhouette at the back.

"The window!" The Iute pushes me towards the opening. He stands in the doorway to block the enemy and buy me time to flee, but it's a futile gesture — he succumbs to the hatchets and clubs before I even reach the frame. Wortimer's men scramble to grab me down and pull me to the floor. I wave my sword and slash one through the stomach. The others start kicking and punching me.

"Enough," says Wortimer.

He stands above me holding a long cavalry sword. His nostrils flare. He's not smiling.

"Pick him up."

The roughs fulfil his order. Wortimer lowers his sword and cuts through my leg, in the same exact place where I slashed him in the Battle of Crei. I bite my tongue not to let out a cry. He cuts again, on the shoulder and on the side, reopening my old wounds. This is too much and I howl in pain. This, finally, makes him smile.

"Take him outside."

Out in the courtyard of Masuna's palace, the brief fight is already over. All the Iutes lie scattered where they fell, guarding the entrance and the ramparts. Wortimer's roughs and Ambrosius's legionnaires roam around the place, making sure all their enemies are dead. The rebel Londin courtiers all stand in one corner under guard, chained — all except Postumus, who's dead body lies thrown in the dirt under the palace wall. I note that Wortimer's men failed to take him alive, and it gives me the last glimmer of satisfaction: freshly dried blood pools around the Councillor's slit wrists. I catch a glimpse of the traitor Masuna, staring down at the destruction from his chamber at the top floor of the palace. His eyes meet mine and he pulls away from the window.

Then a hatchet butt strikes the back of my head and I slide back into the fiery mist.

TO BE CONTINUED IN THE SONG OF ASH, BOOK THREE: THE SAXON MIGHT

Printed in Great Britain
by Amazon